CHASING DIGNITY

A novel
By **Rachhpal Sahota**

Book Title: Chasing Dignity
Author: Rachhpal Sahota, USA

Published by Tirchhi Nazar Media

Arth Parkash Bhawan, First Floor, Sector 29-D, Chandigarh 160030

Tirchhi Nazar media is a conglomerate of Babushahi, Babushahi.com, Babushahi Times and @BabushahiKhabar

Phone: +91-90233 77722, +WhatsApp: 91-78884 02170
Fax: +91 172-4668583
Email: tirshinazar@gmail.com

ISBN: 978-81-961923-2-7

This is a work of fiction. Names, characters, places, and incidents either are the product of the author's imagination or are used fictitiously, and any resemblance to actual persons, living or dead, business establishments, or locales is entirely coincidental. The publisher has no control over and assumes no responsibility for the author, third-party websites, or their contents.

Copyright © 2023 Rachhpal Sahota

All rights reserved.

No part of this publication may be reproduced, distributed, or transmitted in any form or by any means, including photocopying, recording, or other electronic or mechanical methods, without the prior written permission of the Copyright holder, except in the case of brief quotations embodied in critical reviews and other specific noncommercial uses permitted by copyright law.

TNM

Foreword

Chasing Dignity is a beautifully written novel. Though it is his first, Rachhpal Sahota has made a noticeable entry into the world of English fiction written by Punjabis, especially Sikhs. Through the story of different phases of the life of Jaggi, the main character, Rachhpal has written a social history of contemporary Punjab in a fictionalised form by giving centrality to the caste system as it operates in Punjab, especially among the Sikhs in both the rural and urban settings. What is most admirable is that the novel does not present the caste system as either ever present in a rigid fashion or as a vanishing practice. What emerges are the complexities and contradictions of the caste system both through its presence and absence in varied forms. Several characters both from the so-called lower castes as well as the so-called upper castes defy it and those defiances are beautifully captured. It is a depiction of the beauty of those defiances coexisting with the violence- mainly verbal but sometimes physical- of the system that lends this novel a distinctive character. The novel ends with the depiction of some forms of low-level casteism (mainly in the form of caste biases) migrating to the West along with the migrants. So, the journey to chase dignity continues.

The village retains the central plot of the story even though it covers facets of life in schools, colleges, universities, hospitals, religious places, cremation grounds, cafes, cinema halls, tourist spots, courts, media outlets and embassies (more specifically US embassy). This imparts another distinctive character to this novel. English fiction on Punjab has been written almost exclusively by urban-based Punjabis. This novel is written by someone who has been successful in his career as a scientist in the US (and his knowledge of science filters through the novel giving it another distinctive feature to this literary creation by a Punjabi) but has deep roots in the Punjabi village society and has a first-hand feel of the economy, society, cultural norms and religious practices of rural Punjabis.

Rachhpal's use of the language shows remarkable versatility. The main form of the language remains simple and direct- this lends the narrative a raw and earthy character. The simplicity of the language represents the simplicity of life in rural society. This simplicity is so powerful that at times, a reader may feel that s/he is reading a Punjabi language novel and not an English language one. The simplicity of rural life should not be confused with innocence. Far from innocence, the social life in the village has many scary blemishes and those blemishes emerge at several points in different forms. The character of Banta, a rogue right from childhood to adult life, personifies the ugliness of rural life. The simplicity in the description is about being direct without any polish or spin. However, when Rachhpal moves the plot away from the village to the university in a big town and deals with the relationship between Jaggi and Navi, amidst the culture of the university where they are studying, the language beautifully captures the tenderness of the young lover's feelings and expressions. The simplicity and beauty of the following para stole my heart:

'It was a warm, pleasant evening. Usually, Navi took the straight path by the administrative block. But today, she wanted to take the T-point road, a more extended way that wove around the botanical garden. When they passed by, Navi drew him into the garden. "Let's sit down here for a few minutes," she said. It was dinner time, and there was not a soul in sight. She selected a bench under a Kachnar tree.'

Jaggi and Navi's relationship assumes an independent status within the novel of a touching love story amidst all the social tensions associated with caste.

What I especially enjoyed in this novel was the prominence given to women characters and their strength, humanity, intelligence and decisiveness. The characterisation of Bindo, Rani, Navi and Dr Gill represents them as real-life wonderful women who transcend many forms of caste barriers. However, Rachhpal does not allow this positive characterisation of women to romanticise womanhood because he also presents another type of woman (such as Gurdev) who can harbour designs of honour killings.

Rachhpal has so constructed the narrative that because there were tragic deaths, there was always a lurking fear of something dreadful happening even when the joyful turn of events was taking place. Rachhpal is able to keep this suspense till the end. However, there is a feeling of relief at the end that despite all the sadness of losing loved ones and the unpleasant reality of the reappearance of caste even after moving far away from the village to the US, there is a joyful family life transcending the caste barriers. Chasing dignity seems to end with a message of hope.

The only criticism I have is about the empirical and historical reality of the US as presented in the novel. Rachhpal's narrative presents the US as a model country and society which it is not with all its problems-racism, police killings (the highest of any country in the developed/industrialised world), massive inequalities, terrible role of the American state and army in Vietnam, active role of its intelligence agencies/military in overthrowing progressive governments in different parts of the world. The most gruesome and internationally known of these interventions was in Chile when on September 11, 1971 (a different September 11 which should not be forgotten!), the socialist government of President Allende in Chile was overthrown, the brave President was murdered while resisting the army take over and a military dictatorship was imposed which during its 15 years rule, committed unspeakable level of human rights violations. The brave people of Chile, after huge sufferings, are now retrieving their proud socialist traditions.

Rachhpal is a scientist who has taken to fiction writing and can be excused for a historical error. Though it is necessary to inform the readers of the ugly reality of the US state which many Punjabi readers may not be aware of and remain seduced by the charms of the widely touted 'American dream', the factual error about the US state and society does not and should not stand in the appreciation of the sociological and literary beauty of this wonderful work of Punjabi fiction.

A Punjabi translation would mark a new genre in Punjabi fiction. I strongly recommend this.

Dr. Pritam Singh, DPhil (Oxford)
Professor Emeritus in Economics
Oxford Brookes Business School
Oxford, UK

January 30, 2023

For my wife Manjeet, mother Surjit Kaur, Children Hermondeep, Jasline, Amneet, Granddaughter Sachi,
and
To the memory of my father, Sucha Singh Sahota

Prologue

April 2, 1984, Village Kundyan, Punjab, India

As the night breaks, hazy mud houses take form; a lone figure lying in a cot stirs, gets up, and walks inside a hut. The figure will reemerge, holding a tumbler of water in one hand, slouching down the unpaved lane, disappearing toward the fields. The morning will yawn, stretching its limbs with the florid orange growing from the east. More cots will squeak around the shacks, and more figures move to traverse the same path. The earthen stoves burning dung cakes will come to life in front of the mud huts while the cacophony of shouts begins for youngsters to wake up.

People in dirty clothes will start walking out of the shantytown—singly, in pairs, or small groups. They will pass by the brick house at the end and turn left to the main village, where the women will clean barns for Jats all morning, hauling away cattle dung for scraps of food. The men will toil, helping Jat farmers in the fields for small sums.

At noon, the women will return, carrying small vessels containing cooked lentils and vegetables doled out by the Jat ladies. Seeing their sisters and mothers return, the scantily clad children will abandon their play and run to the huts for lunchtime. Their empty stomachs will not balk at the unusual texture and taste of the vessels' mixed-up curry concoctions. A few scrawny cows, buffalos, goats, and sheep tethered around the shacks will grunt and bleat for attention.

This is the Keera[1] basti, the shantytown of Kundyan where the Keeras live. It is no different from other Keera bastis of Punjab, set up on the southwest outskirts of the main villages. The Keeras are the untouchables, the outcasts of the Indian caste hierarchy,

---

[1] The use of original terms to describe outcaste categories has been outlawed in India; Keera—कीरा—from kirtee (laborer) is used as an alternate expression.

outside the four Hindu varnas. They are neither allowed to live in the main villages, nor permitted into Jat homes, nor to eat from the same kits the Jats eat. They carry their bowls and tumblers with them when they go to a Jat home and eat sitting on the ground at the door.

The upper caste Jats live in the main village. Jats are the farming community, and they own all land. Their brick houses are spacious, often containing two to three rooms, separate kitchens, walled-in courtyards, and barns for the cattle. Men work in the fields with hired help from the Keeras in the basti. The Jat women take care of the household chores, milk buffalos, churn milk in the morning, clean, launder, cook, and spin yarn.

Besides Jats, a few other castes also live in the main village. They belong to the broad caste category of Sudra, the lowest of the four varnas of the Hindu Shastras. Sudras provide various services to the Jat community and live in the main village, though not amid the Jats. They are allowed into Jat homes, and the Jats do not mind sharing their eating utensils.

A well-traveled, wide, paved road separates the main village of Kundyan from its Keera basti. Except for one brick house, the houses in the basti are one-room mud huts, two or three of which share a small, open courtyard that houses their earthen stoves. Twenty-some of these shacks are spread along an unpaved street, which at the end splits at right angles to left and right. The brick house stands at the corner where the main lane turns toward the village. The house is a basti oddity. Its boundary wall covers the main house and the cattle barn. The house has one spacious bedroom, a guest room, a veranda, a kitchen, a small bathroom, and a flush toilet in one corner of the yard. It has a metal door toward the basti and another double door through the barn that opens to the street to the main town. The brick house exudes a feeling as if it has been dragged here to exile from the main village.

Chasing Dignity

Very few Keera children go to school. Most drop out after a year or two of primary school; rarely does anyone finish high school. Keera girls are discouraged from going at all. Once in a blue moon, one may encounter a Keera woman with a high school certificate. Bindo, an occupant of the lone brick house of the basti, is one such exception.

PART 1

Only mothers can think of the future - because they give birth to it in their children.

Maxim Gorky

Chapter 1

Jaggi woke up at the first clinking in the kitchen. The six-year-old was excited; it was his first day of school. His mother, Bindo, had already set water to heat on the mud stove. Jaggi took no time to brush his teeth and take a bath. He quickly ate a thickly buttered flatbread with yogurt.

Jaggi was thrilled; whenever he passed by the school he had watched with awe the children playing inside. Now he'd have the chance to be there with his friend Himmat all day long and play marbles. It made him giddy with anticipation. Bindo smiled at her son's excitement.

After eating, Jaggi was ready for Bindo to tie a turban on his head. She combed his hair and rolled it into a small bun. She took out the long soft cloth and folded it lengthwise into a long two-inch-wide strip with the help of Jaggi's tiny hands. It was both of their first time tying a turban. Bindo never needed a turban as a woman, but her little boy had to be dressed no less than any other in school. Jaggi anchored one end of the cloth with his left hand while Bindo carefully stacked one round over the other around his head, turning the fabric into a beautiful turban, befitting his striking handsomeness. She stepped back to admire her handiwork.

How handsome my son looks, with that face like the moon! Bindo quickly moved her gaze away, lest her captivated eye caused harm to him. She had an urge to put a soot-mark on his forehead with her pinky to ward off the evil eyes. But she did not, not wanting the other children to have any reason to mock her boy.

His nose was just like his grandfather's—the thought brought her the memory of her father's face. His eyes were certainly like hers, and Bindo was very proud of her eyes. And why wouldn't she be? "You have gazelle-like eyes, like those of Dimple Kapadia," she was often told. Women from the villages did not go to the cinemas without a male company. And so, as soon as they married, Bindo's first demand from her husband Teja was to take her to the cinema to watch *Bobby*, a Dimple Kapadia film.

She blushed when she thought of a match for Jaggi's chin: It reminded her of her cousin, Baldev, who she held as a standard of handsomeness. She had harbored feelings toward Baldev that she knew she shouldn't have.

"Wh-wh-what are you loo-loo-looking at, maa?" Jaggi's question broke her trance.

"I was thinking how handsome my son looks," she said, caressing his cheeks. Jaggi's face reddened, and he lowered his gaze.

Himmat, a boy in class three, walked through the door to take Jaggi to his first day of school. Himmat was from a Jheor family, a low caste Sudra, living on the Jat side of the road.

Bindo took the small, handcrafted cotton tote bag off the peg in the wall. The bag contained a small wooden slate and a clump of clay to coat the slate with, an inkpot, a reed pen, a little book of Punjabi alphabet, and his lunch—an omelet rolled in a thickly buttered flatbread, wrapped in a small kitchen rag.

Bindo hung the bag on Jaggi's shoulder and sent him off with Himmat. She stood in the door watching the boys walk away, her heart pitter-pattering in sync with Jaggi's tiny steps. Her son was going to school in new clothes, sandals, and a new bag on his shoulder. Her eyes were gleaming with pride.

Jaggi was her only child, her life. "You shouldn't get pregnant again," the doctor had advised her after a complication with Jaggi's birth. It was difficult to digest his words, as if he were declaring her womanhood invalid. However, as time passed, she reconciled. After God's such handsome gift, who needs more children?

Chasing Dignity

Bindo was born into a Keera family. Her father, Soma, had finished school till class eight. A constitutional provision that eased outcasts to get government jobs enabled Soma to secure a security guard post with a bank. The position paid modestly, but it ensured that his wife and two daughters did not have to clean cattle barns or do other humble jobs for the higher castes. A consistent, regular income and his girls' freedom from the menial work was congenial for their schooling. In a way, Soma was ahead of his time; he wanted both of his daughters to go to school.

It wasn't easy, though; he had to overcome much resistance. He had to deal with comments from the community, and his wife was dead set against sending the girls to school. "What is the school going to give them? In the end, they will bear children and cook bread like the rest," she argued. However, Soma was too determined to be swayed.

Unfortunately, Bitti, the older one, did not show much interest in studies; she hated being referred to by her caste in school. She dropped out after class five and was married three years later, barely fifteen at the time.

Bindo, on the other hand, loved books and did well in her studies. But her liking of books did not bode well with her mother, Piaro, who wanted Bindo to do all the household chores. As Bindo advanced in her classes, Piaro's interference increased, becoming emotionally manipulative. She would feign sickness and fall ill when Bindo had to work on her school assignments. She would demand Bindo's full attention, making her cook certain things or heating water for her to take a bath. "Do you know how I took care of my mother when I was your age?"

But the more Piaro tried to interfere with Bindo's studies, the more determined Bindo became to succeed. There was a stop near her school where two Jat girls boarded the bus for college. Bindo was fascinated by them and would stop working to look at them get on or off the bus. She, too, wanted to dress up like them and get on the bus, carrying a bag of books. Frequently, she dreamed of being in college or a position meant only for the educated.

After Bindo finished high school, Soma broached the subject with Piaro of sending Bindo to college.

"What? Are you going to sell me to pay for her college?" she snapped. Piaro was beside herself. "Stop that rubbish right now!" she thundered. "The girl finished high school, and that's enough. No need for any more of that nonsense. Do you know any other girl from the basti going to college? And when will you find her a husband?" Bindo was seventeen, fair-skinned, tall, and beautiful, and Piaro could not bear the thought of her roaming among the Jat boys, who considered low caste women their collective property.

Soma could see his wife's viewpoint; they were barely making it with his meager salary at the bank, and a college-going woman would need money for decent clothes, books, tuition, and other expenses. How would he provide for all that? Where would he find a matching Keera husband for his college-educated girl?

Piaro's outrage did not surprise Bindo, but she couldn't understand why her father sided with her mother. She was proud of her father and had always counted on his support. She desperately wanted to go to college and get an admirable job. It did not excite her just to get married, produce children and cook meals for them all. 'Why do I have to live the same life my mother and her mother before her lived? Why doesn't she want me to be independent? Why is she so jealous of me?'

One day, disappointed, she sat her father down for a discussion. "Baau ji, why don't you support me anymore?" she asked. Soma explained their meager financial resources.

"I will buy used books and never bother you for fancy clothes," she pleaded.

"It doesn't work like that, bete," Soma said. "If I send you to college, I wouldn't want you to be any less than your classmates. And bete, where will I find a suitable husband for my college-educated daughter?"

"Who wants to get married?" Bindo snapped. "I want to be independent and not depend on someone else for my livelihood."

"That kind of talk is total nonsense, and you know that. Do you believe society will let you or us live in peace if you stay unmarried?"

Soma shared other reservations about working women; they made a tiny percentage in his bank or other workplaces he visited. "Their male coworkers don't treat them as equals or show the respect these ladies deserve. And these Jat girls who go to college; how many you think will work in offices? Most just aim to get a good husband, and that's about it."

Bindo talked about being a nurse or a teacher, but all these required years in college, and Soma could not afford it. She didn't know what to do or whom to talk to. No one in her education-deprived neighborhood sympathized with her; why did she need more education than she already had? Bindo understood; it was the end of her dream.

Bindo was determined not to depend on her husband for survival. *What if I have three kids and something happens to him? Who will take care of my children and me?* She thought of learning a trade, but what? The available agriculture and allied activities didn't pay enough; none needed a high degree of skill or specialization.

Bindo went to see Parkash, the village tailor. Tailoring was Parkash's hereditary occupation. He had two daughters and a teenage son. The daughters were married off, and the son was helping him in his trade.

"Uncle ji, how much money can one make from tailoring?" Bindo asked

Parkash smiled.

"Bete, you know tailoring is our familial occupation, and this is all I know. My son will take over the trade after me, as I did after my father, and he after his. We are not rich, but we never had to worry about our livelihood. How much money you make depends on where you live and how good and hardworking you are. I believe tailors living in cities make much more than we do."

Parkash's answer satisfied Bindo. Being a seamstress was not her idea of getting a job for the educated, but it could afford her the independence she sought.

Bindo asked Parkash if he could train her to be a seamstress.

"Why not, puttar ji? Ask Soma to talk to me, and we will get you going."

Bindo talked to her father, and within a day, she was training with Parkash.

Parkash used part of his house as a shop. He was busy, and he had an employee to help him in addition to his teenage son. Bindo liked the work and quickly got good at it. After two months, Parkash started to pay her. The pay was modest, but Bindo pursued the confidence to be independent more than she desired the money.

Soma started searching for a suitable husband for Bindo, and two years later, he found Teja.

Bindo was not thrilled to learn her future spouse had not gone past primary school, but what Soma told about Teja was intriguing. Teja and his father farmed someone else's land as sharecroppers. Being a farmer and hiring his labor was honorable for a Keera, even as a sharecropper.

"Teja has a brick house, the best in the entire village, not just the basti!" Soma told Bindo with pride in his eyes. Bindo trusted her father's judgment. She was excited to live in a lovely house, different from the four mud walls she grew up in.

Her mother's argument still rattled Bindo. My children will go to college and not be denied like I am, she resolved.

Like all the brides of her time, Bindo did not see Teja before their wedding. During the holy Granth's ceremonial circling, she walked with her straightest posture to compare Teja's height with her own and couldn't figure out if he was taller than her. He would fit below Baldev's chin, she thought. The thin red dupatta pulled over Bindo's eyes was like a filter through which she saw everything, including her new husband's face. It wasn't until the ride to the in-laws that she saw him openly. Bindo sat in the back seat with her lady companion and Teja next to the driver. He is good enough, she decided.

Her first night in Kundyan had followed a grueling day of wedding ceremonies and a long line of ladies who came to see the new bride. When she was finally in the bedroom, she wanted to sleep but was afraid of offending Teja and stayed awake, waiting. She had heard so many stories from her friends and had no clue what to expect. One had told of her husband, who expected her to initiate everything because it would signify his weakness if he had to ask. Another told her how they had stayed awake all night, making love. Then the one whose husband came in drunk and forced himself on her, and the one whose husband was so nervous he couldn't even perform.

Finally, the door squeaked open. Someone entered the room, closing the door behind. Bindo was sitting on the bed, still dressed in her wedding clothes. He slowly walked closer, and she waited to hear him say something, but nothing. She scooted over a little, and he gently sat beside her. After a couple of minutes, he put his hand on her shoulder.

"Do you want to lie down? You must be tired," he said. Teja's compassion put her mind at ease as he lay back, softly pulling her with him. They straightened on the bed with him lying on his back and resting her head on his shoulder. He took her free hand, put it on his chest, and tenderly moved his hand over her arm. A long time seemed to pass, and he was still gently stroking her arm. She became more comfortable each minute and began to doze off. Then he said something bizarre that she couldn't grasp: "Bindo, do you know Chandgi Ram opened an *Akhara* in Delhi?"

Bindo did not know who Chandgi Ram was. What kind of foreplay is this? He must be nervous, she thought. Then he was quiet for a couple of minutes, still stroking her arm. "Bindo, we will have two sons, two strong sons."

A son and a daughter, she wanted to say but kept quiet and slowly dozed off in his arm.

Teja turned out to be a good husband, though Bindo did not like his non-confrontational nature. He spoke only when there was no other way. But he was a loving and hardworking man.

Three years later, when Jaggi was born, Teja confessed.

"I'm glad I have an educated wife. I know nothing about schooling and would not have known what to do with a child," he said.

"I'm sure you would have sent him to school," Bindo answered lightly.

"Yes, I would've, but I wouldn't know how to help him with his studies and what to do when he finished. Now I'm not worried; you will know what to do."

Chasing Dignity

"I don't know all the answers, but I'm sure of one thing," Bindo said.

"What is that?"

"Our son will go to university, and nothing will stop him—nothing!" she said with a conviction that made Teja's face glow.

Today, sending Jaggi to school was the proudest moment in Bindo's life. She stood watching the boys until they disappeared behind the small hillock, and in those few moments, she saw Jaggi grow up to be collegiate. My son will go to university, and nothing will stop him—nothing!

Chapter 2

Jaggi's exhilaration increased as they neared the school.

"The man at the table," Himmat said, as they turned the lane facing the school, "is masterji."

Jaggi's heart pounded a little faster.

"Are we l-l-late?" Jaggi asked, worry in his little voice.

"No, the bell isn't dinged yet," Himmat said.

Jaggi considered the Sikh man sitting behind a table under the neem tree in the school courtyard, wearing a dark blue turban and a light blue Punjabi *Kurta-pajama*—a loose, long shirt and drawstring trousers. He looked older and much more significant than his father.

Jaggi dragged his feet, entering the large compound he had seen many times, though only from the outside. Unconsciously, he grabbed Himmat's shirt. A row of children was sitting near masterji on his left. He wondered if the children would play with him. At the end of that row, Jaggi's gaze fell on Banta, the village sarpanch's son, making him cringe. He knew Banta from the gurdwara, where he and his rowdy friends were always running around, noisy, ignoring repeated warnings by the priest. Jaggi didn't want to sit in that row.

There was another line of children sitting on the right of masterji. Maybe I'll sit there, Jaggi thought; he wanted to sit with Himmat, though, and there were older children, the age of Himmat, sitting in the veranda. There were two rooms beyond them, and the students looked much older through the windows.

The boys stopped by the table, and Surjit Singh looked up. He knew Himmat, but the younger child was new.

"Masterji, please write his name in your register," Himmat said.

The schools did not require verified documents. An older student, or a family member, if one accompanied the student, would provide the necessary information—the child's name, birth date, parentage, etc. That would become their permanent, official record for getting admissions to other schools or applying for jobs for the rest of their lives. Since Bindo was confident, Jaggi could provide the required information, and because Himmat was with him, she did not think she or Teja had to accompany him.

"Son, what is your name?" Surjit Singh asked the child.

Curiosity about the newcomer made the two nearby classes attentive.

"Ji Ja-Ja-Ja-Ja-Jaggi," the boy stammered.

The children burst into laughter, and Jaggi's body collapsed into a slouch.

Surjit Singh motioned the boy to his side, "Come here, son. It's okay; this is your first day."

Jaggi nodded.

"What's your father's name?"

"Ji Te-Te-Te-Te—"

Before he could finish, the children burst into laughter again, even louder this time.

"Silence! Get back to your work, all of you," Surjit Singh yelled, quieting them.

"Tell your baau ji to come and see me tomorrow, okay?" he said, and Jaggi nodded. "Now, you two go and sit in your seats. Bete, that is your class," Surjit Singh said, pointing Jaggi toward a space where Banta was sitting.

As Himmat went to the veranda to join his classmates, Jaggi was frightened at being alone. His heart was beating hard as he went and sat next to Banta.

Chasing Dignity

"He is hakla," whispered Banta to his friends, informing them Jaggi stuttered. A few others echoed his hushed laughter.

Each morning, students from the third and fourth classes were assigned to teach the first graders to write the alphabet. The year-one students wrote on wooden slates, called *phatis*, smeared with a thin layer of clay. The older students would draw letters with pencils, which the younger traced in ink with reed pens. Himmat was assigned to help Jaggi. Jaggi watched intensely as his friend drew each letter, and when he got back the phati, he traced the letters methodically and accurately.

"Do you know the alphabet?" Himmat asked.

"Yes," Jaggi said, nodding. He recognized all the letters; his mother had taught him the alphabet to get him ready for school.

"After you finish, prop it against the wall to dry. Someone will look at the phatis before you all go to the pond to wash them," Himmat said before walking back to his class.

Jaggi was thrilled with his achievement. He finished before everyone else and proudly stood up to put his phati against the wall. Banta, sitting next to Jaggi, got up and pushed him. Jaggi lost his balance, hit his inkpot as he fell, and smeared ink over his phati, right sandal, and part of his right leg. Fiercely, he straightened back up and pushed Banta, who fell hard. The thud of Banta's fall got attention, including that of Master Surjit Singh. He looked at the spilled ink around Jaggi and motioned for him to come to his desk. Jaggi was acutely aware of the children watching as he made the long walk over.

"Why did you do that?" the teacher asked sternly. Jaggi was about to tell him what happened, but then recalled the children laughing and kept silent.

Surjit Singh prodded him for an answer, but Jaggi wouldn't speak. "I see!" said Surjit Singh. "Be Murga for five minutes."

Jaggi looked up, confused.

Surjit Singh looked at Banta and motioned him over. "Show him how to be Murga."

A big smile crossed Banta's face. He leaped forward at the opportunity and demonstrated the Murga position, bending forward, weaving his arms around and through his legs to hold his ears. To enhance the severity of the punishment, he raised his buttocks as high as he could.

Jaggi got into the pose. It was more embarrassing than painful. Although Master Surjit Singh let him go back to his seat after a couple of minutes, it didn't help. He was humiliated in front of the whole school and didn't want to be there anymore.

Later, the students ran to the pond to wash and recoat their phatis. On return, they leaned them against the courtyard wall for drying. Some of them, to speed up the process, started to swing the phatis around in the air and sing:

Surja, Surja phati suka,
Aj teri mangni, kal tera viah

[O dear Sun, make my phati dry; if you do,
it'll be your betrothal today and the wedding tomorrow.]

Jaggi had the urge to swing his phati around and sing like them. Instead, he set it against the neem tree to dry and sat quietly on one side. There was a neem tree in front of his house that Jaggi loved to climb. His mother made soap from the neem tree fruit.

"You won't get skin rashes if you use neem soap," he remembered her saying. But this neem tree did not look friendly.

During the lunch break, he and Himmat took their lunch packs outside the courtyard to eat and sat on a tree stump.

"Why did you push Banta?" Himmat asked.

"He p-p-pushed me f-f-first."

"Why didn't you tell the masterji then?"

Jaggi didn't answer, and Himmat did not ask again.

They hadn't finished eating when some of Himmat's friends came to play marbles.

Jaggi knew the game well. They would draw a small circle on the ground, and each player put one or two marbles inside. Taking turns, they would aim at the marbles from a marked position, with a larger striker-marble, to win the marbles by hitting them out of the circle.

Two of Himmat's classmates drew their circle close to where they were eating.

"Marbles, Himmat?" one called.

"In a minute," Himmat answered. "Finish up quickly; we'll play."

"I don't have any m-m-marbles," Jaggi said.

"I have enough," Himmat said, pulling a few from his side pocket and giving those to Jaggi. They quickly joined the others.

Jaggi and Himmat had just placed their marbles in the circle when Banta came running and put his pair in the ring, announcing, "I wanna play, too."

Himmat picked up his marbles and threw them out.

"Get lost and play with your class," Himmat yelled, pointing to where Banta's friends were playing.

"Why's he playing then?" Banta said, pointing to Jaggi.

"Our choice," Himmat said sternly.

Banta shot daggers at him. Himmat was older and bigger than Banta, and he stared him down. Banta turned around to pick up the thrown marbles.

"Sala Jheor, the lowly caste," he said as he walked away, spewing contempt. Though *sala* means wife's brother, its abusive usage is "I fuck your sister."

Jaggi saw Himmat's eyes flare up and thought he would go after Banta. But instead, Himmat took a deep breath and returned to the game.

The next day Teja came to school and introduced himself as Jaggi's father.

Master Surjit Singh looked at the diminutive figure before him; nothing in the man's language or appearance indicated an ounce of education. When Surjit Singh asked for Jaggi's date of birth, he described it in the Indian calendar, forcing Surjit Singh to convert it into Georgian—June 16, 1978.

"Teja Singh, I'm not sure if the boy is ready to start school yet. He cannot even say his name."

"Jagjit Singh is his name, but we call him Jaggi," Teja said, looking uncomfortable.

Teja recalled Bindo's face and how excited she was to send Jaggi to school. She would be devastated if the teacher didn't admit Jaggi.

Not making out if Teja understood, Surjit Singh said, "Teja Singh, can you wait another year for him to enroll?"

"No, we want him in school now," Teja said. He seemed proud and relieved at his answer.

"It's up to you, Teja Singh, but the boy is slow; children usually speak well by this age," Surjit Singh said.

"The doctor said Jaggi would speak well in a few years."

"Every child develops at their own pace. Your boy may have difficulty keeping up with other children."

Chasing Dignity

Teja was alarmed at the comment. He recalled his pride when Jaggi started to walk at not even eight months. He showed all signs of being intelligent, learning everything much quicker than other children his age. However, Jaggi always had trouble speaking, and by the time he was four, they got worried and took him to a doctor. Dr. Khera told them it was a developmental stutter which would likely go away with age. But it had nothing to do with Jaggi's intelligence. In Teja's mind, Jaggi was more brilliant than any other child his age.

"Jaggi is smart," Teja said softly. Surjit Singh did not understand Teja's words.

"Don't you worry, Teja Singh," he said, "leave it to me. I will take care of him."

Teja had gotten up to leave when Surjit Singh remembered the incident from the day before, and he shared it with Teja. It baffled Teja; it did not sound like Jaggi, but he didn't say anything.

When Jaggi got home from school, Teja brought up the issue of his fight in school. Jaggi explained what happened. When asked why he didn't tell the teacher, he looked down. Bindo could see his small body tremble and knew what was going on. She remembered her childhood—how the shame of being from a low caste had made her timid, withdrawn, and unable to stand her ground. After all her work to make sure her son wouldn't endure what she did, here he was, reduced to cowering because of their unfortunate lot at birth.

She got up to hug him, her eyes moist. "Don't worry, bete, you are better than them." She knew how better her son was than them all.

Chapter 3

Teja was a hardworking man, and his world consisted of farming, cattle, and the half-mile run between his house and the fields. His social life was limited to showing up at events related to deaths or religious ceremonies in the basti. He did not like attending celebrations and would only participate in a festive activity like a wedding party when he had to. He never indulged in drinking at parties or associated with the revelers.

Teja's late grandfather was a jamadar in the British Indian army. Since the military paid for his food and living expenses, he could save most of his salary. Thanks to the grandfather's thriftiness and foresight, Teja lived in a lovely house. Standing at the entrance to the basti, the house was visible from the main road, giving the basti a dignified look.

After Bindo came as Teja's bride, she insisted on installing a flush toilet. It was ground-breaking in a place where people knew no better than the privacy of the crops or the hillocks. Their house became the only house in the whole village with that luxury.

Even though Teja was not educated, he had a highly educated person, Professor Tara Singh, as his close friend. Tara Singh was younger than Teja only by a couple of months. Their friendship drew attention—Tara Singh was from an upper-caste Jat family and had a PhD from Oxford. He worked as a professor of geography at a renowned university in Punjab. He owned a significant amount of farmland in the village.

Their unlikely friendship had its origin before their births. Teja's father, Hari, worked for Tara's father on his farm. Tara's parents were not as exclusive about their high caste and did not prohibit their workers from entering their home, even though that invited the ire of the villagers. Sometimes Teja would accompany his father to Tara's house and play with Tara.

When Tara started school, Teja was already a student and Teja went with him to his home after school. Teja's mother tracked Teja down and came to get him.

"Would you like a glass of warm milk?" Tara's mother asked.

"I didn't bring my cup," said Teja's mother apologetically.

"Oh, rubbish, have a seat."

"No, bhen ji, sit on the charpoy here," Tara's mother said when Teja's mother tried to sit down on the floor. Such friendly treatment in a Jat's house was new to Teja's mother. No other Jat woman had ever addressed her with the sisterly term, bhen ji. She reluctantly sat on the charpoy. Tara's mother brought two glasses of milk and sat with her.

"Teja can come here with Tara whenever he wants to. The two seem to get along well," Tara's mother said.

A few years later, Tara's father had a stroke. He survived, but his health was not the same, and he decided to retire from farming. He gave his land to Hari for sharecropping. That raised many eyebrows in the Jat community. It was common for a farmer to give his land for sharecropping, but no one ever shared their land with a Keera. People did not believe Keeras had the skills or the means for independent farming, and they certainly did not want to see a Keera working on par with them. Still, Hari received all the farming equipment he needed for which he paid over a few years.

Hari's association with Tara's family could probably lead Teja further with schooling. However, Hari needed reliable help with his new venture, and after primary school, Teja quit to help his father. Tara continued his education and eventually finished college.

Tara was still in college when his father died. Tara won a Rhodes scholarship and went to Oxford for a PhD.

Chasing Dignity

Tara was still away when Teja married Bindo and lost his father to an accident. He continued farming Tara's land despite all the changes, and they maintained their friendship.

Teja was highly thankful for his family's good fortune, comparing himself to others in the basti, who had it far worse. He had a beautiful, educated wife, enough to eat, and a lovely house. More importantly, his son had it better as a result.

Soon after their wedding, Bindo launched her tailoring business and quickly established herself as the village seamstress. She tailored women's garments and got extremely busy. Typically, the Jat ladies from the village didn't come near the basti, but Bindo's house was right on the other side of the road, and it looked like any of theirs. They began visiting her home, bringing unstitched clothes to place their orders or picking the readied products, gradually building a routine. Bindo upheld herself well and her house was always clean and better maintained than most of theirs. Still, many couldn't overcome the fact that Bindo was a Keeri. Though they would accept her hospitality, they would refuse if she offered them a drink.

One day a married young woman from the basti visited Bindo. She wanted Bindo to read her a letter from her parents because she couldn't read.

"I will do it this time, but promise you will learn to read and write. I will help you with that," Bindo told the young lady.

The woman was excited at the prospect of learning and became Bindo's first pupil, motivating a few others in the basti who also wanted to learn. Soon Bindo had a regular one-hour class at her home that met three days a week. Bindo asked them to pay, not with money, but with their time. They had to help her clean the basti lanes and the surroundings to upkeep the neighborhood. With persistent effort and coaxing, Bindo organized a dynamic basti-cleaning crew. They planted and nurtured trees, creating a rich landscape—a new concept to the area.

Her activities roused jealousy and the ire of a few Jats, who saw her as audacious—a low caste trying to look superior. Some would go out of their way to put her in her place. On one occasion, Bindo needed to make a delivery, and Jaggi insisted on accompanying her because a child from that house was in his class. Jaggi had done so before, mainly when the home they were visiting had a child he knew. It had never been a problem before; the children would play while the ladies chit-chatted.

The two played on a cot while the ladies were engaged in their business. While waiting for payment, Bindo stood drinking tea by the door, and the head of the household came home for something. He saw Jaggi playing with his son on the cot and, enraged, charged toward them. He pulled Jaggi by the arm and threw him down, yelling, "Sala, ill-gotten Keera! How dare you climb on a Jat's bed?"

That unleashed Bindo's fury like never before. She flung the brass tumbler into the floor, spilling tea all over, picked up Jaggi, and marched out without bothering to collect her money. Bindo learned later that the farmer had been an outspoken critic of her for not behaving as she should and had promised, given a chance, to teach "the Keeri" a lesson.

Not every Jat family was like that, though. Many Jat women regarded Bindo with respect and dealt with her as an equal; many sought her advice on matters besides tailoring. Many men from the village appreciated Bindo's efforts, honesty, and boldness. A few would not hesitate to stand with her against their kind.

Bindo learned this from an incident at the Gurdwara, which was situated on the tallest hillock outside the village and had a limited-capacity concrete veranda floor. Without fail, Bindo took Jaggi to the Sunday service, where people wouldn't mind sharing the space with the low castes on most days. However, when the crowds swelled on special occasions, the upper castes occupied the main floor while the Keeras and other low ranks sat on the grass outside.

Bindo and Jaggi went to the Gurdwara early and casually took seats on the main floor on one such day. People soon crowded the veranda; still, more were coming when a young man asked Bindo to get up and sit outside on the grass.

Bindo was about to move when she heard someone behind starting to speak to the young man. "Why don't you, yourself, sir, sit outside? The lady is here with her child, and they arrived before you." His voice was sharp and strong. She saw Jai Singh, a middle-aged farmer from the village she knew well. Jai Singh had already gotten up to confront the young man and motioned Bindo to keep sitting.

"I am talking to her, not to you. All the Keeras are sitting outside; why can't she sit with her lot?" the young man shouted.

"This is the Guru's house, and in the presence of the Guru, everyone is equal. Keep your high caste to yourself and leave her alone," Jai Singh said with a tone that didn't leave much room for negotiation; the young man backed off. Bindo sensed a spectacle involving more people emerging on the issue and did not want a scene created on her account. As soon as the service was over, she prompted Jaggi to get up, and they left.

Chapter 4

Master Surjit Singh was the sole employee of the Kundyan school for the past eighteen years and was responsible for teaching all the subjects to all five classes. He lived in a village a forty-minute bike ride away and was always on time. The students would compete to take his bike to park it in a corner, an exciting job for them. Master Surjit Singh was well-liked both by the students and the parents. He owned a beautiful little metal canteen, a gift from his brother in the army, which he kept in an almirah in the room for the fifth class. Every day around mid-morning or on the rare occasion that a teacher from another school or an official from the District Education Department visited, he would send a student with the flask to get hot tea from home. The moms would gladly accommodate, sometimes even packing a few cookies to go with the tea.

Surjit Singh depended on his students for many tasks. Each class had a monitor to ensure the students stayed engaged and completed the assigned task. The students had to inform the monitor of water and bathroom breaks. The fourth- and fifth-class students were responsible for cleaning the premises in the morning before school started. They would sweep the brick-covered floors of the rooms and the uncovered courtyard and sprinkle water over the yard to let the fine dust settle before spreading the long, narrow jute rugs for the students to sit on. Cleaning school premises was sacred, and all students did it, regardless of their caste.

Surjit Singh paid personal attention only to the upper three levels; he taught classes one and two by proxy—the upper-class students were responsible for teaching them. He spent a significant chunk of his time on years four and five. An outside high school tested grade-five students, and class-four students were eligible for a district-wide competition for a scholarship with a nominal amount of money for the student and bragging rights for the school.

The year-one students were required to memorize times tables up to ten, and they were tested on their progress twice a week by a senior student. Bindo helped Jaggi learn the tables early on, even before joining the school. The first day Jaggi was asked what two times two was, he quickly answered "char." The next question was two times seven, and Jaggi immediately knew the answer "chaudan." But he got stuck at the first syllable; the rest wouldn't just come out of his mouth. Before he could finish, the whole class burst into laughter, and he stopped trying. He was asked another question, but he did not answer. Anyone missing two items incurred five *Kan-phar-Baitthak*—squatting down while holding your ears. Jaggi took the punishment.

Jaggi would practice saying numbers by himself at home to avoid embarrassment, and he could do it without much stuttering. However, his voice would fail miserably during the test. Eventually, he found it easier to take the punishment than stutter trying to answer. Surjit Singh frequently saw him doing the Kan-phar-Baitthak, and one time, while he was watching, Jaggi got down into the squat, even before he heard the question.

Despite his inevitable punishment, Jaggi enjoyed the rote exercise in which they recited the tables. The children would stand shoulder to shoulder in a single file. One would step out to lead, facing the rest, and rhythmically sing the table, one line at a time. The rest would roar their lungs out, chorusing after the leader. Shouting with force would overcome Jaggi's stutter, drowning any remnants of it in the collective roar.

The situation was even worse with reading assignments. Jaggi could read better than any other student in the class; his mother had been reading with him at home. However, he found it easier to be Murga over reading aloud in the study. Jaggi never talked about his punishments at home, lest it saddened his mother. He enjoyed getting into her lap to read and recite all the times tables he knew. Bindo never acknowledged Jaggi's stutter and would beam listening to him read and do multiplications by memory. His classmates did not write beyond practicing the alphabet, but thanks to Bindo's tutoring, Jaggi began to write, and soon he could write with the ease and command of an above-average class three student.

However, at school, Banta's taunts had increased. He would call Jaggi Murga, and, often to intensify the insult, would combine the slurs, calling him hakla-Murga.

There was no formal year-end testing for class-one students; generally, all students who were in school for at least six months got promoted. Jaggi had been in school for the entire year but having witnessed him be Murga or do Kan-phar-Baitthak all year, Surjit Singh was not ready to advance him to class two. He sent for Jaggi's father one day to discuss the matter.

Teja remembered the master doubting Jaggi's abilities and thought Jaggi had proved him wrong. But he was startled when Surjit Singh said that he was considering holding Jaggi a year back. "I have observed him very closely this year, and I feel he is not yet ready to move to the next class. I suggest we keep him in the same class for another year. It will be in his best interest."

"What?" Teja almost screamed.

Surjit Singh was surprised to see Teja suddenly have that much energy. "Sir, please sit down. Listen to me before we begin to fight. Jaggi cannot read from his elementary textbook and has not learned any times tables. Those are the minimum expectations we have from them."

Teja was not involved with Jaggi's learning because he didn't know enough to help him. But he knew well that Jaggi could read beyond his grade. After dinner, Teja always sat on a low stool to watch mother and son envelop themselves in books for third- and fourth-year classes. He would enjoy the glow in his wife's eyes when Jaggi showed interest in a new book she brought home.

Bindo suggested that masterji had invited Teja because he must be considering Jaggi skipping a year.

Teja was very attached to Jaggi, who always went to the fields after school and on their way home in the evening would ride on Teja's shoulders to the bullock cart. He would sit in Teja's lap during dinner, taking nibbles from his food morsels.

Teja tilted his head in frustration. He wished he had the courage and respectability to prove the teacher wrong, but he didn't know how.

"I will talk to Bindo," he mumbled, getting up to leave.

Surjit Singh took it as his acceptance of the proposal. "I wanted to talk to you before I announced the results on Monday," he said.

Bindo jumped out of her skin as if she had touched an electric wire.

"You are not serious, are you?" she asked, knowing that Teja would never lie like that, especially when it concerned Jaggi. "What do we do now?" she said.

There was dead silence while she paced around.

"I'll talk to Tara," Teja said, giving Bindo a glimmer of hope.

The professor often visited the village on weekends to visit his mother; luckily, this was one of those weekends. The next day Teja went to Tara's house. He was having breakfast sitting under the mango tree when Teja walked in. His mother was sitting on a separate charpoy next to him. Tara Singh pulled a chair for Teja and offered him breakfast.

Teja declined and, without much ado, told them the whole story.

Chasing Dignity

"How can he do that? Your boy is smart," said the professor's mother. "One day, he came here with his mother. He picked up my Punjabi newspaper and read it. He is a lovely boy," she added, looking at the professor.

"Yes, something seems to be amiss here. Let me finish eating; we will go to your place. I'd like to talk to the boy," the professor said.

Jaggi had gone to play with Himmat. While Teja went to get him, Bindo showed a book to the professor. "I had this textbook in my fourth class. Jaggi can read it without any problem. Also, the master says Jaggi cannot recite any times tables," she said, picking a notebook from the shelf and handing it to the professor. "This is Jaggi's notebook; take a look for yourself; he can do tables up to twenty by twenty."

The workbook was full of two-digit multiplications interspersed with pages of written text.

"Did he write all this?" he asked.

"Yes, I dictate him from that book," she said, pointing.

"What am I missing? I wonder how that teacher could miss a smart boy like him. Did Jaggi ever tell you he had a problem at school?" the professor asked.

"No, never. But from what the master said, Jaggi may not speak enough in the class to show his intelligence. Children can be cruel—maybe they are making fun of his stutter. We never wanted to make Jaggi self-conscious; Dr. Khera told us not to discuss it. So we don't."

"I agree with the doctor," the professor said. His gaze moved to a pencil drawing sitting on a stool.

"Jaggi likes to draw," Bindo said, following his eyes. "Let me show you," she said and brought him a small stack of papers with drawings.

"The boy is very expressive," the professor said, slowly going through the stack.

As he examined the drawings, the front door opened, and Jaggi ran inside. Teja followed.

"Sasrikal, un-un-uncle ji," Jaggi said, getting close to the professor.

"Sasrikal beta," the professor said, ruffling his hair. "Do you play all the time like this, or do you study too?"

"I do s-s-study!" said Jaggi.

"I see, and you like to draw," the professor said, pointing to the stack of papers Bindo gave him. "Can you tell me what this is?" he said, pointing to the sketch of a large, round, brown animal with curly hair and horns.

"Meeni," Jaggi said; Meeni was one of their buffalos. At a bit of prodding, Jaggi went over all the drawings. One included him with maa and baau ji, and one with Himmat. The one that intrigued Tara Singh the most was Jaggi's depiction of their basti. It was de facto a map that showed the two streets of the basti drawn as double lines with the houses shown as little rectangles. The shapes of the squiggly lines resembled the actual curves of the lanes.

"I'm impressed, Jaggi. Do you know what this is?" the professor said, putting his finger on the paper.

"It's Tai Kau-Kau-Kauro's house," Jaggi answered quickly.

"No, not that—this whole paper that you drew. What do you call it?"

Jaggi shrugged. "Paper," he said shyly.

The professor smiled at his answer. "Bete, what you drew here," he said, "we call it a map. You did a wonderful job at drawing this."

Jaggi shrugged again.

Chasing Dignity

"And I hear you are very good with numbers."

Jaggi looked at his mother with big eyes; she smiled at him and softened.

"You see, Jaggi, I need your help," the professor said. "Can you tell me, what would be seventeen times seventeen?"

Jaggi seemed amused at the question. There was a spark in his eyes, but he glanced at his mother instead of answering.

"Bete, answer uncle ji. You know, we did this last night," Bindo said.

Jaggi looked back at the professor "t-t-two eighty-nine," he said and ran toward the staircase that led to the rooftop.

"Come back here, Jaggi!" yelled Bindo, and Jaggi came to her. "It is not polite to run away like that, bete. Uncle ji is talking to you," she said.

"And that was very good, Jaggi. Now one more question," the professor said. Jaggi looked at him. "What is thirteen times seventeen?"

"Two hundred twenty-one," Jaggi answered without a glimmer of hesitation or stutter.

"Yes! You are a smart boy!"

Jaggi's eyes lit up.

"What were you and your friend playing just now?"

"They were playing marbles," Teja answered for Jaggi.

Jaggi looked at his father.

"Oh? Do you know your baau ji and I are very good at marbles?"

Jaggi looked up at the professor, amused.

"You don't believe me, do you?"

Jaggi shook his head; he had never seen adults play marbles.

"Okay, let's see how good you are. Bring some marbles. Do you have any?"

Jaggi nodded and ran inside to get some. He then drew a circle on the ground, put a few marbles inside, and drew a small marker to hit from a few feet away. Finally, he offered the striker to the professor.

"No, you go first," Tara Singh said.

Jaggi went to the line and aimed at the marble pointed to by the professor. It was a nice hit, hitting the target and one other marble out of the circle.

"Oh, you got two," the professor said. "Now, I'll show you how to really play marbles."

The professor went to the line and aimed at the marble Jaggi pointed to and, on purpose, missed the circle entirely.

Jaggi laughed loudly.

"Now that was embarrassing, wasn't it?" the professor said, "I'm out of practice. Let's not play this game today, okay? I need to practice."

Jaggi nodded in agreement, collected his marbles, and put them in his side pocket.

"But I'll play another game with you," the professor said. He picked up the book Bindo had shown him and sat nearby on a cot.

"Come here," he said, patting next to him.

Jaggi sat there.

"Can you read this page for me?" said the professor, opening a random page.

Jaggi knew what that book was, and the request tickled him a bit. He looked at his mother.

Chasing Dignity

"It is okay, bete. Uncle ji is getting old and can't see as well," Bindo said, chuckling.

Jaggi took the book from the professor and started reading the page. The professor could see him struggling with the stutter.

"Can you write if I dictate it to you?" the professor asked.

Jaggi nodded and picked up his workbook while Bindo grabbed him a pen. The professor dictated from one page, and Jaggi wrote it with ease.

The professor reviewed what Jaggi wrote. "You are quite a smart boy!" he said. "You can now go and play with your friend."

Jaggi disappeared, saying, "Going to Himmat's, maa."

The professor went quiet, lost in his thought. Bindo waited for him to say something.

"This boy is not ordinary. He will stand above the crowd," the professor said. "He will make you proud."

Bindo was a little amused at the statement because she was already very proud of Jaggi. She looked at the professor intently.

"Do you think he'll change his mind, Veer ji?" Bindo said.

The professor looked at her. "What?" he said.

"Do you think the master will change his mind about Jaggi?"

"I don't know, Bindo," he said. "He had the child with him the whole year. I don't know how he could miss what Tara Singh got out of the boy in no more than twenty minutes. He is either a total blockhead or biased against a smart Keera boy."

The professor's answer sent a chill down her spine.

"What can we do?" she asked.

"I don't know. Give me some time. Let me think about it."

"But the master said he will announce the results on Monday, and he won't promote Jaggi," Bindo said. The professor didn't say anything.

Bindo was desperate. "Veer ji, it'll devastate Jaggi if the master holds him back," she said.

"I will talk to the teacher," the professor said and got up to leave.

"Veer ji, are you going back to Chandigarh tomorrow?" Bindo asked.

"I was planning to, but don't worry; I will meet with him before I leave on Monday," assured the professor and left.

Chapter 5

It was the last Monday of March; the children were excited about being promoted and off for a week. The following Monday, they would return to their new classes. It was a pleasant morning, and the bell had not dinged yet. Master Surjit Singh was sitting relaxed in his chair, eyes closed, enjoying the coolness of the neem shade when he sensed adult footsteps entering the schoolyard. He opened his eyes and was surprised to see his guest, Professor Tara Singh. The professor was well-respected in the village, and Surjit Singh knew him by his reputation and was well aware of his education at Oxford.

Dressed up in a light half-sleeve shirt matching his elegantly tied turban and the dark blue tie that matched his trousers, Tara Singh lived up to his expectations. He held a small notebook and a Punjabi storybook in his hand.

Tara Singh had never been to the school before, and his sudden presence caused an unconscious feeling of humbleness to run through Surjit Singh. He stood up to greet the professor.

"Hello, Professor Sahib, welcome, welcome to our school! What did we do to have the pleasure of your visit?" Surjit Singh extended his arm for a handshake and offered the chair to the professor.

"I need to talk to you, Sardar Surjit Singh Ji. But I need to get back to Chandigarh as soon as possible, and I don't have much time," the professor said, sitting down.

Surjit Singh was taken aback by the curtness in the professor's tone. "Please, Professor Sahib, how can I help you?"

"I heard you plan to hold Teja Singh's son back in the first class?"

The teacher squirmed in his chair; the professor must have come to chastise him for holding back a first-grader who had been there the whole year.

"The boy is not yet ready to move up. He cannot read from his book. We expect them to memorize the basic, single-digit times tables at this level, and he cannot tell what two times two is. He cannot even speak properly," Surjit Singh said rather forcefully.

"Do you mind if we invite Jaggi in here for a minute?"

"Why?" the teacher asked with defiance. He had, after all, made his decision for the benefit of the student.

"Because I know the boy, and I disagree with your conclusion! It is only fair if we test him a little together."

Surjit Singh glared at the uninvited intruder.

The professor sensed the teacher's resentment.

"Sardar Sahib, I'm not here to disrespect you, and I'm sure you want the best for your students. But what bothers me is why the two of us see the child so differently and why that may be the case."

"So, you are saying my assessment is wrong," the master said scornfully. "All right, I'll call him." He looked toward the first-class, sitting a little farther from his desk.

"Jaggi," he called out aloud, motioning Jaggi over.

Jaggi briefly looked at the professor, but quickly his gaze went down, and he started fiddling with his hands.

"Jaggi bete, can you show masterji what we did the other day?" the professor asked, sliding the notebook and a ballpoint pen toward him. Jaggi didn't react at all.

"Bete, write here the answers to what we ask of you," the professor said. Jaggi nodded.

The professor asked, "What is ten times ten?"

Without thinking, Jaggi wrote one hundred. The professor continued, asking six times eight, nine times nine, five times four, three times nine, and Jaggi promptly wrote the correct answer. Surjit Singh watched in silence.

Chasing Dignity

"What is fifteen times fifteen?" the professor asked.

"We teach only up to ten," Surjit Singh interrupted.

The professor put up his hand to hush him.

Jaggi looked off to the side, then wrote down 225. The professor continued to ask questions from double-digit times tables to twenty by twenty, not skipping over even the hardest computations. Without fail, Jaggi promptly wrote all answers correctly.

The professor shot the dumbfounded teacher a look of intensity. "Now write what I speak," he said, turning back to the boy. He began dictating from the storybook he had brought with him, and Jaggi wrote every word without a single spelling mistake.

"Bete, now, you can go back to your seat," the professor said, patting Jaggi on the head as he left.

The teacher looked up at him, bewildered.

"Sardar Surjit Singh Ji, please tell me how you concluded that you need to hold him back in the first class?"

He had no response.

"I assume it has nothing to do with the fact that he's a Keera…" The insinuation stung Surjit Singh.

"Professor Sahib, please! That is one insult I won't take. I'll be the last person to discriminate against a student because of his caste!" he said, feeling a lump in his throat—his voice had started to shake a little. "But you must know," he continued, "I am the only teacher in this school, and I have to take care of all five classes. The upper two classes take up most of my time. I have to get help from the older students to teach classes one and two, so I've had little one-on-one time with him. And, above all, the child cannot communicate," the teacher said.

"I think he communicated very well with us, don't you? He has a stutter. He feels ashamed when people laugh at him," the professor said. "If I were his teacher, I would have him promoted to class three instead of holding him back. And even there, I can bet you; he will be better than most in the class."

Surjit Singh didn't say anything.

"Sardar Sahib, I have to go, but now you know why I had to stop by. I will leave these with you," the professor said, leaving the books he had brought with him on the table. Surjit Singh did not say anything, nor did he get up to shake the professor's hand.

After the professor was gone, Surjit Singh got up from his chair and paced around in the courtyard, recollecting Jaggi being Murga day after day for not reading or reciting tables. He thought of his class-threes, realizing how most of them and even many class-fours struggled with multiplications beyond sixteen.

He looked at the children, excited for him to announce the results, his gaze stopping at Jaggi. He called him to his desk. "Jaggi, can you do me a favor?" The boy nodded. "I want you to write down what you do when you go home. You can write whatever comes to mind. There are no wrong answers," and he gave him a pencil and a notebook. "I want you to fill one page of this notebook."

Jaggi took the notebook and the pencil, but he did not write anything. He seemed utterly confused. "It is okay, bete; I want to see how smart you are. Take your time; there is no rush. I will be back; I need to go to the bathroom," Surjit Singh said and went outside to leave him alone.

When he returned, the notebook was on his desk with the pencil inside. He opened it and saw the following:

First, maa hugs me. She gives me milk and one cookie. She makes tea for baau ji, and we go to the fields. My baau ji drinks tea. I go to the pastures to get berries from the bushes. I get on baau ji's shoulder. We sit on the cart. We go home. My baau ji eats roti. My maa eats roti. I eat one egg, one roti, and dal. I again drink

Chasing Dignity

milk. My maa reads to me. I read to my maa. She hugs me. She tells me a story. I go to sleep. The end.

"I read to my maa," stuck with Surjit Singh. No wonder the boy had advanced so far, separate from his instruction!

He called the student assembly. They all came and sat in rows according to their classes. Surjit Singh started to tell them who was promoted, one class at a time, beginning with the fifth class.

All fifth-class students had passed, and all but one from the fourth class got promoted to the fifth. All students from the third and the second class passed. Clapping followed each announcement.

Then he looked at the year-one class and said—"You all pass." There was a big clap.

"And Jagjit Singh," he said, looking at the small boy, "is promoted to class three."

Jaggi looked around as if the teacher was talking to someone else. Everyone was quiet—how could a school Murga skip a class?

"That is all for today, students. You can go home," he said, adjourning the assembly.

"*Sipharsh*—unscrupulous recommendation," Balbir, Banta's older brother from the outgoing fifth class, mumbled. "Professor's *sipharsh*—Keera-hugger professor and his baau are cronies."

The following Monday was unpleasant for Surjit Singh. The news of the professor's visit had spread, and nepotism was the only explanation available. Surjit Singh got a visit from Sukha, Banta's father. Sukha was furious because Jaggi's undeserved promotion had humiliated his son. He demanded Banta and Jaggi be in the same class, which meant either Jaggi to be put back in year two or Banta promoted to year three. Banta was more intelligent than Jaggi, who the entire school knew was the worst child, who couldn't even speak.

Sukha was financially well off and had established clout. He was sarpanch, elected head of the village. Even though he knew the professor's influence, how could an outsider—the professor had a house in the city where he spent most of his time!—manipulate their school teacher and have an outcaste boy promoted over the son of the village sarpanch?

"Isn't the government already doing us great harm by reserving so many jobs for Keeras? And now this? At the bidding of that Keera-hugger professor, you promoted a Keera ahead of our boys. Do you want these Keeras to grab all jobs before ours even finish their degrees?"

Surjit Singh had known Sukha for many years and was always able to coax his fiery ego in moments like this. But today, none of his arguments was good enough. To avoid having the scene continue in front of the students, he took Sukha out for a walk, taking along the notebook the professor had left behind.

"Sardar Sukha Singh Ji, it is my responsibility to place a student in a class that matches his mental caliber. I have tested Teja's son myself. He already knows far more than what I teach in class two. It is only fair to promote him to class three."

"That light came to you with the professor visit! I heard, all year, the boy did nothing but be Murga!"

The teacher took a deep breath. "Yes, you are right, and I am ashamed of my oversight. As a teacher, I should have been able to see how intelligent he was despite his difficulties." The teacher was almost in tears.

He then told Sukha everything that transpired between him and the professor—how Jaggi performed the double-digit multiplications and took perfect dictation. "He is the best student I have seen in years."

"Are you telling me that the hakla, Keera boy is more intelligent than my son?"

"We can test your son in your presence, and if he is equally capable, I'll gladly promote him to class three," proposed Surjit Singh. "I will do this for any student, not just your son. I can't do it otherwise," he said firmly.

The teacher's story made Sukha think hard; he did not have the nerve to put his son in a losing position against a Keera, especially against someone the professor had vouched. Sukha had known the professor all his life and had never doubted his integrity before this. He decided to back off.

Surjit Singh struggled with his own feelings for a while. On the one hand, he was resentful for his wounded pride, but on the other, the memories of Jaggi's taking punishment every day troubled him. How could he have been so oblivious to the plight of a small hapless boy?

He started paying more attention to the first two classes, being particularly observant of the shy and reserved, and becoming overly conscious and protective of Jaggi.

Getting promoted to third class was bittersweet for Jaggi. On the first day of the new class year, Jaggi instinctively joined his former classmates during playtime, hoping for familiarity and acceptance.

"Hi, hakley, we won't play with you. Go back to your class," Banta said, getting in front of him and blocking him from putting his marbles in the circle. The rest of the children didn't pay much attention and continued to play. Jaggi walked over to the third class playing their games; they paid no attention to him either. Even in the first class, he was the youngest student, and now, not only was he the youngest by an extra year, but he was also the littlest, and his older classmates casually left him out of games.

Luckily, Jaggi was better at playing marbles than many in his new class, and they did not exclude him from the game he enjoyed most.

Surjit Singh, aware of Jaggi's speaking issue, did not require him to recite anything. During book reading exercises, he would let Jaggi write his assignments instead. Getting this special treatment often drew sniggers, and it confused Jaggi. He wished he was treated like everyone else, even if it meant taking punishment.

Jaggi's isolation continued for a little while. However, slowly, his classmates started to see how smart he was and began to warm up to him; the resentment of his promotion slowly dissipated.

Chapter 6

Every day, Jaggi returned from school around four. After giving him a glass of milk, Bindo would make the afternoon tea for Teja, and they would go together to the fields. She would hand Teja the small round brass vessel full of tea, pick up a sickle, and head to the sorghum field to cut forage for the cattle. Little Jaggi would run to the hillock along the farm's side to pick up wild berries from mallah bushes. There were plenty of thorny mallah bushes that bore berries. Kids loved to pick them up even though they would get bruised. "Jaggi, be careful of the thorns," Bindo would shout.

"Let him be, Bindo," Teja would interject. "This is how he will learn to be a man."

It would take about half an hour for Bindo to cut the forage and put it on the cart before heading home to return to her sewing. Jaggi would stay behind and play around, sometimes playing close to his father, pretending to help him.

"Baau ji, why doesn't the bullock get hurt when he steps on the plowshare?" he would ask when running in the furrow behind Teja's plow.

"He can get hurt if you aren't careful," Teja would say. "You need to keep the plow straight."

If he saw his father leveling or harrowing, he would run to sit between his legs. Holding on to one leg with his tiny hand, he would try to grab the wheat stubbles with the other before they went under the leveler or into the teeth of the harrow.

"Be careful; don't let go of my legs," Teja would warn.

Often Himmat and sometimes Rani would come and join Jaggi. They would run around in the fields and the bushes on the hillock.

During busy periods of sowing or harvesting, Teja would hire extra help from the basti. Teja took so much upon himself that Jaggi rarely saw this extra help regularly, except for Chhaju.

Chhaju would show up without asking, whenever he felt like it, to help Teja with whatever Teja was doing at the time. He did this with other farmers, too, the ones he liked. Chhaju was a lanky man in his forties. His left leg was shorter than the right, which gave him a funny, asymmetrical gait. He always carried a pitchfork with him. Because of the limp, people called him *langra*, or sometimes *pitchfork-langra*. A few would call him *pitchfork-mouse* because he never confronted anyone and would walk away if he even smelled a fight around. He would work for a few hours and accept whatever he got as remuneration, even if it were just a petty meal. He wouldn't take food unless he worked for it.

Chhaju had no family. He was a low caste but not an outcaste. Even though people wouldn't mind Chhaju living in the village, he lived near the gurdwara, in a hut under a banyan tree. His shack contained the meager possessions he had, which besides his pitchfork that he never left behind, included a small cot covered with burlap rags, a couple of blankets, a pitcher of water, and a few utensils to cook or eat food. He did not eat much, and no one remembered him ever being sick.

Chhaju did not speak much and would jerk his chin up whenever he did, as if by the force of the words. He would ignore if someone ridiculed him, and if he didn't have an or didn't want to answer a question, he would throw up a *hunh*, shake his head and walk away.

Jaggi always addressed Chhaju as Chhaju Chacha, the respect Jaggi showed to all adults. He never used derogatory words other people used toward Chhaju and considered Chhaju his friend.

"Chh... Chhaju Cha... Chacha, why do you always c-c-carry a p-p-pitchfork with you?" he asked one day.

Chasing Dignity

"One needs to be prepared," Chhaju answered. Often his answers were in short, funny phrases like that.

"Pre-pre-prepared for wh-wh-what, Chacha?"

"Hunh," Chhaju said with his chin jerking up.

Jaggi asked his mother why Chhaju Chacha always had to be prepared.

She laughed, thinking about Chhaju's idiosyncrasies. "He is prepared to attack if someone tries to hurt him," she said light-heartedly.

Jaggi imagined Banta trying to hurt Chhaju and Chhaju going after him with his pitchfork. Jaggi tried to run like Chhaju, with his right leg swinging around the left. He made it his goal to perfect that run, mimicking Chhaju's gait for many days, even holding a stick for Chhaju's pitchfork. One day Bindo caught him doing that and gave him an earful.

"It is not polite to mimic a handicapped person," she said. "It is not his fault if he cannot walk like you and me."

Even though Jaggi stopped perfecting his Chhaju-walk, Chhaju continued to fascinate him.

The following year, when Jaggi was in the fourth class, he got a chance to indulge in his fascination. Every month the fourth class had a storytelling day. The month Jaggi had his turn, he wrote a story about Chhaju. In his three-page narrative, a hero with a limp saved an old lady's house from being robbed, defending the lady and the place with just a pitchfork while the entire village feigned sleep during the robbery.

On his turn, Jaggi got up, holding the neatly written pages.

"Do you want me to read it for you?" offered Surjit Singh

"No," Jaggi said, "I w-w-will read."

"All right, go ahead," Surjit Singh said.

Everyone was curiously watching. Sweat formed on Jaggi's forehead as he started with a heavy stutter. It took him much longer to tell the story. However, the patience of the students pleased Jaggi. As he got into the account, he got more comfortable, and his stutter reduced. He didn't realize while speaking, but he had unwittingly infused his Chhaju-walk into the performance. That brought laughter from the students and big applause at the end.

That was a turning point for Jaggi, and he gradually gathered the courage to speak in front of the class more often. Although he didn't win over everyone, the novelty of his stutter started to fade. Most had begun to accept it as part of his being, just as one would someone for being overweight, underweight, too short, or too tall. More importantly, as Jaggi got friendly with the students, his stutter reduced, and so did his need to hide it, making it less burdensome for him.

At the end of the fourth year, Jaggi won the coveted scholarship. It was a special moment not only for Jaggi but also for Surjit Singh. Jaggi's achievement validated his decision to have Jaggi skip a class, and he felt exonerated.

Bindo and Teja planned a secret gift for Jaggi. Jaggi had been asking for a dog for a long time, so they arranged to get an Alsatian puppy for him from a neighboring village. Without telling, Teja took Jaggi to collect his gift. When Jaggi realized what was waiting for him, his face was worth everything for Teja. Instead of laughing, Jaggi started to cry. Tears flowed down his cheeks as he hugged the puppy over and over. Jaggi named the dog Teepu, and he could say it without the stutter. Jaggi's confidence increased, further reducing his stutter. He was progressing faster than the doctor had projected. The next time Dr. Khera saw Jaggi, he prognosticated Jaggi would entirely lose his stutter before college.

The doctor's words made Bindo ecstatic. She could envision her son walking through the college corridors with notebooks in his hand. There'll be no stigma attached to my son!

Chasing Dignity

Bindo's chest fluffed up with pride, imagining people wooing her for their beautiful daughters' hands for Jaggi in marriage.

Jaggi was ten now, and he was in the final year of his primary school. Himmat had graduated and gone to a high school in the nearby town. Though Jaggi missed Himmat, he had made friends with other boys and was comfortable without him.

One day, Jaggi was walking to school in the morning when a noise from his right startled him. He hadn't even fully turned his head to the sound yet when something hit his head and someone jumped him.

"Sala Keera," he heard as he rolled on the ground, trying to avoid a kick to his ribs, "the sister-fucker hakla has grown wings; we'll clip your wings, hakley."

It was Banta with two of his friends. They were kicking him all over as he tried to protect himself with his arms and legs.

"Let's go. I hear someone coming," one said.

"We'll kill you if you tell anyone," Banta said, staring fiercely into Jaggi's eyes.

Bewildered, Jaggi got up and saw his assailants running toward the school. His turban had fallen off. He picked it, put it back on, and readjusted it. He shook the dirt off.

Embarrassed, he entered the school. The bell had already rung. From the corner of his eye, he saw Banta and his friends peering through the window from class four, and he sensed them grinning.

Jaggi avoided his assailants all day; they, too, left him alone. He had pain in his ribs under the right arm from a hard kick, which troubled him all day.

At home, Bindo asked what had happened to his pants.

"I fell, maa," he answered.

Then she noticed the bruise on his side when he changed his shirt and asked him what it was.

"Nothing," he said.

She was curious and moved to take a closer look. Jaggi winced when she gently pressed the area.

"You did not just fall to get this bruise. What happened, bete?" Bindo inquired.

"I fell from the peepul," he answered. Bindo knew he loved to climb trees, so he thought she'd believe him.

"Be careful. You can get hurt climbing those trees." She was not satisfied with his answer but didn't press further.

The following day, Jaggi was scared to walk to school alone and kept an eye on other children leaving to tag along. Bindo was still packing his lunch when he noticed a third- and fourth-classer walk by his home.

"Going, maa!" he shouted and got out the door.

"Hi, wait, take your lunch," Bindo yelled, but he was already out of the door. Bindo followed him, still wrapping it.

"Come back, take this," she yelled.

Jaggi ran to grab the lunch rag and ran back to join the two children.

With Himmat gone, he needs to make new friends, she thought.

Even with his friends, Jaggi was watchful, looking for any trouble lurking around while they walked. That day, nothing untoward happened, but Jaggi made a routine not to walk to and from school by himself.

Surjit Singh had after-school lessons for the fifth grade every year to prepare them for the finals. Usually, he would start

Chasing Dignity

the extra class once a week and increase its frequency as the year progressed. A couple of weeks after Jaggi's terrifying experience, Surjit Singh began to hold that class on Mondays. There were no other children with Jaggi from the Keera-basti, and he had to walk home alone.

Jaggi would almost run home after the class, alert for any sign of Banta or his friends. He was barely getting comfortable when, one Monday, he saw Banta and the two of his friends moving out from behind the same tree to block his path. They were hiding there, waiting for him. He thought to run back for a moment, but that felt cowardly; besides, where or who would he run to?

"Sala Keera, you thought we forgot about you," Banta said; he held a small shaven tree limb.

"Leave me a-a-alone," Jaggi said.

"What did you say, hakley? Leave you alone?" Banta laughed and swung his stick at him. Jaggi dodged, and the limb hit his bag. The other two jumped on him with their fists, and soon Jaggi was getting blows from every direction. He tried to protect himself with his pack as much as possible, but Banta's stick made a gash on his left eyebrow. Suddenly everything stopped, and the three ran away. Jaggi looked around and saw Chhaju coming from the school side. As usual, he was carrying his pitchfork.

He stopped by Jaggi.

"Okay?" Chhaju asked.

Jaggi nodded.

"*Pukka?*" Chhaju repeated to make sure.

Jaggi nodded again. Chhaju's face showed genuine concern, and it comforted Jaggi.

With this, Chhaju limped on. Jaggi walked with him for a short distance, but the path split and Chhaju went toward the village.

No one was home when Jaggi arrived. Teja usually came late from the fields, and Bindo had gone to someone's house. It gave Jaggi time to change and clean the wound. He washed it and put some neem oil on it.

"What is that?" Bindo asked, pointing to the cut when she came home.

"I fell," he answered.

Bindo pulled a cot and sat down.

"Come here, bete," she said, inviting Jaggi to sit by her. She put her arm over him. "Chhaju just spoke to me," she said. Bindo extracted the whole story from Jaggi without much encouragement, including his previous encounter with Banta.

Although Bindo tried to keep a calm face, Jaggi's situation shook her to the core. She talked to Teja in the evening, and he, too, got agitated.

"I think you need to go to the school tomorrow and talk to masterji about it," Bindo said. Teja didn't say anything, and Bindo seeing his reluctance, grimaced in pain.

"Okay, we will go together," she said.

The following day, they went to see Surjit Singh. He listened to them and promised to look into the matter, but he said he couldn't talk to the boys in their presence.

After they left, Surjit Singh called the boys, who denied they had ever beaten Jaggi. When Surjit Singh told them that someone from the village had seen them hit Jaggi, they said the man was lying. "All low castes lie," Banta said with a sneer. Surjit Singh bristled at his student's crass remark. He took a deep breath and told them to have their fathers come and see him the following day.

All three fathers came to see Surjit Singh. He explained the situation to them in his cramped office.

"Did you see our sons beat that Keera boy?" one asked.

"Did they beat him inside your school?" another asked.

"You are taking the word of a Keera over that of our sons?" the third said.

Surjit Singh pleaded with them to understand, but they all got up and left.

"Don't even think about punishing our boys; it won't be good for you," one said.

Although Surjit Singh fully trusted Teja and Bindo, he could not do much without proof; even if he had the evidence, favoring a Keera and taking action against the Jat boys would have been unpleasant. He conveyed his situation to Bindo and Teja.

Bindo, not knowing what to do, went to the mothers of the boys. The women were already aware of the situation and aligned with their husbands.

"How dare you go to the teacher against our boys?"

"Why did you not come to us before running to the teacher?"

They called her names and told her to behave like the Keeri that she was and not provoke the Jats' ire by pretending to be equal.

Bindo tried to band together men from her basti to go to the police and file a complaint.

"Have you forgotten what happened when Guddi's father went to the police? It's their police, not ours," someone reminded her. A couple of years earlier, Guddi, a basti girl, was raped by Jat boys, and Guddi's father filed a complaint. The Jats bribed the police, and the police let them go free. Afterward, the police harassed Guddi's family, accusing them of reporting a false case, and the family ended up bribing them to stop the harassment.

Chhaju also would not say what he saw, and when Bindo pushed, he got up.

"A man got to do, what a man got to do," he said, one of his favorite phrases, and limped away.

"Coward," Bindo said, disgusted. Unfortunately, Jaggi heard her and was hurt. How could the hero of his story be a coward?

Left with no viable options, Bindo let the matter go. Teja and, sometimes, Bindo began walking Jaggi to school. To not embarrass Jaggi, they would walk a safe distance behind. Bindo focused ever more keenly on his education and well-being. Overcoming obstacles required more focus on one's goal, she believed.

Chapter 7

Jaggi finished primary school topping his district. The boys-only high school in town was half an hour's bike ride from the village, offering classes six through ten. It was the next and often the last level of schooling for boys from Kundyan; rarely did someone from the town ever move on to a four-year college. Balbir, Banta's older brother, was already there in the ninth class, and Banta would be joining the following year in the sixth. The mere thought of sending Jaggi to the same school Banta would attend stressed Bindo.

During the year-end break, Bindo and Jaggi visited her older sister Bitti, who lived in Kotla, a village a few miles from Kundyan.

"We have a nice middle school; why don't you send Jaggi here?" Bitti suggested. The middle school offered classes six through eight. Jaggi could spend three years in middle school and go to high for years nine and ten.

By the time Jaggi graduated from Kotla, Balbir would be out, and they could reassess the situation. Although Bindo wanted to keep Jaggi distant from that bully family as much as she could, sending to Kotla meant adding another couple of miles each way to Jaggi's bike ride.

"He is a young boy, and riding a few extra miles wouldn't hurt him," Bitti said. "Besides, he wouldn't have to share the road with all those cars, buses, and trucks." The dirt roads and trails connecting Kundyan to Kotla were pretty safe, devoid of any significant automobile traffic.

Jaggi was overjoyed; going to Kotla meant visiting his cousins more often, and he was excited to ride his new bicycle. Upon return, Bindo discussed it with Teja, and he was quickly on board.

The route to Kotla meandered through fields and villages, over cart paths and bike trails. For a couple of miles, they had to ride on the dirt embankment of Budki Rao, a seasonal river that stayed dry most of the year.

At one point, a vast water canal passed beneath the river using an underbridge. For that stretch, tall, three-foot-wide brick walls replaced the dirt banks of Budki Rao. The flat tops of the walls were level and continuous, with Budki Rao's dirt embankments on the two sides, and one could continue to walk on top of the wall uninterrupted. However, crossing the bare top wasn't safe, and side-rail-protected walkways facing the canal existed at a lower level for people to travel.

One cyclist came from behind as they walked down the steps and crossed the canal over the wall without dismounting. Jaggi shuddered as he watched him cross, imagining him falling, hitting the concrete walkway ten feet below, and bouncing down into the deep water.

Jaggi knew precisely where the middle school was; he had been to the school compound to play with his older cousin during his visits to Bitti Mausi. He enthusiastically led Teja there. The school building was more prominent than the Kundyan primary. A shoulder-high boundary wall enclosed the school grounds, next to a football field. The gate opened into a large square exposing the main structure at the farthest end. A volleyball court occupied the middle of the yard, and the left and right-side corners had tiny bathroom enclosures.

A few staff members were getting things ready for the next school year. The headmaster spotted and greeted them, asking how he could help.

When Teja told him the reason for the visit, the headmaster was surprised someone wanted to join their small middle school instead of attending the high school in town.

Chasing Dignity

"Jaggi just started riding a bicycle. His mother is scared of him sharing the road with all the cars and the trucks," Teja explained.

"Didn't a child from Kundyan top the district class-five exam this year?"

"Yes, masterji, it was him, my Jaggi," Teja said with pride, adding, "he also won a scholarship in class four."

"Oh, is that so?" said the headmaster admiringly.

Jaggi's eyes brightened, and he looked down shyly.

"That is wonderful," the headmaster said with a smile. "I hope you can bring honor to our school as well. And the scholarship money this time will be more than they offer in the primary school."

The headmaster took them into the lobby and registered Jaggi. Each class had two sections, A and B. Before they left, the headmaster showed Jaggi his classroom, 6-A.

The middle school served Kotla and the three nearby villages. Mostly Sainis, a farming community like Jats but with smaller landholdings, made up the population. Considered a notch below Jats, Sainis were above many lower castes in the caste hierarchy. The news of a brilliant student preferring their school over a high school in the city got mixed reactions from the faculty, ranging from excitement to fierce opposition. The main opposition came from Ranjit Singh, who argued that when the school explicitly catered to their Saini villages, why should they accept students from far away and that too from a low caste? However, his argument did not go far with most staff, and the issue quickly disappeared from their discussions.

Jaggi timidly walked into the school, facing strange looks. Imagining all students from the nearby villages knowing each other made him feel being an oddity.

He was not late, but the entire class was already there. Ranjit Singh, the homeroom teacher, sat behind his desk on the right side of the door, with his back against the wall. The girls sat on jute rugs along the right sidewall and the boys along the left and the far sidewalls. Jaggi put his bag down, spotting an available seat opposite the girls. He discreetly counted six girls and ten boys, including himself.

Ranjit Singh taught English. After independence, India adopted Hindi as its national language but temporarily retained English as a second official language in response to opposition to Hindi from the Southern States. Although more commonly used in large metropolitan cities, English was not popular in rural Punjab. After Punjabi and Hindi, the students would start learning English in the sixth grade as the third language. English teachers were poorly trained, had limited vocabulary, and couldn't speak the language. All class communications were in Punjabi, except when a student, or the teacher, was obliged to read aloud or parrot out a memorized piece from the class textbook. Ranjit Singh was no different.

"*Apna apna ate apne school da naam dasso*," Ranjit Singh said at the start of the first day, asking them to state their names and the names of their primary schools.

The students started to introduce themselves from one corner. Jaggi noticed a girl in the middle gawking at him. Her name was Punit as she spoke in her turn. She whispered something to the girl sitting next to her, and they both giggled, making Jaggi nervous.

Girls, in general, made Jaggi nervous. He had little interaction with them during primary school. There were not that many girls in the school, to begin with, and they were all from Jat families. The shame of his stutter and caste consciously led him to avoid them.

There was one exception: a girl named Rani; she was a year younger than Jaggi. Rani was from a Jat family, and the farm Teja cultivated shared a border with Rani's family. Rani's father, Sohan Singh, was not stuck on his superior caste and had a cozy relationship with Teja. The two would borrow farming equipment from each other and help each other in need. Their farmhouses were close, on the two sides of the boundary, and their children grew up playing with each other. Rani had no brother; she treated Jaggi like one and even called him Veer. Her sister, Ginder, was four years older, and both Rani and Jaggi addressed her as *bhen*. Rani and Jaggi were two years apart in classes and did not interact much in school. Jaggi was a role model for Rani. She was in class four when Jaggi graduated and joined Kotla Middle.

Sohan Singh and his wife, Lakhwinder, treated Teja and Bindo as equals, and Lakhwinder liked Bindo. The girls were fond of Bindo, and since neither Sohan Singh nor Lakhwinder had much schooling, Rani often sought Bindo's help with her homework. "I won't miss having a son if my daughters grow up to be like you," Lakhwinder would tell Bindo. Bindo treated Rani like a daughter and had quite an influence on her.

But the girl sitting opposite Jaggi against the wall was not Rani, and she was making his heart pitter-patter.

"Jaggi, Kundyan," he said shyly on his turn in a manner that hid his stutter. He felt proud for getting through the words and quickly sat down.

After introductions, Ranjit Singh moved on with their first lesson. He drew four parallel lines with a ruler on the blackboard for writing the alphabet. He asked if anyone knew what the first letter of the English alphabet was. Ranjit Singh's son, Bablu, who was in the same class, instantly raised his hand. It was perhaps not astonishing that no one else knew the answer. Ranjit Singh pointed toward Bablu, who proudly said, "*A*." Ranjit Singh wrote the letter *a* on the board. He repeated the process with each letter from *a* through *j*, and only Bablu would raise his hand to answer the question each time.

The headmaster taught mathematics, and his was the third period. "Let's see where you stand in math," he said to the class after a bit of pep talk, and distributed a three-question test, which Jaggi thought was easy. After they finished, the headmaster went over the math books and told them what to expect during the year.

Ranjit Singh considered Bablu the most intelligent student in school and didn't like that rank going to Jaggi. He developed an obsession to show Jaggi to be of merely average intelligence. As days passed, Ranjit Singh's passion intensified, and he would yell at Jaggi for minor mistakes and invoke Bablu's intellect by having Bablu answer the same question after Jaggi misspoke. Jaggi had great enthusiasm to learn English and had begun the class with zest, but he would sit stupidly silent to avoid arousing the teacher's fury and exciting his stutter. Ranjit Singh's anger rekindled every time anyone, especially the headmaster, praised Jaggi. Slowly Jaggi's interest in the language diminished to merely survival.

Jaggi avoided long discussions with other students and generally nodded or gave brief monosyllabic answers. However, it didn't take much for his stutter to come out. Some students would try, on purpose, to engage him in lengthy discussions and chuckle when they succeeded in getting him to stutter.

One day the sixth-class students were playing catch during the physical activity period when Jaggi heard from behind, "Can you th-th-throw the b-b-ball to me?" Bablu was standing behind him, laughing with another boy who answered, "Y-y-yes!" with a big roar of laughter.

Chasing Dignity

A group of girls from the class were within earshot. Jaggi looked viciously at the other boy, who immediately stopped laughing. Though Jaggi was used to this kind of ridicule, being demeaned in Punit's presence made it unbearable, and the thought of hitting his chubby tormentor crossed Jaggi's mind. But, envisioning Ranjit Singh's reaction, he controlled himself.

With all this torment characterizing his school day, Jaggi eagerly looked forward to his bike ride home. He was getting comfortable on the bike and trying new tricks like steering with his feet or riding without holding the handlebar. There was a hairpin turn in one section, and Jaggi always tried to make it without slowing down. The turn was too sharp, and he fell into the mud on one side a few times. But he mastered the corner in a month and could now make it without holding the handlebar.

Soon Jaggi memorized the turns and twists of the entire route and timed the distance between various points. He would go home and draw the course and all the landscape on a piece of paper, and within a couple of months, he had a nice-looking, realistic map to scale, which showed the route with exciting landmarks nicely marked. When he showed the drawing to Bindo, she was so excited that she framed it and hung it on a wall.

The drawing class excited Jaggi; it allowed him to express his artistic prowess. The course included two-dimensional cross-section representations of three-dimensional objects and freehand drawing. Although Jaggi was also good at 3D to 2D scaling of objects, it was the freehand part he wowed people with. He would draw things as if writing a story, often adding details the teacher, Krishan Kumar, didn't ask. His classmates were constantly amazed by his talent, and even Krishan Kumar would look at his drawings with interest, sometimes for prolonged periods. However, Krishan Kumar was hard to please; no word of praise ever came from his lips.

Krishan Kumar was a man of medium height and a stocky build. He shaved his beard but kept a defining, short thick mustache covering his nostrils, making Jaggi wonder how he breathed. He was harsh on students and did not hesitate to use the cane beside him.

Krishan Kumar and Jaggi lived on the same side of Kotla and shared part of the route. They had to cross the dangerous bridge where the canal passed underneath the Budki Rao river. Jaggi generally would start a little before Krishan Kumar, and often, Krishan Kumar would catch up as Jaggi reached the bridge. Unlike Jaggi, Krishan Kumar would ride on top of the wall. It fascinated Jaggi—was he not afraid at all? Jaggi would imagine Krishan Kumar falling steeply into the deep canal after hitting the ledge below and breaking his ribs.

Although Jaggi did very well in drawing on his midterm test, he felt Krishan Kumar was becoming hostile toward him and did not understand why. Then things became apparent when Jaggi noticed the close friendship between Ranjit Singh and Krishan Kumar; they were always together in the teachers' area between classes, spending most of their free time together. Even though Jaggi did poorly in English on the midterm exam, he did much better than Bablu in the combined score. It annoyed Ranjit Singh, and he started to ignore Jaggi. When Jaggi noticed Krishan Kumar's behavior change negatively, his enthusiasm in the drawing class waned, and he stopped asking the teacher any questions.

One day Krishan Kumar asked them to draw a *teetar*—a partridge.

"I drew one for you to see what a teetar looks like; take a look if you have never seen one," he said, putting the sheet on his desk.

Chasing Dignity

All students, except Jaggi, went to the desk to look at the drawing. Besides being reluctant, Jaggi did not see the need to know how a teetar looked; his neighbor raised black domestic turkeys, and in local parlance, these birds were called *Kala teetar,* or mostly just teetar. However, teetar referred, more frequently, to various partridge species smaller and different than Kala teetar. Jaggi drew a male Kala teetar, and he did a superb job detailing its wattle, beard, fluffed feathers, and fanned-out tail plumage, a pose the bird takes to attract hens.

"What have you drawn?" Krishan Kumar asked when Jaggi went to him to show his work.

"A teetar," Jaggi answered.

"Is this a teetar?" the teacher said. He exhibited the drawing to the class. "Look at this! Do you think this is a teetar? It looks like a Keera fowl," he said, aiming at Jaggi's caste because, typically, Keeras raised Kala teetar.

Bablu and a few others laughed. Jaggi muttered something under his breath, which Bablu noticed.

"Masterji, he swore at you," Bablu said.

"Oe Keere, did you do that?" Krishan Kumar asked.

Jaggi shook his head in a no.

"He is lying, masterji. I saw him do that," Bablu said.

"No, I did not," Jaggi said, shaking his head again, looking desperate.

"Why would Bablu lie?" Krishan Kumar asked. Picking up his stick, he caned Jaggi's buttocks and bare hands.

Jaggi tried to stay quiet, but after the fifth strike, he yelped, tears escaping his eyes.

"My class is not for the faint-hearted," the master shouted. "Quit if you can't handle our teaching!"

Jaggi controlled his pain as much as possible, trying to stand straight. Briefly, his eyes met Punit's bubbling tears. She looked down as soon as they connected.

The drawing period was the last bell of the day. *My class is not for the faint-hearted*—the master's words rang in Jaggi's head, fomenting a rebellion that simultaneously made him nervous and excited. Jaggi started for home after making sure the drawing master was ready to leave. He sensed Krishan Kumar behind him and stepped up the paddling to stay ahead about a mile into the way. Jaggi, reaching the bridge, knew the drawing master was close behind and did not get off the bike to climb down to the walkers' ledge. He rode on top of the forbidden wall, Krishan Kumar following. Past the bridge, the master sped up to pass Jaggi and stopped as if to talk to him. Jaggi ignored him and continued his way. He felt tremendous the rest of the way; I'm no faint-hearted! He was amazed that he wasn't afraid of falling from the wall, even for a second.

Jaggi couldn't share his excitement with his mother; what he did was forbidden. But his itch to share was intense. After having a snack, Jaggi went to the fields with Teepu. He was throwing balls for Teepu to fetch when the urge to tell overtook his restraint, and he embraced the dog. "Do you know I rode on the wall today," he whispered in Teepu's ear. "You too can do that, but you can't be scared!"

"Are you talking to the dog?" Jaggi heard. It was Rani walking toward them.

Jaggi grinned.

"What's it, Jaggi veer? Why are you laughing like that?" Rani asked.

Overwhelmed with pride, he told Rani the whole story, making her promise not to tell anyone.

"You are stupid," Rani said.

Chasing Dignity

Jaggi looked at her, deflated.

"You risked your life because you wanted to show someone you are not faint-hearted. That's insane," she added.

A year younger than him, Rani suddenly looked grown-up.

Soon they both began playing with Teepu and forgot about it. But when Rani left to go home, she turned to him with a stern expression. "Jaggi veer, I won't talk to you if you do that ever again," she said.

The following day, in the drawing period, Krishan Kumar called Jaggi to the front. Jaggi looked at him defiantly.

"Why are you staring at me, Keere? Don't you forget who you are!" said the drawing master slapping him. Suddenly, Krishan Kumar sensed someone watching and looked at the door. It was the headmaster passing by. The headmaster moved on without saying anything. However, a few minutes later, he sent a student to call Krishan Kumar to his office. That was the last time Krishan Kumar bothered Jaggi. Now he, too, ignored him, just like Ranjit Singh did.

Chapter 8

Jaggi was now in the seventh class.

The Sikh Punjabi teacher from Kotla got transferred to another school, and Ram Kapoor, a clean-shaven Hindu man, replaced him. Ram Kapoor had a corpulent body that spilled out of his chair, making Jaggi imagine the chair caving under his weight. Ram Kapoor was an intriguing character who liked to tell stories. Like the one-thousand-and-one nights, Ram Kapoor's narratives were open-ended. He would embark on a new account in the middle of a tale, which would quickly meet the same fate resulting in long strings of unfinished parables. By the end of the class everyone, including Ram Kapoor, would forget the original story. During his discourse, Ram Kapoor would reference Hindu epics, Sikh biographical narratives, Christian Biblical tales, storybooks, or even novels. Jaggi discovered the school library stocked Punjabi translations of many of the books he referred to. That got Jaggi interested in literature. Besides Punjabi writers, he read translations from foreign languages, especially Punjabi adaptations of Russian novels and storybooks. Jaggi would check out books to take home and stay up reading way past midnight, covering his small, electric table lamp with a blanket. Bindo would occasionally scold him or take his book away so he could go to sleep.

Soon, Jaggi's mind began to ferment his own stories, and he felt an urge to write. During one of his lectures, Ram Kapoor narrated the tale of love between a boy and his dog, Lassie. Lassie was separated from the boy, making them both miserable. Eventually, the dog escaped from her new home and made a hundreds-of-miles-long journey, inundated with obstacles, to unite with the boy. Jaggi asked the teacher where he could find the book. Unfortunately, the teacher did not recall its name; all he remembered was a Hindi translation of some English text. The narration excited Jaggi, and he decided to write a story in which the hero, his own dog Teepu, finds a child who had wandered far away from his home and brings him back safely. Jaggi was proud of his creation, and he read it to Rani, Himmat, and Bindo. They all liked it. Jaggi realized that writing allowed him to express himself freely and fluently without worrying about his stutter.

One day Jaggi was sitting in the library reading when Punit came in.

"Did you bring back *Pavitar Pappi*," she asked. "I saw your name in the checkout register."

"No, I didn't f-f-finish it," he answered.

There was only one table in the small library with five chairs. Punit sat down next to him.

"Do you like it?" she asked.

"Yes," he nodded.

"I want to read it," she said, "when you finish."

"I'll bring it t-t-tomorrow," he said and got up. He put his book back on the shelf and got out.

It was the first time Punit had talked to him, making him anxious and thrilled.

"Jaggi veer, you seem very happy," Rani commented when she saw him that evening.

He smiled.

"I need to finish *Pavitar Pappi* tonight," he said.

"What is *Pavitar Pappi*?" Rani asked, surprised.

"It's a book I'm reading; Punit wants to read it."

"Who is Punit?" Rani asked.

"A girl in my class," Jaggi said, smiling and looking down.

"You like her, don't you?" Rani said.

"No," Jaggi said.

Chasing Dignity

"You like a girl; you like a girl!" Rani started jumping and repeating her tease.

"No, I'm not talking to you," Jaggi said and ran away.

That night Jaggi stayed awake until he finished the book.

Even though the Indian caste system has an irrefutably defined hierarchy, local demographics play an important role in how people feel about their castes. The majority dictates behavioral superiority. There was a Jat boy, Kuljit, in Section B of Jaggi's class, who, as the only Jat student in the school, was the butt of the jokes about Jats. He was quiet and generally took those jokes in good stride. Still, one could feel Kuljit's caste was a barrier in his interactions with other boys, as if, like Jaggi, he too was an outcast, albeit not discriminated against the way Jaggi was.

Starting in the seventh grade, Kuljit and Jaggi became friends and began to have lunch together. Kuljit was tall, robust, athletic, and an excellent football player. He was the only sixth grader to make the school team the previous year.

"You talk like that at home, too?" Kuljit asked Jaggi one day, referring to his stutter.

"Yes," Jaggi answered, and Kuljit didn't ask further.

Jaggi didn't notice any ridicule or sarcasm in Kuljit's question or take offense to it. Instead, it made him feel closer to Kuljit, and he began to hang around him more often.

The social studies teacher Sunil Mehta coached the school's football team. He needed two squads to practice but didn't have enough players. He invited Jaggi to rehearse with them.

Jaggi hesitated; he had never played football before and was smaller and younger than other players. Kuljit encouraged him, and with Kuljit's inspiration, Jaggi joined. He and Kuljit would go to the playground to practice with a ball during their free time. Jaggi immediately liked the sport, but his skill and speed could not keep up with the older players during practice. He bought a football to practice dribbling at home and started running in the evenings. Soon Jaggi was running eight kilometers. Though he did not make the team that year, Sunil Mehta was pleased with his progress and let him substitute in a couple of games in real matches.

That year Jaggi went through a growth spurt, and when he returned for class eight, he was not a little boy anymore. He easily made the football team, becoming one of the better players.

One day Jaggi was in the library working on his math assignment when Punit came and sat next to him.

"Jaggi, can you help me with this question?" she said, leaning close to him.

Jaggi nodded and showed her how to solve it. She continued to sit there, working on the rest of the assignment. A couple of times again, she asked for his help, and he would feel her elbow touch his, setting a jolt up his arm.

That night he had a beautiful dream. He was comfortable talking to Punit, and suddenly they were embracing each other, and then they didn't have any clothes on. He woke up the next day with a vivid dream memory and messed-up underwear. When he went to sleep the following night, he hoped for a repeat. But then he remembered the sermon from the Gurdwara priest.

"Bhogī Kao dukh rog viāpai," the priest had explained. "Painful diseases afflict those who indulge in sex."

Jaggi felt guilty and tried to get rid of his sinful thoughts, closing his eyes and praying to God to cleanse his mind whenever he felt the arousal stirring. But the more he tried, the stronger his thoughts became. Jaggi eventually fell asleep. The following

Chasing Dignity

Sunday, he prayed for forgiveness in front of the holy book at the gurdwara.

One day the headmaster called Jaggi to his office. Jaggi found him in his usual good mood.

"I hear you play outstanding football. Sunil Mehta is all praise for you," the headmaster said, extracting a smile from Jaggi.

He had called Jaggi to discuss preparations for eighth class finals. Jaggi did exceptionally well in all subjects except English.

"You seem to be struggling with English."

Jaggi looked down.

"Jaggi, we all know you are intelligent. You did so well in your primary school. The state awards several scholarships to eighth-class graduates. If you can work on English, you stand a good chance of winning one."

The headmaster paused for a response but didn't get one.

"Do you have anyone in your village who can tutor you English?"

"No, sir," Jaggi shook his head.

"Can you spend extra time if I find you a tutor?"

"Yes, sir," Jaggi nodded.

After a few days, the headmaster called Jaggi again and told him about a teacher, an old student of his, who lived in Kotla and was willing to tutor Jaggi for free.

"He will teach you, but he is available only on Sundays."

"I'll talk to baau ji," Jaggi promised.

The following day, Jaggi informed the headmaster that his parents had consented, and the headmaster put him in touch with Navjot, a young businessman.

There were three months to the finals, and Navjot started teaching Jaggi basic grammar. Jaggi would diligently work on his assignments before returning the following Sunday. In addition to grammar, Navjot worked on his writing skills, including essay writing and summarizing a poem from the textbook.

In the Board exams, Jaggi did much better than his performance in the sixth and seventh classes. However, English proved his Achilles heel; the dozen Sundays Navjot spent with him were insufficient to compensate for three years' neglect. Jaggi missed winning the scholarship by a small margin.

During the three years, Jaggi grew both physically and emotionally. From a scrawny, awkward little boy in primary school, he developed into a tall, handsome, athletic young boy who was not an easy pushover anymore. Even his doctor admired his ability to overcome his stutter. "It won't be long before he forgets he even had a speech issue," he told Bindo at their last appointment.

Jaggi's sense of self-worth improved after he stood up to the bullying of the drawing master. He was beginning to observe things deeply. Noticing that even Kuljit, the highest caste boy in school, could feel ostracized, he realized the caste hierarchy was not an absolute concept. The caste labels like Jat, Saini, Jheor, Keera, and whatnot were convenient ways for people to exclude each other.

Kuljit and Jaggi had grown fond of each other. Kuljit would not pursue education any further. His father was a man of modest means and needed Kuljit's help in farming. It made Jaggi appreciate his own blissful kismet; he was better than others in many respects. He had supportive parents, capable of providing everything he needed. Jaggi never had to go to bed hungry, as many children in the basti did, and he could easily be one of them, working in someone's fields instead of going to school. Jaggi could, instead, get as much education as he desired.

Chasing Dignity

Punit's memory was another yearning Jaggi would take with him. They never interacted much, but he fell head over heels in love with her. Jaggi hated the days when school was closed, and he could not have a glimpse of her. He would never have a chance of that glance; Punit was from a different village and stayed in Kotla with her aunt for schooling. She would go back to her parents and get married. Unfortunately, Jaggi could not express his love for her, or any higher caste, for that matter; it would be a mortal sin for his lot. Sometimes he sensed Kuljit knew about his feelings, but they never talked. Nonetheless, she left warm memories for Jaggi to carry for years.

PART II

It isn't what we say or think that defines us, but what we do.
Jane Austen

Chapter 9

Jaggi was in the ninth class when Bindo's cousin Baldev came to visit. He was a large-framed, tall man, twice the size of Teja. He wore a nicely trimmed snow-white beard, free of any knots or gnarls, and the tips of his curled mustache pointed upwards like bicycle handlebars.

Baldev met Teja when he came with Bindo's father to propose her hand to Teja. The two met a couple of times at family events again. Baldev left for the USA shortly before Jaggi was born. When Baldev first visited India, Jaggi was seven. Baldev had brought impressive toys for him—an electric horse that could flip backward, a car racing game with two toy cars, and a course. Baldev himself set up the track in one corner of the veranda, and Jaggi loved him for the attention he gave him. Jaggi had never seen such unique toys, which made his friends jealous. Baldev's stories sparked Jaggi's interest in America. Jaggi began to read about that country any chance he got.

Baldev and Teja sat on the charpoys, talking, and Jaggi listened to their conversation intently. Bindo had made *pakoras*—the spinach leaves coated in seasoned batter and deep-fried. She served the pakoras with tea and a few ladoos and joined them on a low stool.

"What do you do over there, Mama ji?" Jaggi asked.

"Bete, your mama ji has hotels, and now he makes a lot of money," Bindo said.

Jaggi didn't miss her use of the word "now."

"What did you do before that, mama ji?"

"Let your mama ji drink his tea; it'll get cold if you keep asking questions," Teja interrupted.

"Don't worry, Teja Singh," Baldev replied. "The boy is curious, and I like that."

"Before?" Baldev said. "Well, I did everything you can think of. I did the framing and paint jobs for a construction company, picked berries on the farms, did laundry, cleaned rooms in a hotel, and washed dishes in a restaurant. I drove a taxi and then a big eighteen-wheeler truck at one time. To survive, you do whatever comes your way."

"So, you work a lot, mama ji," Jaggi said, imagining Baldev doing all those jobs simultaneously.

"These days, I don't work nearly as much. I have a dozen hotels, and more than two hundred goras and gories work for me," Baldev said with a tinge of self-admiration that white men and women worked for him.

"Did you have a lot of money to buy the hotels?"

Baldev was enjoying the awe in Jaggi's eyes. "No, I did not," he continued. "When I left India, I had just eighty-five dollars in my pocket. I worked my way up. I had one goal and one goal only—to save enough money to buy my own business. No matter what I did, I never spent more than half of what I made.

Baldev was a natural storyteller, and the twinkle in Jaggi's eyes set him on a roll.

"Can you imagine ten parallel lanes of cars, going over one hundred twenty kilometers an hour in one direction, and then a separate road, just as wide and full of speeding cars, going in the other?"

Jaggi had read about clouds-touching skyscrapers of the USA. He imagined standing atop one, looking down through thin clouds, admiring a beautiful city around him. A vast road cut through the tall buildings; it was full of beautiful, gigantic cars that seemed to be flying and touching the ground simultaneously. Many had no roofs, and riding in them were Punjabi men and women in turbans and Punjabi suits.

Seeing the boy lost in thought, Baldev tried to guess what he was thinking, "You must be wondering about the accidents, aren't you? Well, son, you won't see many accidents over there, not nearly as many as you see on these narrow roads full of pits and potholes. And, if an accident happens, a chopper will descend from above, drop a huge clamp that looks like a god's hand, grab the offending car, and haul it away within minutes, and you will see the traffic proceeding at the same insane speed as if nothing ever happened."

To Jaggi, Baldev's white beard was beginning to appear integral to his immense wisdom. The sparkle in the boy's eyes was ramping up Baldev's enthusiasm, and his stories were getting spicier by the minute.

"One can't help but marvel at the police. If you get into an accident in the US, the police will be there in minutes, and you wonder how they knew you were in trouble. It is unlike here, where the police won't show up for hours after an accident. They will tow your car to a mechanic's shop, with you riding in that truck."

Baldev took a pakora from the plate and put it in his mouth, giving him a little break from talking. Bindo looked up at Jaggi and Baldev at the same time. She smiled to see how Jaggi had taken after her side of the family.

"Mama ji, do you have to work with any Jats?"

Baldev smiled at Jaggi's question. "No, I don't have to. But do I work with Jats? Yes, I do," he said, "My first partner was a Jat."

"Your partner was a Jat?" Jaggi seemed shocked.

"Yes, it's incredible, isn't it?" said Baldev smiling, "He is a good man; we are still partners."

"And he knows that you are not a Jat?" Jaggi asked.

"Yes, he does," Baldev said, smiling—and knowing his concerns, explained further. "You see, most Indians marry within their castes even when they come to the US. But they don't carry those social burdens into everyday life; they interact without paying much attention to caste. More than a dozen Jats and other upper-caste Indians work for me."

"And you can kick them out if you want to?" he asked.

"No, not just because I want to. That wouldn't be fair, would it? There are stringent laws that protect workers, and one has to be careful as an employer. However, if someone doesn't work as expected, I can fire that person, and I have done that."

Jaggi's mind was soaring. His imagination had taken him to a far-away, heavenly wonderland. Indeed, there was a place where he would not be inferior to Jats. No one will call him *Oe Keere*.

Baldev's stories were beginning to grab Teja and Bindo's attention too. All three were listening with heightened interest.

"Mama Ji, what kind of work do most Indians do? Are they all successful?" Jaggi asked.

Baldev thought for a second, "I'll say yes, most Indians are successful. I have never seen an Indian in the US not making a comfortable living. They own stores, drive taxis and trucks, own hotels; they do all sorts of stuff."

"Do Indians work in government jobs, too?" inquired Jaggi.

"Yes, they do. Many Indians work in high positions with big companies. But only the educated ones. I was not educated."

How did Baldev, without education, make it to the USA and interact with Americans without their derision? Jaggi wondered.

"How did you go to the USA, mama ji?"

Chasing Dignity

"I was lucky," Baldev said, "very lucky. I was working with a construction company in New Delhi. I did house repairs on the side and learned skills as a handyman. One day I found the US embassy was looking for handymen. I applied and got hired. I worked there for over two years and learned to speak English. They, too, liked my work. Then a big opportunity arose. A US construction company was hiring skilled labor, and they hired me. Many Americans knew me since I worked inside the embassy, and the visa officer who processed my visa was friendly. 'We'll miss you, but I'm sure you will do well in the US,' he told me when he gave me the visa."

"You see, bete, your mama ji is a hard-working man," Bindo said.

"Do you think it makes sense for Jaggi to go to Amrika?" Teja asked with wide eyes.

"It is a great idea!" Baldev said. "Jaggi is a smart boy, and he can go there to study. There are many students from India, and after they finish their education, they get jobs with big companies, and the companies help them get settled."

He looked at Jaggi. "Son, you have to work hard at it. Get good marks and learn to speak English well. No one can stop you. How old are you now?"

"He's thirteen," Teja said.

"You are too young to understand what I'm saying," Baldev continued, "but listen close. You will have to bribe someone even to get a small job in India, which has nothing to do with your caste. The bigger the job you seek, the higher the bribe you will pay, and your parents may not have the money for that. You don't have to bribe anyone to get a job in the USA. They respect hard work and motivation. You can do anything if you are smart, educated, and hard-working. The sky is the limit!"

Jaggi repeated the last sentence in his mind; his face sparkled.

That night, Jaggi fell asleep, reminiscing on his uncle's words. He had a delightful dream; he was flying without any machine. He flew around Kundyan, touching the treetops. He went higher and higher until all the clouds were left behind, far above, till he could not see them anymore. 'The sky's the limit," he said, smiling to himself when we woke up to the noises of his mother working in the kitchen. Immersed in happiness, he lay awake in the bed, with a sense of freedom and control of his life. He saw his goal clearly defined for him. No one could stop him from getting to his dreamland, from touching the sky.

Mama ji's words, "learn to speak English well," generated a new urgency in Jaggi to master that language. His interest in Punjabi literature had already evolved into a passion, and he had read many authors. He loved writing and was on his third story, even though his audience included only Rani, Himmat, and his mother. But, so far, English had failed to capture his attention; the resentfulness of Ranjit Singh, his middle school teacher, had nipped Jaggi's early enthusiasm in the bud, so to say. His lazy high school English teacher, dull and lackluster, was not much help; Jaggi would find himself yawning in his class.

Jaggi subscribed to the *Tribune*, an English daily. His vocabulary was so limited that he could not navigate even the simplest of the news. Jaggi had never failed an English exam, but one didn't require much vocabulary to pass as he pondered. And how would he learn to speak English? No one around him did that, including his teachers and fellow students. It was so annoying to connect all those complex sounds and illogical rules.

Jaggi bought a dictionary and started to create a wordlist to enrich his vocabulary. One day, an idea struck him when looking up a word. Wouldn't it be lovely if he memorized the dictionary a couple of pages daily? 'I'll have the best vocabulary in the whole world,' he grinned and started on his quest with page one. However, the futility of his approach dawned on him in just a couple of days.

Jaggi recalled the professor's help when his teacher tried to hold him in class one. Jaggi had never needed his help since. Could he help him with his English? Consulting the professor on a crucial matter excited him and made him feel grown-up. The professor's mother told him the professor would be home on Friday and advised him to visit them Saturday morning.

The professor was in a jovial mood when Jaggi arrived. Sitting in a comfortable chair under the big mango tree, he browsed through the *Tribune*. An extra chair awaited Jaggi.

"So far, what have you done to learn English?" the professor asked.

Jaggi just shook his head.

"Do you read any English Newspapers?"

"I try, but I don't understand. The papers use hard language."

The professor asked Jaggi to go to the living room and bring the Punjabi version of the *Tribune* that he had subscribed to for his mother.

Laying it next to the English version of the *Tribune*, the professor pointed to specific news items. "Look at these two versions of the paper. Seventy-to-eighty percent of the news is the same."

Jaggi had never thought about that.

"I suggest you subscribe to both. First, read Punjabi and then the English version every day. Slowly you will start to observe the translation. Next time I come, I'll bring some easy-to-read storybooks."

Jaggi's face brightened.

The professor continued. "Bete, the key to learning any language is practice. Practice, practice, and practice; read, write, and speak daily. That is how I learned English."

"But how do I practice speaking? No one speaks English around here," Jaggi said.

"The main reason for hesitation in speaking a foreign language is our ears; they are not used to hearing our own voice making unfamiliar sounds. Read aloud to get used to yourself speaking English. Most dictionaries have a pronunciation key to help pronounce unfamiliar words," the professor said.

These were very doable, practical tips, Jaggi thought.

"Practicing to write is also important. The important thing is you write every day. Start a diary and write something in it every evening before bed. The entries can be as short as one or two lines."

The professor was relaxed and slipped into a storytelling mode, telling Jaggi about his college days. Jaggi listened faithfully. The professor often published articles in magazines and journals, Jaggi learned.

At one point, Jaggi mentioned the stories he wrote.

"Oh, that's great. I'll like to see those," the professor said.

Jaggi got excited about the professor wanting to read his stories. He went home and returned immediately with his folder.

"You have excellent penmanship, Jaggi," the professor said, browsing through the folder. "This is beautiful. I didn't know we had a writer among ourselves."

The professor asked Jaggi to leave the stories with him so he could read in leisure.

Chasing Dignity

Jaggi bought a diary the following day. The thought of rewriting his stories in English tickled his mind.

Chapter 10

Jaggi grew faster than most children his age. Though a year younger at fourteen, he was the tallest boy in his class, and his broad chest made him look formidable. He was addicted to football and set up an arduous practice routine; he would run ten kilometers before school and take his football to the fields in the evenings to practice dribbling. He easily made it to the high school team the first year, and in the final, he played the center half.

Besides schools, the villages had their own sports teams and inter-village tournaments. Kundyan hosted a two-day annual contest in kabaddi, hockey, and football, where more than a dozen teams from nearby villages would compete in each sport. Kundyan had a strong kabaddi team, but their hockey and football squads were barely average.

In the final year of high school, Jaggi also played on the village team, and his inclusion made them the title contenders. Jaggi played exceptionally well during the tournament and was the squad's star. His last-minute goal in the final game earned them the championship.

The villagers threw the team a party to celebrate. Many adults, including the players' fathers, joined the celebrations. Teja abstained; he did not enjoy parties and had never been to a Jat party where he felt they wouldn't treat him equally. However, Teja was happy Jaggi was going—his intelligent, educated son wouldn't have trouble getting the respect he deserved.

There was music, abundant food, and free-flowing alcohol. Jaggi had played a vital role on the team, and everyone was buzzing about Jaggi's performance.

"We owe today's party to Jaggi," one of his teammates said. "I never imagined we would ever pick a football trophy."

"Jaggi's goal turned the tables. The Sangatpura team was up three-zero. Who thought we could still win?" said someone else.

"And, that last goal—that was a beauty. Jaggi dodges one fullback, then the other, and bam! He shoots past the goalie. Man, I've never seen that before," someone sitting at a bit of distance shouted.

Jaggi floated in ecstasy, sitting with his teammates inside a Jat's courtyard where people showered praises on him. And then something happened. The courtyard was not large enough, and people set up cots across the entrance, spilling into the street. It was still daylight when a large, wandering stray dog decided to poop right by the door.

Suddenly, a voice came from the street, demanding, "What is that Keera boy's name?"

"Jaggi," someone answered.

Jaggi looked back and saw Cheta, an older man. Cheta's son was on the team as a substitute. When he had Jaggi's attention, he motioned him over, "Hi boy, come here!" Jaggi got up and walked to the man.

"You see that dog poop? Clean it before someone steps on it."

Jaggi stood there confused, deflated.

"What are you looking at?" the man yelled in front of everyone, "Get a spade from the animal shed," he said, pointing toward the barn across the street.

Not knowing what to do, Jaggi went to the barn. He saw a spade sitting in one corner but didn't pick it up. He stood there, numb, for a few minutes. The barn had a door to a side street. Jaggi went through that door and around to his home.

Trilok, the host's son, was also on the football team. "You didn't have to ask Jaggi to do that. I could have called Pappu," he said to Cheta. Pappu was their domestic servant.

"What is wrong if I asked a Keera to clean up the poop? It's their job to clean. Letting him sit with you and have him eat from your plate doesn't make him a Jat."

Jaggi stood outside to recompose before entering his house.

"You came back early. I wasn't expecting you till later," Bindo said.

Jaggi nodded.

"Is everything okay? Did you eat at the party?" she asked.

"Yes," he said, "I'm tired."

"You must be. You have been playing for two days. Go to bed."

Jaggi went to bed, but it took a long time for sleep to come.

The next day was a Sunday, and Jaggi still felt terrible when he woke up. After breakfast, he went to the fields. But instead of taking the usual route, Jaggi turned toward the village and went to Himmat's house. The door was open, and he went inside.

Himmat's mother greeted him. Jaggi asked if Himmat was home.

She nodded. "Are you okay, bete?" she said.

"Yes, auntie ji, why?" Jaggi said.

"You seem lost. You didn't even say your *Mattha-Tekna* today." Jaggi had never missed his bow-to-you greetings before.

Jaggi apologized and bent down to touch her knees.

"Upstairs," she said, pointing to the roof, and Jaggi climbed the old wooden ladder.

Himmat was a pre-university science student in college and was busy with his math assignment. He was surprised to see Jaggi.

"I thought you would be sleeping after two grueling days of the tournament."

"Yes, it was exhausting. I am still tired," Jaggi said, pulling a charpoy to sit opposite him.

"You played fantastically well; everyone talked about you in the tournament. Who thought Kundyan could ever play in the championship game, let alone win?" said Himmat.

"Yea, we won," Jaggi said unenthusiastically. "Enough of football; let's not talk about it."

That surprised Himmat, and he changed the topic, but Jaggi seemed distant. And then, unexpectedly, he stood up.

"I was going to the fields. I just stopped by," he said.

"Are you all right?" Himmat asked.

"Yes."

"I could go with you, but I need to finish this. It is due tomorrow, and it is rather long," Himmat said.

"No, you finish your assignment. I'll see you tomorrow," Jaggi said and left.

Jaggi walked to the farm. He saw Rani sitting with a book; she was in the eighth class now. Jaggi always admired her incredible way of simplifying complex matters, and she was never judgmental.

"What are you reading?" Jaggi said, pulling a cot near her.

"My history textbook," she said, showing him the cover. "We have a test tomorrow."

"I shouldn't be sitting here then," Jaggi said.

"Oh no, I am ready for the test. I didn't have much else to do, so I came here," Rani said.

Rani enjoyed talking to Jaggi and would do so even when buried neck-deep in work. Jaggi needed to speak to someone, and

Chasing Dignity

Rani was a good listener. He sat down. Rani closed her book and put it on the side to give Jaggi her full attention.

"I heard you won the football tournament? That is fabulous, Jaggi veer," she said.

"Whatever," he said, shrugging.

"What's wrong?" Rani asked.

"I want to run away from this place. I want to disappear," Jaggi said, covering his face with both hands. Rani was suddenly worried. She had never seen him so upset.

"What happened?" Rani asked. "I heard you went to the party last night. Did something happen?"

Jaggi nodded and described the story, how he played, how people praised him, and how Cheta singled him to clean the dog poop.

"Is that all?" said Rani, "You want to disappear because of that buffalo-head Cheta?"

"No, it is not just Cheta. None of the people sitting there, praising how good I played, said anything in my defense. I was so ashamed. How will I show my face to anyone?"

Rani got up, sat beside Jaggi, and hugged him. "Jaggi veer," she said, "you are silly. Why should you run away? Let those who have no sense of right and wrong run away," she said, tightening her hug. She held him for a couple of minutes before getting back to her cot. "I know this isn't fair. But it is their problem, not yours. Don't give much thought to what they say; they are not worth the trouble. Why should what others said bother you when you didn't do anything wrong?"

Jaggi suddenly felt calm. They changed the topics, discussing her school and his English-learning project. He asked Rani if she would like to practice speaking English with him, and she readily agreed.

Jaggi saw Himmat coming from the village and took Rani's leave.

"I thought you had to finish your assignment," Jaggi said.

"Yes, I did. But the way you left abruptly got me worried. Something didn't look right," Himmat said.

"Yes, I wasn't feeling well," Jaggi said, and he described the story to Himmat.

"I'm glad you left the party. It should send them a message," Himmat said.

"Am I silly being mad about what happened at the party?"

"No, you are not being silly, Jaggi. The damn Manu Smriti inscribed caste on our foreheads. We can't run away from it," he said. Manu Smriti, a Hindu scripture, cataloged people's diminishing rights as they fell down the caste ladder.

"But how to live with humiliation every day? I thought I was somebody during the tournament. Finally, they all loved me. But then someone reminded me who I was—a nobody Keera!"

"I know, but don't overthink about what one person did. The whole village knows you were the best player in the tournament. Many were talking good about you."

"It's garbage," Jaggi said. "We need to prove ourselves so much even to hope for fair treatment."

Jaggi finished his tenth class, the last year of high school. He would now go to a four-year college, a year of pre-university followed by three years of the BA degree program. To decide on a career path, Jaggi went to seek the professor's help.

The professor asked him how he did in the high school exams.

"I didn't win any scholarship, but overall I did well. I can get admission to any college I want," Jaggi answered.

Chasing Dignity

In the past, Tara Singh had advised Jaggi against spending four years of college in the small rural town of Rupar—"it would hamper your social development," he had said. But going to a college in a bigger city like Chandigarh meant living in a dorm, and Jaggi did not want to put that extra financial burden on his parents. When Jaggi told him he would be going to Rupar, the professor smiled but said nothing.

"Uncle ji, I want to thank you for your help with my English," Jaggi said, his tone showing more confidence.

"So, you found the books I gave you useful," Tara Singh said.

"The books were useful, but what helped me the most was your suggestion to read the Punjabi and the English versions of the newspaper together."

"I see," the professor said, "did you try speaking?"

"Not much; reading English aloud to myself did not work. It was boring. However, Rani and I read to each other. We take turns reading from the books you gave me."

Jaggi then asked him what subjects to pursue in college.

"It depends on what you want to do in life," the professor said.

"I want to go to the USA!"

"I know that, but you will still need a career once you are there. What work interests you?"

"I just want to do something that qualifies me to go to the USA," Jaggi answered.

"I don't think that is the right approach. People of all professions go to the USA. To succeed in life, you should focus on what you enjoy doing."

"I like literature, and I like to write stories, but I don't know what jobs involve writing and reading," Jaggi said.

"Writing is a competitive field. Whether you succeed as a writer, only time can tell. You don't have to make that choice now. You like to write in Punjabi; keep it as a hobby. English is a mandatory subject for you, so keep working on your English. As you get comfortable with the language, start writing in English. And if you decide writing is for you, you can make it into a career. The Indian Mantra for success in foreign countries is developing technical skills. Technical skills are always in demand, and one can usually make a comfortable living."

"What does that mean?"

"Many successful Indians go for medicine or engineering, which are always in demand. Do either of those areas interest you?" he asked.

"Both areas require chemistry, and I don't like it. I have seen Himmat's chemistry books. They are boring. And I don't like biology, which is required to get into medicine."

"Hunh," the professor said. He recalled seeing the map Jaggi made, one of his basti as a child and the other of his bike path to Kotla that Bindo still displayed on her wall. "Do you have much interest in maps?"

"A lot. Last year I made a map of Kundyan, and I'm working on one that will include all villages within seven kilometers from here," Jaggi said with a smile.

"How do you calculate distances?"

"I see how long it takes me to bike or run it. I have gotten pretty good at it," Jaggi answered.

"You know, son, you would love cartography—the study and the practice of mapmaking. Cartography is a sub-discipline of geography, my specialty. I suggest you take geography. The cartographic process is more than drawing maps; it involves data capture, image processing, and visual display—all technical skills!" The professor then explained what jobs would require a cartographer's skills. Jaggi was ecstatic. After hearing Tara Singh's speech, Jaggi felt he was a born cartographer destined to succeed in the US The other subject they decided on was economics.

Chapter 11

Finally, the day arrived, the day Bindo had always dreamed of; Jaggi was going to college. To express her gratitude to God and pray for Jaggi's success, she arranged an *Akhand Paath,* a two-day uninterrupted reading of Guru Granth—the Sikh holy book. She invited all their friends and relatives to the celebration.

It was the first week of July; the morning was delightful, and the temperature surprisingly pleasant. Jaggi finished his breakfast, set a backpack on his bicycle carrier, and pulled the bike off the stand.

"Okay, maa," Jaggi said. Bindo dropped whatever she was doing, got up to embrace him, and came out behind him to see him get on his bike. Her boy was now an adult, embarking on his life. He was tall, sturdy, and handsome and knew how to tie a beautiful turban. Bindo stood there misty-eyed, just as she had done years ago on his first day of primary school. Her chest swelled as her son, a young man now, paddled away for his first day of college.

The college building had two stories, with three hallways extending like a T from the lobby. Jaggi arrived half an hour before class. Lost first-year students were trying to find their schedules on notice boards. Jaggi's first class was English, and he was in section C. After ascertaining his classrooms, he decided to walk around. Mehar, an overweight young man Jaggi had just met, joined him. They both shared the English period.

The principal's room was on the ground floor. There were two large rooms at the end of that hallway; one labeled "Faculty Lounge" and the other "Students." They went upstairs. They were in the science arena, and the "Chemistry" label on one side brought Himmat to Jaggi's mind.

A room in another hall got Jaggi's attention. A glimpse of maps and a large-sized globe through the glass door established where his geography class would be.

They went out and walked around the campus, passing by a few single-story buildings in the back; one had the sign "Library" above the main door. They walked around toward the main road. On one side of the main building, bordering the main road, was a structure that looked like a cafeteria; there was no sign for it, though. It had two lawns on each side, with beat-up tables and chairs. Across the road from the main building were the student dormitories, two tennis courts, and hockey and football fields.

The sight of the football ground stirred a desire in Jaggi, even though he had decided not to participate in college football. He admonished his itch—*focus on your studies and English.*

A few buffaloes grazed on the other side of the college property, reminding Jaggi Rupar was a small rural town.

The two made it back just in time for the class. The teacher, an old Sikh gentleman, eyed them, settling into their seats. The classroom had the traditional lecture arrangement, with rows of fixed seating. A dozen girls were sitting in the first row, and the male students were only in the back. Twenty percent women—Jaggi did a quick calculation. After introducing the prose and poetry textbooks, the teacher explained how the marks were assigned to various syllabus parts and adjourned the class.

Himmat found Jaggi before lunch, and they went to the cafeteria—two small halls with separate entrances for men and women. The service counter separated the men from the women who placed their orders through a door-size opening. The room had only a few empty chairs available when they got in, all with backs to the counter. They ordered some channa bhatura and took their seats.

"We need to get here earlier if you want a seat on the other side of the table." Himmat laughed. "Many come here just to ogle at that door," he whispered, signaling back with a neck twist.

When Jaggi went to his geography class, he saw a young, dark-complexioned woman standing on the teacher's side, her arms akimbo. She was talking to some female students in the first row. Tall and well-built, her confident posture made her seem even more prominent. Jaggi assumed she was the teacher. But then, an older man in his forties walked, carrying a couple of books in his arm, and stopped to look at the woman.

"Oh, sorry, sir," she said and turned around to sit with the other girls. The girl's name was Simran Grewal, Jaggi learned during introductions. Simran's face and imposing posture stuck with Jaggi for a while.

Though mixing of the sexes was present, to a degree, among upper-level students, pre-university boys and girls seldom talked to each other. Upper-level students interacted mainly on-campus—crossing each other on the lawns or having lectures in the same room. Outside mingling, whether for lunches or other reasons, was usually in group settings; it was inappropriate for a woman to go out with an unrelated man alone.

Simmie—the nickname everyone used for Simran—was a glaring exception. She could talk to anyone, boy or girl, without hesitation. Most students rode buses or bicycles to college and a few motorcycles or scooters, but none had a car. Simmie rode a lovely Vespa, and occasionally, someone would drop her off or pick her up in a Fiat car. That gave her an aura of being from an influential family, and no one ever questioned the liberal mannerism of this pre-university girl. Over the year, Jaggi became comfortable with Simmie.

Jaggi decided to make a map of Rupar, which had a complex network of streets. He would go out and walk around, familiarizing himself with the town in his spare time. Many roads changed direction quickly and frequently, making Jaggi lose his sense of direction fast. Frustrated, he talked to his geography teacher.

"Get a compass," the teacher advised.

That was easy, Jaggi thought. 'Why didn't I think of it before?'

•Jaggi's map, detailing even the not-so-prominent shops, was complete by the end of the year. A charitable group acquired the map to help small businesses in remote nooks get noticed. They offered Jaggi some money, but he declined. Seeing people picking copies of his map from storefronts was exhilarating; he had never thought his effort could be worth more than feeding his curiosity.

The pre-university year passed quickly. All of Jaggi's geography classmates were now in BA part 1. One day, when they came out of their class, Simmie caught up to Jaggi.

"Have you ever been to Naina Devi?" she asked.

Sitting on a hill in the Himalayan ranges, Naina Devi temple was a popular tourist destination. During the deity's festival, it attracted thousands of devotees from hundreds of miles around. Many braved the distances doing *dandaut*—lying down stretched on the ground, making a mark with extended hand, and then getting up to that mark to repeat the process—often spending months conquering the distances from their homes. The temple was about sixty-five kilometers from the college.

"No, I have not. Why?" Jaggi asked.

"It's a beautiful place. I went there as a child with my parents. We drove to the base and walked up the steps to the temple."

Jaggi looked at her questioningly. He didn't understand why she had brought up Naina Devi.

"Are you going there again?" he asked.

"No," she smiled. "I wondered if a few of us from school could go together. I talked to my parents. They are okay with us going as a group. We can go to Naina Devi and the Bhakra-Nangal dam and back in one day."

Bhakra-Nangal was a 740-foot-high concrete gravity dam, the highest in the country. It was built across the Sutlej River to produce hydroelectric power. The blocking of the river resulted in Gobind Sagar's creation, a breathtaking 170 square kilometer water reservoir used to irrigate over ten million acres of farmland. Jaggi had seen pictures of the lake, which generated a particular interest for him. He had read the recent news of the government building another power plant, Nathpa Jhakri, upstream on the same river Sutlej. He had tried to map the river's run between the two power plants by extrapolating Gobind Sagar's dimensions from a map.

His heart skipped a beat with anticipation of a visit.

"Who else is coming?" he asked.

"Right now, it's me and my friend Jhinder. We wondered if you and Mehar could join us, and maybe you could ask your science friend. What's his name—Himmat?" Simmie said.

Jaggi had butterflies. He had never gone on any excursions other than with his parents. Not only that, going on a trip with girls, especially the one who so often visited his nighttime thoughts, was almost too much to digest. He thought it would be the class's talk for a while.

"My mama ji is an SP. He has a Jeep, an MM540, that he will lend us, along with the driver."

The word SP—Superintendent of Police—stopped Jaggi in his tracks. Not only was her family financially well off, but they also had links in higher bureaucracy. That made Jaggi conscientious of his low status she wasn't aware of. His impulse was to say no, but he did not.

"I'll let you know tomorrow," he said.

"Can you talk to Himmat, please? I already spoke with Mehar, and he was thrilled about it," Simmie said.

On his walk home, Jaggi replayed the conversation in his head, perplexed over being asked on the trip. Why him? Sure, he and Simmie were comfortable with each other, and she had occasionally borrowed his geography assignments. But she was friendly with almost everyone in the class.

Jaggi mentioned the invite to Himmat. He was equally surprised. Himmat was not even in their class and had barely met her.

"She likes you, man!" Himmat said.

"But she invited you, too," replied Jaggi.

"Only because I'm your friend, obviously," Himmat laughed. "I'll go for your sake. When are we going?"

"I need to talk to baau ji and maa before accepting the offer," Jaggi said.

Jaggi talked to his mother about the outing. He had previously talked about this Jat girl, and the request made her tense up. Bindo was proud of her son, growing up and making friends with women his age, but getting associated with a high caste girl could spell trouble. On the other hand, Bindo did not want to dampen his enthusiasm and have him go through life constantly worrying about his caste, as she did. Jaggi got the approval but with a gentle warning. "Bete, it's okay to go on the trip. But be careful. Do not get involved with any girls. You are too young for that."

Chasing Dignity

Jaggi's face reddened. "We are just friends, maa."

They selected a Sunday for the trip. Jagdeep, the driver, pulled up in front of the college gate in a police Jeep. The Jeep was modified to replace the back two seats with cushioned, sectional stools to provide seating on three sides. Jhinder had a camera, and she took the front seat with the driver. Himmat and Mehar sat facing forward, and Simmie and Jaggi on the side stools, facing each other. Since they had to pass through Anandpur Sahib, Simmie suggested they stop for a few minutes to pay respects at Kesgarh Sahib, one of the Sikhs' most revered, holiest places.

Jagdeep talked non-stop. In the first half an hour, they learned, without prompting, almost everything about his thirty years of existence, his family, work, likes, and dislikes.

"We need to put tape on his mouth," Simmie whispered, extracting smiles. "Do you have any music, Jagdeep?" she asked.

"I have everything. What do you want to hear?" Jagdeep asked.

"Anything. I don't care," Simmie said, shaking her head. Jagdeep seemed to get the hint, but he put on high-beat Punjabi music too loud for them to have any conversation, making Simmie roll her eyes.

Soon they were at Anandpur Sahib; the Gurdwara was up a small hill, a few minutes from the road. Jagdeep waited in the car while they went to pay their obeisance. As most Sikhs do, they kowtowed in front of the holy book, except Simmie, who fully prostrated herself on the bare floor for over a minute and then got up and encircled the sacred Granth with folded hands.

"Jagdeep, please keep the volume low," Simmie said as they got back in the car.

"You are very religious," Jaggi said to Simmie, "Do you do *Nitname?*" Nitname was the daily routine of reciting five specific compositions from the holy Granth, which devout Sikhs followed religiously.

"Yes, I do," she answered, "don't you?"

Jaggi shook his head. Although Jaggi did not follow the Nitname protocol, he knew those opuses well. Bindo had worked with him to ensure he memorized the verses and understood their meaning. Jaggi did not say anything, though.

Soon the terrain became hilly, exciting Jhinder, and she became unusually vocal.

"Wow, looks like the road is piercing through the mountains!" she exclaimed.

"Wait a little; it will get exhilarating soon," Jagdeep added. Jagdeep had forgotten that his talking annoyed those sitting in the back. Jhinder would comment on the tall, sharply cut, stony sides of the hills, the vast expanses of green land, or a small house she saw on a mountain in the distance. Jagdeep would take his eyes off the road to look at her and say something to add to her excitement. The road meandered through the hills, and at times, it sloped down sharply while bending around a deep gorge on one side and a steep mountain on the other. Jhinder would scream with excitement making some comments. "You are distracting the driver," Mehar would yell, intensely focused on the road.

Jagdeep had driven on this route multiple times and was very familiar with it. He would randomly point and say, "Shiv Mandir is over there," or "That on top of that hill is Baba Balak Nath Ji's mandir," or "Over there is Hari Davi's mandir."

Jhinder would try to find it, "Where? Where?" she would inquire, making Mehar squirm in his seat, anticipating the driver taking his eyes off the road to show Jhinder where whatever that was. His flabby, terrified body was now beginning to sweat. Twice, with the cliff edge on their right and the hill on the left, they approached a sharp left turn where the road wasn't visible beyond the arc, giving a feeling the car was headed straight into the canyon. Both times Mehar gasped, gripping Jaggi's knee tightly. "Relax, man," Jaggi said, putting his hand on Mehar's shoulder. "Look how beautiful it is outside."

Jaggi was soaking in the breathtaking views. At times he would get the impression of being in the midst of clouds. The chasm between them and a water body in the distance offered no obstruction; sometimes, it would feel as if they were driving over water. "Is it Gobind Sagar?"

Mehar was relieved when they arrived, and Jagdeep parked the car. There were several other vehicles, and people were walking around.

"I'll wait here while you visit the mandir," Jagdeep said.

"Where's the mandir?" Mehar asked.

"On top of the hill. That way," Jagdeep said, pointing toward the steps that seemed to be winding around the hill. "There are seven hundred fifty steps. It will take you a while."

The site of the steps dampened Mehar's enthusiasm, though everyone else was excited. It took them about half an hour to reach the top. They were running and then stopping to take a breath or enjoy the expanses of the hills around, Jhinder capturing the beauty of the surroundings in her camera. They spent another forty minutes on the top, visiting the sacred places. They had a snack on return and were on their way to the Bhakra-Nangal dam by eleven.

The road to Bhakra Nangal was narrower, running parallel to the Sutlej River, which at this point, was growing broader as the Gobind Sagar Lake, providing a stunning spectacle. Jaggi had switched seats with Mehar, so Mehar didn't look straight to the front. Mehar was now more relaxed and did not object to Jhinder's distractions.

"Do you have any siblings?" Simmie asked Jaggi. He shook his head.

"I have two brothers, both older," Simmie said. "They are both into farming. One finished his BA, but the other dropped out of college." They must have a significant amount of land, Jaggi thought. "My father is a very skillful farmer. After high school, he took special agriculture courses," Simmie added.

Jaggi had never volunteered his social status to anyone for a good reason. When people learned about his caste, their interactions changed, and many treated him as inferior. The only person in the vehicle—in fact, in the whole college—who knew Jaggi's caste was Himmat. Himmat's caste ranking, though higher than Jaggi's, was still below society's perceived respect threshold—the boundary between the Sudra and the twice-born, the wearers of the sacred-thread, janeu. Like Jaggi, he, too, would not voluntarily share his caste.

Because Jaggi was from a farming family, his experiences were similar enough to Simmie's, and they could comfortably talk to each other at length. There was no reason for either to wade into the caste territory. Jaggi shared his upbringing, closeness with Rani's family, and how they grew up playing together. "So, Rani's like your sister," Simmie commented, sensing Jaggi's admiration of Rani.

Simmie's calling out about his relationship with Rani perturbed him—Is it because she isn't my real sister? Jaggi wondered. "You could say that" he answered, "she calls me Jaggi veer."

Their stop at Bhakhra-Nangal was memorable. They rented a motorboat and were in the water donning safety jackets for more than an hour; none knew how to swim. It was well after sunset when they returned to Rupar. Jhinder had filled four rolls of film.

Chasing Dignity

Jaggi had never imagined the trip to be so gratifying. He felt like a grown-up, traveling without his parents, being in the Himalayas, and boating in such a massive body of water. It felt surreal. He found Simmie's confidence charming and was tickled that, of all the boys in the class, she invited him. *Do not get involved with any girls. You are too young for that.* Jaggi understood what his mother had precisely conveyed. Simmie had no idea about his caste, and Jaggi didn't doubt what getting involved with a Jat girl could mean. Divulging his caste was not in the cards; he didn't want to lose his position and respect or embarrass himself after gaining new friends. Jaggi decided it was best to keep his interactions with Simmie as muted as possible.

Their short excursion had another unperceived outcome. By the evening the trip ended, the five had gone from mere classmates to being a family. The new dynamic of their interactions percolated through the entire class; the students began to be at ease with the opposite sex.

Chapter 12

It was the start of February, and Rani had less than two months to go into the final year of higher secondary school when an unfortunate accident happened. Rani's father, Sohan Singh, went to Rupar one morning to pay utility bills. Lakhwinder had some shopping to do, decided to go along on the outing, and hopped behind his scooter. A fallen tree had blocked part of the road, which no one had moved for a few days. People just drove around it, forcing traffic in both directions through the narrow, unblocked part of the road.

    Two young children were riding their bikes ahead, and Sohan Singh slowed down to let the children safely get around the blockage. A speeding car behind knocked Sohan Singh's scooter, which hit the fallen stump, tossing them off. The offending vehicle did not stop. Lakhwinder flung farther, miraculously, escaped only with minor scratches. She gathered herself and got up to find her husband lying on the ground, face down, a few feet from the fallen scooter. She came to him and shook him, but he didn't move. She pulled him by the arm and turned him face-up. A few walkers ran to them. Two men from a roadside bike repair shop also came running to help.

    "I saw his head hit that sign," someone said, pointing to the nearby concrete milestone. The older man from the bike repair shop examined Sohan Singh. "He is breathing, thank God," he said, "Veerpal, get a glass of water from the shop." His younger colleague, a man in his mid-twenties, ran and brought a tumbler of water. The man spattered Sohan Singh's eyes with a palmful, repeating a couple of times, failing to revive him.

    "Bhen ji, you need to take him to the hospital," the man said to Lakhwinder. She looked at him, bewildered. She had been dependent on Sohan Singh all her life. She didn't even know how to ride a bicycle independently.

The man realized her plight and asked the onlookers to flag the vehicles in the town's direction. People wouldn't stop, and if they did, they would refuse to carry Sohan Singh.

After about twenty minutes, a truck driver agreed. The gentleman from the bike repair shop sent Veerpal along to help. They put Sohan Singh in the driver's cabin, and Lakhwinder sat with him, holding her husband's head in her lap. Slight and agile, Veerpal quickly climbed into the vacant cargo area.

The driver dropped them at the emergency door and left. Neither Lakhwinder nor Veerpal knew what to do. Though breathing steadily, Sohan Singh was unresponsive. None of those walking or standing around came to help.

"I'll find someone," Veerpal said and went inside. After a few long minutes, he returned, pulling a stretcher with a faulty wheel. A bystander helped them put Sohan Singh on it, and they wheeled him inside. Few patients and relatives were scattered, but no staff was in sight to attend to Sohan Singh.

"You need to get a *parchi*," Veerpal said, pointing to the lady at the reception window. "It's for ten rupees."

Lakhwinder never kept any money on her when she was with Sohan Singh. She did not even have a pocket. She looked in the side pouch of Sohan Singh's shirt, and luckily, his wallet was there. Sohan Singh had brought enough money to shop and pay the electric bill.

The receptionist gave Veerpal the admission ticket and said, "Put him in a bed," pointing in the general direction of the hall.

A door on the left opened into a sizable room with a dozen beds, half occupied by patients and the rest by their friends and relatives. Many didn't have sheets, pillows, or blankets, and there were no stands for IV hookups. Two men got up to make room for the new patient and helped them transfer Sohan Singh onto the bed. Lakhwinder had been proud of her husband's tall, well-built, robust physique and always felt secure in his company. Today, for the first time in her life, he was the one who needed help, and she felt so vulnerable, and his body so heavy for her aging hands.

"Where is the doctor?" she asked someone only to get shrugs.

"There may be someone in the other room," another said, pointing to the door. Lakhwinder found a similar but more organized room on the other side of the corridor. She noticed a nurse in the room. There were patients with attached tubes and bags of fluids hanging from stands.

"Bhen ji, please help," she pleaded to the nurse with folded hands. "My husband had an accident. He is lying unconscious in the other room."

"Give me a minute," the nurse said, and after finishing what she was doing, she came with Lakhwinder.

"Let's move him to the other room," the nurse said and helped them put Sohan Singh on the stretcher and wheel him out. His new bed, at least, had a sheet and a pillow. The nurse took his vitals, wrote them on a sheet, and put it on a clipboard. She then pulled a stand close and hung the board from it. She made a list on paper. "Get me these things from a chemist's shop. These should cost around two hundred." There were a few chemist shops outside the hospital entrance, thriving on the hospital's inability to provide such basic things.

"When will the doctor look at him?" Lakhwinder asked, giving Veerpal three hundred rupees.

"He is gone out for a cup of tea and should be back soon," the nurse answered, "call me when you get the supplies. I need to start the IV."

The next hour was long for Lakhwinder. She would look at Sohan Singh, sleeping comfortably, without any sign of trauma.

But why wasn't he waking up? She remembered hearing he had hit the concrete milestone. His head must hurt, she thought and wondered if he could listen to her or the people around.

"Can you hear me? Wake up," she whispered, shaking him a little. She tried to move his arms and legs, one at a time. Everything seemed to work normally. Satisfied, she relaxed.

When Veerpal returned, the nurse prepared Sohan for an IV hookup. Soon after, the doctor returned, and the nurse explained to him briefly what had happened.

The doctor took the paracetamol Veerpal had brought and hooked the medicine to Sohan Singh.

"Doctor Sahib, when will he become conscious?" Lakhwinder asked.

"I don't know," the doctor said. "The neurologist, the head doctor, will tell you better."

"When will he get here?" she asked.

"He comes around one," the doctor answered and walked away.

Lakhwinder looked at the clock on the wall. It was a little past noon. Seeing Sohan Singh hooked to a tube gave her assurance; he was under care. Lakhwinder realized that neither of her daughters had any idea about the accident. Rani was a bright girl, and Lakhwinder would not feel as helpless if she were there with her.

Veerpal, wanting to take his leave, handed Lakhwinder the remaining money—a little over one hundred.

"Can you do me one more favor, puttar?" she asked, giving the money back to him. "My daughter is in the girls' higher secondary school in town. She is in the eleventh class. Her name is Rani. Can you take an auto-rickshaw and bring her here?"

"Ji, auntie ji," Veerpal said and hurried out.

Chasing Dignity

Veerpal had never been to a high school, much less a girls' high school. Rupar was a small city, and though the girls' higher secondary school was on the other side of town, it was only about a fifteen-minute ride. Getting off the auto-rickshaw, he looked at himself. His clothes were dirty and greasy. He tried to comb his hair with his fingers as he entered the high boundary wall gate. A chowkidar noticed him and came over. Veerpal gained confidence at seeing someone in a low-rank uniform.

"What do you need?" the man asked.

Veerpal explained the situation, and the chowkidar went inside, quickly returning with Rani.

Rani was frantic as Veerpal tried to explain what had happened. "Let's go," she said. The auto-rickshaw was waiting. They had just started when she stopped the driver and asked him to go to college first. The college was less than five minutes from her school.

Rani got off in front of the college and ran toward the building steps, asking them to wait. She saw two girls coming down the steps.

"I'm looking for my brother, Jagjit Singh," she said in a very anxious tone. Before the girls could say anything, "He is in BA part two," she added. The urgency in her words seemed to transfer to the girls. They looked at each other.

"Jaggi, the tall, very handsome?" one asked.

"Yes," Rani said.

"He was in the library. We just came from there," the girl said, and they turned back to help Rani.

Jaggi shook his head in surprise to see Rani in the library. She explained the situation in gasps, and before she finished, he'd packed up his things and begun pulling her toward the door. Veerpal squeezed into the front with the driver, leaving the back seat for Rani and Jaggi. On the way, he brought them up to date with the situation.

The sight of Rani and Jaggi gave immeasurable relief to Lakhwinder; now, she wasn't alone and helpless. It had been three hours since the accident, and while she had been fortunate to have Veerpal with her all this time, he could do only so much, and she didn't know how long he could stay with her. Veerpal took his leave, and Lakhwinder gave him fifty rupees for his help.

Jaggi looked for the doctor and found him reading a newspaper in his office. All doctor told him was that Sohan Singh likely had a trauma to his head, and they were waiting for the neurologist to order a CT scan. "Can't you have the CT scan done now to be ready when the neurologist comes?" Jaggi asked.

"No, it is his job, his specialty," the doctor said, frustrating Jaggi because he would not listen to any argument.

Jaggi sent a taxi from a taxi stand outside the hospital to Kundyan with a note for his parents.

It took another hour before the neurologist showed up. There was a new nurse on shift now, and she looked experienced from her demeanor and how she talked to the doctors and the patients' relatives.

"Nurse," the neurologist said, "please take his vitals and arrange a CT scan for him."

The nurse looked for Ramu; Ramu was the hospital's general service employee, to help with errands like getting supplies from the store, moving the patients, acting as a messenger, etc. She spotted him and asked him to alert the technician.

While the nurse collected Sohan Singh's vitals, which were still good, Ramu returned with the news that the technician was not in the lab.

Chasing Dignity

"Go and find him. Tell him Dr. Narain needs this CT scan immediately. We are going to the lab directly," she said. She pulled a stretcher and put Sohan Singh on it with help from Jaggi and Rani.

They had to wait in the lab for twenty minutes for the technician. It was an hour later that Dr. Narain announced the results to them.

The doctor said that Sohan Singh had a small epidural hematoma. "There's blood inside the skull. It will take some time, but it should cure itself," he explained.

The doctor's statement calmed them down. When the doctor went away, the nurse signaled Jaggi, to walk out the door. She stopped where it was a little private.

"Take him to PGI," she said.

PGI was a Post Graduate Research Institute with excellent staff and facilities, about an hour away. Being the only institute to cater to four states, PGI was overly crowded, resulting in long wait lines for the outpatient department and the emergency wards. However, it was the only hope for thousands of patients who needed critical care.

"Don't take hematoma in the skull lightly. It's up to you, but I wouldn't waste a minute," the nurse emphatically said. "The Narula chemist shop, outside the hospital, provides private ambulance service. It will cost you a few hundred rupees, but it is worth it."

Jaggi wasn't sure how much cash Lakhwinder had with her, but he was hopeful one of his parents would arrive with money any minute; he had explained the situation in the note. He went to inquire about the ambulance. The ambulance was available, and the cost was seven hundred rupees, 'not too bad for a thirty-mile ride for four, especially under the circumstances, and the driver will have to drive the empty ambulance back.' Jaggi told them about his money situation. The person was friendly, and Jaggi seemed believable. "Let's get your uncle in the ambulance first. Hopefully, your father will arrive shortly." Jaggi told him where to send the ambulance. Bindo was entering the hospital gate when Jaggi returned. She had brought with her a little over a thousand rupees. "This is all we had at home. If you need more, I have the bank passbook with me. I can get you more."

"This should be enough. Lakhwinder auntie should have some. She had come for shopping," Jaggi said.

Jaggi explained to them what the nurse had advised.

Soon the ambulance arrived. It was no more than a modified van with the word *Ambulance* printed in big letters on the sides and a flashing light affixed on top. It didn't have a separate driver's cabin. Two long sofa seats were behind the driver and the passenger chairs, set lengthwise along the sides. The vehicle had no medical equipment, and the driver was not a medical professional. Nevertheless, it was a convenient option for people in need.

Lakhwinder, Rani, and Jaggi accompanied Sohan Singh. Before they boarded, the driver put a pillow and spread a thick bed sheet on one of the sofa seats. They laid Sohan Singh there, and Lakhwinder sat with him holding his head on a pillow in her lap. Rani and Jaggi sat opposite.

The driver took the back roads to save time. "It would be just a forty-five-minute drive," he said. On the way, Lakhwinder told them how things had unfolded after the accident in greater detail.

"Are you okay, maa?" Rani asked, suddenly realizing that her mother, too, was thrown off the scooter in the crash.

"Yes, I'm okay," she said. "I just had a couple of small scratches."

The discussion shifted to the nurse, who advised them to go to the PGI.

Chasing Dignity

"Why didn't she tell us that earlier?" Rani asked.

"She had just come on duty. There was another nurse in the morning," Lakhwinder answered.

"Why did she call you out? Couldn't she just tell all this inside where we were sitting?" Rani asked Jaggi.

"She wanted to be discreet. I don't think advising against her superiors could have been a simple decision," Jaggi said. "She seemed to know how things work there. Remember how she sped up things, calling Ramu to get the technician to quicken the CT scan?" he added.

As Rani thought about it, the nurse was efficient and friendly with patients and their family members. She suddenly felt more gratitude for the nurse than for the doctors who diagnosed her father.

"A good nurse can make a real difference in someone's life," Rani contemplated.

Lakhwinder ventured down memory lane. Being the only one to take care of farming, Sohan Singh had a lot of responsibilities, but whenever he could, he would help Lakhwinder with milking the buffalos and other chores. And how good he was to their two daughters! Ginder was two; Rani wasn't born yet. It was the middle of the harvest season, and Sohan Singh was extremely busy, barely sleeping four hours a day. Lakhwinder developed pain in the lower abdomen. On the second day of her discomfort, Sohan Singh dropped everything and took her to the hospital, even though she told him the pain was not intolerable and she was okay. "What will I do if something ever happened to you?" he had said. Lakhwinder's eyes moistened. She looked into his closed eyes; 'I need you; the girls need you."

Rani frequently looked at her wristwatch, calculating how far they were from PGI. She was in the eighth class when Sohan Singh bought her this watch. "How beautiful it looks on my

Laddu's wrist," she remembered him saying. He was the only one to call Rani *mera Laddu*. She remembered climbing on his shoulders as if it were only yesterday. Sohan Singh didn't have much schooling but took pride in how well Rani did in school.

Lakhwinder held Sohan Singh's head, and the back of her left thumb was right below his nostrils. She suddenly realized she was not feeling his breath anymore.

"Rani, I can't feel your baau ji's breath," she said with panic.

Rani got up and put her finger in front of her father's nostrils. She did feel the breath, but it was weak and irregular.

"How much longer, sir?" Rani shouted to the driver, "Can we go faster?"

"We are close. We should be there in five minutes," the driver answered as he pushed down the gas pedal.

The driver had been to the PGI many times, and as soon as they reached the emergency door, he parked the ambulance and ran to grab a stretcher. After securing Sohan Singh on it, he pushed it toward the door; Jaggi helped.

People crowded the emergency area.

Rani ran to the register counter while Jaggi looked around for help. He saw a nurse.

"Sister, urgent, please, we have a patient with trauma to the head. The accident happened many hours ago, and we can't feel his breath," he pleaded, pointing toward Sohan Singh.

"Come with me," the nurse said and approached a doctor with another patient.

"Dr. Sushant, a head trauma patient needs your urgent attention," she said.

The doctor had just resuscitated and stabilized a heart-attack patient. He quickly wrote instructions for the ICU before examining Sohan Singh. Jaggi briefed him on the accident and their visit to the Rupar Hospital.

"Do you have that CT scan report?"

'No," Jaggi said, feeling foolish for not bringing the report.

"We need a CT scan," the doctor said. He took a small notepad from his coat pocket and prescribed the scan. "I need the report right away," he said to the nurse.

"Let's take him," the nurse said. Jaggi pushed the stretcher, the nurse guiding it from the front.

Within half an hour, they were back with the report and the scan images.

"Severe hematoma. We need to evacuate it immediately," the doctor said.

"What?" Jaggi said.

"When his head hit the concrete object, it caused bleeding under the skull. The blood is collecting inside, and it has nowhere to escape. It is now putting pressure on the brain. We will have to cut his skull and remove that blood," the doctor said.

"Is it dangerous?" Rani asked.

"Yes, it is major surgery. But if we don't operate right away, the patient will not survive. It is an extensive hematoma, and it may already be too late. Shall we proceed?"

Jaggi looked at Rani and Lakhwinder. "Whatever you two think is right," Lakhwinder said.

"Let's do it," Rani said, and Jaggi agreed.

They took Sohan Singh immediately for the surgery. After about an hour, a little past six, they saw Sohan Singh wheeled into the ICU. In addition to the IV hookup, an oxygen line was attached to him. His head was all bandaged, and his hair was shaved off.

The doctors had successfully evacuated the hematoma, but his condition remained critical for the next 24-to-48 hours. "We don't know if the delay in proper treatment caused irreversible damage to the brain. We'll have to wait and see," the doctor said, leaving them to speculate what time had in store for them and Sohan Singh.

It was six-thirty in the evening, and they huddled in a corner outside the ICU; the excruciating wait could last many hours. Jaggi decided to go out and get something to make them more comfortable. He got an auto-rickshaw, went to a mall a couple of kilometers away, and bought three small blankets. The shop had only two pillows, and Jaggi purchased both. He also brought sodas and packets of biscuits.

They settled in that corner on the floor with their backs against the walls, Rani and Lakhwinder sharing a pillow.

A nurse woke them up a little before five in the morning. She was shaking Rani's shoulder.

"I'm sorry we could not save your father," she said.

The news rattled them from their groggy state, and, startled, they sprang to their feet.

"What?" said Rani. She thought it was some weird nightmare.

"The blood's damage to his brain was irreversible," she explained.

Jaggi noticed a man in hospital apparel standing beside a gurney, looking at them. Jaggi stepped closer and uncovered Sohan Singh's face under a white sheet. Someone had nicely tied a cloth around his head that looked like a small turban. His eyes were closed as if sleeping. Rani and Lakhwinder followed. Rani bent over, looking at her father's face, and held it in her hands, parts of her hands buried in his flowing beard. Lakhwinder was looking at him expressionlessly, replaying the events from the previous day in her mind.

"You can get a taxi at the door, and Chandan will help you get your uncle in," the nurse said, and the man by the gurney blinked his consent.

Jaggi was almost out of money by now. He went around to ask Lakhwinder if she had any. Lakhwinder handed him the wallet.

The taxi Jaggi found was a medium-sized car with a back sofa seat for three. Chandan and another man helped them put Sohan Singh into it; Rani and Lakhwinder sat in the back, squished in the small space along the front of Sohan Singh's body. Neither would accept Jaggi's offer to swap with his front seat.

Lakhwinder turned back to look at her husband's face. "What will I do if something ever happened to you?" A wry smile traversed Lakhwinder's face. "Did it ever occur to you what I would do without you?" She had never imagined a life without Sohan Singh. They had two daughters. Lakhwinder had no qualms about the girls, one day, getting married and moving out of the house, but they would have each other. Now what? How would she deal with this mountain of life alone? Suddenly Lakhwinder regretted not having a son. A son's family would live in the house, and she wouldn't have to worry about being lonely.

"I want people to call me your wife, Sohan Singh's wife, forever and ever, not just some widow," Lakhwinder's eyes welled up. People identified women by their husbands; becoming a widow meant losing that identity and respect in society. Female infanticide put women in short supply, and a widow, especially a young one, would become a quick target in that sex-starved society. The lack of a man in the house would make her daughters vulnerable.

She thought of Jito, one of her cousins. Jito had lost her husband to cancer years ago, and Jito's in-laws always blamed Jito for his death; "She's a man-eater," they would say. People would not invite Jito to auspicious occasions like weddings or children's parties because she carried bad luck. Many would refer to her as *randi*, a common synonym for a widow and a prostitute. To show remorse, widows would only wear white, discarding colorful clothes and jewelry for the rest of their lives. "I'm a living corpse," Jito once confided in Lakhwinder. The thought made Lakhwinder shudder.

A car cut in front of them, and the driver hit on the brakes, giving them a jolt. Both Rani and Lakhwinder hit the back of the seats in front. Rani looked back at Sohan Singh to make sure he was okay. He can't feel pain anymore, she thought, but still, it would hurt to see her father get hit. He would be hurt if I were hit. Rani always thought she was her father's favorite. If an argument with Lakhwinder got Sohan Singh agitated, he would relax the moment he talked to Rani. Sometimes Rani felt her father saw the son he didn't have in her. "My Laddu will be an officer when she gets educated." He would let Rani help him in the fields, seek her advice on essential matters, and show pride when she did well in school. He never missed praising her when she learned something new and comforted her when she needed cheering. She looked back at him, caressing his leg. "Don't you worry baau ji, I'm here, your son's here. I'll take care of everything."

It was about seven in the morning when they reached Kundyan. Bindo had stayed with Ginder for the night. Seeing her father return dead, Ginder broke down entirely, and soon they were all crying.

Rani remembered getting ready for school the day before; Lakhwinder had just returned from milking Fullo, their prized buffalo. Ginder made breakfast while Sohan Singh ate, sitting next to her. He will never sit by the chullah again to have breakfast with us, Rani thought.

The day began to lighten, and the news spread quickly through the village. People started to pour into the house. Messages went out to Sohan Singh's sister, Lakhwinder's parents, and other close relatives. People arrived by late afternoon and were ready to take Sohan Singh for cremation; they had to do it before sundown. Gurdev, Sohan Singh's sister, took Lakhwinder inside. "Change into these," she said, handing Lakhwinder a plain white attire. "And, let's remove these," she said, helping Lakhwinder take her jewelry off. Lakhwinder complied without resistance.

Lakhwinder's brother and his wife stayed with the family for two nights, and Gurdev through the final rites on day ten.

The immediate problem was taking care of their wheat crop, which was coming up for harvest in less than a month. It had to be harvested and taken to the market. None of the women knew what to do. Teja volunteered:

"Don't you worry, bhen ji," he assured Lakhwinder. "I will take care of it just as I care for mine."

Bindo visited them every day and helped them with whatever they needed.

"Rani, I think you should go to school tomorrow," Bindo suggested. Sohan Singh died on a Wednesday, and Rani did not go to school for the remainder of the week. "Getting back to the routine will help." Rani did not respond, but she went back to school on Monday.

The relatives and Friends gathered for the final rites. Everyone except Gurdev left. Gurdev lived only a couple of miles away and was with the family for another two days. All sorts of worries occupied Lakhwinder's mind—Rani's education, farming, a match for Ginder, and paying for her dowry. She shared her concerns with Gurdev. Gurdev garnered respect and influence in the family; Sohan Singh and Lakhwinder always listened to her and solicited her opinion on important matters. Gurdev's husband had two nephews of marriageable age. There had already been a discussion of Gurdev taking Ginder's hand for the older when Sohan Singh was alive.

"Bhabi ji, you know I have quite a say in my family. I will take Rani's hand, too, for the younger," Gurdev offered. Lakhwinder's face brightened. The offer was enticing.

Rani, listening, blurted out immediately: "Talk about Ginder, not me. I want to go to college."

Gurdev had never gone to school, not even the primary. She was married into a farming family that, though financially well, was just as illiterate. In Gurdev's mind, the only practical purpose education served for women was to read letters, road signs, or destination tags on the buses. College education made no sense in their lives, none whatsoever.

"You are seventeen years old," Gurdev said, "it's time to settle down. You cannot find a better match than that boy. He is taller than his older brother, and he is handsome. He will inherit six acres of land. Plus, he doesn't drink or have any other vices. Do you know how many Jat boys are on drugs these days?" Gurdev snapped.

Rani was taken aback by her bhua ji's tone.

"Rani, with your father gone, I cannot afford your college," Lakhwinder said.

"Maa, I want to be independent, and attending college at Rupar is not expensive," Rani argued.

Gurdev scoffed. "Independent," she said, "what is that nonsense? You think our home is a jail?"

She turned to Lakhwinder, "The sooner the girls are married, the sooner you will be worry-free, bhabi ji. You don't have to agonize over dowry. We'll take the girls in their plain clothes."

"Bhua ji, we will talk about it after my exams," Rani said.

"You can take your exams. But I need to know soon. Everyone eyes boys like that. They're already getting offers from well-to-do families," Gurdev warned.

Over the next few months, Rani's education remained a thorny issue. Lakhwinder was unsure if she could afford her education and did not want to annoy her sister-in-law. Rani convinced her mother, but Gurdev wasn't thrilled. Finally, Rani prevailed. Lakhwinder long-term leased her land to Teja, and Rani's education was easily affordable with the lease money. Rani took her bhua ji into confidence with a vague promise of considering her marriage proposal.

Rani excelled in her final exams. While considering her career choice, she could not get out of her mind the nurses' help they received during her father's hospitalization. Rani wanted to contribute to society, and becoming a nurse was the best way forward. So, the following year, she joined the one-year pre-medical program at Rupar, the same college where Jaggi was.

Chapter 13

Jaggi would arrive at college at 8 a.m. and spend at least four hours in the library before and between his classes. He needed about an hour to finish his class assignments, and the rest of his time went into reading fiction.

One day, browsing through the English literature, Jaggi noticed *I take this woman*, Khushwant Singh's translation of Rajinder Bedi's *Ek Chadar Maili Si*. Jaggi had read the Hindi version and was curious to compare the two.

Knowing the story well, Jaggi found reading the translation easy. He noticed significant differences between the two versions compared word for word. Here and there, the translator rearranged sentences and added or deleted some to recreate the scenes.

Jaggi began to develop a taste for English literature. An excellent way to learn English, he thought and expanded his reading of translations. He found a few versions of Russian works like Maxim Gorky's *Mother*, which he had read before. He slowly began to appreciate the efforts and skills involved in translating foreign-language works. Sometimes he would come across a social concept so alien that he would wonder how one could convert it into Punjabi without losing its sense and meaning. He realized that creating the same intensity of feeling in a different language was more than a literal sentence conversion. One had to be imaginative and fluent in the languages and the culture. Slowly, he started to notice the range of writing styles—from Hemingway's detached and succinct prose to the social and cultural realism in Khushwant Singh and Mulk Raj Anand.

Still, by far, Jaggi read Punjabi fiction. He was in love with Amrita Pritam's writings and often hummed her poem "Aj aakhann Waris Shah Nu"—Today, I call upon Waris Shah—a cry of anguish over massacres that followed the 1947 partition of India. Another of Jaggi's favorite authors was Shiv Kumar Batalvi, whose imagination and profound symbolism fascinated Jaggi, and many of his poems got permanently etched into his memory.

The writers often focused on age, race, gender, and inequality, the issues that negatively impacted a group of people one would ignore in day-to-day life. The more Jaggi read, the more keenly he began to notice the injustices in the world. To understand the Indian caste system, he read the Hindu Shastras and carefully read Manu Smriti, the so-called 'mother' of the Hindu social structure. Incidentally, he stumbled on Dr. Ambedkar's works. Dr. Bhim Rao Ambedkar, a scholar and an untouchable himself, was one of the architects of the Indian constitution. His works gave Jaggi an insight into the origin of the caste and how it became a dominant part of Indian society.

Jaggi entertained the idea of becoming a career writer. *Whether you succeed as a writer, only time can tell*, he remembered Professor Tara Singh. Jaggi decided to try his luck and wrote two articles, one based on his experiences in college and the other about human prejudices. Not wanting his social status disclosed, he made roundabout references to any issue that involved caste. Jaggi sent the articles for publication in reputed English newspapers, confident they would be published. Neither got accepted. Maybe I don't have it in me to be a writer, he concluded. I should abandon writing if my primary goal were to succeed in the US. Jaggi decided not to do writing as a vocation and limited his penning to capturing his reflections in a diary.

Academically, Jaggi liked economics and geography equally well and couldn't decide what to pursue for his master's. But then his geography professor got transferred, and they had a new, young teacher, Aditya Kumar, a trained cartographer. Aditya Kumar's M. Phil. focused on "the importance of physiographic understanding to plan for land conservation effectively." An energetic person, Aditya Kumar was enthusiastic about his work, and he taught this esoteric subject in a way that piqued everyone's interest, especially Jaggi's. One day he introduced the idea of GPS. No one in the class had heard of it before.

Aditya Kumar explained. "GPS stands for Global Positioning System. The US military developed the system about twenty years ago, and shortly after, in 1980, the US allowed its use for civilian purposes." He discussed how handheld devices used stationary satellites to pinpoint any location's exact coordinates on earth.

"Speed is the primary benefit GPS provides. It's a good tool in the hands of a cartographer," Kumar said. "The quickness with which one can find a location's coordinates on earth makes a difference in how one reacts to a situation."

A hand went up.

"Atlases rarely change over the years. How does it matter if GPS can speed up the map-making process?" the student asked.

"True, drawing political boundaries and road maps does not always demand the quickness of a GPS. But there are other scenarios where mapping speed can save lives and property. Can you picture such a scenario?" Aditya Kumar asked.

No one answered; a few shook their heads.

"Did any of you read about the Oakland Hills firestorm that happened a couple of years ago? It was in the newspapers."

Again, no response.

"Oakland is in California, a western state of the USA. A fire started there on a hillside, and it took them four days to control it. It killed dozens and injured scores. GPS was not widely available then, and people think such a loss of life was preventable had the GPS been fully operational. One could dynamically map how the fire spreads and direct the resources to contain it more accurately. Knowing the exact locations of buildings, people, and emergency resources is critical in reducing the time it takes to mobilize support."

Quickly, the discussion veered toward other disasters like the big oil spills and disastrous avalanches. Aditya Kumar explained how quick, accurate, and dynamic mapping of disaster-stricken areas could help manage such calamities. Predicting the locations of looming catastrophes like volcanos could be more precise. The technology could help endangered species by dynamically mapping their migrations and understanding the forces behind such movements.

Jaggi quickly became fascinated with GPS technology, and Aditya Kumar's lectures became highly appealing. Jaggi's questions began to venture into areas beyond the class's scope, often prompting Aditya Kumar to ask him to meet afterward. A friendship grew between them, and their discussions cemented Jaggi's interest in geography as the major for his master's.

Jaggi was eighteen at the start of his fourth year and had grown another three inches since high school. The gaunt little boy with a stutter was now a sturdy, agile, six-foot-one spectacle to behold with confidence that matched his physique.

Simmie showed keen interest in Jaggi, and Jaggi liked her, but what could he do about what society so strongly forbade? While it gnawed at Jaggi's heart, he felt all he could do was keep his feelings at bay. But, the more Jaggi attempted to stay aloof, the more Simmie tried to forge a connection. She frequently suggested going to lunch, which eventually became regular. However, Jaggi ensured someone accompanied them, usually one of their Naina Devi trip companions. But when Himmat graduated, only Jhinder and sometimes Mehar was available to give them the company.

Chasing Dignity

Simmie's conversations became increasingly personal, and Jaggi wouldn't be surprised if she suggested pursuing a relationship one of these days. It was becoming difficult for him to hide the reasons for his avoidance. However, he was comforted knowing that Simmie was a devout Sikh, and Sikh scriptures and history touted equality among all humans. Jaggi would imagine her to be tolerant toward lower castes and thought of sharing his social status with her, so she understood. But would his secret be safe with her? What if she told Jhinder and the news spread? What his classmates and friends would think of him? Since they would be graduating in less than two months, Jaggi decided not to take the risk of ruining their friendship in its last days.

One day, Jhinder did not come to college; it was just the two at lunch. Jaggi dreaded Simmie broaching the subject. If she did, Jaggi saw no escape but to tell her the truth. Strangely, the thought of sharing his caste with her relaxed him.

"You haven't talked much today," Simmie said, breaking his reverie. "What are you thinking about?"

"Nothing; I think I'm just tense about the finals."

"Oh, hush!" she said. "If you are worried about the exams, what will happen to the rest of us?"

Jaggi smiled; his academic reputation was strong.

"What do you do in the evenings?" she asked.

"Nothing much," Jaggi answered nonchalantly.

"Jhinder and I plan to go to *Dilwale Dulhania Le Jayenge* tomorrow." It was a popular movie, released a while ago and playing in the local cinema. "I hope you can go with us."

Jaggi saw no good reason to say no and agreed.

Simmie was already there when Jaggi arrived for the movie.

"Jhinder's not here yet?" Jaggi asked.

"She isn't coming," Simmie answered. "She couldn't stay late today."

Jaggi became apprehensive, but he didn't say anything.

"I already got the tickets," Simmie said when she saw Jaggi pull out his wallet. She had two tickets for the upper floor, where they found a relatively secluded corner to sit.

A few minutes into the movie, she held his hand, linking her fingers with his. His heartbeat was on the rise. She's friendly, Jaggi rationalized and relaxed in his seat. He was enjoying the touch of her skin and involuntarily squeezed her hand. They went out in the intermission to get sodas and popcorn. Once the second half started, she held his hand again. This time Jaggi was more relaxed.

A few minutes before the movie ended, Simmie suddenly pulled Jaggie's neck and planted a kiss on his mouth. It was a brief kiss, but the first for the nineteen-year-old young man, and it jolted his system. When they separated, he let go of her hand, and she didn't try to get it back.

It was early in the evening when they got out of the theater.

"See you tomorrow," Jaggi said when they parted.

"See you," Simmie said with a meaningful smile.

"You seem distracted today, bete," Bindo said during dinner. "What's going on?"

"Nothing," Jaggi said. "Just thinking about my exams. We have less than a month to go." The results would determine Jaggi's perspective on getting admission into his choice master's program.

"Don't worry about it. I have faith in my son's abilities. You should, too," Bindo said, patting his shoulder.

That night Jaggi could not focus on his assignment and lay tossing for a while before sleep came to him.

"Do you have a few minutes? I want to talk," Jaggi said to Simmie after their class.

"Aren't we going to lunch? We can talk there," she said.

"No, let's go to the lawn by the library." The place had benches, and Jaggi didn't expect anyone to be there during this hour.

"It's about yesterday, isn't it?" Simmie said, sitting by his side as he sat on a bench.

Jaggi nodded but didn't say anything.

"It must have come to you as a shock," she laughed. "I thought that was the best way to convey my feelings. By the way, I never kissed a boy before."

Jaggi kept quiet.

"I know it was bad on my part. A woman shouldn't be that forthcoming," she said.

"Yes, it took me by surprise, but that's not what I want to talk about," Jaggi said.

Simmie suddenly seemed nervous.

Jaggi noticed her expression.

"Simmie, I like you, but—"

Simmie looked at him, confused.

"Do you know—" He again stopped midsentence.

"Do I know what?"

"That I'm not a Jat?" he said, relieved at his admittance.

"What? Are you a Bhapa? You don't look like one," she said. Bhapa was a slightly derogatory term Jats used for the business community Sikhs. In the caste hierarchy, Bhapas were considered equal to Jats. They were generally more educated and more open to inter-caste marriages. However, Jats considered them cowardly and cunning and frowned over such unions. If one ever materialized, it would become a permanent target of their ridicule.

"No, I am a Keera," Jaggi said, barely whispering the last word.

"What was that?" For some reason, her bewildered face didn't unnerve Jaggi.

"I said, I am a Keera," he repeated with a poise.

"You are joking, right? You don't look like a Keera!"

Jaggi was familiar with that hurtful comment. Centuries of segregation and suppression had created perceptions that the lower castes had darker complexions and smaller bodies, and people expected them to exhibit servitude.

"I didn't know Keeras looked any different from others," he answered.

"How could you have lied to me?" she said.

"How did I lie?"

"You didn't tell me who you were." She appeared to choke. "And now you ruined my life!"

"Simmie!" Jaggi said, now growing frustrated. "What are you talking about?"

"Everyone knows I like you. We've gone to lunch every week for the whole term; people think there's something between us. What will they think of me now? That I was spending time with someone like you? And," she paused, "I kissed you!"

"That's why I wanted to tell you before we went any further."

"Further? How can you even think of that? How could you think of going further with a Jat girl?" She yelled and got up, turning to walk away.

"Simmie, wait..." he said, in despair to explain himself.

Chasing Dignity

"Don't you call me, ever, just stay away! Imagine what my brothers will do to you if they find out! You Keera! Oh, God, I kissed a Keera!" Her disgust sent chills through Jaggi. One moment, she was in love with him, and the next, she treated him as if he were a leper. Jaggi's mind went into a swirl. Flashes of the humiliation he had endured over the years passed through his head. He recalled when someone asked his mother to move to the grass outside to make room for the Jats; the Jat who threw him off a cot, the smiling faces when Cheta called upon him to clean the dog poop.

As Jaggi walked away, he felt like an insecure little boy with a stutter, ridiculed and bullied by children, beaten down for the reasons of his birth, for something he didn't do. The memory of Simmie prostrating in front of the Sikh holy book became vivid, and he shook his head in disgust.

It was a Wednesday. Jaggi still had his economics period left, after which he usually spent time in the library. But today, he didn't feel like going to his class or the library and went straight home. His mother was not there. He wished to talk to Himmat, but Himmat studied in Ludhiana. Teepu, sitting in the yard, looked at his master with a submissive grin. Jaggi took a ball and tried to incite the dog into a game of catch. But Teepu just licked his lips and lowered his head, to get more comfortable in his position. The old soldier preferred sitting to playing fetch.

Jaggi decided to take a walk and unconsciously strolled in the direction of their farm.

"You are early today, Jaggi veer," he heard. It was Rani. She was reading her chemistry book. Rani liked to set her cot on Jaggi's side of the boundary; "It is more serene on this side," she would say.

Jaggi pulled a cot next to her. Rani was now eighteen. She looked stunning: she had a perfectly symmetrical face, big bright eyes, and a flawless nose. Jaggi's gaze moved from her full lips to her ample bosom.

"Rani, I have a question for you," he said. "Do we Keeras look different from you Jats? How do I look?"

"Did you run into that buffalo-head Cheta again?" She wanted to tell him she did not know another man half as handsome as he was. But she did not; she could not. "What's going on, Jaggi veer?" she asked

Jaggi told her the entire story, the trip, the lunches, the movie, and the kiss he got from Simmie.

Rani knew Simmie; she had met her with Jaggi in the library. Jaggi's detail was so vivid that Rani's eyes narrowed, imagining she was sitting with Jaggi watching that film, and she was the one who kissed him.

"This morning, I told her I am a Keera. And s-s-she," Jaggi stuttered. "She acted as if she had touched some filthy, rabid dog."

Rani closed her eyes, shaking her head.

"Why do high caste people get polluted when they touch a Keera?"

Rani extended her arms to hold his hands.

"I'm a Jat, and I'm not getting polluted."

He abruptly pulled his hands away, making Rani startle. A lump was growing in Jaggi's throat.

"Veer ji, you give too much importance to what others think."

Jaggi did not say anything, and they sat quietly for a while.

Rani spoke when she saw Jaggi relaxed.

"I know things are bad, and I am not in a position to say how you should feel. But the times are changing, though slowly. I read that there was a time when people from many castes had to beat a drum to announce their presence while walking, so the upper caste could move aside."

"I know," Jaggi said. "Maa tells me that when her grandmother was young, the villagers wouldn't let our kind fetch water from the wells. She would sit by the well, sometimes for an hour, for some kind-hearted passerby to pull a bucket of water for her and pour it in her pitcher."

"Jaggi veer, the best thing for you is not to waste your time on these people. When you graduate and go to the USA, you won't have to worry about your caste and can do whatever you want. 'The sky is the limit'—isn't that what your mama ji said?"

Chapter 14

One evening, Jaggi returned home on his bike when he sensed a high-speed vehicle approaching from behind. He quickly shifted to the unpaved shoulder, turning his neck to see. A speeding Jeep veered from the center of the road passed, almost brushing him. The jeep stopped about a hundred yards ahead of him. It had its top pulled down. When Jaggi came close, he saw three people inside. One sitting in the front passenger seat was Banta. He looked back at Jaggi and grinned. Then he said something to the driver, and they took off. The car moved as if the driver had pushed the pedal to the floor.

A shiver went through Jaggi. Were they trying to kill him? Maybe they just wanted to scare him. But they had him, had he not moved to the shoulder so quickly.

Jaggi recalled his last confrontation with Banta. Jaggi was in the ninth class, almost fourteen then. By then, he had grown tall and robust and was on the school's football team. One day, returning from practice, Jaggi and his friends walked past a group of eighth-graders fighting. Two boys were pummeling a weaker student, and he was trying to protect his face from being hit.

"Stop that!" Jaggi yelled, halting.

"Do you need a thrashing too, hakley?" said someone. Jaggi looked; it was Banta. Only he would mention Jaggi's stutter, which he had long outgrown.

The boys stopped hitting, and the attention shifted to Banta and Jaggi. Although he hadn't noticed Banta before he spoke, Jaggi was not surprised. He had played this encounter many times in his head since joining the school and was ready for it.

"Do you wanna try, you gitthu?" Jaggi said, getting in Banta's face.

Jaggi was taller, though Banta wasn't tiny that one would call him *gitthu*. Banta wasn't thin either, by any means. Two of Jaggi's friends moved right beside him.

"Who is this clown?" asked Daljit, a tall, stocky tenth-grader.

"No one I can't handle," Jaggi said, looking piercingly into Banta's eyes.

Banta was caught off-guard. Never in his dreams had he expected such a stand by Jaggi. He took a step back without saying anything.

"Let's go," Daljit said, tugging at Jaggi's arm.

Walking away, Daljit turned to Banta and his buddies. "If any of you touches that boy again, we'll find you and teach you a lesson that you won't forget," he said, pointing to the boy they were abusing. "Remember that."

Banta had to repeat class eight and was still in the ninth when Jaggi left for college. That year, Banta got arrested with two others for burning a house. Luckily, no one was hurt, but he spent six months in jail. Banta never returned to finish school.

Then people started hearing about him being close to a politician known to be corrupt. Banta had joined the politician's "voter-motivator" team. Many spiritual gurus in Punjab had varying followers, ranging from a few hundred to a few hundred thousand. They voted en masse for any politician the guru favored. Banta's team was assigned to motivate these gurus to direct their followers to vote for specific candidates. The motivation strategies ranged from outright threats of violence to bribery and other favors, including protecting them from unnecessary scrutiny by the government or independent social groups.

Quickly, Banta's influence grew, and he worked with a politician heavily involved in drug trafficking. Banta joined the gang responsible for moving drugs coming through neighboring Pakistan to India.

They were also involved in vacating properties. Sometimes the tenants, using the protection of the existing laws in their favor, would refuse to leave the rented properties. For a share in the property, the gang would make the lives of these tenants miserable and force them out. At other times, a wealthy or influential person hired them to motivate an unwilling owner to sell a strategic property.

As an individual, Banta did not scare Jaggi. Jaggi was taller and more muscular than any three in the Jeep. But Banta's being a part of these nefarious circles that enjoyed political and police protection made him dangerous to everyone, not just Jaggi.

The incident disturbed Jaggi beyond reckoning. Fortunately, it was past his exams for the incident to impact his results. Jaggi did not want to scare his parents by sharing the encounter. What could they do, he thought. He couldn't discuss it with Rani either. She, too, would worry to death about his safety.

Jaggi stopped by Himmat's house. Himmat had finished his B. Ed. degree and was back with his parents, relaxed and waiting for the results. He had already started to look for a job.

"There's a good chance I'll find one close by, within thirty kilometers."

"Thirty kilometers will be a long commute," Jaggi said.

"I didn't say thirty; *within* thirty kilometers is what I said," said Himmat. "I plan to buy a motorcycle. Thirty kilometers on a motorbike isn't bad."

Jaggi agreed. "Hi, I came to talk to you about something. Please keep it to yourself. I don't want to scare anyone."

It got Himmat's attention, and he nodded in agreement. Jaggi narrated his encounter with Banta.

"Shouldn't you contact the police?" Himmat asked.

"What would I report? They didn't hit me, so I have nothing to tell. Plus, people say they have protection from the police. Reporting will only aggravate them," Jaggi said. "This is insane. That man is becoming uncontrollable," he said.

Himmat saw his point.

Jaggi sat with Himmat for a while; they decided that sharing the incident with others would not solve anything. All he could do was advise Jaggi to be watchful whenever he went out.

"I hope your plans to go to the USA succeed," Himmat said with unmistakable sincerity in his voice.

PART III

My soul will find yours.

Jude Deveraux

Chapter 15

Rani received an admission offer from a reputed Nursing college in Ludhiana, a couple of hours away. The annual tuition of 30,000 rupees was easily affordable with the money they received for their six acres leased to Teja.

But, there was a problem—Gurdev, Rani's bhua ji, who, after Sohan Singh's death, regularly visited Lakhwinder, who depended on her for advice and moral support. Gurdev was present when Rani received the offer.

"No good family will accept a nurse as their daughter-in-law," Gurdev lashed out at Rani. "It's a man's job to earn money. Your job is to care for the house, raise children, and keep him happy."

Nursing carried a unique taboo in rural areas, where people raised questions about a woman's morality and sexual purity the moment she stepped outside the familial realm. Since nurses worked in close quarters with male doctors, society harbored a markedly unfavorable attitude toward them. Many considered male doctors to have a free pass with the nurses. How could a nurse be morally upright when she must witness nude patients in the company of male doctors and discuss human anatomy?

Besides, Rani would be staying in a hostel, away from her mother's eyes.

"Who knows what these young women did when they stayed by themselves? Don't you have any respect for your family?" Gurdev looked at Lakhwinder scornfully.

Lakhwinder sat in silence, enduring the assault blow by blow. Gurdev was her closest and most trusted relative, and with Sohan Singh gone, she did not want to annoy and alienate her. In addition, she shared Gurdev's perceptions and concerns.

Gurdev left the following day, considering the matter settled.

Rani felt betrayed and did not talk to her mother all day. The tension in the house was thick, with no one else to talk to for either of the two. Rani decided to speak with Bindo and went to see her. She explained the situation.

"I'll talk to your maa. Don't worry; we'll figure something out," Bindo assured her.

When Bindo went to see them the following day, she could feel the stress in the air. But it didn't take long before Lakhwinder relaxed and raised Rani's desire to be a nurse and her bhua ji's concerns.

"It is not my place to question your decision, bhen ji. But I hope you decide what is best for Rani," Bindo said.

Rani looked up at Bindo to request more support than that blanket statement.

"Do you ever see Raina? How is she doing?" Bindo asked Lakhwinder. Raina was a divorced woman in her forties, and she was living with her parents. Her brother's wife did not treat her well.

"Poor Raina," Lakhwinder said, "what do you expect when you have no place to go? You take whatever someone doles out to you." Raina's parents were old, and their daughter-in-law was a dominating woman; Raina's brother did whatever she wanted.

"I wish Raina could get a job," Bindo said.

"She barely passed ten classes. Who will give her a job?" Lakhwinder said.

Rani smiled.

"Lakhwinder bhen ji, you may want to rethink your decision about Rani," Bindo said, drawing Lakhwinder's attention. "You have a chance to help her, to give her insurance for the future. God forbid she has to go through what you and Raina went through! If Rani has a job before she marries, she will be financially secure and handle her life much better if she ever has to live independently. And what if, like Raina's parents, Gurdev bhen ji, and you are too old to help her? I wish I could have gone to college. But I was lucky to have a father and a husband who supported my business as a seamstress. My husband's income alone couldn't support Jaggi through college, but now, we don't have to worry about it. And imagine how easy things would have been for you if you had a job."

Lakhwinder nodded in agreement.

"Nursing is a secure career; all hospitals need nurses. And about your concerns. Nurses are people just like you and me, maybe even better. They save lives, take care of the sick, and give hope to families. Isn't that what our gurus would want us to do? You know more than I do how nurses helped when Sohan Singh veer ji was in the hospital. Were those nurses immoral or unclean? I'll be proud if my Jaggi marries a nurse. Don't let your thinking be impaired by what others say."

Bindo's comment, "I'll be proud if my Jaggi marries a nurse," caught Rani's attention more than anything else she said.

After Bindo left, Lakhwinder was relaxed, though neither she nor Rani said anything to each other. Rani got up and sat down next to her mother, putting her arms around her neck.

"Please, maa, let me be a nurse. Let me do it for baau ji," Rani pleaded, looking into her eyes. Her voice did not have the anger or the hurt of yesterday; it instead posed the innocent confidence of a little girl asking her mother for a cookie, a request she knew her mother wouldn't deny.

Lakhwinder looked into her pleading eyes and took her in her arms. How could she be deaf to her daughter's pleas? "Yes, bete. If I am not on your side, who else will be? You can do whatever you want to." Lakhwinder said. Then after a pause, she made her plea, "But bete, please don't do anything to make me hide my face in shame."

Rani gently wobbled her head against her mother's neck. "I won't, maa," she said.

When Gurdev visited again, Rani had already moved to Ludhiana. That did not, at all, bode well with Gurdev.

"I did it for Rani," Lakhwinder said. "I spoke with Bindo; she was very supportive of Rani getting her degree."

That took Gurdev over the edge.

"So, this was all her doing. Does that Keeri know better than me? That immoral slut! I don't think you should let this girl associate with that woman or her son. How dare that boy talks to your girl? Do you know of any Jat who will let his daughter be this close to a Keera?" She moved her face close to Lakhwinder, miming how Rani and Jaggi would sit next to each other. "Do you have any shame left in you?"

Lakhwinder did not know how to respond.

"I don't think my opinion matters in this house anymore," Gurdev said. "Remember the offer I made to take this girl's hand for my husband's nephew? Forget about it. They will not accept a nurse into their family."

Chapter 16

Jaggi finished college—one more achievement, one more milestone, and one more *Akhand Paath* by Bindo to thank God and get His blessings. She was on top of the world.

Four-year colleges in India did not offer Graduate Programs, but the universities did—on their main campuses. Jaggi was accepted at the PB University Patiala, though the university still had to verify copies of the documents he sent against the originals. Two weeks before the session, Jaggi went to the university campus to get his documents validated.

The bus dropped Jaggi at the university gate, an impressive entry leading to a wide double road. The hustle and bustle of scooters, motorcycles, cars and people surprised Jaggi. After half a kilometer's walk, the road split, and a decorative sign indicated the administrative building to the left.

Jaggi realized he was coming to a more liberal and sophisticated place. A young man and a woman walked hand-in-hand ahead of him. Further on, a group of three women and two men ambled along, laughing, and nudging each other. Trying to avoid being poked, one of the women almost bumped into an old cyclist, inciting angry looks from him.

The administrative building was huge and set at a higher elevation, with more than half a dozen wide marble steps leading to it. The admissions office was on the third floor, and a dozen-long line of students awaited, with no one on the other side of the counter.

"Lunchtime," the last woman in the row told Jaggi sarcastically. Jaggi nodded.

"They should not allow them to go to lunch all at once," the woman had now turned around to face Jaggi, and he nodded again.

"I came from Ambala and had to get up at six. Would you believe that? It takes me two hours to get ready and make my food.

Would you believe that? The bus was so crowded that I couldn't find a seat. A healthy young man was sitting on the seat where I stood, and he didn't have the courtesy to offer me the seat. Would you believe that?"

"Yes, I would believe that," Jaggi said a bit comically, "and we're in luck. There's a lady behind the counter now. They are opening a second counter."

The lady momentarily turned her neck to look back.

"My name is Preeti, would you bel…"

But Jaggi cut her off. "Yes, I would."

"Oh, I suppose I have a habit of saying that," she smiled. "I'm here to do my MA in Hindi." She was still fully turned toward Jaggi, "I have a younger brother. He just finished high school." She talked about her and her family, slowly moving back to keep up with the moving line. She was of average height, had a fair complexion, and had sharp features. Suddenly, the three people ahead of her left.

"It's your turn," Jaggi said, and she moved to the counter on the right.

Jaggi was at the counter on the left in less than a minute. He gave his certificates, and the lady brought his file, compared the documents, and returned his originals, marking the file verified.

"The fee and class schedules are over there," she said, pointing to a display board in the corner.

Jaggi had a single occupancy room in the graduate dormitory. He looked at his tuition and dorm expenses, which included two meals, and calculated over thirty-five thousand rupees for the first year. That's half the salary of a college teacher, Jaggi thought. Jaggi's heart melted as he reflected on his parents' hard work. Despite not owning any farmland or being educated enough to secure well-paying jobs, they had managed to save enough, so he didn't have to worry. Bindo worked extra hours, stitching as many garments as possible, and Teja worked double due to the additional land leased from Lakhwinder. Even though they had saved enough for his degree, he did not want to be a complete burden on them. He had planned to find a part-time job.

He looked around; Preeti was babbling off with another lady not too far from him about having lunch. Only one student was at the counter, and the other lady was free. Jaggi went to her.

"Where can one find a part-time job?" he asked.

"I have no idea, sir," the lady answered. "All jobs here at the university are full-time jobs."

"Do you know of any off-campus jobs available to students?"

"I wouldn't know, sir," she said, shaking her head.

Jaggi had just turned around to leave when the other lady clerk called after Jaggi. "Sir, what kind of work are you looking for?"

"I don't care; I'll do anything."

"A few days ago, my husband and I were at this car mechanic's shop. He was complaining about not being able to find good help. Maybe he will hire you."

She jotted down the place's name and rudimentary directions on paper.

Thanking the lady, Jaggi left to find an auto-rickshaw.

After about twenty minutes, the auto-rickshaw turned the bend, and a faded sign, "Nirmal's Car Repairs & Painting," appeared over a double-door workshop. Three cars were inside, and an older man sat, working on a tire.

"Are you the owner?" Jaggi asked.

The man shook his head and pointed to the small back door.

There was ample open space, with a few vehicles parked on the other side of the door. Jaggi didn't see anyone around, but a screeching sound came from the other side of a Jeep, and Jaggi went around. The Jeep's rear tire was jacked up, and a man on his back had crawled under. The man's torso wasn't visible. Jaggi waited.

After a few minutes, the man bent his knees to pull his creeper from under the car. He must be in his mid-thirties.

"Are you here for repairs?" he asked without getting up.

"No, I am here looking for part-time work," Jaggi answered.

"Have you ever worked on cars before?" the man asked, sizing up the well-dressed man.

"No, bhaa ji, I have never worked on cars before," Jaggi answered. "My workshop experience has been limited to taking our tractor for repairs."

"Have you ever driven a car?"

"No, bhaa ji."

Instead of getting up, the man slid close to his toolbox, got a long metal bar with a hook at one end, and slid back under the car without saying anything else.

Jaggi wasn't sure what to do next. Was the man's response negative? Should he wait until the man pulls himself out again?

Jaggi had to wait at least five minutes before the man pulled himself out and got up, wiping his hands with a greasy towel.

"I see you are still here; you passed my first test. So, young man, where are you from?"

"I am from a village near Rupar."

"You must know how to drive a tractor, right?"

"Yes, bhaa ji," Jaggi answered.

Chasing Dignity

"Come inside," the man said, motioning to Jaggi and offering him a chair. "Would you like a glass of water?" he asked while filling himself one from the pitcher. Jaggi nodded, and the man served him a glass as well.

"Tell me, why are you looking for a part-time job? Are you a student?"

"Yes, bhaa ji, I will be doing my MA at PB University."

"Oh, you must be smart. I didn't go beyond high school. I didn't care much for the books." Jaggi was impatient but needed the job and didn't want to be rude. "I have two sisters. They were to be married off. I had to work to help my father." And the man continued with his small talk.

"Bhaa ji," he finally interrupted, "do you have any work for me?"

"Yes, I do. But I will need you here at least three days a week and no less than six hours a day. Can you do that?"

"Yes, bhaa ji, I can do that, but I'll give you a definite answer once my classes begin and my class schedule is confirmed. I should certainly be free on the weekends."

"You said you are from near Rupar. What village?"

"Kundyan."

"I'm from Knaur. A girl from my village is married in Kundyan. She is a few years older than me."

That got Jaggi's attention. Knaur was his *nanke*—his mother's parental village.

"What is her name?" Jaggi asked.

"Bindo."

Wow, the man was undoubtedly talking about his mother.

"She's my mother," Jaggi said hesitatingly.

"Oh, isn't that a small world? I know your mother very well."

Then Nirmal shared something very private with him. He was from the Jheor caste. "Growing up, I was very conscious of my caste. On the other hand, your mother was different, and I learned from her to accept myself for who I was. I have a lot of respect for her."

Jaggi felt a great relief. Instead of needing to hide his caste from Nirmal, he had found an ally. Hearing someone from Bindo's distant past shower her with respect, Jaggi had a renewed reverence for his mother. He wished he could marry a girl like her one day.

Nirmal offered Jaggi a job. Jaggi would decide the exact days he could work, after he joined classes.

"Please say my Sasrikal to your mother," Nirmal said when Jaggi parted.

At home that night, Jaggi told his maa about Nirmal, and she smiled, her jaw dropping a little. She seemed to gaze off into some distant memory of a little boy she used to help in his studies.

"He had been to our house frequently," she told Jaggi.

"I almost didn't tell him you were my mother, thinking Nirmal was a Jat," Jaggi said.

"Bete, as I've said before, being born in a low caste is not fair in any sense. But hiding your caste is worse. It can lead to more embarrassment. I'm not saying you walk around with caste written on your sleeve. But don't feel ashamed if you need to reveal it. It's bad enough how others look at us. But it can be quite burdensome if we do it to ourselves, walking around with a secret."

When Jaggi confirmed his class schedule a few days later, he returned to Nirmal as promised.

Chasing Dignity

Jaggi had been stutter-free for a while now. However, the new university environment created anxiety, and he got nervous during introductions in his climatology class. Jaggi was sitting second from left in the second row. I will be the seventh, he figured, after counting five in the front. Worried his stutter would declare its evil presence, his heart started to pound as his turn approached, and he couldn't pay attention to what anyone said.

"Jaggi, from Rupar," he said speedily on his turn and sat down.

For Jaggi, this was his first time living independently, away from his parents. However, the transition was smooth and short; within days, he felt like his usual self. Jaggi's room was spacious, with a bed, a table, a chair, and two closets. The dorm had a cafeteria called 'mess,' His tuition included Lunches and dinners, though he had to pay for breakfast and other snacks. Each hostel had a lobby and an entertainment area with a TV, a few carrom boards, two table tennis tables, and one billiards table.

Unlike the ethnically homogeneous Rupar, university students came from all walks of life. Jaggi began to notice a curious rural-urban divide. The students from rural backgrounds were readily distinguishable from those from the cities; they flocked together, and generally, men and women clustered separately. Men were louder and boisterous when among themselves but shy in mixed company. Punjabi was their sole medium of communication.

On the other hand, the students from the cities exhibited a more liberal and westernized attitude. They were more poised and casual in their interactions with the opposite sex, were at ease in classrooms, and interacted more freely with the teachers. Many spoke English with as ease or better as they spoke Punjabi.

Jaggi's reading and writing fluency had become admirable thanks to his fondness for English literature. However, he was not used to conversing in English. Other than reading loud with Rani, he never spoke English. Because of his thick accent, Jaggi worried about the hushed smiles it would incite. Besides, he feared his stutter could resurface under stress, and conversing in English was stressful.

Jaggi's natural inclination was to hang around men from a rural background like him. But somehow, the idea of crossing the divide into the urban cliques promised strange excitement. He could improve his spoken English by being with the city folk, and Jaggi followed his instinct to meet his fears head-on.

Harry and Nisha, two of Jaggi's classmates, spoke fluent English and Jaggi made special efforts to befriend them. As it turned out, they were both very relatable and open-minded. Harry's room was in the same hostel as Jaggi, and he was a phenomenal table tennis player. They could converse in either language with equal ease and didn't care whether Jaggi spoke English or Punjabi, and they didn't pay attention to his accent.

Jaggi developed a circle of close friends from his dorm. Harry and two others were from Delhi, one was from Gurgaon, and two, besides Jaggi, were rural boys. Three in the group, including Jaggi and Harry, were geography majors, one botany major, and another engineering student. Sunny, whom Jaggi got quickly close to, was doing a PhD in Punjabi literature. Jaggi and Sunny would get into long, in-depth discussions about books and authors, and often Jaggi would feel he had a firmer grasp on the subject than his friend. Jaggi wondered, what if he had chosen Punjabi over geography? Would he be on track for a PhD and a life in the stories he'd loved when he was a boy? But before he went too far down that road, he remembered how he enjoyed geography and was convinced geography provided him with a much better opportunity to go to the US. The promise of living in a place where no one cared about his caste was worth more to him than his love of storybooks, which would always be there in his spare time.

Chasing Dignity

They had a routine of going for a walk. The road next to the hostel had distinctive rows of eucalyptus trees. They would start at their hostel, go around the stadium to the Engineering College Road, turn around the Bebe Nanki hostel for women, and then to the T-point road on the other side of the campus. The T-point passed by the Botanical Garden, completing the circle. They would walk around in the Botanical Garden before heading back to the hostel mess for dinner.

Female visitors were allowed in the dorm's common areas, and frequently, Nisha and her friend Nimrata would visit them for a game of table tennis or carrom board. Slowly they became an integral part of their ethnically diverse circle, where no one ever talked about or bothered about each other's background. Though he had no reason to dwell on his social status, Jaggi felt, if found out, he would not get the severe rejection from any of these friends as he would from a typical rural band of people.

The university offered free German, French, and Spanish foreign language classes, and Nisha had signed up for German. One day during a carrom game, Nisha asked Jaggi if he would like to take a German class.

"I don't know if I should start another foreign language; I'm still struggling with English."

"Come on, Jaggi, your English is fine. It's as good as anyone else's. You just need to relax when you speak," Nimrata said.

"Do you know how to make a line shorter without touching it?" said Sunny.

"No, how?" Jaggi asked, confused by his non sequitur.

"Draw a longer line next to it."

"Okay…" said Jaggi, smiling, "but what does that have to do with learning German?"

"It's not about German. I'm talking about your concerns about speaking English. Start learning a new language. Your struggle with it will diminish your concerns about English," Sunny said, laughing.

That made sense to Jaggi. He had already thought about learning another language, but not German. He wanted to learn Spanish because of his interest in the US, which Jaggi knew had a sizable Hispanic population. Jaggi registered for Spanish.

The Spanish class had ten students, and six were women. Jaggi knew one of them.

"We ended up in the same class! Do you believe that?"

"Yes, I believe that," Jaggi answered with a grin.

The teacher, a young female PhD student of Latin American literature, was witty and friendly. Jaggi liked her; she could easily engage with the students and make comical mistakes using a deadpan voice. She called students to the front of the class for simple Spanish conversations and summoned Jaggi a few times. He was nervous in the beginning but quickly got used to it.

Sunny was right; Spanish shifted his focus to learning new vocabulary and grammar rules. Suddenly English felt like his mother tongue by comparison, and Jaggi's self-consciousness about his accent disappeared.

Most students didn't have classes immediately following Spanish; they, as a group, would go to Chacha Chimna's for tea.

The canteen, a relic from one of the campus villages, was a small, two-room adobe brick building. It had a sizable courtyard, with a big old peepul tree in the middle. Several weathered wooden tables, each with its assortment of chairs and benches, peppered the yard. The canteen bordered two intersecting streets, providing free access to passersby. The room on the left was Chacha Chimna's kitchen, where he greeted customers while making tea or frying samosas. Its open shelves displayed biscuits, sweetmeats, half-fried samosas, pakoras, and jars of salty snacks. The room on the right had a door and two windows, a ceiling fan, and a few tables with better chairs.

Chacha Chimna's fifty years of fatigue had faded his heavy mustache to salt-and-pepper. He walked around in an undershirt that did not cover the bottom of his potbelly, leaving nothing to the imagination about how he tied his pajama drawstring. He carried a thin cloth towel around his neck to wipe anything that needed cleaning—from his poorly shaven face and hands to tabletops. He always had a pencil perched on his right ear and a small notebook nestled in his pajama pocket for keeping a record of the money the customers owed him. He never bothered to ask them their names. He had unique identifiers for all of them:- "The little lover," "dark-skinned woman," "the bullies," "earrings," etc.

Chacha Chimna had a waiter, Mundu, a young man in his early twenties from the neighboring country of Nepal. Mundu was not his real name; it was a condescending term meaning "little boy" to address young domestic servants from outside of Punjab. Since Chacha Chimna was typically busy in the kitchen, Mundu took most orders.

The Spanish class cohort always gathered around the farthest table in the courtyard. Anil was invariably the first to order: "Mundu, two samosas, and tea." Preeti would follow, asking for a ladoo with her tea. Jaggi seldom took anything other than a cup of tea.

Preeti and Esha had the same rural background as Jaggi, and soon Preeti started to show interest in Jaggi. Jaggi was not interested; he found her babbling a bit overwhelming. Besides, it had not even been a year, and he had not yet recovered from Simmie's hateful rejection. He had no desire to be put in a similar situation again.

"Hey Jaggi, we are going to the movies tonight. Would you like to join us?" Preeti asked him one day at Chacha Chimna's.

The film she suggested, *Saali Aadhi Ghar Wali*, was a lowbrow comedy. Its immodest, trite title, meaning 'in half of the ways, your sister-in-law is your wife,' offered no hint of a serious story, and Jaggi preferred movies that probed deep into the human psyche.

Jaggi could go to directors like Shyam Benegal and Satyajit Ray anytime without worrying about the subject matter. Knowing Preeti would not like those movies, he suggested going to *Suraj Ka Satvan Ghoda* instead. It was a Shyam Benegal movie, playing in a theater nearby.

"Who watches those dumb movies? There's no entertainment in them," Preeti said. Jaggi didn't answer, and luckily Anil threw in a new topic, and the discussion shifted to something else.

When they were ready to leave, Preeti changed her mind.

"Esha, why don't we watch *Suraj Ka Satvan Ghoda*? We can go to *Saali Aadhi Ghar Wali* some other day," she said.

"No, thank you," Esha said. "I don't have the same motivation you do to endure the pain," she whispered with a gentle elbow nudge.

Preeti would seek out Jaggi's company, making different pretexts, but Jaggi would avoid her making one excuse or the other. Though Jaggi liked Preeti's attention, he could not imagine getting into a relationship with her. One day she asked Jaggi when he would have a free period.

"I brought something for you from home," she said.

"Today, I finish class at three, but I must be at work by five."

"Work?" she asked. Preeti was surprised. Working while going to school was not the norm. If he had to work, he was from a low-income family.

"I work in a car body repair shop," Jaggi answered. "My parents can afford my studies, but I don't mind working a few hours a week. Less pressure on them!" he said, noticing her discomfort.

"Will you have time before you go?"

"Yes, my class ends at 3; I'll be free till 4:15."

"I'll come to your hostel around 3:30, then. Is that okay?" She asked.

"Sure, 3:30, that's perfect."

Jaggi's class ended a little early, and he was at the hostel a few minutes before three. To his surprise, Preeti was already waiting in the common room.

"I wasn't doing anything. I thought to wait here in case you came early."

She had a large can of *panjiri*, a treat of dried fruits fried in flour and ghee. Jaggi loved panjiri; his mother made it frequently. They went to the hostel cafeteria and ordered tea to go with the treat.

"It is delicious," he said.

"I took special care in making it," Preeti said with her typical coy smile.

Jaggi did not answer. But he was increasingly getting uncomfortable and wanted her overtures to stop. But. How could he tell her no? she hadn't made her intentions explicit.

A few days later, when they were leaving Chacha Chimna's, Preeti said she wanted to talk to him, and they sat back. She asked Jaggi if he would take her to a movie. Jaggi felt an acute sense of déjà vu, and a shiver crept down his spine.

"No, I'm not interested," he said, getting up and walking away.

Afterward, Jaggi felt terrible. He did not want to get into a relationship, but that was not the way to tell someone no. What did she think of his reaction, walking away without even looking at her? She had never been mean to him, and he insulted her. He could do better, he thought and decided to talk to her.

In the evening, he went to Preeti's dorm and sent her a message. She came down quickly and did not seem to be in a bad mood.

"I have come to apologize for my behavior at Chacha Chimna's," Jaggi said, broaching the subject. Preeti just looked at him, not knowing where it was going, but he did not say anything else. Preeti, not liking silence, started to talk about something she had done that day. Before soon, she was on a roll describing what she had done lately. She and Esha had gone to a movie last night, and she told him about their interactions with the rickshaw driver, all about the story of the film, how they had to take seats in the middle of a row and fight dozens of knees, trying to get out to get to the bathroom halfway through.

"Don't you ever get tired of talking constantly?" Jaggi asked her mid-sentence.

"Are you saying I talk too much?"

"No, I mean, you talk a lot, but I think it's charming. I enjoy talking to you," Jaggi said. "Preeti, the way I responded to you was wrong," Jaggi said, returning to his acknowledgment. "I sometimes get jumpy, but it has nothing to do with you. I like your company," he continued after a brief silence, "You are an excellent friend. But we cannot be involved romantically."

"Because you don't like my talking?" Preeti asked.

"Oh no, not at all. I don't have a sister, and sometimes I wonder what it would have been like to have a chatterbox as a sister," Jaggi said, smiling.

Preeti did not respond.

"Preeti, I want to continue our friendship, and as friends, we can go to the movies or other activities. I hope you can agree to my limits."

"Okay," Preeti said. She went to the canteen to order them tea and snacks. They sat there for a long time talking. Before leaving, Jaggi told her about his friends' circle and invited her sometimes to join them for carrom board or billiards game.

Chapter 17

It had been a few months since Jaggi started at the university. One day, he was waiting for a bus to the city when a polite female voice from his right made him turn.

"Are you waiting for the city bus?"

He was suddenly tense. It was a lovely woman dressed in jeans and a loose top, and she was tall, slim, and slightly dark-complexioned. She looked straight into his eyes, and her straight posture, poise in voice, and confidence reminded him of Simmie.

"Yes," he managed to say and felt his stutter rising in his throat—a sudden feeling of trepidation and rejection besieged him.

"I am Navi, Navi Chawla," she extended her right hand.

He nodded a *Hi*, uneasily shaking her hand. After a while, he realized he had not introduced himself, but it seemed too late then. All he had to say was, "Hi, I am Jaggi." He repeated the four words in his mind a few times while he stood there, mute. He could not separate her face from Simmie's, which paralyzed him. Still, he felt a strange attraction and a draw toward her.

Several other people were waiting, and when the bus came, forgetting all manners, Jaggi climbed through the rear door as if to claim the only available seat. The bus had a few places left, and he moved to the front and sat next to an older man. He did not look behind to see if the woman had even gotten a seat. A man stood in the aisle next to Jaggi, meaning the bus was packed, and she might not as well have found a place to sit. The bus stopped near the primary market. Jaggi hurriedly got off and disappeared into a shop far away, walking briskly.

That evening, Jaggi did not talk much with anyone. The hostel cafeteria began serving dinner at seven. Usually, he and his friends ate around eight, but he was there at seven sharp, ate quickly, and went back to his room to be with his thoughts. He didn't know why the woman elicited such deep anxiety and a feeling that she rejected him. 'I don't even know her; why do I feel rejected?' he closed his eyes to calm down. But the woman's face reemerged, accompanying a taunt, *I kissed a Keera*. Shaken, he opened his eyes.

Jaggi thought of praying, but he was not religious, not even sure God existed. If God existed, Jaggi rationalized, as always, He should be above all favoritism and nepotism, and praying was no different than asking for a favor. But Jaggi's upbringing had rooted an image of God in him that he could not just evacuate, making him timid. He feared his ego might offend the Almighty, and to beg seemed the safer bet. He sat on his bed, cross-legged, eyes closed, hands folded in prayer. He tried to imagine God as a light encompassing him and cutting across the universe in all directions. He uttered: "God, please help me!"

Jaggi knew his anxiety was entirely unfounded but didn't know how to deal with it. He wished to talk to Dr. Khera, his childhood doctor, but he was too far away. There has to be a medicine to calm me down, he thought and went to the university clinic the following day.

It was a small building with only one doctor on duty—a woman. The thought of sharing his feelings with a woman was as terrifying as the feelings he came to discuss. But he gathered himself and filled out the form with the receptionist.

The doctor was in her fifties, and she seemed kind. Jaggi described his problem.

"How do you feel when you get nervous? What makes you think you are nervous when so?" the doctor asked.

"My heart gets faster, and I begin to sweat. I can't speak well. I begin to stutter. I used to stutter when I was young," Jaggi said in quick bursts.

"Are you nervous now?" the doctor asked.

Jaggi nodded. "A little."

Chasing Dignity

The doctor got up, pulled out two small plastic cups from a shelf, and poured water from a jug.

"I am thirsty. I have been working all day today," she said, taking a sip from her cup while offering Jaggi the other. Jaggi took it and felt himself relax a little.

Dr. Gill was not a psychiatrist. Since there was no psychiatrist or psychologist on the university staff, she would refer any patient who showed signs of depression or other severe mental illness to the main city hospital. However, the new students had frequent anxiety issues, and Dr. Gill handled them herself in the clinic. She would try a relaxation technique before prescribing them any medication.

"What village are you from?" she asked.

"Kundyan, madam. I went to college at Rupar."

"I am from Dadu Majra," she said. "It is on the other side of Rupar."

From how Dr. Gill dressed and talked, Jaggi could not believe she was from a village. She had also gone to school in Rupar and had done her pre-medical at the same college as him. She was compassionate, and Jaggi was ready to share his feelings with her.

"So, Jaggi tell me, what makes you nervous?"

"Girls. I mean, some girls."

"Do you have a sister, a cousin, or any other girls your age that you are comfortable with?" she asked, and Jaggi told her about Rani and the girls from his current friends' circle, including Preeti, Nisha, and Nimrata.

"I see. Girls generally don't make you nervous, but you say some girls do. Could you be a little more specific?"

Hesitatingly, Jaggi explained the incident at the bus station. The name Navi Chawla and her description alerted Dr. Gill. Dr.

Gill was confident Jaggi talked about Navi she knew—a family friend's daughter from Delhi. Navi's father, Karmjit Chawla, was a jeweler, and before moving to Delhi, he lived in the same neighborhood as Dr. Gill. Navi had started her MA in English this year and had dropped by to say hello to Dr. Gill a few weeks back. However, Dr. Gill did not mention her relationship with Navi.

"Why do you think she made you nervous?" she asked.

"She resembled a girl I knew in college at Rupar," he said. With a bit of prodding, Jaggi described the entire incident in detail.

"I see. That is unfortunate. The centuries-old caste system still shackles our society. Only God knows how long it will be before we free ourselves from these chains. But let's talk about your problem," Dr. Gill said. "You have anxiety. People can have anxieties for different reasons. Many new students have it simply because they are in a new environment, away from home. However, yours seems to be a case of rejection anxiety."

"Is there a medicine for this?" he asked.

"There are medications, but they can be addictive, and I recommend those only as a last resort. I prescribe another technique. Many students have benefited from it, and I believe you can too. Try it for a few weeks, and if it does not work, I'll write you a prescription."

"What is the technique?" he asked.

"It's a workout for your mind. We can train our minds to get stronger with special exercises."

"Are you talking about meditation?" Jaggi asked.

"Kind of; do you do meditation?"

"No, I just heard about it. Isn't it like sitting still and looking at something for a long time?"

"There are many techniques. The main purpose is to direct your mind so it does not wander unnecessarily or become anxious about things you can't control or aren't real."

Jaggi looked at her with curiosity.

"The technique I am talking about is self-relaxation. The purpose is to relax your mind, sharpen its focus, and confront the situation that bothers you from a detached, objective viewpoint. You will learn to understand and control your feelings. Do you want to try it?"

"Yes," Jaggi nodded.

"Today, we'll do it together. But at home, you can do it yourself. Find some time when you are relaxed and not rushed. Find a quiet secluded place. You can sit in your bed or on the ground. It'll work even if you are sitting in a chair, as you are now."

Jaggi nodded.

"Let's try," Dr. Gill said.

She asked Jaggi to close his eyes and take a dozen deep breaths. Then, starting with his toes, she began to slowly and deliberately name parts of his body, going from ankles, calves, knees, etc., to his scalp. She would ask him to relax in the region she called before moving to the next. Once he settled, she asked him to imagine talking to Navi, making small talk—like, "Navi, how are you?" "Navi, I am Jaggi," "I am from Kundyan, I am doing a master's in geography," etc. He was supposed to take a deep breath and relax whenever he felt tense.

When she ended, Jaggi was deeply relaxed and happy in a way he hadn't felt in a long while. She asked him to try this technique for at least two weeks and promised to write him a prescription if the method did not work.

Dr. Gill sent Jaggi on his way and returned to her office for lunch, which she usually brought from home and ate alone instead of in the busy cafeteria. Jaggi's visit brought back the frightening memories of an honor killing of one of her classmates from college. The woman was burned alive by her own father and brothers because she wanted to marry a low-caste man. They had also tried to kill the man, but he escaped the trap miraculously. Dr. Gill tried to imagine the girl's face, which Jaggi said resembled Navi. The meeting with Jaggi unnerved Dr. Gill. What if the woman had involved her family—her father, brothers, cousins, and friends—and done something to this poor boy?

Jaggi was handsome, and he left an elegant impression on Dr. Gill. Did he feel love or fear when he saw Navi? Would he put himself in harm's way for Navi? Navi was lovely, and Dr. Gill had known her since she was a child. She imagined Jaggi and Navi as a couple and smiled unconsciously. Could Navi's father consider an honor killing? Naa. A businessman like him won't engage in risky behavior without monetary incentive. Honor killings were known only among rural Jat families, and Mr. Chawla was neither rural nor Jat.

The receptionist's knock broke Dr. Gill's reverie.

"Dr. Gill, the next patient is here," she said, handing Dr. Gill the admittance ticket.

Dr. Gill straightened in her chair. "Please send him in."

Jaggi had an instant positive opinion of Dr. Gill; she was bright, he thought. Gill was a prevalent Jat last name, but Jaggi felt comfortable confessing his caste and sharing his concerns with her. Their interaction loosened Jaggi, and he got excited about the technique she taught him.

That evening, he sat in the middle of his bed and, starting with his toes, attempted to relax his body parts the way he had at the doctor's instruction. Jaggi had barely reached his knees when his mind wandered away. He started with the toes again. The second time Jaggi made it to his thighs. He made a few more attempts, but sometimes his mind would go to dinner or his mother or an assignment from school, or he'd have the overwhelming urge to take care of an itch—always some inevitable distraction. Eventually, he gave up and went downstairs to eat.

That evening, when Jaggi went to bed, different thoughts occupied his mind, and he had difficulty falling asleep. He kept tossing and turning. After wrestling with his sheets, Jaggi decided to try his mental exercise. Too lazy to get up, he did it lying on his back. This time, Jaggi could control his focus much better, and on the third attempt, he could maintain his attention from the toes to his forehead, and his whole body was relaxed. Before he could think about anything else, sleep took over.

Over the following few days, he gained control over the technique and could relax his body in a couple of attempts. He could keenly hear his heartbeat and differentiate the low, prolonged lubs from the high-pitched dubs when instructing his chest to relax.

Once relaxed, Jaggi would imagine himself being in Navi's company, talking to her. If he got tense in her presence, he would breathe deeply and guide his body into relaxation.

A week passed. Jaggi had been doing his mental exercise without a miss, sometimes even twice a day. He wished he could somehow run into Navi. He would often search for her while walking around campus and even went to the bus stop several times, hoping to find her there.

Why am I looking for her? What will I talk to her about? Jaggi would muse. I need to prove to myself that I'm not afraid anymore, he would reason. *No, you are lying—you are just looking to tell her you're a Keera so she can reject you,* a voice would counter. *Maybe she was visiting a friend and is not a student at the university*. Nevertheless, her face had etched in his mind, and he hoped to one day run into her.

Meanwhile, Preeti had started to visit his group of friends in Jaggi's dorm, and she became an excellent carrom player. Seeing Sunny's particular interest in Preeti, Jaggi arranged a short weekend trip for the group to Kasauli, a nearby hill station. It was an enjoyable excursion for all, and to Jaggi's delight, Preeti and Sunny hit it off quickly.

Jaggi remembered his visit to Dr. Gill fondly. He continued to practice the relaxation technique and found it helpful in falling asleep quickly and waking up more refreshed in the mornings.

Chapter 18

At the end of November, the Red Cross scheduled a blood drive on campus in collaboration with the university clinic. It was a Friday, and toward the end of the day, Jaggi went to donate. A dozen chairs were outside the collection room, but only one other student, a woman, was waiting. A few minutes later, a nurse came out with a male student and returned with the woman.

Jaggi saw a little bureau by the wall with a few magazines on top and looked through the pile; he did not find anything interesting. But then he spotted an old copy of *Reader's Digest* on the ground and picked it up. He had barely started browsing when he heard his name.

"Hello, Jaggi, how are you?"

He looked up; it was Dr. Gill. Returning her greetings, he got up.

"You have a good memory, Dr. Sahib. You remembered my name even after three months. You see so many people every day. How do you manage to remember them all?"

"Not all of them, Jaggi, just the ones that make an impression," she said with a wink that made him blush.

"How is your dorm life? Do you miss being with your family?" she asked, walking inside with him.

"My dorm life is excellent," he said. "I have friends, ranging from literature scholars to those working on their PhDs in science. It's an incredible experience to be surrounded by such knowledgeable people. I miss maa's cooking, though. Dorm food, though not bad, is quite repetitive."

Dr. Gill smiled, noticing his way of conversing and entire manner was much more easeful.

"My parents installed their telephone line, and I talked to them yesterday. It felt so great," Jaggi added.

"That's nice. But make sure you don't cut on your visits home. Phone conversations do not replace those you make huddled together," Dr. Gill advised.

There were three beds inside. The young woman who came before Jaggi was lying on one with a needle in her arm. She had a squeeze ball in her hand. Another person was getting ready to leave.

The doctor made Jaggi sit on the vacant bed, took his temperature and blood pressure, and pricked his finger to take blood for testing.

"Hello, Dr. Gill. How are you?" Jaggi heard a female voice. Navi; Jaggi recognized her from the bus.

"Hi Navi, come on in," the doctor said.

Navi looked at Jaggi quizzically.

"Do you know each other?" the doctor asked.

"No," Navi said, "your face seems familiar, though."

"I am Jaggi. We met at the bus stop to go to the city a couple of months ago," Jaggi said with a poise that surprised even him and extended his hand for a handshake.

"That's great; we're all acquainted!" the doctor said. "We can go out to dinner after this. My treat! But first, we have to collect blood from you two."

Dr. Gill started the process on Jaggi first, and all the while, she chatted with Navi about Navi's family and school.

Jaggi's mind was racing the whole time. So they are family friends, and Dr. Gill knew who I was talking about, and that's why she remembered me. What if she has already talked to Navi about me? Jaggi suddenly felt embarrassed and thought of declining the doctor's offer to dine with them. However, he didn't want to miss the excellent opportunity.

Chasing Dignity

They were the last donors for the day; when finished, Dr. Gill provided further instructions to the staff and asked if she could leave.

"No, problem, Doctor, you can go. We will finish up," one of the nurses said. "A successful drive—eighty-two donors."

Dr. Gill had to take care of a few things, so they went to her office before dinner. Jaggi took the copy of *Reader's Digest* which he picked up earlier outside the clinic. He sat in a chair reading while Navi stood looking at the elaborate human anatomy poster on the wall. Dr. Gill wrapped up her work quickly.

It was already five-thirty; the sun had just gone down. The temperature was falling, and Dr. Gill put on her heavy coat. Navi had a thick shawl over a cardigan. It was reasonably warm during the day, and since Jaggi had not planned to stay out late, he had only a light sleeveless sweater. Looking at Jaggi, Dr. Gill opened a cabinet, pulling out a full-sleeve man's sweater.

"This is my husband's. I think it will fit you," she said, handing it to Jaggi.

"No, please, I am fine," Jaggi said. But she insisted, and he put it on.

"Uncle leaves his clothes in your office?" quipped Navi.

"A couple of weeks ago, he came to pick me up for a party and had to wait. He left it here, deciding he didn't need it." Davinder Gill was an engineer in the construction business.

It was a big, beautiful restaurant with luxurious sofa booths along the wall—it could easily accommodate a hundred customers and was about half full. Jaggi had never been to such a nice restaurant and felt overwhelmed; his heart started to race, and he felt heat rising under the borrowed sweater. They were seated in a booth by the wall.

The waiter came to take their order.

"Jaggi, are you a vegetarian? I know Navi is not," Dr. Gill asked, looking at the menu.

"No, I'm not," Jaggi said.

"I hope you don't mind, but I will have a glass of wine. It has been such a long day. What would you both like?" Dr. Gill asked.

Jaggi was dumbfounded. He knew only two kinds of drinks, hard liquor and beer, and he figured wine was a type of liquor. Plus, he had never seen a woman drink an alcoholic beverage.

"I'll take wine, too," Navi said.

"Is merlot all right?" she asked Navi.

"Yes, I like merlot."

Dr. Gill looked at Jaggi, asking with her eyes if he'd also like a glass.

Even though Jaggi's father, who was not the drinking type, drank occasionally, Jaggi did not drink; he always had water with his dinner. Both the women were drinking, and he thought not joining them would be unmanly.

"I will take wine, too," he said.

"Merlot?" Dr. Gill asked.

Jaggi bobbled his head, having no idea what he agreed to.

"Any preference for appetizers? I like their Tikka Fish and Tikka Paneer."

"Sure," Navi said, and Jaggi also nodded.

Dr. Gill ordered the drinks and the appetizers.

"Jaggi, where are you from?" Navi asked.

"Kundyan," he answered. Navi looked at him, confused.

Dr. Gill smiled. "Kundyan is a village on the east side of Rupar. Do you know Rupar, Navi? It is a small town about eighty kilometers from here, and you have to go through Sirhind, the city where the Chhote Sahibzadas were martyred," she explained.

"So, you are from a village! That is nice," Navi said, "I have always wanted to see a village but never got a chance. Can you take me to your village one day?"

"Sure," Jaggi said, and his heart sank at the thought. He envisioned her on the road just before entering Kundyan—the main village to the right and the Keera-basti to the left. There were no basti signs, but except for his own house, the mud-walled huts of the basti spoke volumes about who lived there. Beads of sweat were now forming on his temples.

It can be quite burdensome if we do it to ourselves, walking around with a secret all the time, he heard his mother whisper. But didn't you say I don't need to walk around with caste written on my sleeve? he quipped.

"Do you have any hobbies?" Navi broke his trance. The question made Jaggi even more uncomfortable. Sitting in a posh restaurant with two high-caste, sophisticated ladies, he felt out of place.

"No, I don't have time. I work in a car body shop," he answered.

"Which one?" Dr. Gill asked.

"It is in the city. It is called Nirmal's Car Repairs and Painting."

"That is a sweet little body shop. I know Nirmal Singh, the owner. I took my car there once, and he did an excellent job," Dr. Gill said. "Does he pay you well?"

"It's not bad. I work there just three days, Tuesday and Thursday evenings and Saturday mornings."

The waiter brought their wine; it was dark red, almost black. Merlot must be English whiskey! he guessed. He looked for the waiter to wave him for water to add to the liquor when he realized the doctor was already sipping it. Neat! he thought, reminding him of Tara Singh, who liked his whiskey neat.

Jaggi lifted his glass and took a sip; it had a strange thick leathery taste, not bitter as he expected. He took another sip, longer this time, and let the flavor bloom in his mouth.

"Jaggi and I have the same alma mater. We both went to Government College Rupar," shared Dr. Gill.

A few moments later, the waiter came over with the appetizers.

"So, for your PhD, what universities will you apply to?" Dr. Gill asked Navi.

"I haven't decided yet. My top preferences are the University of California, Berkeley, and the University of Chicago. But it's tough to get into those. I may have a better shot at the University of Michigan or the University of California, Davis; those are good schools," she said.

Jaggi's ears perked. She was talking about the universities in the US. Jaggi had planned to go to the US for a long time, but he had not done much besides selecting geography as his sailboat. This woman seemed to know the process well and was far ahead of him. He took a big swallow; the glass was now two-thirds gone. Navi had barely touched her drink.

"When will you start applying?" Dr. Gill asked.

"About this time next year, when I am close to finishing the degree. I will take TOEFL this year and the GRE next. The University of Michigan requires a sample of critical writing. I plan to publish a few articles before applying," Navi said.

"How did you find out about these universities? It must be a lot of work to research all this on top of your studies," Dr. Gill asked.

"It was quite simple. We have an office for international studies at the University of Delhi. They have all the information on international universities. I also bought a book on universities in the US It has all the details I need, the requirements, the application process, the tuition, and more."

"Do you have the book here with you?" Jaggi addressed Navi for the first time and sensed his voice tremble.

"Yes, I have it in my room. You can borrow it if you want."

"Yes, that would be so helpful," he said.

A smile flashed across Dr. Gill's face; she had hoped to see Jaggi comfortable in Navi's presence.

"Sure," Navi said. "Are you planning to apply to American universities?"

"Yes," he said. Soon, they were talking about the admission process. Navi was working on her MA in English and planned to continue with English literature in the US.

By the time their dinner was over, Jaggi was relaxed and comfortable. Dr. Gill dropped them off at their dorms. She dropped Navi first so Jaggi could get the book from her.

That night, Jaggi was in heaven. He could not get the image of Navi sitting across the table out of his mind. I'm in love, he thought and smiled. The little sane voice that usually kept his emotions in check was not there to reason. No one can stop us from going to the US now, he said to himself, delighted that he said *us* instead of *me*.

Chapter 19

Jaggi blew through the book over the weekend. It was highly detailed. Each university listed individual departments' student populations, the majors offered, the average number of students, applied versus accepted, admission requirements, the lowest test scores, and other relevant statistics. Jaggi thought admission to schools with prestigious programs in geography, like Boston University, the University of Colorado, and the University of Maryland College Park, would be tough. He remembered Navi mentioning the University of California, Davis: he looked at their requirements and felt comfortable getting into a university like that. He had many questions for Navi and decided to go to her department instead of joining his Spanish crowd at Chacha Chimna's.

Jaggi was inside the building, looking for Navi, when he saw her coming, carrying a small backpack.

"I went through the book and had a few questions," he said.

Navi was headed for the library, but since they couldn't talk in the library, they went to Chacha Chimna's instead.

"So, you read Somerset Maugham?" Navi said, looking at *Of Human Bondage* Jaggi put on the table. He had brought it to return to the library.

"Yes, very enjoyable."

"I like Somerset Maugham. Do you know he was gay?" she said with a smile.

"No," he answered, getting red-faced.

"I am sorry; I embarrassed you, didn't I?" she said.

Jaggi was not embarrassed by her comment. He was thinking about how beautiful she looked. He turned red because he thought she caught him gazing at her breasts.

Navi changed the conversation. They talked about literature, the universities in the US, Western culture, and about themselves. Navi learned about Jaggi's keen interests in Russian literature, his small village, and his little family.

Navi came from a progressive environment. Her family lived in Vasant Vihar, an affluent residential colony near New Delhi's diplomatic enclave, and she went to a prestigious English-medium, co-ed school. Indian and British literature was part of her BA curriculum, and she was particularly interested in literary theory and criticism. Navi had two brothers; Bitu, who was younger than her and still in college, and Raman, her older brother, an engineer, working for an international corporation. Jaggi realized there was a world of difference in their backgrounds. However, his usually cautious mind refused to dwell on this small detail.

"What else do you like to read?" Navi asked.

"I like Punjabi literature. My school library had mostly Punjabi books, which I read early on," Jaggi explained and said he got interested in English literature in college. "What do you like to read?" Jaggi asked.

"Oh, I'll read almost anything. I like Indian as well as foreign authors, short stories in particular. I loved Alice Munro's 'Dance of the Happy Shades.' However, my favorite of all time is Victor Hugo's *Les Misérables*."

"That's impressive. I can't get myself to read such a long novel," Jaggi said.

"It is less intimidating if you consider each of its volumes a separate book," Navi said.

"Did you read that in French?" he asked.

"No, unfortunately not. I took French in college, but I read the novel before that. It was an English translation by Norman Denny."

Jaggi again caught himself scanning her body.

"Do you write?" she asked.

Her question brought Jaggi back to the table. "Yes," he said, "I wrote a few stories when I was in the eighth class, but only a few friends saw them. I tried to publish a couple of articles in college. No success, though."

"What did you write about?"

"Various things. A story about my dog, one about someone from my village. One of the articles I tried to get published was about college life, and the other was about society's biases."

"Do you write in English or Punjabi?"

"A little of both," Jaggi answered.

"That sounds interesting," Navi said. "You shouldn't get discouraged. Many writers experience rejections in the beginning."

"Do you write?" he asked, remembering, during dinner, Navi had talked about publishing a few articles."

"Yes, I write short stories. I used to publish in our college magazine. Now I have another opportunity. I'll be on the editorial team of the *Sunup*"—a student-run English-Punjabi bilingual magazine published monthly. "I was selected to replace a PhD student who finished his dissertation and left the university," Navi explained.

"Congratulations," Jaggi said, "Maybe I'll try my hand in the *Sunup*."

"Yes, why not? College magazines are the best starting place."

Though Navi spoke Punjabi well, she used it sparingly, and Jaggi felt comfortable conversing with her in English. His main problem was how to stop his mind from continually shifting to her body. He had to make a conscious effort to focus on her face. Everything about her was so attractive.

They sat there for over two hours, unaware of the time passing.

"Jaggi, you are pretty happy today. You've been humming to yourself all morning. What treasure did you step into?" said Nirmal as Jaggi lowered the car from the jack.

"Bhaji, I feel good today," Jaggi said. "Everything looks so beautiful!" It had been two days since his tea with Navi, and he was still ecstatic.

"You are talking like Ranjha. His world was beautiful when his Heer was around," Nirmal said. "Did you find your Heer?"

"Bhaji, you don't need a Heer to see the beauty around you. It is all there. You just need to open up your heart to it."

"Okay, Great Sage, if you are done with the Fiat, bring that Ambassador in," Nirmal said, pointing to the blue Ambassador parked outside. "It needs work on the front right door."

The work at the shop was tiring. Jaggi routinely worked till late in the evenings to finish the work Nirmal piled for him. But Jaggi did not mind working extra hours; more work meant more money and less bother to his parents.

Jaggi had been regularly writing in his diary through college and was on his fifth book. However, he had slackened off lately and decided to make an entry to capture his love for Navi. He kept his diaries in the bottom drawer and pulled out the whole stack when digging in.

Jaggi opened the first book he hadn't opened in years and smiled as he went through it. The initial entries were concise, the first being a single line, *I will write in my diary every day.* The one a few pages down, *I scored two goals today. The PT masterji hugged me,* brought back fond memories of his Physical Training teacher, who coached his high school football team. His motivation and training helped Jaggi become an excellent football player. As Jaggi moved through the entries, nostalgia for his high school football team overcame him. The entries in the other books were lengthier and included his college experiences, thoughts on the books he read, discussions with his teachers, and other incidents. Then there were entries about his feelings and fears about Simmie. Reading the one after Simmie berated him was painful. He glossed over the last few pages, but that one stuck with him as he sat solemnly, reliving the hurt.

In his interactions with Navi, Jaggi had his guard down and had not consciously dwelled on the differences in their caste and social statuses, ignoring any ideas of rejection. He was physically attracted to and madly in love with her. However, the diary juxtaposed his time with Simmie and his infatuation with Navi, pulling a distinct discord that jerked him out of slumber.

Finally, he sat at the table to jot down his feelings he had not initially intended to write and pulled out his special fountain pen—he never wrote in his diary with a ballpoint pen. He opened a new page; starting an entry on a fresh leaf made it special. Jaggi gave titles to his notable entries, and today's entry was significant. His deliberate, beautiful cursive handwriting began to flow.

Tuesday, December 2, 1997

My Cursed Love

My mother told me how elated she was when the midwife put me into her hands. She said it was the most beautiful thing that had ever happened to her. She looked at only the part she could see, touch, and feel. She couldn't possibly see the invisible fragment, the aura of the dark curse that had to follow me through my life. Didn't she know I'll never have the right to express my feelings without fear?

I've been in a fool's paradise, believing a chance with Navi. I wonder if she would smirk or lash out like Simmie did when she finds out I'm a Keera, someone beneath the lowest of the low. Why would she be any different?

Why do I fall in love and writhe in agony? Haven't I gathered enough experience at being insulted and rejected?

I enjoy her company. Why can't I just be friends with her, friends for life? Yes, that's what I'll do. My heart will ache, but I will learn to live with it.

Mirza Ghalib must have been in my shoes when he wrote—

'Merī qismat meñ ġham gar itnā thā, dil bhī yā-rab kaī diye hote—'

[If my fate had to have that much anguish, O God, you should have given me many hearts (to endure).]

Satisfied with his decision and the entry, Jaggi closed the diary, clasped it to his chest, and put it back in the drawer.

Navi and Jaggi's interactions became more frequent and less fraught for Jaggi. They went to the library simultaneously, ate lunch together, and often met at Chacha Chimna's in the evenings. Navi was undoubtedly the woman Jaggi wanted to be with, and she reciprocated his caring.

Their friendship resulted in the revival of Jaggi's interest in writing. He wrote an article on the effects of stress on self-esteem and how to cope with it, describing the technique Dr. Gill gave him, enhanced with additional research on meditation. He submitted the piece for publication in the *Sunup*, and Navi edited it a little before publishing. It received a lot of attention from both the students and the faculty. Many talked to Jaggi about it, saying how helpful it was for their anxiety, which boosted his writing morale.

Chasing Dignity

The following month Jaggi wrote another article on the same subject titled "The Power of Seeking Help." It did not need editing at all. Jaggi's consistent comment was his choice of topics, which people pointed out was relevant to student life. Slowly, Jaggi felt his voice was getting more robust and unique. The attention his writing received and his pleasure from it were worth more than his time writing. As Jaggi became a frequent contributor to the *Sunup*, his name became recognizable on the campus.

Whereas Jaggi focused on nonfiction, Navi wrote short stories. Navi's writing style reminded Jaggi of Anton Chekhov, his favorite Russian author. Her stories were poignant and moved the reader emotionally.

Though many friends viewed them as a couple, their relationship remained platonic. They enjoyed being together, sharing writing ideas, going to the movies, etc. Jaggi enjoyed the nonsexual nature of their friendship, taking pride in keeping his physical desires in control.

Jaggi's friend Sunny was from Chandigarh, home to Tagore Theater, the region's leading center for cultural performance. It attracted prominent performing groups from all over the country. Once Sunny invited Jaggi to a performance by Gursharan Singh, the distinguished Punjabi dramatist. The show was late evening, and Jaggi had planned to stay with Sunny at his parents' house. Knowing Navi was interested in and involved in stage dramas in college, Sunny invited her as well.

When they went to sleep after watching the show, Sunny's mother arranged for Jaggi and Navi to sleep in the same room with a nice size bed enough for two.

"Maa, let Navi sleep in my room. Jaggi and I will sleep here," Sunny said to his mother.

His mother looked at them suspiciously, "Aren't you two married?" she asked, looking at Navi.

"No, we are not married," Navi answered, shocking the lady; it was unimaginable for her to see an unmarried woman traveling and staying with a man overnight at someone else's house.

"We are good friends, auntie ji—like a brother and a sister," offered Jaggi. His quick save seemed to appease their hostess.

Jaggi's words might have warded off the lady's shock, but his characterization of their relationship surprised Navi, and she looked at him with dismay. Jaggi shrugged and the subject never came up for discussion.

Chapter 20

It was the end of May. They were done with their first-year final exams and would be off for six weeks. Navi went home to Delhi, and Jaggi to Kundyan. Rani's college calendar ran parallel to theirs, and she had returned home a few days earlier.

Jaggi was brimming with excitement; he had so much to tell. Every moment he spent with Navi and every praise he got for his writing was newsworthy. Bindo had already seen a copy of the *Sunup* containing his first publication; Jaggi had brought it home previously. He brought Magazine issues containing his more recent articles.

One day during dinner, Bindo asked him if he had found a girl he liked.

Jaggi's face reddened at his mother's question, and he avoided her eyes.

"What's the matter, Jaggi? What are you hiding? Who is she?" Bindo asked cheerily.

"It's nothing," Jaggi answered, his cheeks reddening. "We are just friends. She is from a wealthy family. She is doing an MA in English. She is the editor of the magazine where I send my writings."

Bindo smiled. Jaggi talked about his latest writings and the response of the readers.

Teja didn't ask many questions but was equally excited, listening to Jaggi. "Yours is a good college," he added contentedly.

The next day Rani came. That was the first time Jaggi saw her since she started nursing; she was now a grown woman—no longer the girl he played with and teased.

"How is school?" he asked.

"Very nice," she answered, "I was anxious initially, living away from home. But once I got used to the surroundings and made a few friends, It felt like a second home!"

"Do they let you interact with the patients yet? I imagine you spend the first year entirely in the classroom," Jaggi said.

"No, we are exposed to the hospital environment right away. We had two months of clinical. Mostly we watched the nurses and helped them with small tasks. But each year, our responsibilities and hands-on will increase."

Rani always had calm in her voice. But the new poise in her speech spoke volumes about her confidence.

"I read your article in the issue of *The Sunup* that you left behind. It is beautiful," Rani said.

"I have written more since. I brought those with me."

"There was a story in it, 'The Smoldering Sticks.' I loved it. I read it three times, and every time, I cried," Rani said.

Jaggi smiled. "Navi wrote that story," he said, "my friend."

Rani noticed Jaggi's facial expressions change as he mentioned Navi.

"She is a close friend, I imagine?" Rani said mischievously.

"Yes," Jaggi said, missing Rani's playfulness.

"How close?" Rani asked.

"Very," Jaggi answered.

"Do you love her?" she asked.

"Why do you ask?" Jaggi said.

"Because I see love written all over your face!"

"Yes," Jaggi answered without hesitation. "She is from a wealthy family. They are jewelers. But she doesn't know about my caste. I'm afraid to tell her, lest I lose her even as a friend."

"I think you should tell her how you feel and your concerns. You never know. There are good people in the world. Your caste may not matter to her. Even if it does, I don't see any reason you will lose her as a friend."

"You are right. I need to be brave to have the life I want," Jaggi agreed.

Jaggi and Navi started the second and final year of their master's, and it was time to prepare for admission to US universities. Most programs required TOEFL to demonstrate command of English and GRE for general aptitude. Overall, Navi was better prepared than Jaggi, and he decided to take a couple of months extra to prepare.

In late September, graduate students from the English department decided to go on a picnic at the Moti Bagh Palace, and Navi invited Jaggi to go along.

The old Royal Palace, Built-in 1847, spread over 160 acres. The weather was enjoyable when they arrived at the palace. No one desired to tour the building. They instead set up two makeshift badminton courts, and a few of the men set to play bridge. Women were more interested in badminton than card games, and so was Jaggi.

There were over a dozen in the group, and everyone assumed Jaggi and Navi to be a couple. Whenever the game needed pairs, Navi and Jaggi would play together.

By lunchtime, they were all tired and hungry. There was more than enough alcohol for the occasion. Although women drank mostly sodas and juice, the men sipped beer the entire morning. Navi, Ritu, and a couple of other women had a glass of wine with lunch. They were all relaxed and enjoying themselves.

"How long have you two been together?" Akash, a friend of Navi, asked Jaggi.

"We are just friends," Jaggi answered. Ritu's ears perked up.

"So, you are available, then," Ritu said.

Navi's face contorted, and she gave Ritu a stern stare.

Ritu, raising her eyebrows and shoulders in apology, silently mouthed *Sorry* to Navi.

They were there for another couple of hours before returning to campus.

A few days later, Jaggi was sitting in the library, reading Mark Monmonier's *How to Lie with Maps*, when he heard Navi's voice from behind, "Maps, distortion, and meaning." She was reading the title of one of the books Jaggi had laid out in front of him.

Jaggi looked back. "Hi, come on, have a seat," he said.

"What kind of book is that? Why will anyone want to distort maps?" she said.

"Oh, it is a beautiful book, one of Monmonier's earlier works. It is a prelude to *How to Lie with Maps*,'" he said, showing her the title of the book he was reading.

Navi sat down. "You are a little too obsessed with maps, aren't you? Did you always like maps?" she asked.

"I guess so. As a child, I liked to draw maps. I would draw the route to my school, riding around to get additional details to add to the map. I would measure distances based on the time it took me for the ride. After a while, I got pretty good at it."

"Do you still have any of those maps? I would love to see them," she said.

"Yes, I do. Maa framed one of those, which still hangs from a wall in our house. Our family friend, a professor, saw a map I drew as a child. He was so impressed that he remembered it years later. He's the one who encouraged me to take geography."

"But the book you are reading is not about making maps; it teaches you how to *lie* with maps," she laughed.

"Well, if you don't know how to lie with maps, you are not a good mapmaker," Jaggi said, smiling back.

"Seriously, how can you lie with a map? By showing the wrong boundaries of a country or something?" she asked.

"People look at maps as if these represent absolute truths. Which is a lie."

"How do you mean?" she asked.

"If you take a 3-D globe and flatten it into two dimensions, you must leave a lot out and distort the rest. Leaving information out is just one way of not telling the truth," he tried to explain.

"But that's inevitable. I'm sure one has to delete the superfluous information, to make maps simpler and easier to read," Navi argued.

"Exactly, that is the problem! The cartographer decides what is superfluous and sometimes intentionally leaves certain information out to meet a specific agenda," he said.

"You mean some of these maps are drawn incorrectly on purpose?"

"I wouldn't use those words; it's more like misleading," Jaggi explained.

"I am lost," she said with a laugh.

"Let's take an example. Suppose I want to map India into four regions based on per capita incomes. I can color each state and the union territory based on what tier it falls in. New Delhi will certainly show up in the top tier. However, if I do not want to draw attention to New Delhi, I can remake the map using the same four colors, but I'll divide the country into fewer contiguous regions this time. I will lump New Delhi with the low-income state of Uttar Pradesh to make it appear in the bottom tier. Neither map would be incorrect, but they would look very different," he explained.

"I am starving, Jaggi. Let's find our way to some food."

Jaggi couldn't tell if she changed the topic because she found it boring or she was hungry. "Let's go to Chacha Chimna's," she said.

"Sure," he said, picking up his notebook.

Mundu greeted them; Chacha had momentarily gone out.

The canteen was almost empty; two students at one table were getting ready to leave, and at another, a male professor and a female student sat, immersed in conversation.

"That looks too intense," Navi whispered, looking at them.

"I wouldn't read too much into it," Jaggi said.

Mundu came and got their order.

"I have a question to ask of you," Navi said.

"Fire away."

"How do you feel about us, about our relationship, I mean?"

"Did I do something wrong?" Jaggi asked.

"Please do not joke that you don't know what I am talking about," Navi said. "I just want to know where we are going with this."

Jaggi made a serious face. He looked at her, deciding where to begin.

"Navi, you know you are my best friend, not only here on campus but also in my life. We have known each other barely for a year, and it feels like it has been forever. I have shared almost everything with you—my aspirations, weaknesses, and many of my fears. I am a different person now, and I owe you all the positive changes in my life and personality."

"And...?" said Navi.

"I know what you are asking. I am just trying to find the words." He took a big breath before he went on. "I enjoy being with you and would love to be with you f-f-f-forever. But..." he added after another gulp of air.

"But what?"

"Well, how can I dream of owning a Mercedes-Benz when I can't even afford a Vespa scooter?"

Perplexed, Navi gave him a blank glance.

"I see," she said, dropping her eyes.

"I hope you understand my analogy," Jaggi said apologetically.

"No, I understand. I am just surprised you would think this way."

"How do you mean?" he asked.

"I'm asking about giving a name to our relationship and taking it forward in the name of love. But maybe you are one of those who think a husband owns his wife like a car, and I am not good enough a model."

"No, that is not what I meant at all, Navi!" said Jaggi with a lump in his throat, and he became aware of his stutter looming beneath the surface. Was this going to end the same way as with Simmie? No, he couldn't handle another rejection like that.

"I am sorry, Jaggi, but how else should I interpret that statement?"

"You don't know me, Navi, not all of me. I would never put a price tag on another person, let alone on you, of all people. It's the honor of marrying you that I'm not sure I can afford. I never told you; there was a woman in my life who I thought loved me, and I loved her back. But the moment she learned who I was, everything changed. 'Don't you ever call me, just stay away,' she said, and those words still ring in my head. I can't afford to lose you."

"Jaggi, what do you mean 'who I was'? I know who you are!"

"No, you don't," he said meekly, looking down. "I am a k-k-Keera."

Navi had not expected this. The only Keeras she ever knew were those who cleaned city streets; she never imagined meeting one as a university student. Jaggi looked miserable, and he was not making any eye contact with her. Suddenly she found a great deal of empathy for him.

"What if I tell you that it will be my honor to marry this Keera?" she said, holding his hand and looking straight at him.

"What?" he said, startled, almost confused. For the first time in his life, he had heard the words Keera and honor in such proximity.

Navi squeezed his hand, "Jaggi, I love you as you are and for who you are. I did not make these castes, nor did you. I don't care about it if you don't."

Jaggi did not say anything. He looked at Navi, and his eyes began to water; he squeezed her hand. He told her the rest of what happened with Simmie. While he talked, Navi's face stayed calm and lucid.

"It's not easy to deal with ignorance," she said. "It wasn't her fault. Our whole society is screwed up. Most people can't unlearn what they learn growing up in a society that has been rigidifying for centuries."

Jaggi sat silent, but then spoke. "That incident with Simmie encouraged me to understand our caste system's underpinning. I had read some of Dr. Ambedkar's work, but after that incident, I read him more thoroughly. He seems to have read the Hindu scriptures inside out, and following his references, I began to read the Hindu scriptures, like the Rig Veda, the Yajurveda, the Puranas, and the Smritis."

"That is impressive," Navi said. "So you are a Pandit! Aren't Brahmin Pandits supposed to know everything about Hindu scriptures, but how many of them do?"

Jaggi shrugged.

"Have you ever considered writing a book about the caste system?"

"The thought has crossed my mind…"

"Can you please walk me back to the hostel, Jaggi?"

"Sure," he said, and they got up.

It was a warm, pleasant evening. Usually, Navi took the straight path by the administrative block. But today, she wanted to take the T-point road, a more extended way that wove around the botanical garden. When they passed by, Navi drew him into the garden. "Let's sit down here for a few minutes," she said. It was dinner time, and there was not a soul in sight. She selected a bench under a Kachnar tree.

"It is a nice night," Jaggi said.

Without saying anything, she put her arms around his neck, her lips coming close to his. He could feel her breath blowing across his face. He was not shocked, as if expecting or even wanting it. Slowly his arms rose behind her back, his right hand holding her head in place. They were kissing! And it seemed so natural. When their lips parted, she rested her head on his chest. He held her tenderly.

"You just kissed a Keera!" Jaggi said.

"Does the Keera have a problem with that?" she calmly questioned.

"No," he said, puppy-faced. Navi gently stroked his back.

After being accepted without prejudice, Jaggi was oddly confused, exhilarated, and frightened simultaneously. Besides his caste, what had also bothered him was the disparity in their financial statuses. These differences were significant, and Jaggi had rehearsed a discussion multiple times in his head. Still basking in the feeling that his caste didn't matter to Navi, he was reluctant to broach the financial aspect. But, I must, he decided. It wouldn't be fair to her.

"I have a few other questions."

"Like what?" she said, separating from him and sitting straight to look at him. She had a compassionate look that promised to dissolve all his worries.

"Does your family have a car?" he asked.

Navi was sure that he knew the answer to his question. She had discussed her family and their lifestyles with him on multiple occasions.

"What kind of question is that?"

He didn't answer. "Yes, every family member has a car, including me. I kept my car even after coming to Patiala, so I can use it when I am home," she said.

"Do you know that my family doesn't even own a scooter?"

"Jaggi, what's your point?"

"Poverty and riches, they say, are like the two riverbanks that never meet."

"Interesting, we just decided to cross the centuries-old contours of caste but can't sail from one riverbank to the other! Now let me ask you a question," she said.

Jaggi sat at attention.

"Are you a happy man?" she asked.

"I would say yes."

"If you can be happy with or without what you have, why can't I?" she asked. "Am I not capable?"

"It's not a question of your capabilities, Navi. I was born into this lifestyle and never knew any different. On the other hand, you are used to the comforts you'll lose by becoming a part of my life. I feel guilty about that."

"So, it is not me, but the guilt that bothers you!" she said.

"You're twisting my words—my guilt or not; it won't count if you become unhappy and start regretting your decision," he said.

"You sound just like my father. He believes that I will die if I am deprived of the luxuries he has raised me with."

"He seems to be an intelligent man. I already admire him," Jaggi said, lightening the conversation.

"I am sure he will admire you, too. You two can admire each other. Who needs my opinion?"

"Can I ever win an argument against you?" Jaggi asked.

"Whatever!" she said. "By the way, he may be coming to Patiala, and I am sure he would like to meet with you."

"Do you think he will like me?"

"Why one smart person won't like another? Two smart men can meet and decide what is in my best interest," she said with sarcasm.

"Okay, you win," he said and took her into his embrace.

"You know what I sometimes think when I can't get through to you? Maybe I should be a nun," she said, laying her head on his chest.

He started laughing gently at her comment, holding her tighter now. His broad chest pulsated with laughter, and she liked her head moving with the vibration.

"It's funny to imagine you in a nun's habit, milking a buffalo," he said. "I hope you know that you will have to deal with buffalos if somehow we live in the village."

"Of course, and why not in the US? We can take a couple of them with us and have fresh milk all the time," she lifted her head to answer him.

He held her chin with his left hand and kissed her, a slow, gentle kiss she did not want to end.

"Can you take me to your village one of these days?"

Jaggi remembered her asking to go to his village when they first went out to dinner. He didn't think then she was serious.

"Why do you want to go to my village; there isn't much to see in a village. You won't find any excitement."

"I can't explain what I'm asking. Sometimes I feel trapped in the city and don't know how most people live. I eat things made of wheat, rice, and corn and yet know nothing about how they look when they're growing. I know these grains are produced and harvested in the villages but have no idea how," she said.

"Tell me what you want to know."

"I don't even know what kind of tree rice grows on. How do these trees look different from the ones corn grows on?"

Jaggi started to laugh. "Navi," he said with a more thoughtful look. "I wish we had grown up together as children." His eyes became distant as he continued. "Our parents would plant rice shoots, and we would run around, pushing each other in the water-filled paddy fields. They would yell at us to stop, and we would forget all that yelling in a minute and get going at it again. It was so much fun then."

Chasing Dignity

"I thought you did not have any siblings?" Navi said.

"I do not. But I grew up with Himmat and Rani, my friends from the village, and we were just like siblings."

"What are rice shoots?"

"The rice grows on small plants, not even two feet tall, not on trees. In July, the farmers plant these; they first seed rice densely in small nurseries. When the plants grow to about eight inches, they uproot them, and we call these little plants rice shoots. They replant the shoots more thinly in larger areas, greater than ten times larger, so each plant has enough space to grow. The replanting process is very elaborate. The fields for replanting are prepared by plowing and filling them with water. During the replanting season, it's common to see men and women everywhere, holding little bunches of rice saplings and replanting those hunched over the water-filled fields. The view is breathtaking, with the tops of the new rice shoots swaying above the waters like dancers."

In describing rice, Jaggi's mind got transported to a faraway place, and the serenity of his face was beautiful to Navi.

"Jaggi, I want to see your village and those rice shoots. I want to meet your parents and your friends Himmat and Rani. I will even wear a Punjabi suit and cover my head with a nice dupatta, like a traditional Punjabi girl," she said.

He held her cheek in a gentle pinch. "It doesn't matter how you dress. I don't want you to change because of me or my parents. I like you the way you are, and they will, too." Navi could feel his words filled with devotion for his parents and for her.

"I have to ask you something, though," he said.

She looked at him.

"What kind of questions do you think your father will ask me?"

She started laughing. "You think I am going to make it that easy for you? Forget it," she said, laughing. They sat there for a long time, neither wanting the embrace to end. He lifted his arm to look at his watch. She grabbed it to stop him from looking at the time. "I'm not hungry at all. Let's sit here all night."

He smiled and held her tightly.

PART IV

Courage is grace under pressure.

Ernest Hemingway

Chapter 21

Bindo had been sweeping the brick floors, mopping concrete rooms, and daubing the earthen courtyard for the past two days. She cleaned and refreshed the furniture and set up the beds with fresh bedsheets and newly refilled, fluffed quilts. Neatly arranged firewood and the dried cow-dung chunks lay by the mud stove in the kitchen. To regale their special guest, Teja traveled to town to buy a new pair of chappals, soap, towels, sweetmeats, salty snacks, and other supplies. Bindo had already prepared the main dishes for the evening, and they were anxiously waiting, dressed in newly stitched Punjabi clothes. Bindo went out a few times, hoping to spot them; one could see as far as half a mile up the road before the bend where the road turned left and disappeared behind the tall-hardy-grass-covered mounds.

Navi's image in Bindo's mind was of a beautiful, educated, high-caste young woman from a wealthy family who didn't care about caste or financial wealth. However, she was still nervous: 'Will she accept me as her mother-in-law? Will her family accept our son without hatred or prejudice?' Setting aside doubts, Bindo wanted to put her best foot forward, anxious about how the young woman would take their humble dwelling, speak to them, and interact with them.

People frowned if a man and a woman met before marriage. A woman first saw her husband after having already wedded him. Navi's traveling alone with Jaggi tickled Bindo a little as if her son's education had earned him that right. She imagined how women from the village would invent stories of them going to school together, roaming around unhindered, or living in the same room.

There was no direct transportation to the village, and the nearest bus stop was about two miles away. Considering the half-hour walk, Navi packed light, fitting everything into Jaggi's backpack; Jaggi seldom brought anything for himself.

They got off the bus around three in the afternoon. The weather was good, and the scenery was beautiful. The road had tall, hardy eucalyptus trees along the sides. The lush green fields stretched into the horizon on both sides, and the crops were lilting with bouts of light wind.

Jaggi walked on the familiar path, holding his head high with pride. After being so apprehensive around girls for so long, it was a proud moment for him to arrive at his village with a beautiful, educated woman by his side who had agreed to spend her life with him.

A farmer with a spade on his shoulder walked through the fields. Navi remembered Jaggi describing the rice plantation scene.

"Is this rice?" she asked, pointing to the fields.

"No, this is wheat. You won't see rice in February. It is grown in July during monsoon."

"Will they plant rice here in the same fields?" she asked.

"Yes, the wheat is almost mature. Over the next few weeks, it will turn golden brown. We harvest it and get the fields ready for paddy plantation."

The paved road was barely broad enough for a single vehicle, though its dirt shoulders were broad. Navi looked around curiously with a satisfied expression when a tractor-trolley came from behind. The driver used the dirt shoulder to pass them, causing a dust whirl, and Navi tried to shake the dirt off with her hands.

"Do you think your mother will have me make roti, like a test?" she asked once the swirl of dirt had passed them.

Jaggi smiled. "Oh, you don't know how to make roti! She will be disappointed."

"But seriously, do you think I should keep my head covered in chunni all the time?"

"It would be nice if you cover it when someone visits. I don't think maa would care otherwise."

The road veered through another settlement along the route, where a few stray dogs barked their welcome. Finally, it turned right, and a village came into view.

"That is Kundyan," Jaggi said. Just then, a cattle herd passed by from the opposite direction, and the dust raised by the ungulate hooves fell everywhere.

Navi stomped on the paved road, trying to shake the dust off. Jaggi took a handkerchief from his pocket, wiped her face and bare arms, and brushed her hair and back.

Bindo approached them, smiling as they entered the courtyard. She and Navi looked at each other.

"Sat Sri Akal auntie ji," Navi said and bent down to touch Bindo's knees. Bindo held her midway and pulled her up in a long hug. They parted, but Bindo kept her hands gently on Navi's shoulders, admiring her with awe. She pulled her into another embrace.

Jaggi looked at the two women with fascination: each graceful in her way, measuring up well to the other.

Navi approached Teja, standing beside Bindo. "Sat Sri Akal," she bent down to touch his knees. "Sat Sri Akal puttar," Teja patted her head like his own child.

Navi, Jaggi, and Bindo sat in chairs around a small, short table, and Teja sat on a charpoy. Bindo brought tea and a plate of sweets, and salty snacks.

Bindo's joy knew no bounds. She was now at ease; the woman, her son, loved and wanted to make his wife, the daughter-in-law she always imagined, sat right in front of her.

The curious ladies from the neighborhood interrupted them a few times, coming in without knocking on the pretext of blessing the new girl.

Soon, it was dinner time. Bindo had already prepared her favorite dishes: fried cheese curry, mustard *saag*, yellow-lentil soup, yogurt for the main course, and *kheer*—rice boiled in sugared milk, for dessert. To her delight, Navi enjoyed all dishes and ate a bowl full of kheer, a testament to Bindo's culinary skills.

Bindo asked Navi about her and her family, and the two ladies were quickly comfortable. Teja usually left all decisions of importance to Bindo, but today, he was uneasy with questions popping up in his head. Once he got used to Navi's demeanor and casual manner of the conversation, he spoke.

"Beta, what's your caste?"

Both Jaggi and Bindo looked at him, surprised.

"Uncle ji, I was born in a Sikh-Khatri family," Navi answered casually. Sikh-Khatri fell in a category higher than the Jats. Most princely families came from that caste, and in the Indian caste hierarchy, Brahmins were the only category above Khatris.

"Do your parents know we are Keeras?"

"I know, but I haven't had a chance to talk to them yet."

"Do you think they will approve of your decision?"

"I think they will. My mother always taught me our guru's philosophy,"

Ek noor se sabh jag upjya,

kaun bhale kaun mande.

[How could few be good and the others wrong when the entire creation originated from the same light?]

Knowing Navi wasn't religious, and they had never discussed Gurbani, Jaggi was impressed by how casually she inserted the sacred reference into the discussion.

Bindo spoke.

"Bete, this is an important matter. I think you should talk to them as soon as you can. Suppose they disapprove; at least you will know whether you can go ahead with your decision or not."

Navi looked at her and didn't say anything for a few seconds. Jaggi also got curious about how she would respond. Then she spoke with poise and clarity.

"I am not sure if I am the type of girl you had envisioned for your son, and Jaggi may not have everything my father is looking for in his son-in-law. But I know one thing for sure. Jaggi makes me happy. I love him very much, and I will make him happy. What caste we each marry into should be our decision alone. With due respect, my mother and father, and for that matter, even the two of you, cannot override that decision."

They were all taken aback by what she said. Bindo did like that Navi was a strong woman, but how she had, in a single stroke, deprived them and her parents of the right to have a say in their marriage alarmed her. It defied social norms; marriage decisions were considered the parents' prerogative.

Though Jaggi never considered his parents would question his judgment, the thought that they had no right in his marital decision-making had never crossed his mind. He sensed the hurt Navi's statement caused and quickly intervened to mitigate it.

"Maa, as I mentioned before, both Navi and I will likely move to the USA, which will make our castes a non-issue."

Bindo ignored him and addressed Navi directly. "Bete, we are lucky that Jaggi found a girl like you. But I'm worried—the difference in our castes is huge. Most high-caste families cannot swallow the humiliation of their daughters marrying into low-caste families. We all have heard the horror stories that result from these relationships. I cannot approve of this relationship if it is against your parents' wishes. Please, get them to agree before we discuss it further. I don't want it to come to a point where your family tries to protect their reputation by inflicting physical harm upon you or Jaggi."

"I will talk to them, auntie Ji," Navi said respectfully.

Bindo had already made sleeping arrangements for them. Bindo and Navi would sleep in the large bedroom; Jaggi would take the guest room that, since boyhood, he had used as his bedroom and study. Teja set up his bed in the veranda.

Not accustomed to the surroundings, Navi found it hard to fall asleep. Unfamiliar sounds coming through the window—the distant hoot of an owl, the howl of a street dog, or even cricket chirping were disquieting. She felt as if her brain was in surveillance mode, on night watch. What would it be like to live here? she wondered. She imagined her parents on a visit to see her, her mother's cot set up next to Bindo's, and her father's beside Teja's. Slowly, the sound of Bindo's comfortable breathing relaxed Navi, and she slid into sleep.

Navi was still asleep when she felt a presence beside her bed.

"Bete, I am starting tea," and she heard the footsteps going away.

Navi woke up disoriented before realizing where she was. She grabbed her watch under the pillow; it was five thirty-one in the morning. Navi put on her sweater and grabbed her toothbrush from her bag. The bathroom was outside in the courtyard, she recalled.

Chasing Dignity

"I had Jaggi put a bucket of hot water and a fresh towel in the bathroom if you want to take a bath," Bindo said when Navi passed through the veranda.

It was the middle of February, cold and dark outside. Navi spotted the light switch by the door frame. She knew she was in for an experience when she opened the door. Used to western-style toilets, Navi looked at an authentic Indian squatty potty. Instead of toilet paper, there was a water tap next to the latrine to wash afterward. Navi was still trying to assess the situation when she spotted a sizable toad sitting by the loo. She jumped back with a scream, backing herself up against the door. A knock startled her for the second time. She opened the door to find Jaggi. She pointed at the toad, unable to speak from the chaos of it all.

Jaggi's face melted into a smile; her fright was adorable. She was always so confident and yet, terrified by a little toad, one of the animal friends he had played with as a boy.

"I am sorry you were surprised, Navi," he said with a wink after he shooed the creature out of the bathroom. "Here in Kundyan, we live in harmony with all creatures."

Chapter 22

After tea, Bindo was going out to milk the buffalo when Rani entered the courtyard.

"That must be Navi didi," she chirped.

"Rani, I assume," Navi said, greeting. "I finally meet with the girl Jaggi talks about so much. I thought you would be in Ludhiana," Navi said.

"So Jaggi veer told you about me?" Rani said, laughing.

"Oh yes, I have heard a lot about you. Jaggi thinks the world of you."

"Ah," Rani said, brushing aside the praise. "I read your stories. 'The Smoldering Sticks' is a masterpiece. When I found out you were coming to Kundyan, I made sure I was here," Rani said.

Navi instantly liked Rani, who was more proud of her writing than her siblings.

"Since Rani is here to keep you company, can I go to town for a few hours?" Jaggi asked Navi after they had breakfast. "I can run some errands while you two get to know each other." Jaggi always used his visits home to take care of any pending official business like renewing the tractor's registration, bill payments, etc. These chores were often lengthy and involved dealing with bureaucratic red tape. Jaggi had begun to take over these responsibilities in high school to save his father from taking valuable time away from farm work.

"Didi, don't worry; we'll have more fun without him," Rani said, noticing a doubt on Navi's face.

"Sure," Navi said.

Soon Rani was off with Navi to give her a tour of the village. She took her through the village lanes, pointing to the friendly Jat houses. She took Navi to her home; Lakhwinder was delighted to see Navi.

"Balkar Singh's family is running a *ghuladi* today. Take this and ask them to make a *tikki* for her," Lakhwinder said, handing Rani a small packet. "You will see what it is," Rani said, seeing Navi confused.

"That is ghuladi," Rani said, pointing to a small setup for making brown sugar. Navi was fascinated with the design. They collected juice by squeezing sugarcane through a bullock-operated machine and turning the liquid into brown sugar by concentrating it in a large, round metal pot sitting on a giant furnace.

Balkar Singh's family excitedly greeted the young ladies, offering them ginger-laced sugarcane juice, which Navi enjoyed immensely. They took the packet from Rani, which contained a mixture of raisins, almonds, cooked peanuts, fennel seeds, and other nuts and spices, and mixed it with the concentrated juice to make a thick, large-size chunk of raw sugar. "This is your tikki. Trust me; it is delicious," Rani said. They stood there for more than half an hour, Navi watching the process with curiosity. They were leaving when Hamirkur, Balkar Singh's wife, held Rani back, whispering, "Did this girl come with Jaggi alone?"

"No big deal, Chachi, they go to university together," Rani whispered back, laughing, before joining Navi.

"What is she doing?" Navi asked, pointing to a woman taking big handfuls of lumps from a pile of cow dung, shaping and placing them in orderly rows on the ground. Rani explained that these chunks, called pathees, would fuel their earthen stoves when dried. She showed Navi the big conical stacks of stored pathees for use throughout the year.

It was amazing how people made everything they needed from scratch, using simple ingredients and tools. Toads, sugarcane, dung—these were things Navi had never seen in her childhood.

Chasing Dignity

How little she knew about them and how casually Jaggi would insert these narratives into their discussions at the canteen.

They passed by a light blue, single-story building in the middle of a sizable courtyard a while down the road. "This is where I went to school," Rani said. Navi looked at her in disbelief, then walked closer to the low boundary wall.

In one corner, twenty-some students sat on the ground. A girl about ten years old was reading to them from a book, and the young female teacher was sitting in a chair on one side. Farther away in the veranda, a male teacher was teaching another class, writing something on a blackboard. Four children played hopscotch on the left, and a girl ran by them, singing.

"Did Jaggi go to this school?" Navi asked.

"No, there was no school in Kundyan when Jaggi veer was little. He had to go to the next village," she said. "They moved here the year he went to middle school. I was in class four then."

None of the children were wearing uniforms. Navi thought of her school—a beautiful brick building, and the classrooms, clustered around a multipurpose shared room, were furnished with student desks. The school had a cafeteria, a library, and boys' and girls' restrooms, and the courtyard had colorful slides, swings, and seesaws. All students wore uniforms. It couldn't have been more different from this. She had renewed appreciation for Jaggi, who, coming from a rudimentary place like this, was able to go to university and write so well in a language foreign to this corner of the world. She wondered if she could have accomplished the same had she been brought up under these circumstances.

Teja's farm wasn't too far from the school. Rani followed a cart track that led them to lush green fields on both sides. There was no one in sight, and Navi took off with a sprint on a whim. Rani followed without questioning. After about a hundred yards, the track came to a T junction, and not knowing which way to turn, Navi stopped. Rani caught up with her. They were both huffing and began to laugh, looking at each other.

"This is wheat, right? It is beautiful!" said Navi, pointing to green stalks that spread into a vast expanse in front of her. She recognized it from her walk to the village.

"Yes," Rani said and plucked a spikelet for her. "These are young stalks. The grain is just beginning to form." She explained that these would be ready for harvesting in a few weeks.

"Once, Jaggi told me how they planted rice and how you would all play as children in the water-filled fields."

"Oh yes, it was so much fun for us, children," Rani said, remembering how they ran about, threw water, wrestled, and horsed around and if someone scolded Rani, how Jaggi would rush to take all the blame upon himself. Navi saw Rani's eyes space out, a smile spread across her face, and her gaze lost in some lovely, distant past.

Navi looked around. There were no cars, trucks, ear-blowing horns, elbowing walkers, or hollering cart vendors, just peace. "Want to go for another run?" she asked.

Rani nodded with a smile and took off again, Navi leading with Rani at her heels. Navi stopped at the end of the track and dropped to her knees, breathing vigorously. Rani stopped, too, and pointed to Navi's knees, "You dirtied your pants."

Navi got up and looked at her soiled knees. "Oh well," she said with a shrug and a laugh.

The first acre and a half of the farm had vegetables—Muskmelons, bitter gourd, Tinda Gourd, Okra, and *Kakri*, the Armenian cucumber. Rani found a ripe muskmelon, washed it in the water channel set to irrigate berseem, and broke it by hitting the stone ridge. After clearing the seeds, she gave half of it to Navi. The melon was sweet, but how Rani plucked it and quickly prepared it for eating added extra deliciousness to its taste. The water in the channel was fresh and bright, and Navi took off her shoes and stood in; the cool water tickling her feet.

A couple of acres down, they stopped at the sugarcane field. Two men were chopping off stems from a thick grove with short-helved axes, collecting them into piles. Three others, two women and a man, cleaned the stalks of their leafy layers with sickles. So, this was the plant she saw them crushing for juice at the ghuladi. "Why don't we have a ghuladi if we're growing sugarcane?" Navi whispered to Rani. Rani liked her use of *we*.

Rani explained that Gur making process was labor-intensive, and unless people had enough family members, they preferred to sell the sugarcane to sugar mills.

Rani was an excellent guide; she showed Navi how every inch of the land was used and sometimes for multiple crops. The wheat fields had rows of beautiful yellow flowering mustard and rapeseed plants, blossoming to the fullest without much extra space. Along the ridges were white and yellow flowering varieties of fenugreek. "Teja Chacha doesn't talk much, and at home, he does not interfere with what Chachi does, but here, he is very astute with the land," Rani said. "He produces more per acre than anyone else in the village."

"I haven't seen uncle Teja at all," Navi said.

"Chacha may be doing something on the far side, behind the sugarcane," Rani said, and he was. He was plowing the harvested sugarcane fields to prepare them for the next crop. Teja saw them and stopped the tractor, turning it off.

"Do you like it here, bete?" he asked Navi.

"Yes, uncle Ji, it's lovely out here, in the country."

"I hope Rani didn't give you a hard time." Teja knew Rani enjoyed teasing; given a chance, she wouldn't spare even him, who barely said a word to warrant it.

"No, uncle Ji, she showed me so many things," Navi answered as she looked at the tractor. Rani followed her gaze.

"Do you want to ride it?" she asked.

Navi nodded with a smile. Rani hopped in the seat and extended her hand. "Come on!" she said.

"Careful, Rani," Teja warned. He was worried Navi might get hurt. But he was pleased to see the girls getting along. Navi was relaxed and down to earth.

Navi climbed into the side seat on the wheel guard. Rani started the tractor, put it in gear, and plowed like a pro. After one round, Navi wanted to drive, and they switched. The clutch was much more challenging to push down than a car, and the front of the tractor jumped up as she released it. But she quickly got the hang of it. The tractor had disk plows attached. Navi tried to align the furrows with those made by Teja and Rani, but it was difficult. She wanted to continue plowing—and she wanted to do it right.

"Chacha, you can go. We'll finish it," Rani yelled to Teja. Teja waited for a few minutes and then left.

Navi and Rani were still on the tractor when Bindo showed up with a tea pitcher and two tumblers.

"Let's finish these two last rounds," Rani yelled. The sight of the girls having such fun together enthralled Bindo,

Just then, Jaggi arrived. He stood behind Bindo without her realizing he was there. He was astonished to see Navi behind the wheel, plowing so comfortably. She sure would fit in Kundyan, he thought.

"What do you think of that, maa?" Jaggi said, startling his mother.

"Oh, you are here!" she said. "They are so happy. They look like sisters."

"Can you tell Navi is not a farmer's daughter?" Jaggi said.

Bindo gave him a big smile. "Maybe not, but perhaps a farmer's wife."

Soon they finished plowing, and Navi pulled the tractor up to them. Her face beamed with pride as she looked at Jaggi, who helped her down.

"Aren't you two tired yet?" Bindo asked Navi.

"No, it was fun," she responded.

Bindo poured tea into glasses for the girls. Jaggi had no glass, but he took the jug and started sipping directly, inviting "He's an animal," from Bindo, snickering and shaking her head.

"You both are covered with dirt. You should wash up before dinner," Bindo said to the girls.

"The tube well is still on. We'll take a dip in the *auluu*," Rani said. Since she was a little girl, she loved bathing in the masonry trough, letting the torrent of water flowing from the aqueduct run over her back and hair. She looked at Navi to see if she agreed. "Of course!" Navi said her face brightening. She was excited; there were so many nuances about life in the country, all new to her.

"Okay, you two do that, and Jaggi and I will head home. Take this to wrap yourself with," Bindo gave them her shawl, "and look inside for a towel."

The tiny two-room adobe building housing the tube well was the first thing Navi saw when they came to the farm in the morning, but she hadn't thought anything of it then. A long, four-inch-wide pipe stuck from one of its walls, carrying a steady gush of water, which fell into the *auluu*, a six-by-five-foot trough with thigh-deep water.

The two didn't even have a change of clothes and did not find a towel inside.

"This is how I will change," Rani said, reading Navi's mind. "We'll use the shawl as a towel." She then held the shawl in her teeth, making a screen between them, shed her clothes, shook them vigorously, put them aside, and gently slid into the auluu, pulling up the shawl and throwing it at Navi.

"Your turn, didi! Remember, this is our private place. No one will come here. There's no need to worry!" she said fearlessly.

Navi hesitated, looking around nervously. Bindo and Jaggi had already left, the farmhouse was obstructing the view from one side, and the vast wheat spread all around, bordered by distant tall sugarcane fields, providing Navi a clear sense of privacy. Comfortable, she followed suit.

It was an exhilarating feeling. The lukewarm water and its gushing sound were mesmerizing. A sense of being free overtook Navi, and, holding her breath, she dunked her head beneath the surface. She had learned to be discreet and proper around other people, but this was a new feeling of liberation. Though the turbulence caused by the strong water torrent afforded them privacy from each other, still being nude under the open sky, barely a foot away from another naked woman, was thrilling and fostered a connection in Navi's mind she hadn't thought of before. She felt as if Rani was her sister, the one she never had but always wanted. I can get used to this life, she thought and smiled under the water.

After a while, they got out, first Rani, then Navi, and toweling off with the shawl Bindo gave them, they put on their clothes.

"Do you often bathe in here?" Navi asked.

"No, not here. Sometimes I bathe in our auluu," Rani said, pointing to a similar farmhouse on the other side of the boundary between their farms. "Let me show you our farmhouse," she said and took Navi to her side of the farm.

Rani had organized part of that farmhouse for her use. It had a small table, two chairs, and a built-in bookshelf. Navi noticed three old issues of the *Sunup* on the table. "I borrowed these from Bindo Chachi."

"This looks more like your office than a farmhouse," Navi said, settling into a chair. Rani took the other chair.

"Ever since baau ji passed away, Teja uncle has been farming our land, and he doesn't have much use for this space. I like to come here and have set it as my office."

They talked at length. Navi described how it was to grow up among lots of people, noise, and smells.

"Ludhiana isn't as huge as Delhi, but I feel lost in that big place the moment I step outside my hostel," Rani commented.

"I don't think of Delhi as a cumbersome, bulky place. For me, it's just home, where I know my way around. The hustle-bustle of people around you becomes the norm, I guess." Navi explained.

Rani described the accident in which she lost her father and how Jaggi's family had helped them. "Growing up, I played more with Jaggi veer than my sister. He was my role model, and I would try to mimic whatever he did, even his stutter sometimes," Rani described with radiance in her eyes.

When they got back to the house, Jaggi was apologetic.

"I'm sorry for being out all day, leaving you alone," he said to Navi.

"Yes, I've been sitting around all day, sulking," Navi said with a smirk, realizing she hadn't thought much about Jaggi.

Rani took their leave, hugging Navi. She declined Bindo's offer to dine with them, "Maa must be waiting for me."

"She's a wonderful girl," Navi told Jaggi.

"She's very much like you—just as stubborn," Jaggi said.

"Stubbornness must be the quality you like in girls," Navi said playfully.

Bindo brought them samosas and a pitcher of a white drink. "Navi worked very hard today. She plowed over two acres!" Bindo's face was glowing with pride.

"Yes, hard work felt good!" Navi said. She liked the drink, diluted milk with salt and pepper added—*kachi-lassi*, as they called it

"Is uncle ji still at the farm?"

"Yes," Bindo said, "he is setting up the sugarcane load to take it to the mill tomorrow."

"Let me show you our Gurdwara. I go there to enjoy the serenity of that place. I think you will like it too," Jaggi said of the Sikh shrine of the village.

"Sure," Navi said.

Bindo gave them twenty rupees each for the offerings when they were ready to leave.

"I have money," Navi protested.

"I know, bete, but this is from me," she said, forcing the bill into Navi's hand.

The Gurdwara perched on top of the tallest hillock, and a walking track snaked around. The gurdwara building stood on one side of the three acres of the irregularly flat summit. Various trees filled the rest of the compound, giving it a wild forest appearance.

The sun had disappeared into the horizon, but its red glow was still intense. The Gurdwara priest greeted them; he knew Jaggi well.

Jaggi introduced Navi as his friend from Delhi.

"Wherein Delhi?" The priest asked. He had lived in Delhi during his early years.

"Vasant Vihar," Navi told him.

"I lived in Shahjahanabad, Old Delhi. It has been more than twenty years since I lived there. I'm sure it's very different now—more modern. I must have been around your age," the priest said.

After offering their prayers, Jaggi walked with Navi to his favorite spot near a rosewood tree far from the main building. They found a big broken old log to sit on. One could look over the vastness below, stretching in all directions.

"I'm not sure if I believe much in religion, but I enjoy coming here, especially in the evenings. So peaceful. Sometimes I come here just to gaze into the distance," Jaggi said, pointing to the void.

Several small hillocks were scattered around. A few remnants of the sunlight remained, and bulb lights started appearing in the distance. "Have you been to those other villages?" Navi asked.

"Oh, yes. I know these villages, and they know me. I have jogged and ridden my bike through them and have played football against their teams," Jaggi said with satisfaction. "How have you liked my village so far?"

"I love it."

Jaggi grinned at her reply. "Really, what do you like so much about it?"

"The quietness—it's so tucked away from the city's stir. And I like the simplicity of the people living here. Your family, friends, everyone knows everyone else, and they know how to take care of themselves."

"I am glad to hear you like this simplicity, but it can get boring after a while, especially for those used to a big city's hustle and bustle," Jaggi said.

"I can imagine that, but it's a beautiful getaway place whenever you need a break."

Jaggi smiled, realizing she sincerely liked this place. Interestingly, her longing for a remote, quiet place contrasted with his desire to succeed in the bustling USA. But, no matter what part of the world I live in, I will always belong here, and each of my visits will be a pilgrimage. A powerful, endearing sentiment gripped Jaggi.

"It's past eight," he said, looking at his watch, "We should get back."

"Look at those," Navi said, pointing to the lightning bugs on their way back from the Gurdwara. "Aren't they beautiful? Why are so many in one place?"

"This is a berseem field," Jaggi said, bending down to point to the small green plants. "The lighting bugs love berseem."

Navi bent down to touch the soft, densely grown, foot-tall plants. The dark green, lobed leaves were barely the size of the tip of her middle finger. The softness of the touch and the fragrance emanating from the field were soothing. "What do you do with berseem?" she asked.

"It's the cattle's favorite food," Jaggi explained.

It was pretty late now, but the moonlight provided some visibility. A voice came from a distance; it was low but clear, "He is getting too big for his boots." Jaggi looked in that direction and saw two silhouettes against the dense sugarcane field. Jaggi couldn't be sure, but one appeared to be Banta.

"What was that?" Navi asked.

"Nothing," he said as they walked toward the home.

Teja had eaten by the time they got home, but Bindo was waiting for them.

"How have you liked your visit so far, bete?" Bindo asked Navi.

"If I have to say one thing, it is that this trip has strengthened my trust in my choice. I feel comfortable and close to you all, especially to Jaggi." Jaggi put his hand on Navi's, looking tenderly into her eyes. Teja, who was listening, sitting a little farther away, quietly wiped away a tear. *Protect them, Guruji,* he prayed silently.

That night, Navi fell asleep as soon as she hit the bed. When Bindo came after finishing in the kitchen, Navi had already turned off the light, but the moonlight lit her face through the window. Her eyelids were closed, her muscles relaxed, and her breathing was deep and calm. Immersed in the surroundings, she was at peace with herself.

Chapter 23

Navi's visit had created a rumbling in the village. The news that Jaggi's girl was a high caste Chawla became the subject of village gossip spreading through the town like a fire. The more people talked about it, the more it seemed something wasn't right. Those who thought Jaggi was working above his station itched to do something about it. A few talked about putting a stop to it, but others interfered in their plans. "The woman is from the city," argued the peacemakers, "how is this any of our concern?"

But when Banta learned about it, he did not see it that way. Watching Jaggi and Navi descend from the gurdwara hillock had enraged him. Jaggi once beat Banta by skipping a year, getting a class ahead of him. He had also not forgotten how Jaggi and his football buddies stopped him and his friends from beating a high school student. Banta was now pacing back and forth along the ridge. He swung his arm around in a rage, hitting a sugarcane stalk. The unfortunate plant broke in half, the top ungraciously falling to the side.

No, it cannot happen again. How dare a Keera from my village, especially this one, make me feel small? Banta was beside himself. He has to be taught a lesson.

Banta did not like the centuries-old tradition broken by a Keera, and of all the Keeras, Jaggi. He could not be allowed to blur the caste boundaries. Banta remembered someone telling him that the only way to maintain the caste system over centuries had been preventing inter-caste marriages.

Banta enjoyed how the area's people feared the terror he could inflict. His group was close to the police and the politicians, making him feel above the law. Just recently, an episode of his horror had gripped the area. In a nearby village, they shot dead an opponent, tied his body behind a jeep, and dragged it around town to send others a message. Police did not register a case because people were afraid to become witnesses.

Banta guessed Jaggi and his girl would be there only for the weekend, so he had to act fast. He made a quick scheme, deciding to reapply the terror strategy they had used in the neighboring village.

"This is what we will do," he said to his friend. "Tomorrow morning, we'll pick him up from his home, tie him behind the jeep and drag him around the village alive."

"Why don't we do it tonight? We can go and just kill him. No one will ever know about it," the friend said.

"What's the fun in doing that? I want people to watch what we do with him. I want his lover to see what worth he was hanging around. It will teach Keeras a lesson to stay in their place. We will go to his house at the break of dawn," continued Banta, laying out the plan to his friend, "That's when Keeras start getting out of their huts to work. I don't want them to miss the spectacle."

The friend looked around and felt secure standing in the dark, with a dense sugarcane field behind and the wide-open area in front, with no one in sight.

"Who else do you want to take along?" the friend asked.

"We will take Mika. Going in with revolvers, the three of us are more than enough. Don't you agree?" Banta asked.

"Yes, I do," the friend said, and they walked toward the village.

The sugarcane stalks stirred; someone was inside the field listening. He had gone in to ease himself and waited for them to leave. Carrying a pitchfork, he came out, made his way toward a nearby hut, went inside, picked up all the money, and limped toward the gurdwara.

The priest had just finished *Kirtan Sohila*—the last Shabad to conclude their day. He was getting ready to go to bed when Chhaju showed up. The priest was surprised; Chhaju was not the praying type, and though he knew Chhaju well, he had never seen him at the Gurdwara.

"What do you need, Chhaju?" he asked.

"Bhai sahib, say my *Ardas*," Chhaju replied, offering him a handful of change and a few roughed-up bills to say a prayer for him.

In Sikh tradition, the prayer has a formal format in which one invokes the Sikh Gurus by their names and makes a few other entreaties before putting down the actual request. Many believe prayer to God is more effective if made in the proper format. *Ardas* is essential when embarking on a critical mission, and since very few know how to do it, often one goes to the priest and makes some monetary offering to make the prayer for them.

"What do you want me to pray?" the priest asked, baffled.

"A man got to do what a man got to do," Chhaju said.

The priest didn't follow what Chhaju meant; he asked again.

"Chhaju, what do you want me to pray for?"

Chhaju was reasonably intelligent and knew right from wrong, but he could not articulate his thoughts well. The short phrases he often spoke contained deeper meanings in his mind, and each of these axioms conveyed a wide range of concepts.

"That is my prayer," Chhaju replied. "A man got to do what a man got to do."

"So, you want me to pray—a man got to do what a man got to do?" the priest asked.

Chhaju nodded his head in a yes.

The priest shook his head. Assuming Chhaju planned to undertake some project for which he wanted God's help, he invited Chhaju inside the prayer hall.

The priest put the money Chhaju offered in the coffer and stood beside him in front of the holy book to say his prayer. He condensed the prayer but included, "Please help Chhaju do what a man got to do."

Smiling gratitude for the blessings, Chhaju hurriedly limped back.

Jaggi got out of the bathroom. Bindo was making breakfast, and Navi sat by her side, having already taken her bath. They were basking in each other's company in the warmth of the Chullah.

"When will you revisit us?" Bindo asked.

"Soon, I hope," Navi said. "I would first like to discuss our plans with my parents."

The day had just broken, and things were visible. The basti was fully awake.

A jeep stopped close to Jaggi's house. Banta and two of his friends got out.

"Remember, get rid of anyone you have to, except the Keera and his lover," Banta said as they moved toward the house. He was carrying a rope.

Chasing Dignity

Suddenly a pitchfork emerged from behind the neem tree, and Chhaju's form followed, blocking their way.

"Don't do this," Chhaju said.

"What is this pitchfork mouse doing here?" said one as he tried to get past Chhaju.

Chhaju emitted a shrieking sound as he drove his pitchfork into that man's neck, immediately pulling it out. A jet of blood squirted back up into Chhaju's face. The attack took them by surprise; Banta had to fumble to get his revolver out. He immediately shot at Chhaju. Chhaju screamed, lunging at Banta, and drove his pitchfork through Banta's ribs, piercing his heart. Banta was able to put three bullets into Chhaju before falling. The third person fled the scene and drove away in the Jeep.

Their screams and the noise of the bullets drew attention, and a few people ran to the scene. The door to Jaggi's house opened. Teja, Bindo, Jaggi, and Navi all came out.

A terror to the whole area a minute ago, Banta was lying dead next to his companion. Chhaju was still alive. Bindo ran to him and, sitting next to him, lifted his head in her hands. Chhaju's eyes brightened, and a smile spread across his face.

"A man got to do…" he tried to mouth.

"…what a man got to… do," Bindo choked, completing the sentence for him. Chhaju's eyes closed slowly, and his lifeless head tilted in Bindo's hands. Even in death, there was satisfaction and peace on his face. *I chose the right hero for my story*, Jaggi thought.

Navi was bewildered. She held on to Jaggi's hand, and he took her in his arm.

Chapter 24

Navi shuddered, realizing what Chhaju had prevented from happening. She had read about hate and honor killings but had never thought such a story could have something to do with her, even in her dreams; they had such a close call. Though, neither Bindo nor Teja, talked about it in context to her and Jaggi's marriage, she could see the fear in their traumatized eyes. Navi had a renewed awareness of the power of the caste construction that had, over generations, kept lovers apart. Now she fully understood Bindo's worries and why it took so long for Jaggi to express his love.

All along, Navi had been confident her family would accept her choice without question, but she wasn't sure anymore. Her father and brothers were no less proud of their superior caste, and she couldn't say for sure they weren't capable of what Banta had attempted to do. She had planned to call her parents as soon as she returned to Patiala, but now she couldn't gather the courage. She picked up the phone a few times only to put it down.

A week passed. Navi knew she had to resolve the matter. She decided to start with the easier of her parents, her mother, Parveen. The two were close, and Navi had always been able to discuss anything with her, like a friend. Born into a wealthy family, Parveen was a compassionate and strong-willed woman, and she set the general direction for the family. Her husband was different; he was a motivated businessman with a competitive personality. His measure of success was outperforming his friends and business acquaintances. He came from a relatively mediocre background, inheriting a small jewelry business from his father. He slowly expanded it and later got into diamond trading. Karmjit spent most of his time working and left most family affairs to Parveen.

Karmjit and Parveen did not oppose dating. Navi's older brother, Raman, had a steady girlfriend, and the younger Bitu was on his third. Navi was the middle of the three, and though her friends often included boys, she never had a boyfriend. Karmjit treated her tenderly, never refusing anything she asked. However, he was protective of her and took an interest in who she made friends with, always encouraging her to select from affluent families.

Navi called her mother.

"I have news for you, Mommy. Finally, I have a boyfriend!"

"Really? When did that happen?" Parveen asked. She did not sound excited.

Navi described the entire story—well, almost. She told her how long she and Jaggi had seen each other and how handsome, intelligent, and confident Jaggi was, giving her as much detail as possible without divulging the caste issue. Navi decided to tackle it when she met with them in person. However, she did discuss her visit to Kundyan, giving her mother a flavor of her feelings about the place.

"So, he is a Jat?" Parveen guessed when Navi told her she plowed two acres of their land with a tractor. Marrying a Jat was a step down for Khatris, but it wouldn't be the end of the world.

"He's a farmer, yes," Navi answered, avoiding an outright lie. People used the terms Jat and farmer almost synonymously, the farmer being more common in large cities.

Her mother's simple mention of caste crumbled Navi's confidence that she could easily beat the centuries-old system.

"What are your thoughts about Gippy, Gurdial's son?" Parveen asked.

"What about him?" Navi asked. Gurdial was friends with Karmjit and a big-time exporter of clothes. Gurdial's business took off much faster than Karmjit's, and Navi felt her father always tried to catch up with him.

Gippy was two years older than Navi, and the two went to the same college. He was a typical, spoiled son of a wealthy father and never came across as a person of serious thought.

"Has your father talked to you about him?" Parveen asked.

"No."

"Gurdial uncle has shown interest in your hand for Gippy, and your father is excited about it," Parveen said.

"Mom, I know Gippy rather too well. He cannot talk beyond drinking and flirting. He is a womanizer and treats women like trophies."

Her mother did not respond, and their call ended soon after.

The next day, she called her father, ready to start the story from the beginning. But Parveen had already updated Karmjit, and he was not in the mood to discuss.

"Next month, I plan to come to Patiala. I would like to meet him in person," Karmjit said of Jaggi.

"Will Mom be coming with you?"

"No. I'll have a busy schedule, and it won't make sense for her to come along."

Navi was disappointed; without her mother, she had even more doubts about persuading her father.

Karmjit Chawla arrived in Patiala on the second Thursday of March. He planned to take Navi and Jaggi to dinner the following day and invited Dr. Gill and her husband, Davinder Gill. The Gills were one of his few contacts in Patiala, and Navi's joining the university refreshed that connection.

Jaggi was nervous; he had no idea what to expect from Karmjit. Besides the anxiety of meeting his girlfriend's high-caste father, being in the company of wealthy and sophisticated was not his idea of fun. Simple things like ordering food in an expensive restaurant were challenging for him. He hated to say "the same for me." Sensing his discomfort, Navi tried to put Jaggi at ease by telling him her father was just as friendly and easy-going as his; if nothing, it extracted a smile from him.

The Shershah Society of Patiala was the meeting venue—a private, members-only club attended mainly by business people, doctors, engineers, government officials, and politicians. The club premises spanned a few acres and had a beautiful stone perimeter wall. A massive courtyard behind the main building offered a scenic garden with amaltas, gulmohar, bottle brush, camphor, amla, and mango trees. It had rained during the day, creating a slight chill in the evening air. The courtyard was busy with other diners. Men in dress slacks, full sleeve collared shirts, or turtlenecks, neatly tucked in, and women in colorful Salwar Kameez, Saris, and expensive jewelry were chatting leisurely around the tables.

Dr. Manpreet Gill walked into the club with Navi and Jaggi. Her boxy-fit loose buff blazer paired with wide casual trousers carried an aura of confidence. Jaggi wore off-white chinos and a beautiful turban that matched the dark blue of his striped shirt. Navi's off-white dress pants and jacket matched Jaggi's pants and the light in his shirt.

Dr. Gill led them to Karmjit and her husband, sitting around a large table; they both got up to greet them.

"Hello Papa, you made it," Navi said, giving her father a tight squeeze. Jaggi went to shake his hand and bent down to touch his knees. He was an overweight man of average height, dressed in a light-color suit and a red tie that matched his turban. Jaggi noticed a beautiful Rolex on his left wrist and, instead of the customarily iron, a heavy gold *Kara*—the Sikh's religious bracelet, on the right.

Davinder Gill, a tall, slender man, was dressed in a dinner jacket. Davinder warmly shook hands with Jaggi.

Navi sat next to her father and Jaggi between her and Dr. Gill.

Davinder and Karmjit had arrived half an hour earlier and were drinking scotch. Davinder ordered tandoori chicken snacks to share, another round of scotch for Karmjit and himself, and a glass of merlot for his wife. "Only half for me," he instructed the waiter. Jaggi and Navi asked for water.

"So, you are graduating this year, Navi," Davinder said cheerily. "What's next for you?"

"Uncle ji, I am applying to a few PhD programs in the US"

"How far are you with your applications?"

"I've sent the applications and am waiting for responses."

"I am certain my brilliant daughter will get more than one offer from the States," chimed in Karmjit. "She did well in all the tests required."

"Jaggi is also applying for admission in the US," added Dr. Gill.

Navi looked at her father, expecting a question or a comment, but none came.

"And how far along are you, Jaggi, with your applications?" Davinder tried to fill the silence.

"I'm behind Navi by a couple of months. I am just starting to send in my applications," he said.

"Jaggi will certainly get accepted," Navi interjected, "he scored much better than me on the tests."

After his second, Davinder switched to water, but Karmjit continued with scotch. Jaggi did not speak much; Navi and Manpreet tried to direct the conversation toward Jaggi a few times, but Karmjit immediately diverted it to something else. The three "adults" talked about their old friends from Patiala and Karmjit's business, which Jaggi gathered was doing very well. Navi and Jaggi were primarily spectators. As Karmjit gulped down his fourth scotch, his ability to listen diminished, and slowly, he took over the discussion, cutting others mid-sentences. He looked past Jaggi as if Jaggi wasn't even there. But at times, when he talked about his successes, he would look at Jaggi to ensure he didn't miss what was said. Navi was embarrassed; she had never seen her father drink like that and make a fool while out in public and with a guest, no less.

Finally, the main course arrived. Karmjit remained indifferent to Jaggi's presence, which everyone now knew, was deliberate, not the effect of the alcohol. Jaggi had prepared so many answers to what he imagined Karmjit might ask. He thought of raising a topic that would engage him, but nothing seemed relevant at the time. Disappointment had replaced Jaggi's initial nervousness. Karmjit began to look like just another short fat rich man, and he didn't intimidate Jaggi anymore.

Manpreet decided it was time to adjourn. Navi did not want to know what her father thought about Jaggi, in his drunken state, especially in front of everyone.

"I will stop by to see you before I leave tomorrow," Karmjit told Navi, hugging her as they got near the car. "Are you free around two in the afternoon?"

Navi nodded a yes. "Okay, I will come by then," he said and shook hands with Jaggi, providing some consolation to Navi.

Karmjit rode with Davinder Gill; he stayed with them for the night. Manpreet drove Navi and Jaggi. Besides Dr. Gill trying some small talk, their ride back was quiet.

As promised, Karmjit showed up at Navi's hostel at two.

"Do you have a place where we can sit down?" he asked her.

"Sure, let's go to the cafeteria. There's no one there at this time."

Navi ordered tea for both, and Karmjit decided to get to the point, looking around to ensure their conversation was private.

"I know you are curious about how I feel about that friend of yours."

"That friend... has a name, Papa," Navi responded forcefully.

"Yes, yes, I know," he said. "The short answer is, I do not approve of this Jaggi."

"Why? What did he do to you? At dinner, he was so respectful, and you didn't even talk to him. I was so embarrassed!"

"I am an excellent judge of people," he said, fingering his beard, "You are naïve, and he knows who you are. You are simply an easy path to success for him. End of the story."

Navi shook her head, "And how do you know that, papa?" she said, looking him straight in the eye.

"You see this grey in my beard? It is proof of my experience. He is a Jat, right? How do I know, you may ask? Because only those scoundrels tie their turbans like him."

Navi had the impulse to declare a full-fledged war by telling her father that Jaggi was not a Jat but an outcaste. What would he have to say about that? But her more rational mind prevailed, and she wanted to preserve, at least for now, the little respect her father still might harbor for Jaggi, even if it was just her illusion.

"I see," Navi said, "all Jats are scoundrels. Then I guess your friend Davinder Gill and his wife are scoundrels too. Why did you spend the night with those scoundrels, and eat breakfast with them, Papaji?"

"I am friends with them, not married to them. Besides, they are well off, living a comfortable life."

"Why do you believe we won't be able to live a comfortable life? We will both be PhDs."

"PhDs in what? You are trying to be a writer, and do you know what percent of writers do not even make a dime? And he? What's his PhD? Is he an eminent astrophysicist that NASA is waiting for him to finish his degree?" Karmjit said scornfully.

"We will be able to find good teaching positions with our degrees. What's wrong with that kind of life?"

"How much land does this boy's father have? Did you know Davinder's father was a landlord? He owned more than fifty acres. They had servants to tend to every chore in the household, a life much better than I could even imagine growing up."

"But why does it matter? We plan to move to America, and how much land he has here does not matter!" Navi said.

"How can you be sure? I work with Americans in my business and have been to the US twice. Thinking about going to the US and going there and making a decent living are two different things. First, you both have to get into a university, and even if you do, so what? Less than ten percent of students get visas. Even if you get visas and finish your degrees, that does not guarantee permanent residence; often, conditions require you to return to your country."

Her father had done his homework. That's why he was so successful in business, she knew.

"How can you be so certain that the life you choose for me will be better?"

Chasing Dignity

"You know how well off Gurdial is. He asked me for your hand for Gippy, and I told him yes," Karmjit said.

"So that is what this is all about! Your promise to uncle Gurdial without even consulting me. I knew it. I know uncle Gurdial, and I know Gippy. I would rather stay unmarried than waste my life with such a womanizing derelict," she said disgustingly and walked away.

"Don't be a fool, Navi. Don't throw away everything I have worked my whole life to give you! Make the right choice!" Karmjit yelled from behind.

"Oh, choice? Yes, papa, who I marry will be my choice—no one else's. Trust me, I will make a choice, but the one that is right for me, not for you or uncle Gurdial," she said, stopping and looking back at him. Karmjit saw anger in her eyes that he had never seen before. Then she walked away.

Jaggi had to work at the car body shop the following day, and he wouldn't see Navi until the day after. He couldn't get over the dinner experience with Karmjit. It was humbling, driving home the gap between the two families. He tried to imagine what might have transpired between Navi and her father. He wondered if she told him about his caste and if he threatened her with the consequences. Jaggi did not expect Karmjit to approve of their marriage. Will Navi marry me even if he disapproves? Will it hurt his honor and endanger Navi's life if she does? Should I put her through all this?

His mind wouldn't stop drawing parallels between Simmie and Navi. One moment, the two would look the same, and the next, totally opposite. If the image of Navi driving a tractor with Rani made the gap between him and Navi disappear, Karmjit's face would emerge and recreate a wedge between them.

Navi's evening was just as disquieting. She didn't remember ever being rude or angry at her father. Nor could she recall her father refusing her anything she ever asked. He had always been a God figure for her, but today, he felt like an arrogant, selfish, greedy mortal. Is her whole family like this? She thought of her mother, whom she loved very much. Would she reject Jaggi for his caste? What about her brothers? Navi couldn't bear the thought of everyone turning against her.

That night she had a dream. She was a baby, playing with her father's majestic beard. She pulled on the hair as he contorted his face pretending to be in pain. She was laughing harder, trying to pull his hair ever so strongly with her tiny hands as he feigned to be in more and more pain. Then the dream switched to a kiss; she was kissing Jaggi, lying in his lap, and their little son was playing by their side. The scene shifted again, and she was scraping cow dung with a wooden scraper, the slimy muck covering her bare feet and the hem of her *salwar*. She woke up in a sweat, got up to get a glass of water, and tried to stay awake long enough to avoid getting back into the dream.

The following day, Jaggi found her in her department lounge, and they went to their favorite Chinese for lunch.

"How did it go?" he asked.

"Not well, to tell you the truth," she said, looking uncomfortable.

Jaggi gave a wry smile and looked at the table as if trying to avoid making contact with her.

"It's not over yet," Navi said, taking Jaggi's hands in her own, "The matter will be discussed in detail when I go home after the finals. I was, however, hoping for more enthusiasm from him."

"Where does it leave us?" Jaggi asked.

"I have thought about my choices in case my family disapproves. They cannot stop me from marrying you, but doing so will have consequences, which I am ready to deal with."

"And what are the consequences?" Jaggi asked.

"In the worst-case scenario, they will cut all ties with me and never speak to me again."

"That is pretty severe," Jaggi said. "Can they try to hurt you?"

"No, they won't. At least I am sure of this much of my family—they cannot hurt us, neither you nor me. As I said, what I laid out is the worst-case scenario. I hope they come around, and it doesn't boil down to that."

"Are you okay with living all your life, never talking to your family?" Jaggi asked. "Will you still think marrying me was the right choice?"

"Jaggi, I made my choice. If I have to choose between you and my family, I choose you. I can't promise you anything beyond this life, but in this life, I am yours," she said, firmly holding his hand.

"That's all I need to know," Jaggi said.

A couple of weeks later, the Political Science department arranged a special one-day symposium titled "The Mandal Commission and Students Protests." Mandal Commission was a government-instituted committee considering caste-based reservations in government jobs to redress caste discrimination. All the backward and suppressed social classes made up 52 percent of India's population, and the commission recommended 49 percent reservations for these classes, a substantial increase in the existing quotas. In August 1990, the government decided to implement the commission's recommendations, and protests led by upper-caste students immediately hit the country. Roads, highways, businesses, government services, and schools were closed. All influential newspapers in the country covered the protests.

A recent article published in the 'November-December 1998' issue of the *Journal of Higher Education* called "Student Protest and Multicultural Reform: Making Sense of Campus Unrest in the 1990s" by Robert A. Rhoads triggered this workshop. Speakers at the symposium included prominent experts; attendees, students, and teachers came from all over the campus. All lectures focused on the Mandal commission-related student protests.

Both Jaggi and Navi attended the symposium. Most of the students and faculty were from upper castes, and the gathering's general mood was against job reservations. Jaggi and a few left-leaning students voiced their favor for the reservations, though they, like the others, defended the students' right to protest.

Jaggi was passionate about the subject and kept on top of the news even after the seminar. He wrote an article on the proceedings. Instead of publishing it in the *Sunup*, he sent it as an op-ed to the *Sindhu*, an influential newspaper, knowing well the field experts contributed these op-eds, not mere students like himself. To his great disbelief and pleasure, the paper immediately published his article.

"I was sure it would be published!" Navi exclaimed when Jaggi told her. "The information you covered was too good to be ignored. So, what's next for you, Mr. Writer?"

"I'm still shocked, but this gives me the confidence to do what I've been planning for a while."

Navi looked at him with a questioning smile.

"Mr. Writer's girlfriend," he said, leaning into her as if whispering a secret, "I want to write a book on casteism in India. I want to focus on its origin, perils, and the possible remedies to render this nasty system irrelevant and toothless."

"That will be wonderful. I'm sure you will do a superb job," Navi said.

"And it will make maa so proud," Jaggi said, leaning back in a blissfully peaceful manner.

"Why? Because she wants you to be a writer?" Navi asked excitedly. She always believed Jaggi would enjoy being a writer more than a cartographer.

"No, I don't think it matters to her what precisely I do. My writing on caste will make her happy because it will show her I'm embracing my caste and am doing something about it instead of running from it."

It was the middle of May, and the finals were underway. The last exams were on Friday the following week; hers in the morning and his in the afternoon. Both would finish their master's.

Jaggi was making notes when Navi entered the library and put a large envelope down in front of him.

Jaggi opened it and read the letter inside; it was from UC Davis. The university accepted Navi to its PhD program. UC Davis was one of her top choices, and they offered her a "Graduate Student Researcher" position based on her "promise as a creative scholar." She would receive a monthly living stipend, and because the graduate research positions were part of the university's work exchange program, they waived her tuition.

Jaggi got up and turned around. He lifted her and swung her around in the air. "Congratulations!" he shouted.

"Shhhh, we're in the library!' Navi said.

"Then let's go to the canteen to celebrate," he said.

Jaggi held her hand, giving her frequent hugs on the street. He once even broke into a trot around her, making her burst into laughter.

"*Sahib* ji, you are cheerful today!" said Mundu.

"Yes, Mundu, I am thrilled, and do you know why?" Mundu shook his head.

"Because my lady is going to Amrika!" he said, hugging her again. "Now, please bring us two ladoos and tea," he said.

"Ji Sahib," Mundu said.

They went to their favorite table.

"'We believe you show great promise as a creative scholar,'" said Jaggi, reciting the line from the letter again.

They were still talking about the letter when Chacha Chimna came with various sweets on a big platter. Mundu brought two smaller plates.

"Congratulations, madam ji. We need to celebrate the news with more than ladoos. This is on me," Chacha Chimna said.

"No, please, they are my treat for Navi," Jaggi said.

"She is mine too—you are my favorite customers," Chacha Chimna said, leaning in closer, "but don't tell anyone. I'll send your tea next." He walked away with a bit of spring in his step.

"That was so nice of him," Navi said, delighted.

"Yes, indeed."

"I wish we could go for our visas together," Navi said between bites. The sweets were delicious, especially the chum-chum.

"That would've been lovely. But it'll be a couple of months before I get an acceptance letter," Jaggi said. "Let's go to Kundyan afterward. Maa and baau ji would love to hear your news in person."

"Ahh, I'm sorry I can't," Navi said apologetically; she had to go to her younger brother Bitu's birthday party the same day as her last final. She had missed it the previous year as well.

Chasing Dignity

"You have an exam that day. Will you make it to the party in time?"

"Easily, my exam ends at eleven, and the party starts at seven-thirty. I'll have ample time to be there," Navi said, "I'll go to the embassy for a visa the following Monday."

"Good luck at the embassy," Jaggi said, squeezing her. "Will you call me when you get any news?"

"Thank you, and yes, you'll be the first to know!" said Navi, "Please tell your maa and baau ji; I'll come to see them. We will celebrate it all together."

Chapter 25

Soon after her last exam, Navi was on the bus to New Delhi, her latest interaction with her father occupying her mind. How would the rest of her family react? Bitu, her younger brother and the baby of the family, wouldn't care, she knew; he seldom had any free time away from girls and his football and never took any interest in family affairs. Raman, her older brother, was much like their father. Navi had a good relationship with him and could talk to him about anything. Would he react the same way her father did, she wondered? She thought about Parveen, her mother, and suddenly her face relaxed. Navi always had a special bond with and considered her mother her best friend.

"There will be a thirty-minute stop. Anyone wanting to use the bathroom, have a cup of tea or eat something, now is the time," the driver's announcement broke her reverie. She had a disliking for these roadside restaurants that lured business by offering free food to bus drivers.

It was late evening when the bus arrived in Delhi. Navi spotted Raman, a tall, slender, fair-complexioned young man, to pick her up. He wore a refined turban, and his beard was nicely tucked-in.

"Where's your Jagga Jat? I thought he was coming with you," Raman said mischievously.

"Oh, hush," she responded, getting comfort from Raman's accepting tone.

"Your eyes are yellow; do you have a fever?" Raman inquired.

"No, just tired. My last exam was this morning, and I couldn't take a nap on this bumpy bus ride."

They had planned to go directly to Bitu's birthday party at the GPL club, about half an hour away. The whole family would be there, Navi knew. However, she was exhausted and did not feel like going to the party. She had been fatigued for the past couple of weeks, which she thought was stress from the exams. She asked Raman to take her home instead. "You can go to the party after dropping me at home."

Navi was fast asleep when the family returned. When she came down the next morning, Parveen was in the kitchen, preparing breakfast. Parveen was tall with a slightly dark complexion and sharp features like Navi.

"I heard you and your papa had quite an argument over the boy," Parveen said when they settled to eat.

Navi didn't respond.

"Do you love him, bete?"

"What kind of question is that? Of course, I love him, and he loves me just as much, if not more."

"Is it possible he is after you just to marry into a well-to-do family?"

"Mama, you have been listening to Papa a little too much. Jaggi is not that kind of a person. I was the one to take the lead in our relationship. He was the hesitant one."

Parveen did not immediately answer. Then she smiled, "Is he handsome?"

That was more like the mother Navi knew, her friend, her confidante.

She handed her mother the envelope she was holding and leaned over to whisper, "Much better looking than the one you found."

Parveen smiled and opened the envelope. It had two pictures, one of Jaggi by himself and one with Navi.

"Yes, he is gorgeous," she said.

Parveen put the photo aside and looked at her daughter, her eyes filled with compassion. She had great faith in Navi's wisdom and judgment, especially regarding decisions as significant as this, but she knew her husband and his pride well.

"Bete, you know your father only wants the best for you."

"Of course, but shouldn't I decide what is best for me? We all make our own choices, mama. I'm an adult, and if I make a wrong choice, I will be the one to live with it."

"Don't take it the wrong way, bete. But they say love mars one's judgment, and you certainly are in love!"

Karmjit had woken up by now, and he overheard the last part of their conversation as he came down. He was in his pajamas and, instead of a turban, had a small off-white scarf tied around his head, hiding his receding topknot.

Under normal circumstances, Karmjit would have gone to hug Navi and ask her how his lovely daughter was doing. But the bitterness of their last interaction lingered in both minds; he held back.

"Good morning, ladies," he said, making his presence known with a generic greeting.

Navi didn't look at him. Instead, she got up from the table, saying, "I will sleep some more. The exams have tired me." She walked away.

On the way to her room, she passed Raman. "I'm still tired and want to sleep more," she responded to his curious gaze.

Parveen handed Raman the pictures Navi gave her. "What do you think of the young man, Raman?" she asked.

"He looks dashing. They look nice together," he said, carefully looking at the pictures.

"What do you think, Papa?" he said, sliding the pictures toward Karmjit.

"Don't worry, I have seen the real thing," Karmjit said, without picking up the pictures but stealing a peek at them.

"Chawla Sahib, I don't think you are fair to Navi," Parveen always called him Chawla Sahib when she wanted to make a point.

"I am not fair? What has this to do with me?"

"Navi is an adult. She is educated and has made all the right decisions so far. The boy is handsome, and from what she tells me, he is nice, loves her, and will take good care of her. Don't you trust her?" Parveen said.

"If she doesn't need my approval, she can do whatever she wants. I am not stopping her."

"She is your daughter, and she does need your approval. She wants you to accept her husband. She has never done anything in her life without your approval."

"I wasn't expecting this nonsense! Why couldn't she find a nice Khatri Sikh boy?"

"May not be a Khatri, but he is a Sikh!" said Parveen.

"What will I tell Gurdial? That my daughter prefers a village boy over his family? It was such a perfect opportunity for our families to connect. This girl has no idea what that means," Karmjit said.

"Chawla Sahib, there's no point going back to it. Navi has made it clear that she does not like Gurdial's son. His behavior toward women isn't something that can make me proud, either. Would you like your daughter to be treated like that?" Parveen said.

Soon Bitu returned from his early morning football practice and joined them for breakfast. Bitu was about the same height as Karmjit, significantly shorter than Raman, and had an athletic build.

"What do you think of this guy?" Raman said, putting the pictures in front of Bitu.

"He looks all right—why?" Bitu said casually.

"He's the village boy your sister wants to waste her life with," Karmjit said.

"Don't be stupid," Parveen looked at her husband. "You don't want to lose your daughter. At least listen to her. We can discuss the whole thing like adults. You are not going to convince her of anything by being stubborn!"

Karmjit did not say anything; he kept sitting quietly.

"Go and talk to her; you don't have to talk about Jaggi. Let's all go out to lunch. I know she won't go if you don't change this cold demeanor," Parveen told her husband.

"*My* cold demeanor?" Karmjit snapped.

"Yes, yours. You are the grown-up here, acting like a child!"

Around noon, Karmjit went to her room and knocked at her door. "It's lunchtime! Come down, bete. We're planning to go out to eat."

"Give me a few minutes, Papa. I will be down," she answered.

They went to Thirsty's, a new Sports Bar and Grill that served American food. "So, tell us more about the gentleman you are dating," Parveen said, not wasting a minute after they settled down.

"His name is Jaggi," Navi said, "and he just finished his MA in geography."

"And how did you meet him?" her mother asked.

"We accidentally ran into each other at a bus stop the first week we were on campus. But we didn't officially meet until last year at a blood drive that Dr. Gill auntie had organized."

"Does Dr. Gill know him?" Parveen asked.

"Yes—she adores him and took us out to dinner."

"Tell us more about him." Parveen wanted the discussion to continue.

"He is from Kundyan. It is a village near Rupar," she said. Then she remembered something that made her face lit up. "He did his BA from Government College Rupar, the same college Dr. Gill auntie went to for her premedical," she added.

"And what about his family?" Parveen asked.

"Jaggi does not have any brothers or sisters. His father is a farmer, and his mother is a successful local seamstress."

"How much land do they have?" Karmjit asked.

"Papa, why don't you ask me why I like him or what he likes? What he wants to do, or what he is capable of doing?"

"So, I gather they don't have much," Karmjit said.

"No," she sighed, her attempt to avoid his question derailed. "They don't. And I have been to Jaggi's house, which like any other in the village is small and not substantial, like ours," she said with her voice raised. "I have known him for more than a year, and he tells me everything. He is a good man, which is all that matters to me. I don't care about his land or his small house."

Parveen was tenderly watching the father-daughter conversation. The two always had a loving relationship, and until now, there was never a significant disagreement between them. However, Karmjit was set in his ways and made few compromises in life.

Although Parveen disapproved of Karmjit's reasons to object to Navi's choice, she wasn't sure if Jaggi was suitable for Navi. So far, Parveen didn't know much about him, except that Navi was in love with him. When home, she talked to Navi alone.

"Navi, bete, I trust your judgment about Jaggi, but I have some concerns that I would like to share with you," Parveen said, getting Navi's full attention.

"I worry that you and Jaggi are two different kinds of people. You may now think that you are in love. But love quickly wears off, and when that happens, your similarities with each other help you pull through tough times."

"Why do you think Jaggi and I are dissimilar?" Navi asked.

"A city girl from a business family versus a village boy from farming? Two people who faced different problems growing up and learned different ways to solve them—should I call them similar? When in disagreement, you two will not look at the issue the same way," Parveen said.

Navi took a minute to think through before speaking.

"Mom, I agree with you in general. But my feelings for Jaggi did not originate from obsession, lust, possessiveness, or even idealism. We are more similar than you think. We both have similar education, love literature, writing, and, more importantly, understand each other. At times, we even finish sentences for each other. You may not see it, mom, but we are similar in more ways than different. If that is not love, I don't know where to seek it."

Parveen was listening carefully and attentively to each word Navi said. Navi's speech carved a picture of Jaggi as an intelligent person who cared for their daughter. She could see why Navi loved him and blessed the relationship. "It all happens with Waheguru's will. Who are we to ignore Him?" she murmured.

"There is something else that I have not shared with you yet," Navi said. Parveen looked up at her. "He is not a Jat," Navi said.

"You said he was a farmer?" she offered.

"He is, but he is not a Jat. He is an outcaste—a Keera," Navi said.

The comment shocked Parveen. She was speechless for a minute. "It will not bode well with your father. Not at all," she spoke finally. Navi didn't say anything. "Let me advise you," Parveen said, "just leave it at that. He is a farmer, which is all your father needs to know. Do not volunteer any more information than you have to."

"Can Papa try to hurt him?" Navi asked.

"I don't think he has that in him. It'll bruise his ego, though, and he may not talk to you for a long time. But if you truly love this young man, your father will eventually come around to accept him."

Navi got up and hugged her mother.

Navi accepted the offer from UC Davis, and the following Monday, she went to the US embassy. She was a little tense as only a fraction of the applicants got visas. But she was ecstatic when, after a brief interview, she heard, "You can collect your passport in the afternoon."

"So, I got the visa?" she said, delighted at the visa officer.

"Yes, you did; congratulations."

Navi could not wait to tell Jaggi the news; she had to call him immediately. She traced him to the library, a library staff Navi knew connected her with Jaggi. Jaggi had to take the call in the library office

"Fantastic! You made it," Jaggi shouted, forgetting he was in the company of the library staff. To give Jaggi privacy, the librarian walked out of the office, closing the door behind her.

"I wish you were here with me now, at this moment," Navi said.

"Oh, no, you wouldn't have liked me around you right now," Jaggi said with a mischievous tone.

"Oh yeah, why not?" Navi asked.

"You haven't seen the beast in me, Miss Navi," he said, "It would have surely come out if I were anywhere near you right now!"

It was unusual for Jaggi, and the talk made her a bit randy.

"Oh really, I'd like to see that beast..." said she, getting a thrill from that little injection of lewdness.

A week passed. The news from Navi had invigorated Jaggi and made him optimistic about his admission and visa. A step closer to his dream, his life was beginning to look brighter by the day.

But a few days later, a visit from Dr. Gill to his hostel took him by surprise. The news she delivered was not good.

"It is about Navi. My husband came from New Delhi last night. He had stopped by to see her family," explained Dr. Gill.

Her voice made his stomach drop. Immediately he thought that Navi's family had persuaded Navi against marrying him, and she decided Dr. Gill should be the messenger.

"She is sick—very sick," Dr. Gill continued.

"What? I just spoke with her last week. She was fine," Jaggi said, visibly shaken.

"I know. My husband told me that. He said she went to the hospital the day she spoke with you. Sometimes trouble comes fast and unannounced," she said.

"What is wrong with her?" he asked.

"She has what they call autoimmune hepatitis."

"What's that?"

"Our body's immune system is designed to attack bacteria and viruses that may invade us from the outside. But sometimes, for reasons that we don't understand, it can attack our own organs. In the case of autoimmune hepatitis, it attacks a person's liver."

"Does this always happen so suddenly?" Jaggi asked.

"Not always. But sometimes, the symptoms can be mild, like fatigue, skin rashes, abdominal discomfort, joint pains, yellow skin or eyes, or funny blood vessels on the skin. One may ignore them for long until the signs get severe."

"How bad is it, Dr. Sahib?" he asked.

"I don't know, Jaggi. She might recover with some medication and be released soon, or she may have to stay there for a while. They were still doing testing on her when my husband left Navi yesterday."

"Where is she now? Is that a good hospital?" Jaggi's voice was shaking; he wanted to get up off the table, run to Navi, and hold her in his arms.

"She is in Ram Dyal Hospital in New Delhi, one of the best in the country," she explained. "I don't know how much schoolwork you have right now, but it will be a support to Navi if you could be with her for a little while."

"My master's is finished. I am here just for the Spanish-speaking group. That is not important."

"Then you should go there immediately."

Jaggi did not answer—his mind was ahead of her, and he'd already started planning the trip. What happened to Rani's father flashed in his mind—the delays in treatment, the cost of their travel back and forth. He knew he needed money, and his first thought was to ask Nirmal Singh, his employer, for an advance.

"I will talk to Nirmal bhaji today to let him know I'll be away from work and get an advance on my paycheck," Jaggi said.

Chasing Dignity

"Okay, that is good," Dr. Gill said. Then she opened her purse, pulled out an envelope, and extended it to him. "Here is some money. I brought it with me in case you needed it."

"No, please, Dr. Gill. You are most generous, but I cannot take this from you. As I said, I think Nirmal bhaji will give me an advance. I have never asked him for one in the past, and I've proven I'm a reliable employee," he said.

"I am sure he will. But you are going to Delhi and may need more money than you think. Please take it, just in case."

"Dr. Gill," he said hesitatingly, "it will be tough for me to repay you."

"Don't worry about that."

He opened the envelope; there was a thick bundle of hundred-rupee bills.

"It is five thousand rupees," she said.

"This is too much!"

"Don't say anything. Just listen to me," Dr. Gill said, putting her hand on Jaggi's and tenderly squeezing it. "Navi was born here in Patiala, and I have known her since she was a toddler. I adored her as a child and love her now as an adult. I might have gone myself, but my work doesn't allow me. You will go there just as much on my behalf as you will for yourself. Navi needs you, the man she loves, more than an old auntie."

They were quiet for a minute.

"I will take the money, Dr. Gill, but as a loan. I promise to pay it back one day, somehow," he said.

"I accept that, but now you must go to our Navi."

PART V

Love sacrifices all things to bless the thing it loves.
                    Edward Bulwer-Lytton, 1st Baron Lytton

Chapter 26

The taxi dropped Jaggi under the large portico of Ram Dyal Hospital. A few people were going in and out of the building through a double glass door, and Jaggi walked into the expansive, huge lobby scattered with people. He was looking around, taking a measure of the place, when he saw Navi's father, Karmjit, walking toward him and, to Jaggi's surprise, he greeted Jaggi as if they were the best of friends. He even hugged Jaggi, telling him that Navi had been sick and had chest pain earlier.

"The doctor asked Parveen and me to wait outside," Karmjit said, introducing him to Navi's mother.

The tall, slender lady looked amazingly like Navi. She got up from the chair to embrace Jaggi, and her cuddle was even more welcoming than her husband's.

"I think we can go back in now. It has been fifteen minutes," Karmjit said, looking at his watch.

They took the elevator to Navi's floor.

Karmjit opened the room door, holding the door for them. Navi lay in a bed hooked to an intravenous drip, and a doctor was talking to her beside the bed. Navi's face lit up as she saw Jaggi.

"Jaggi," she said, trying to sit up but winced immediately. Laying back on her pillow, she extended her arms, and he bent down to hug her. She introduced Jaggi to the Doctor, Dr. Mehta, telling him she and Jaggi were together at the university.

"I will let you two talk. I will be back later," Dr. Mehta said, leaving.

"Doctor, you can talk in front of Jaggi. He is part of the family," Navi said, glaring at her father, who lowered his gaze.

"No, I have to go; I need to finish my round," the doctor said and walked out.

Parveen made herself comfortable on one corner of Navi's bed. There were two stools in the room. Karmjit pushed one to Jaggi and took the other for himself. Karmjit pulled his seat to sit close to Navi, putting his hand on her shoulder.

"So, what happened to you? You were fine when I talked to you last week?" Jaggi asked, his eyes scanning her body, which looked tiny and frail in the hospital bed.

"I don't know. I wasn't feeling well, so I went to the hospital, but they admitted me, saying I had jaundice because my bilirubin was high. I thought I was tired from studying, but now they say my liver isn't working."

Soon, they talked about Patiala and became oblivious to Karmjit and Parveen's presence. Karmjit would interject a comment here and there, eluding he liked Jaggi, which Jaggi felt was embarrassing.

Then Navi began to doze off and told them she wanted to sleep.

"You also must be tired from the bus ride," Parveen said to Jaggi. "Why don't you come home with me and get some rest? We can return in the evening."

"I am not tired. I'll stay. Why don't you and uncle ji go?"

They both were, in fact, tired and gratefully accepted the offer. "We will be back around six in the evening," Parveen said. Jaggi was surprised they'd let him stay with Navi alone, but perhaps her mother had helped change Karmjit's mind about him in the weeks since their meeting.

Seeing Navi had fallen asleep, Jaggi went outside looking for Dr. Mehta and found him talking to a nurse at the end of the hallway.

"I would like to ask you about Navi, Dr. Mehta," Jaggi said. "Just a few minutes, please."

"I'm sorry, but I can't divulge any information about her to anyone other than her immediate family."

"Doctor Sahib, Navi and I are very close. If you remember, she said I'm part of the family, and you could talk to me. You can check with her again if you like."

That jogged the doctor's memory. "All right then; join me. I am going to the cafeteria." said the doctor.

As they walked, Jaggi couldn't help comparing this luxury hospital with the government hospital in Rupar, where Sohan Singh, Rani's father, was taken for treatment. Jaggi was somewhat too familiar with those kinds of abysmal facilities, barely equipped even for basic testing. They didn't have ambulances, leaving the poor to hire rickshaws or auto-rickshaws to haul the patient into an emergency room only to deal with absent doctors, unavailable or broken equipment, and rude staff—that is, if they survived the trip at all. Minimal effort was paid into the equipment's hygiene or sterility, making people sick just from visiting there. Patients were admitted to rooms shared by multiple patients, with more beds than IV stands. Corruption and nepotism were rampant; the doctors would treat relatives and friends with drugs meant for hospital patients.

Here, the rooms and halls were uncrowded; the staff was courteous, and the building was well-designed and highly hygienic. The fact that the doctor readily agreed to talk to him was unique in itself. Facilities like Ram Dyal hospital were rising across the country, creating a parallel, elite healthcare system catering to the wealthy.

The doctor bought a sandwich and a cup of tea and asked Jaggi if he wanted anything. Jaggi declined. "Please, remind me of your name?"

"Jagjit Singh, I go by Jaggi."

"What can I do for you, Jaggi?"

"What is wrong with Navi, Dr. Sahib? How did this happen?"

"She has what we call autoimmune hepatitis with possible underlying cirrhosis."

"Yes, I heard Dr. Gill say something like that. But Dr. Sahib, I am not a medical student and need to know: will she get better?"

"The prognosis doesn't look good. Her condition is deteriorating fast."

"What?" he said, squinting; the doctor's bluntness took him aback.

"This means that the treatment is not working. The disease is progressing quickly. Navi is beginning to show confusion and excessive fatigue. She needs a liver transplant."

The doctor briefly explained what a liver transplant was and where healthy livers needed for the transplant came from.

"Sometimes, a person gets in an accident and has no chance of recovery. Many families make decisions on behalf of the person who has died to save other lives. Many of the person's organs are still functioning properly and can be donated to people like Navi. Unfortunately, the demand is much greater than the availability, and Navi has no chance of getting one in time. In her case, we need a living donor."

"How can a living person donate their liver?" Jaggi asked.

"A person's liver has two lobes. If we cut one out, the remaining liver grows back to its full size and assumes the full functions of the original liver. We can transplant the removed lobe into the patient, where it grows to its full size and, hopefully, full function."

Chasing Dignity

Jaggi was absorbing and analyzing each word the doctor said. He didn't understand a lot, but one thing was clear: Navi had a chance.

"Is it a risky operation?" Jaggi asked.

"Every surgery has inherent risks, and this one is big," the doctor said.

"Does Navi's family know about this living donor option?"

"Yes, they are aware of it. The person must be young, and their blood group should match Navi's group, O. It is a stressful situation for the parents. Both want to donate. Unfortunately, her mother's blood group is incompatible, and, per our guidelines, her father is too old."

"My blood group is O. Can I be the donor?"

"No, you cannot. By law, only relatives can be the donors, her immediate family, or her husband if she were married." Dr. Mehta explained how the law was designed to protect the poor and helpless from exploitation by the wealthy and powerful.

"What about her brothers?"

"I don't know about them," Dr. Mehta said, rising from his seat, "I need to return to my rounds. I'll be back tomorrow if you have any other questions," he said, leaving Jaggi contemplating.

Jaggi could understand why Navi's parents were so stressed. The discussion had raised many questions and possibilities in his mind. Could one of Navi's brothers save her life? Could he somehow save her? But so much could go wrong, and he thought of Navi's mother—and his own mother—getting the news that their child had died. He thought back to Rani and her family the day their father died, seeing the doctor walk out of the room with the awful news.

"Every surgery has inherent risks, and this one is big," the doctor had said. Could he live with himself for causing that suffering—even if he had died? He was not sure.

Navi was awake when Jaggi returned to the room.

"Jaggi, will you please lie down with me for a while?" she quietly asked.

The bed was large enough to accommodate Jaggi, and he lay beside her. She nestled her head on his shoulder, and they wrapped their arms around each other.

"The nurse may not like us lying together," he said.

"That is her problem, not ours," she said.

They lay there in silence, their breathing syncing into the same rhythm. "Why did this happen to me, Jaggi? What did I do to deserve this?" she asked in a choked voice.

"Anyone can get sick, Navi. You are perfect; you did nothing wrong," he said.

"But how could one day I am healthy, taking exams and getting a visa to go to the US, and the next day, in the hospital struggling to stay alive?"

Jaggi heard a sob and held her close while she began to shake.

"I am terrified, Jaggi," she said, tightening their embrace. "I don't want to die."

"You will not die, Navi. I won't let you!"

"I wish you had that power. I wish someone, I mean anyone on this planet, had that power," Navi said, her voice trailing off.

Jaggi did not say anything; he just continued to hold her.

"Navi, do you know my blood group is ..."

"O positive," she said, cutting him and nodding into his shoulder joint.

"How did you know?" he asked.

"From the blood drive day at Patiala."

"Did they tell you what my blood group was?"

"No," she said, smiling and raising her head to meet his eyes. "But they separated the bags by the blood group, and yours and mine were in the same pile," she put her head back on his shoulder.

"Dr. Mehta said you are showing signs of confusion, but you are as sharp-witted as ever," he said.

"Only doctors confuse me. Everything is crystal clear when I am with you," she said, curling into him more closely.

"Navi, I would like to be the living donor for your transplant," Jaggi said.

"I thought of that, but you cannot, Jaggi."

"That's what I believed, too, but it turns out, as your husband, I can," he said, making Navi still.

She slowly looked up at him.

"You will complete my life," he continued, "and I promise to work hard to make you happy. I will cherish you all my life and yours. Will you, Miss Navi, be my wife?"

Her eyes welled again, and she pulled away from the embrace, turning aside. Jaggi gently lifted her chin.

"What's the matter, Navi?"

"I envisioned this day so many times but never like this. Saying yes now, here, makes me feel guilty and selfish. We are only marrying so you can give me part of your liver."

"Hush," he said. "Just ask yourself one question, would you do the same for me?"

She didn't answer. She didn't need to.

"So, will you marry me, please?" he pleaded, "Though I'm too comfy to get up and fall at your feet as I should," Jaggi added with a small smile.

Navi nodded and gently said, "Yes, I would love to marry you, Jaggi."

"Thank you," Jaggi said, welling with emotion. "I will make sure you never regret your decision."

Navi was overwhelmed by the gesture, finding herself lost for words. *Thank you* was certainly not enough. She had already given up hope, but Jaggi just offered her another chance at life, another birth. She remembered telling Jaggi she would be his in this life. 'God, I want to be his, life-after-life, life-after-life.' She returned to his arms, pressing herself firmly against him.

In the late afternoon, Raman came to visit. Even before Navi introduced them, Jaggi noticed the siblings' resemblance. From the prominent metal bracelet on Raman's right wrist, Jaggi assumed he was a devout Sikh

"Navi told me you are an accomplished writer," Raman said.

Jaggi smiled. "It will be a bit too enthusiastic use of the word *accomplished* for a writer of my caliber. Most of my contributions have been to our campus magazine," Jaggi answered. "Navi is the better writer."

"I told Raman of your op-ed in the *Sindhu*," Navi said, "And Raman, Jaggi is now working on a book."

"What is the book about?" Raman asked.

Jaggi described how the book would focus on casteism in India.

"That is a great topic. It will be well received," Raman said.

Chasing Dignity

They diverged into other issues related to caste and politics and were still engrossed in their discussion when Karmjit and Parveen returned.

"Have you eaten anything today?" Parveen asked Jaggi.

"No, not yet," he answered.

"We can eat at the cafeteria. It serves decent food," Karmjit said.

"Or you can come home with me and have a real meal," Raman said.

Jaggi thought for a second. His discussion with Dr. Mehta was on his mind, and he wanted to talk to the family regarding his proposal and the transplant possibilities. But before that, he wanted to hear what Raman had to say about it.

"Why don't we all eat here in the cafeteria—you can eat with us, right?" Jaggi asked Raman.

Raman agreed, and as Navi returned to sleep, they went to the cafeteria. Jaggi brought up the subject after they started to eat.

"Did the doctors talk about Navi needing a transplant?"

"Yes, they did," Karmjit said. "I have the right blood group to give part of my liver, but they tell me I am too old."

"Yes, Dr. Mehta told me about the regulations. But what about Raman and Bitu?"

"Bitu is not a match. His blood group is A, the same as his mother's. Navi is O-positive," said Karmjit. Jaggi looked with widening eyes at Raman, who averted his gaze.

Parveen came to his rescue. "Raman has the right blood group."

Jaggi's heart began to beat faster in his chest. "That is wonderful news! When can they schedule the operation?" Jaggi asked excitedly.

"Bete," Parveen continued, taking Raman's hand. "It is not so simple. The doctors say it's a big operation. There is a chance that we can lose him as well. Raman's girlfriend is terrified at the thought, and so are we. Two children lost. I could not bear it," she broke down and started to cry. Karmjit put his arm around her shoulders.

Jaggi was disgusted by what he was seeing. If this were Rani or Himmat, he'd do anything to save them, considering them his chosen siblings.

After a long, quiet moment, Jaggi broke the silence. "My blood group is O. I wish I could be the donor, but unfortunately, the doctor says the person has to be related to Navi."

"You could marry her and be the donor," Karmjit said. "I checked it with the hospital administration."

Finally, Karmjit's uncharacteristic behavior made sense; he must be hoping for Jaggi to be a match. Jaggi recalled the doctor's words about the wealthy exploiting the poor for their organs. A possible ticket to saving his daughter's life, and if I died, they wouldn't care. It made Jaggi upset to be used this way.

Quickly, Jaggi became disgusted at his sudden hesitation. No matter how personally offended Jaggi was by her father, he could not deny Navi the chance to live. Any risk to his life was worth the reward. With his resolve firm, he decided to broach the subject of his caste.

"Do you know what my caste is?"

"It doesn't matter, bete. We know you are a Jat. Navi told us how she enjoyed driving the tractor when she visited your village," Karmjit answered.

"We do farm, but I am not a Jat," his tongue was slightly sharp now. "Perhaps Navi didn't want to hurt your feelings by telling the whole truth. I am an outcaste, a Keera. My family farms rented land, and we live in the Keera basti of Kundyan."

"What?" Karmjit sputtered, nearly choking on his tea. "How could you do this to our daughter?" No one else spoke a word; even the buzz of the cafeteria seemed to go silent.

Karmjit's response brought Jaggi back to Simmie's reaction, and a feeling of dread overcame him. Deciding he was still too unnerved to stick around for more attacks, he got up and left.

Once Jaggi left the room, Parveen turned with fire in her eyes.

"Karmjit, what is wrong with you?"

"Do you expect me to let an untouchable marry my only daughter? Do a *milni*," he spat, thinking of having to hug Jaggi's father, "with a Keera?"

"If you don't, your only daughter will die." Parveen's said quietly, causing a heavy silence at the table.

"Papa, we can arrange for a court marriage and not go through any ceremonies," Raman suggested.

Karmjit started to nod, coming around to this as the only option to save Navi's life. "Yes, a court marriage, then we do the transplant, and they can divorce immediately afterward. We can pay him whatever he wants. Surely it'd be more than he'd ever earn in his lifetime."

"Mr. Chawla," Parveen said, her voice dripping with contempt, "you make me sick. A man loves your daughter and is willing to make the sacrifice that even your son won't make. She is dying, and you are concerned about his caste? It's perfectly fine with me if you don't want to attend the wedding. I'll do the milni with his mother."

Chastised, Raman looked away as he stood to leave with his father.

"Raman," Parveen said authoritatively, "make sure you take Jaggi home with you."

It was past seven when they got back to Navi's room. Jaggi was sitting in a chair beside her bed; their hands clasped together.

"Jaggi bete, we are going home now," Parveen said, "you will ride with Raman."

"Mom, can you make arrangements for him at the Oberoi-Sheraton?" Navi intervened. "The hotel is practically next door. He can walk to it and spend more time with me."

"It must be expensive," Jaggi said, looking at Navi.

"Don't be ridiculous," Parveen said, "Raman will take care of it. I still wish you would stay with us, though."

It was settled; Raman left to book the hotel and have the front desk hold the key for Jaggi.

They said their byes and left Jaggi with Navi. Parveen returned shortly after. "Bete, can I talk to you for a minute?" she said, motioning to the door. Jaggi followed, gently closing the door behind them.

"Bete, to be a living donor for Navi should be your entire family's decision, not ours. Either way, we have no objection to your marrying our daughter. I knew about your caste before Navi got sick. But before you commit to Navi about the surgery, I would like you to talk to your parents and get their approval." She hugged him and left.

Jaggi looked on admiringly. Navi has taken after her, he thought.

"What was that about?" prompted Navi when he stepped in the doorway.

"Can't I hug my future mother-in-law?" Jaggi said with a smile in his voice.

"They agreed?" she asked.

"Yes," Jaggi nodded, holding her hand as he sat on the stool near her.

The nurse brought Navi's food and left the room, bidding them good night.

"Jaggi, I am done. Can you please move this away?" she said after a few minutes.

She had taken only a tiny bite of fish and nibbled on her rice; the plate looked virtually untouched.

"You haven't eaten anything. How can you stay healthy if you don't eat?"

"I am not hungry," she replied sullenly.

"Let me help you." He cut out a piece of the fish, extending it to her on the fork; she begrudgingly took the bite. He got her to eat half of her food and juice in this manner.

As he left her room for the evening, their last date flashed in his mind at their favorite Guangzhou Moon, a Chinese eatery.

"You like pecking at my food, don't you," Jaggi would say whenever she reached across the table with her fork.

"Your fish looks more appealing," she would answer. Navi always finished her food before Jaggi, almost inhaling it.

"I just have a good appetite," she would say.

The memory brought a sad smile to Jaggi's face.

The next day, Jaggi spoke with Dr. Mehta, letting him know his intention. In return, Dr. Mehta made sure that Jaggi understood the risks of the surgery and the stringent requirement that their marriage had to happen before the surgery. He assured the doctor that he understood and intended a quick trip to Kundyan to get his parents' approval.

Karmjit and Parveen came to the hospital early in the morning, and Karmjit had been sitting stiffly, not making eye contact with anyone. Navi wanted to discuss the nuptials. Karmjit's face went tight. "It will have to be a court marriage," he said without looking at anyone, his voice devoid of emotion.

Jaggi looked at him, unsurprised by the offensive comment. A regular marriage involves celebrations, a mingling, where each family recognizes the other, showing mutual respect. That would signify Karmjit openly accepting him as his son-in-law. A court marriage, one in papers only, would allow saving his daughter's life but keep Jaggi's identity hidden from their community.

Calling from his resolve from yesterday, Jaggi calmly shook his head.

"No, I will not agree with that, nor would my parents."

Karmjit turned to him sharply, opening his mouth to yell abuse at Jaggi presumably.

"And I wouldn't agree to a court marriage, either," Navi quickly interrupted, louder than her lungs allowed, and she fell into a coughing fit for a minute.

"Chawla Sahib," Parveen chastised from her seat, "do you have no shame?" Jaggi looked at her. Tears were beginning to well out of her eyes. She tried to hide her agony, her sense of guilt hitting her hard. There was complete silence in the room. Parveen got up and went to Jaggi to put her hands on his shoulders.

"Why are you saving our daughter, bete? Who are we to you?" she said, looking into his eyes, searching for something.

Jaggi held her gaze. "Because I love her. Because my life would be nothing without her," he said simply.

Parveen's shoulders, seeing the earnestness in his face, sagged in relief.

"Thank you, bete. We owe you a debt of gratitude," she said, holding his hands tightly.

Chapter 27

Jaggi left for Kundyan, intending to return as soon as possible. The dreaded conversations with his parents occupied his mind. Jaggi saw his trip home as having two goals. First was securing official approval for the marriage, which he wasn't worried about—they had tacitly given it during Navi's visit. It was the second conversation, his decision to undergo a complex and risky surgery to save his wife's life, that made him anxious. The irony was not lost on him; the otherwise celebratory news of the first would be completely negated by the second conversation.

Jaggi dreaded conveying the need for surgery without causing pain; the mere thought made him tense and quickened his breathing; no amount of body scanning could relieve his dread.

It was getting dark. Bindo, just having finished her sewing work for the day, was getting ready to make dinner. Teja had also returned from the farm. They were surprised to see Jaggi home, on a weekday, in the middle of his summer term, without calling beforehand.

"I'm happy to see you, bete, but how come you are here in the middle of the week?" Bindo enquired after greeting him.

First, Jaggi thought of talking about Navi's visa and her parents agreeing to their marriage. But then, instead of beating around the bush, he decided to blurt out the dreaded.

"Navi—she is very sick. She is going to die, maa."

Shock crossed her face. "Oh, my puttar, what happened to her? She had no problem when she was here!" she said.

Jaggi explained to them how she needed a new liver and could get a cadaver liver only if one were available to them. He stopped short of talking about the live-donor option for her.

There was a long silence between them.

"Poor girl. Why did it have to happen to her?" Bindo said. She couldn't see her son hurting like that. "What are they going to do now?"

"There's another way." His face grew very calm as he spoke. He needed to be strong when telling them the rest of the story, not emotional. "These days," he continued, "they can take a part of someone else's liver and use it instead, even if they are alive. The remaining liver grows back to its full size in just three months. It's amazing science, maa," Jaggi said, a flash of his intellect piercing through his tears. "However, the person giving the liver has to be related to the patient," he added.

"So that means they can take that piece from one of her parents!"

"Well, that's what they would normally do. But the doctors consider the blood group and age of the donor first. Navi's mother doesn't have the right blood group. Her father does, but he is too old. The hospital doesn't take a liver from people older than fifty."

"She has two brothers, no?" Bindo asked.

"Yes, but her brothers can't give either." He felt terrible telling a lie, but he couldn't tell them the whole truth. For his mother's heart, God would surely forgive a part lie.

Bindo knew her son too well and didn't like where the discussion was heading. In his expression and tone of voice, she could read what he wasn't saying—at least, not yet.

"We must have faith in God, Jaggi, and if He wants, He will make something work, and if He doesn't, may God bless her," she said with sudden terseness, then got up to make the beds.

The discussion ended there. After they retired for the night and Jaggi went to his room, Bindo opened up to Teja.

"I am worried," she said. "Do you think the girl's parents pressure Jaggi to give his liver so their sons aren't put through the risk of a big operation? How can one normally live with just half of an organ? God gave us a whole liver for a reason."

"Didn't Jaggi say the person giving the liver has to be related to the patient? Jaggi is not related to her, so he can't be considered," Teja said.

"Marriage is a relation, Sardar Ji. I bet they will agree to their union just for this procedure," Bindo said, trembling.

Teja took her in his arms; they had both seen the resolve on Jaggi's face. No words would bring Bindo relief.

As usual, Teja left for the fields the following day before Jaggi woke up. When Jaggi was up, Bindo brought him his food.

"Your food," she said and walked away. Jaggi found the silence suffocating. He also knew her well and could guess what went through her mind. He wished she would sit with him so they could talk about it, just like they had always been able to since he was a small boy embarrassed by his stutter.

"Maa, can I have some mango pickle, please?"

She brought the small pickle container and a spoon. She silently set it on the stool and turned to leave when Jaggi grabbed her arm. She looked back at him.

"Can I please talk to you, maa?" he pleaded.

Bindo dragged a low stool to his side and looked at the floor without saying anything.

"Maa, Navi needs my help," he said.

Bindo didn't say anything. She moved only her hands, covering her face, shoulders beginning to shake with unseen sobs.

Stricken by sight, Jaggi moved to gently move her hands, attempting to look into her eyes with the strength he did not feel. He got up and, kneeling by her stool, put his right arm over her shoulders.

"You are all I have! I cannot lose you, not even for your love!" she said, her eyes drowning in tears.

"But nothing is going to happen to me. I promise, maa!"

"If it is so easy, they have two sons, why don't they do it?"

"Maa, I told you—."

"Yes, you told me," she interrupted him. "But I don't believe that for a minute. Her real brothers have bad blood, and you have the right kind? How is that possible? I am not stupid, Jaggi."

Jaggi could not argue with that—she was too smart to fool.

"Maa, her parents have agreed to our marriage," Jaggi said.

Bindo would have been excited to hear the news if not for the circumstances. Now, it came across as an act of their selfishness, as Jaggi knew it would.

"To count you as her relative," she said sarcastically, relieving Jaggi. He could handle her anger, not her tears.

"Maa, I love her with my heart. Even if we are not married, it doesn't mean I love her any less."

"Bete, they live in a big city and have three children. But here in Kundyan, all I have is you, and I always hoped that you would grow up and have a better life than we do. God forbid, if something happen to you, what will we live for? Who will care for us as we grow old? Who will light your father's pyre?"

"Maa, listen to me! I talked to the doctor, and he assured me I would be okay. Besides, it is a perfect hospital, the best I have ever seen. The doctors and nurses are so good, and everything is sparkling clean."

Bindo ignored his comment about the hospital. "They are their doctors, Bete, on their side, not ours," she said. "I don't trust them to take care of my son. All doctors are after money, not making people healthy. The bigger the operation, the more money they make."

Chasing Dignity

"All doctors are not bad, maa! If you want, we can talk to another doctor. Someone you know and trust," he said. "We can talk to Dr. Khera," Jaggi proposed, thinking of the doctor he saw for his stutter throughout childhood.

Bindo didn't answer. Jaggi took this as an assurance to continue.

"Think about it this way, maa," he said. "If you got sick like that, would it be wrong for baau ji to take a risk to save your life? Do you think it would be easy for me to live the rest of my life knowing I could have saved her but chose not to?"

Bindo remained silent, sitting completely still as he finished his food.

Jaggi got up and kissed her on the head as he left, saying he'd be back later, and he went for a walk. He walked toward Rani's house, but remembering she was away at school, he changed his mind and decided to go to the Gurdwara.

There was no one at the Gurdwara when he arrived, not even the priest. Jaggi opened the doors and walked to the holy Granth. He took out a five rupee note from his pocket, put it in the wooden coffer, and kneeled, lowering his forehead to the ground in supplication. He slowly stood up, keeping his eyes closed and hands clasped and prayed: 'I know I have sometimes doubted and argued your existence, and I don't deserve to ask you anything. But you know a part of me always believed you exist; if you do, you alone can help me. I want you to help Navi to recover fully. I want a happy life with her, but if only one of us can live, please let her be the one you save.'

Jaggi spent well over an hour at the Gurdwara, contemplating while sitting in his favorite spot.

When Jaggi returned, Teja was home. Teja and Bindo had apparently talked about the issue because as soon as he sat down, Bindo broached the subject.

"Does that lady-doctor Gill at the university, the one you talk about sometimes, still work there?" she said. Jaggi often spoke highly of her, and Bindo had taken a liking to the doctor from his stories. Bindo felt comfortable with the idea of talking to another woman about her concern.

"Yes, and she is a good doctor," Jaggi said.

"Can you take me to Patiala?" she said. "I would like to meet with her."

"Sure, Maa, we can go tomorrow," Jaggi said and called Dr. Gill to set up the meeting.

That night Teja gave his opinion to Bindo. "If the liver grows back, Jaggi should help Navi.'

Jaggi and Bindo met with Dr. Gill in Chacha Chimna's canteen. They were the only customers at the odd hour. Bindo wanted to talk to the doctor alone and bade Jaggi give them privacy.

"Sure, I'll go to the library," Jaggi said. "Is an hour enough time?"

"Yes," Bindo said with a nod, and Jaggi left. Jaggi was cautiously optimistic; he knew how much Dr. Gill loved Navi and hoped her advice would favor his decision to save Navi's life. On the other hand, she was a mother herself, and he could imagine her sympathizing with Bindo.

"Now, while I am excited to meet you finally, I know this is not a social visit. What can I do for you?" Dr. Gill asked.

"Doctor Sahib, do you have a child?" she asked.

"Yes, I do; my son is a couple of years older than Jaggi. He is married."

"Would you ever let him do what Jaggi wants to do for Navi, this liver transplant?"

Dr. Gill was prepared to answer Bindo's technical questions but had to think hard before answering this one.

"*Bhen ji*, it would be a lie if I told you there is no risk in doing what Jaggi wants to do." She looked at Bindo as if to see her reaction. Bindo sat stone-faced.

"However, having said that, what assurance do we have that any of us will live past today? The two of us could die in an accident on our way home from tea—many terrible things are liable to happen to us at any moment."

Bindo's eyes shifted slightly at that comment.

"I am not saying that I would not hesitate to let my son donate his liver because there is substantial risk involved. But if he is doing it for someone he loves so dearly, it's all worth it, in my opinion," Dr. Gill said solemnly. "Why?" she continued. "Because I am also looking at the other side, for whom it is a matter of life or death. If my son could give the gift of life to his loved one, even if it involves risk, I will make myself agreeable with it."

Dr. Gill watched as Bindo processed her words.

"How much risk will Jaggi take going through this whole thing, doctor? Will he be living healthy just with half the liver? He told us the doctors assured him, but I don't believe him," Bindo asked.

"If the operation is done in a good hospital, Jaggi will most likely come out of the surgery safely. And as far as I know, Ram Dyal Hospital is one of the best in the country; just as good a hospital in the USA or Canada," Dr. Gill explained.

"Is it true that Jaggi's liver will grow back to full size?" Bindo asked.

"Yes, that is true. Doctors have been doing this operation successfully for many years, and from what we know, Jaggi's liver will grow back to full function and almost full size. The bigger question is whether Navi's body accepts Jaggi's liver. No one can guarantee that, but without trying, she will surely die."

Bindo was hanging onto every word.

"How close are you to the girl's family?" she asked the doctor.

Taken aback at the sudden change of questioning, Dr. Gill decided to be completely truthful.

"We are very close. Navi was born here in Patiala, and I have known her since she was a toddler. Navi's father is my husband's childhood friend, and we lived in the same neighborhood in Patiala before they moved to Delhi. We still visit each other regularly."

"May I ask you something personal?"

Dr. Gill nodded with a small laugh, wondering how Bindo could get more personal than she already had.

"It sounds like you love Navi quite a bit."

"I do," Dr. Gill said, "but that isn't a question."

"You wouldn't be hiding any risks from me because you want to save Navi?" Bindo asked with a searching gaze.

Dr. Gill went quiet but refused to apologize, her eyes visibly welling with emotion. But Bindo needed to hear the answer and waited in silence.

After a time, the doctor spoke, wiping away two rebellious droplets. "There are many doctors, but you came to get my opinion because you trusted me, right?"

Bindo nodded in agreement.

"I can't claim I love Jaggi the way you do as a mother, but I've come to love him in my own right over the past two years. He's a wonderful young man, and I could never wish any harm to him. I only want his life with Navi to work out and for them to be happy together."

Bindo cupped Dr. Gill's hands in understanding, and neither spoke for a minute.

"Is it true that neither of her brothers can donate?" Bindo asked.

"I can't answer that question, and I don't know about your family's relationship. However, if I needed a sacrifice like this, I don't think my brother would volunteer before my husband."

Dr. Gill's answer calmed Bindo down. She recalled what Jaggi had said to her, and she could envision Teja doing the same for her before anyone else did.

Bindo thought for a while. "It will shatter Jaggi if something happens to that girl, and he will never forgive me for it. His father agrees with him as well. I suppose I have to agree, too," she said.

When Jaggi returned, he could sense tranquility in the air. The two women sat relaxed, seeing a comfortable camaraderie as they spoke. The earlier agitation from his mother's face had disappeared. Clearly, Dr. Gill had soothed her. He breathed a sigh of relief at the matching smiles on the women's faces as they turned to him, knowing his mother would support the marriage.

"When is the operation scheduled?" Dr. Gill asked Jaggi as he sat.

"The hospital couldn't set a date yet. Navi's doctor told me we had to be married before considering me a donor. The surgery, he said, can be scheduled immediately after that."

"Based on Navi's condition, the surgery cannot be delayed for much longer," Dr. Gill said.

"But what about the wedding, the plans, the family?" Bindo interjected.

"Maa, we can only invite a few people, only those very close to us. Navi is not in a condition to go through a big wedding," Jaggi said.

"He is right—a big wedding will take both time and energy, and right now, we have neither. You can always throw a reception when Navi comes out of the hospital, well and healthy," Dr. Gill said, offering a smile to counter Bindo's fraught expression. Indian weddings are about joining two families, not only two people. The loss of the community joy for Jaggi clearly pained Bindo.

"Doctor Sahib, I still need some time to take all this in, to tell my husband and relatives, to pray."

"Bhen ji, if you decide to go ahead, I'll help you with all the arrangements. I'll come with you to Delhi, and we'll do it together. We have a friend there, Dr. Kooner, an old classmate of my husband, and we can stay at his house," said Dr. Gill.

"Thank you so much for your support. I can see why Jaggi speaks of you so fondly," Bindo said while hugging Dr. Gill tightly. Bindo and Jaggi returned to Kundyan. Later that evening, Bindo eventually called Dr. Gill to tell her their consent.

After a brief call with the Chawlas, they decided the wedding would take place in three days, with only close family attendance. During the wedding and surgery, Dr. Gill would take time off work to be with Bindo and her family in Delhi.

As Bindo later fell asleep, she finally allowed herself to become excited at the prospect of a new daughter-in-law who would support Jaggi in achieving his dreams for the future.

Jaggi departed for Delhi first thing the following morning. While traveling back to Delhi, he felt like he could finally take a full breath. He could not bear the thought of losing Navi. The following day, Jaggi spent a long evening with Navi and her family discussing the wedding. Afterward, when he went to the hotel, he stopped at an internet café to send his only two wedding invitations

Chasing Dignity

to Himmat and Rani. He briefly explained the circumstances and hoped they would be able to attend. He recalled Navi's visit to Kundyan, with vivid images of her and Rani riding the tractor. The two were so similar—bold, intelligent, straightforward. Of course, they got along so well. Both cared for him, and he cared for them both.

Chapter 28

To avoid unnecessary delays in surgery, the hospital administration allowed Jaggi's required testing before their wedding. They drew vials and vials of blood—more than he'd ever seen—and asked him to fill out a lengthy questionnaire about his family's medical history.

Jaggi's parents and Himmat arrived at the Kooners' home early Saturday with Dr. Gill and her husband.

Dr. Harmeet Kooner, an orthopedic surgeon, was an old friend and classmate of Davinder Gill. His wife, Surinder, was a part-time teacher in a private school. Their children were grown and out of the house, leaving the elder Kooners their big mansion to themselves. When Dr. Gill told them about Navi and Jaggi, they were deeply moved and wholeheartedly agreed to participate in the wedding. They promised they would do whatever was needed to accommodate the families and give the event the semblance of a traditional wedding as much as possible.

Jaggi joined them at lunch to plan for the wedding:

The Chawlas would arrange the priest, the holy book, and the food for the guests. The groom's party would meet with them around 11 a.m. at the hospital—the hospital had allowed their conference room for the rituals to avoid undue travel exertion on Navi. Navi insisted she had enough strength to walk independently and go through full-blown ceremonies. Still, they arranged for a shortened formality, opting for thirty minutes instead of the traditional three hours.

That evening, Jaggi went to Navi to relay the plans. He stopped short with surprise and delight; Rani was in the room, putting henna on Navi's hands. That was Rani's hobby, Jaggi knew, something she picked up in school.

"You didn't tell me Rani was coming," Navi complained.

"Honestly, I didn't know if she could make it. I wasn't even sure she would get a chance to look at her email," Jaggi said, "but I'm glad she did."

"Veer ji, you know we have internet access on campus, and I read my email daily without a miss," Rani said, "I responded right away too, but I realize you are too busy with other things to worry about your email."

Jaggi nodded gratefully at Rani, surprised at how relieved he was to see her.

Navi lay back against the raised bed and watched with awe how henna flowed effortlessly from the cone. "How do you like the design I selected? Isn't it beautiful?" Navi said when she noticed Jaggi looking at the open page of Rani's patterns book. Rani was working on her left hand, having finished with the right.

"Oh, it's beautiful," Jaggi said.

Navi's nightly medicine included a sedative, and she soon fell asleep. Jaggi helped Rani finish her design by holding her hand open, even as she slept, so that the henna wouldn't smear. They waited more than an hour in silence, gently keeping Navi's palms open by her fingertips. By the time henna dried, Navi was comfortably asleep, and they left to join the rest of the family at the Kooners.

"Jaggi veer, what you are doing is a perilous endeavor," Rani said on their way to the Kooners. Her statement startled Jaggi, though it shouldn't have. She had always worried about his well-being; he should have expected no less.

"Have you thought about the alternative? The risk to Navi's life?" Jaggi's tone was sharp. Rani did not respond.

That night even the Kooners' luxurious bed couldn't help Bindo fall asleep. She lay awake for hours after dark, nervous and fidgety. She had always dreamed of a traditional two-day wedding for Jaggi; what was happening tomorrow was anything but that. A beautiful scene played out in her mind when she drifted to sleep.

In the dream, the guests had arrived for the ceremony. The men were drinking and gossiping away while the women, divided into two groups—*nankian*—from the groom's mother's side, and *dadkian*—the groom's father's side, were dancing, singing, teasing, and taking the traditional jibes at each other. The dream advanced to the morning of the second day. Jaggi was sitting on a stool in his shorts, getting the ceremonial bath from Rani and his female cousins, rubbing his face, arms, and back with *vatnna*—a paste prepared with oil, barley flour, and turmeric. Then Bindo watched the male guests and neighbors board a charted bus, accompanying Jaggi to the bride's village, while the women stayed back and had their festivities. Jaggi returned in the evening, and all the neighborhood women gathered to see the bride.

She woke up with a jolt when she was about to lift the veil from the bride's face. Jaggi wasn't bringing his bride home; he was going to the hospital to be cut open on a surgeon's table, and a part of his body—the body she had grown and loved inside her own—was to be taken out. Her heart jumped to her throat; she got up and started pacing around the room. It wasn't until four in the morning that she went back to sleep.

At 5:40, she woke to a knock at her door.

"Bhen ji, come out." It was Surinder. "The breakfast is ready."

Bindo was shocked to see the setup. The Kooners had prepared an elaborate spread, and everyone was there eating except Jaggi. Bindo took a cup of tea and a cookie.

"Jaggi isn't up yet?" she asked.

"He's getting ready for the vatnna; we will do that over there," Rani said, pointing to the veranda on the far side.

Bindo's gaze moved to the water vapors rising from a bucket of warm water set on the veranda, and there was a small low wooden stool with a bowl of *vatnna* placed next to it. Her heart melted at the hospitality of the Kooners. They were trying their best to make the wedding appear as normal as possible.

Jaggi was finally ready, and his apparel, arranged by Dr. Gill, was beautiful. Bindo looked with awe at her broad-chested, six-foot-tall son, dressed in a *sherwani*, a chaplet, and an aigrette decorating his turban. 'He looks like a prince.' Bindo smiled, remembering how she tied his turban on the first day of his school, her fingers fumbling at the task. Bindo was overwhelmed with gratitude.

"Is there a Gurdwara nearby?" Bindo asked.

"Yes, bhen ji, it is very close," Surinder said, "we'll stop there on our way to take the Guru's blessings."

They arrived at the hospital at ten-thirty. The first ritual, after a prayer by the priest, was the fathers' milni—their official introduction, where the two would exchange garlands and hug each other. Unaware of the dynamics, the priest invited Teja and Karmjit for the milni. Immediately, Karmjit blurted: "No, we don't need any milni." They looked at him, stunned.

Parveen immediately moved forward. "We mothers will do the milni," she said, inviting Bindo to perform the ritual. Karmjit did not greet any member of the groom's party, including the Gills and the Kooners. The rest of the Chawlas greeted and fed the groom's party and they all settled in front of the holy book.

It was time for the bride's arrival, and Parveen went to get her. Navi walked slowly but elegantly, with one of her arms in her mother's and the other in her friend's. Navi was wearing a red *choli*. An elegant pearl necklace and long dangling earrings accentuated her long neck. Red and golden bangles filled Navi's arms, and her hands were decorated with Rani's exquisite henna. Mesmerized by Navi's beauty and big eyes, Bindo forgot what had transpired just a moment ago or that Navi was sick; she looked like a newly landed angel.

After paying obeisance to the holy book, Navi joined Jaggi. Her face glowed to see him dressed so handsomely. Bindo stood there, admiring the beautiful couple, and all her fears and concerns stood stock-still. Navi and Jaggi bowed to the holy Granth and sat down to let the *Anand Karj*—the sacred ritual of the Sikh wedding—begin.

Eighteen people were present, only a fraction of what the guest list might have been, but the attendance seemed enough for the occasion; all the right people were there to grace the occasion.

As advised, the priest had condensed the ceremony to less than half an hour. After refusing to participate in the milni, Karmjit sat stiffly in his place. Parveen alone assumed all the parental roles. He disappeared immediately after the Anand Karj concluded.

Even the short ceremony exhausted Navi, and Jaggi took her back to her room.

"Hold me tight, Jaggi, my husband," Navi said, hugging him when in the room.

"Congratulations, we did it; we are now husband and wife," Jaggi responded with a kiss and a gentle embrace. Navi lay in the bed, and Jaggi sat by her side. A sweet, comfortable silence engulfed them; they had accomplished a feat.

After the guests had lunch, Parveen approached Teja and Bindo, addressing them with folded hands. "Veer ji, bhen ji, we will be indebted to you forever for this generosity. Our daughter had no hope without Jaggi's sacrifice." She broke down, hugging Bindo, "I'm ashamed of my husband's behavior."

Chapter 29

A day after the wedding, Teja, Himmat, and Rani departed, but Dr. Gill and Bindo stayed behind.

Jaggi had to sit with a counselor to ensure he was emotionally fit for the procedure. "You have the right to change your mind right up to the time of the operation," the counselor told him. Despite his nerves, Jaggi's resolve held strong. He would save his wife's life.

Finally, it was time for the transplant. Jaggi would be the first to go into surgery; Navi would follow an hour later. After the part of Jaggi's liver was taken out successfully, they would immediately start operating on Navi.

Jaggi met with his mother. She hugged him, "Worry not, bete. Waheguru is with you," she said firmly.

Jaggi had been to Navi's room early that morning, but he wanted to see her one last time before he went in. Navi was awake, lying in bed, looking at the door expecting him. Jaggi sat next to her on the bed, holding her hand.

"I am going in. Are you ready?" Jaggi asked.

"Give me a hug," she said, extending her arms, and Jaggi bent down to embrace her. It was a special moment for them; when they met again after the surgery, a part of Jaggi's body would be living within Navi's. "Yes, I'm ready," she said, squeezing him as best as she could. "Thank you."

"No thank-yous are necessary between husband and wife," Jaggi said with a choked voice. They hugged again before he left the room, quickly turning so she couldn't see his tears.

At eight in the morning, Jaggi was taken to the operating room on a stretcher. A man in scrubs set up an IV drip in Jaggi's right arm. After an eternity of questions by the hospital staff, making Jaggi more anxious with each, they once more offered Jaggi the opportunity to back out.

"You still have the opportunity to back out if you desire," said Dr. Hiteshi, the surgeon.

"No, sir, I am ready, " Jaggi responded, bolder than necessary. Before he went under anesthesia, Jaggi's final thought was of seeing Navi again.

It was almost noon, and the waiting room had an uneasy quiet. Dr. Gill, familiar with these long waits, had brought a book that kept her busy. But the other three, sitting in the small, confined chairs, were getting restless and bored by the minute.

"I need a cup of tea," Karmjit announced, getting up. "Let's go sit over there in the cafeteria."

Parveen nodded, and they followed him to the cafeteria without saying anything.

Karmjit ordered tea and asked if anyone wanted a snack. Bindo and Parveen shook their heads no.

"Bindo bhen ji, eat something. You haven't eaten anything all day," Dr. Gill said.

"I am not hungry," Bindo said.

"I will order for all of us," Karmjit said and bought pre-wrapped rolls of paranthas.

When they returned to the waiting room, they had moved Jaggi to the recovery, and two visitors were allowed in; Dr. Gill went with Bindo. After six hours of anxiously waiting and perspiring, Bindo was finally in the same room as her son. She clasped her hands and closed her eyes to thank God.

Jaggi was asleep, with several tubes attached to him. His face was calm, and Bindo gently touched his legs and arms, feeling his body's aliveness. He still looked whole, though she knew a part of him was missing. She judiciously watched his chest rise and fall with each breath. She squeezed Dr. Gill's arm with relief. A little later, a nurse requested that they return to the waiting room. "We will let you know when we move him to the general ward in a couple of hours. By then, he will be awake," she said.

They did not expect Navi to be out of surgery for another six to eight hours.

"I think we should all go home now to get some rest and come back in a few hours," Dr. Gill suggested.

"You all go. I will stay," Bindo said. She wanted to be there when Jaggi woke up.

"We are all going to wait," Parveen said.

As a doctor, Dr. Gill was used to this response from families and knew their good intentions wouldn't help them in the long run. "Jaggi is out of the operation, and Navi will not be out for another few hours," she said. "Your being here does not help either of them. Go home and take a nap so you are fresh when you return. That way, you can be more helpful if they need you."

Bindo was adamant about staying in the building with her son to be the first person to greet him.

Dr. Gill could relate to Bindo's request as a mother. "Bhaji, you two go and come back in a few hours before Navi comes out of surgery," she said to Karmjit. "I will stay with Bindo bhen ji. We'll call you if we need you here."

"Please call us as soon as you get any news," Parveen said, and they left.

"Jaggi is sleeping now, sedated. He won't wake up for a couple of hours. Why don't we go out, stretch our legs, and eat something?" said Dr. Gill.

Bindo agreed; with her tension subsided, she was hungry now.

They drove to a restaurant, and Dr. Gill ordered food for both.

"You know how much I prayed to God this past week?" Bindo said.

"I can imagine. You are a brave woman, and you have a brave son. You gave Navi the gift of life. She'll remember that forever, as will her family."

"I am not brave, bhen ji. I have been so scared!"

"Bindo bhen, getting scared does not mean you are not brave. Everyone gets scared. Thanks to Jaggi's sacrifice, Navi will get better soon. They will live a long and happy life together."

They talked for a while when Dr. Gill brought up the subject of Karmjit's behavior during the wedding. "I'm so sorry, Karmjit refused to do the milni with your husband," she said.

"Being born a low caste gives you thick skin, bhen ji. Slowly, you get immune to this kind of insult. You can't punish yourself for every comment the world makes against you," Bindo said. But then she seemed to be overcome with emotion. "Our son put his life at stake for this man's daughter, and he has no appreciation for it. Now being married to Navi, Jaggi will have to deal with him all his life. I hope they can learn to respect each other one day."

Chatting with Dr. Gill and sitting in a comfortable chair away from the waiting room helped Bindo relax. The drinks came, followed by their food.

"Do you know something, Gill bhen ji? I had always imagined Jaggi's wedding to be so elegant. I even had a dream about it the night before. For Jaggi's whole life, our friends, cousins, and neighbors had been looking forward to his wedding. But we could not invite any of them," Bindo lamented.

"Don't worry; we will have a grand party once Navi gets well."

They ate their food and chatted for a while when Bindo reminded her it was time to return to the hospital. She had been watching the clock on the wall behind Dr. Gill.

Jaggi had been moved to a private room in the general ward. Lying in bed and still groggy, he had a sore throat. Jaggi had some confusion about the surgery. He remembered giving his consent to the operation and almost soon after hearing the surgery was successful. He looked around the room, trying to remember the day's events.

He saw his mother enter. "Maa," he said, gently pushing his right hand on the bed.

Bindo took his hand in her own and bent down to kiss it.

"How are you, Jaggi?" Dr. Gill said, moving to the other side of the bed.

"Fine," he said faintly, with a nod.

"He hasn't fully recovered from the sedation yet," the nurse said, watching their interaction.

"It is all right; we are in no rush. Let him take his time," Dr. Gill said.

Bindo was now caressing his head, moving her fingers through his loose topknot, lost in his childhood memories when she held him in her lap and read stories at night.

The room had a three-seater sofa and two chairs. Bindo and Dr. Gill settled on the couch. They were now comfortable with each other and could touch upon all sorts of subjects, ranging from their families to the funny tales from their lives.

Dr. Gill was impressed that, coming from a rural background with limited education, Bindo was so easy to talk to and had such a liberal outlook. She saw why Jaggi was so proud of his mother and always spoke about her with such reverence.

Dr. Gill called Parveen to let her know Jaggi was out of recovery.

Parveen returned a little past six in the evening. "Karmjit was busy and will be here later," she informed. Jaggi was awake and alert. He knew Navi had been in the operation theater for more than eight hours.

"Her operation will take longer," Dr. Gill tried to reassure Parveen. "They have to remove the diseased liver and ensure the new liver is attached properly."

Around 7:30 p.m., the nurse brought orange juice for Jaggi. He wasn't thirsty or hungry, but it was a nice distraction for them. Everyone pitched in some encouragement for him to drink and playfully clapped when he finished.

Staying in the private room was much less stressful than being among families in the waiting room, whose anxiety for their loved ones was contagious. Jaggi went to sleep, and Dr. Gill went back to her book. Parveen tried to engage Bindo in small talk. But Bindo was tired and fell asleep in her seat.

At ten past ten, the nurse finally brought them the good news; Navi was in recovery, but she would be moved to the ICU as soon as her sedation wore off. They could go and visit her, but only very briefly.

'Why would she be moved to the ICU?' said Parveen with worry.

"That is normal for the patients to go to ICU after transplants. The staff can closely watch the patient," explained Dr. Gill.

Chasing Dignity

Parveen called Karmjit, and they went to the ICU when he arrived. Navi was unconscious, and several tubes were attached to her, one going through her throat.

The nurse went to the doctor in the room and whispered something to him. He turned around to greet the visitors.

"I am Dr. Pandey," he said, walking toward them. "I performed surgery on this young lady. Congratulations, she did very well!"

"Thank you, sir," Karmjit said, shaking hands with him.

"When do you think she will be out of the ICU?"

"Probably in a day, maybe two. We will likely take her off the ventilator by tomorrow."

Two days later, Navi was also moved to a private room on a different floor. They both were recovering well. Satisfied, Dr. Gill and Bindo left for Punjab.

Being on different floors, Navi and Jaggi could not see each other. They knew how the other was doing, but it wasn't enough. One night, after visitors were gone and the hospital staff settled for the night mode, Jaggi snuck into the hallway dressed in his regular clothes and made it to Navi's floor. He was about to turn the door handle when a nurse came out of the next room. Jaggi immediately pulled back and froze. The nurse looked at him, nodded her head, and walked away with a small smile of recognition, saying nothing.

When Jaggi crept inside, Navi was asleep. She opened her eyes, looking confused for a moment, trying to figure out who was sitting on her bed. Jaggi gently took her hand into his.

"Jaggi!" she started and tried to sit up.

"Shhhh," Jaggi said and stopped her from moving.

"What are you doing here?" she whispered. "You should be in bed."

Jaggi smiled, "I know. I couldn't resist," he said, locking fingers with her with one hand and stroking her forehead.

"We did it," he said as they looked at one another. "Together, we did it."

Navi smiled, "Yes, we did it, thanks to you," she said, setting her hand on his cheek.

Jaggi stayed in her room for half an hour, not talking much, just enjoying each other's company. Although he wanted to, he did not lie down with her; Jaggi knew her wounds were not in the same healing stage as his, and he didn't want to hurt her.

After sneaking into her room for two more nights, Jaggi was released from the hospital. Parveen offered their home, but Jaggi preferred the hotel. "It's a lot closer to Navi," he argued. Neither of them mentioned Karmjit.

After six long weeks of recovery, they released Navi from the hospital. Her vitals were normal, but she was to return for weekly check-ups. Doctor Mehta gave Jaggi and Navi special instructions: "You can be intimate if you have the energy. However, you should avoid pregnancy for at least a year." Knowing how blessed they were for Navi to be alive, they accepted the advice without question.

This time Parveen and Navi insisted Jaggi stay at their house. Jaggi relented, his love of Navi being more significant than his dislike of Karmjit. Jaggi and Navi would share her old bedroom. It looked different when she walked in for the first time, much to her surprise: a massive, king-size bed and two elegant nightstands had replaced her narrow twin bed. A hand-painted ceramic pitcher of water, covered with a decorative plate, an empty glass, and a little gift bag, lay on the nightstand; marigold garlands decorated the wall above. A large, nicely framed wedding picture of them was adorning the wall opposite.

"You don't look sick in that picture," Jaggi said.

"I can't describe the exhilaration I experienced wearing that dress. I felt no sickness during that moment. The wedding gave me a new chance to live," she said, closing her eyes and taking a long, relaxed breath.

"That's all behind us now; let's look forward," Jaggi said, hugging her close.

"Well, on that note, how do you like my room?" Navi asked, pulling him onto the bed.

"Excuse me, but I thought, tonight it's *our* room. And how do I like it? It is gorgeous, but it pales in front of its stunning owner," he said, extracting a smile and a hug from Navi.

"What is that?" he said, looking at the little gift bag. Navi picked it up and looked inside. She began to laugh.

"What is it?"

"Looks like Dr. Mehta gave my mom the same talk," she said, pulling a condom strip from the bag.

"Oh, yea? Let's see who did a better job, your mom or your husband," he said, pulling a strip of condoms from his pocket and tossing it to Navi. She laughed; they were the same brand.

"Let's get comfortable," Navi said as she got off the bed and went to the closet. "Mom has set up one side of the closet for your clothes," she shouted.

Navi changed into light pajamas. "Why don't you change, too?" she said as she came out and sat on the bed. Jaggi quickly got into a t-shirt and shorts to join her.

Even though they were open in their relationship and could easily talk about sex and other matters of that nature, neither had experience with intimacy. Their bodies had recently gone through so much trauma that it created even more awkwardness as they tried to get close.

"Maybe just hold me to start," she said, getting under the sheet.

Jaggi wrapped his arm around her and pulled her close. He started stroking her back, and soon his hand sneaked under her shirt and began rubbing her shoulders.

"That feels good."

Her shirt had rolled up by now, and he pulled her left arm out, gently leaning her onto her back while playing with her left ear. His hairy arm, brushing her bare breast, was rousing. He took her shirt off, and Navi instinctively covered her breasts with her hands. He tried to move her hands, but she resisted. "No, first, you take your shirt off!"

He gladly obliged and took her back in his arms. She thought it was so marvelous to be held by a man.

He pushed himself up to take a better look at her body. He was enchanted, hesitatingly touching one breast and then the other, like a little boy who, given two new toys, didn't know which one to play with first. He slowly got rid of the remaining pieces of their clothing, playing gently and hungrily with her desires, making her forget the world around her.

Then he sat up, turning to the nightstand to retrieve the gift her mother had left in the goodie bag.

Navi held her breath in anticipation and nodded, realizing he was seeking permission. He stopped when he noticed her wince. "It is okay," she said, smiling in defiance of the pain, and pulled down on his buttocks.

They did not sleep until after three in the morning.

When Navi woke up, the clock showed 10:30. She smiled, realizing Jaggi was lying naked next to her. She quietly got out of bed and went to the bathroom. When she returned in pajamas, Jaggi was still sleeping with his back to her.

"Wake up, you shameless man, you are sleeping naked in my bed," she said, shaking him. He turned around and pulled her to him.

"It is late. We should go downstairs."

"I know," he mumbled, "just ten more minutes."

Navi slid down and put her arm under his head. Relishing in this new life she had begun, she was in no mood to get out of bed either.

It was past eleven when they finally went downstairs. Parveen was waiting for them. It was her daughter's first meal back home. She once doubted if Navi would make it from the hospital. "What would my puttar like for breakfast?" she asked.

"Your signature omelet with toast, mom," Navi answered. Parveen's omelet was unique indeed. She made it by frying her special ingredients and embedding them between folded omelet layers. Jaggi wanted cereal with milk. Karmjit had to go out for a few days on some business, Parveen told them. Bitu was out at school. Raman was at home, and he joined them at the table.

As they ate, they discussed their plans. They decided that as soon as Navi felt well, they would go to the US embassy to get a J-2, the student spousal visa. During those few days, Parveen went the extra mile to make Jaggi feel comfortable and accepted in the house. She cooked what he liked and ate when he ate. She deliberately chose affectionate expressions to emphasize that she considered him her son. Pency, Navi's little Chihuahua, quickly became Jaggi's best friend. Navi had Pency before she went to Patiala for her master's. Pency was much smaller and had a different personality than Jaggi's old Teepu, but Jaggi loved her. She would follow him around in the house and jump up in his lap at every chance.

Raman was polite to Jaggi. He would come and sit with him and talk to him about politics, his work, or Jaggi's writing. Bitu was indifferent and would interact with Jaggi as needed, but he was out of the house most of the time.

Soon, Navi felt well and wanted to visit the US embassy. Karmjit had returned the night before. He did not communicate directly with Jaggi except by nodding to his greetings. When Jaggi and Navi were ready to go to the embassy, Navi put two stapled papers in Jaggi's folder. It was a letter of financial support, Karmjit had written, along with a few financial documents to help Jaggi get his visa.

Karmjit's letter of support surprised Jaggi. Karmjit had not spoken to him since he learned about his caste. Jaggi understood it was tough for Karmjit to bear his daughter dishonoring him by marrying an outcaste, but he knew Karmjit loved his daughter. Is he coming around to accepting me as his son-in-law? Naa, that would be too good! Jaggi's moving with Navi to the US would be an excellent relief for Karmjit from the social pressure he must be under, and he would do anything to get them out of the picture.

Jaggi's petition was approved, and he got his J-2 visa. Over the next few days, all they talked about was their new life abroad. She wanted three children, one boy, and two girls. "I need at least two copies of me, but four would be one too many," she said when Jaggi asked why not two boys. Finally, they could plan their future in the US.

The main image of the USA set in Navi's mind was that of a southern town called Maycomb, Alabama. Navi formed this picture when she was sixteen and read the novel *To Kill a Mockingbird*. Navi identified with Scout, the energetic, headstrong little girl who lived with her father, Atticus, brother Jem, and Calpurnia, their housekeeper. Atticus seemed to be the perfect father and a moral example for his children and the community.

Unlike her brothers, Navi was fascinated with Jem, a playmate and protective brother to Scout. But the true hero in the novel was Boo Radley, someone whose circumstances Navi began to appreciate when she was older. He was an outcast, hated by the entire town until he saved Scout from being killed by a violent drunk one night.

Ever since reading that book, Navi had wanted to see the town of Maycomb. She imagined Scout Finch's house was real, and she would visit it, like a museum, when she went to the USA. Navi knew it was fiction, but her craving to see Maycomb returned when she met Jaggi. She had always imagined her husband would be like Jem, "almost as good as Atticus at making you feel right when things went wrong." She wanted a man like that to be there for her and their children one day, and finally, she had found him. Jaggi, like Jem, made everything right, and like Boo Radley, he arrived with an outcaste label, and his sacrifice ultimately saved her.

It had been a tumultuous journey for Navi. Life had come full circle. In her musings on sharing an organ with Jaggi, she would ponder the thrill of making children with him, another way their fused bodies would exist in the world. *I'm alive*, she told herself every day, once again hopeful about their future in a land of seemingly endless possibilities.

Chapter 30

Jaggi returned to Kundyan, but Navi had to stay in Delhi for a few more weeks under the doctor's supervision. Jaggi thought of calling Himmat to pick him up from the bus stop but decided to make the two-mile journey on foot, a comfortable walk he used to do.

It was a sunny October afternoon. A gentle breeze broke up the stifling heat. Suffused with happiness, he walked to his village, reflecting on when Navi would be walking by his side. Thinking about Navi and his role in pulling her from the jaws of death filled his soul with joy. He was at the center of the cosmos, with the universe flowing from him in every direction. He passed by a few buffalos wallowing in a pool. Their young caretakers were playing marbles under a fig tree. Jaggi giggled at his sudden urge to jump into the pond and nuzzle the beasts.

Bindo was over the moon to see Jaggi back, happy and healthy. She looked up and down his body. "Does it hurt?" she asked, fixing her eyes on his belly. Jaggi was still sore in the abdomen and felt numbness and tingling in the incision areas even after two months.

"Not really," Jaggi said. "It's a little sore, but nothing unexpected. The doctor said to give it another month, and I will be as good as new."

She was making tea for Teja. She made extra, and they took it to the fields to have it together. Seeing Jaggi, Teja smiled and took him in his arms. It was the first time Jaggi saw his father since the wedding.

"How is my daughter?" he asked.

"She is doing well. She is out of the hospital but couldn't come with me; the doctors have to keep an eye on her for a little while longer," Jaggi explained. He gave his parents the news about getting his visa to the US. "All we need now is to decide when to go to our new home, the new country."

The news was excellent but bittersweet. Jaggi was their only child, which meant they would be alone when he left. But if Jaggi was happy, they, too, were contented. Jaggi and Navi would visit India, even if not as frequently as they'd like, and though Bindo might not be part of her grandchildren's daily lives, she would see them, talk to them, and spoil them when they visited.

"It is wonderful news, Puttar," Bindo said. "We're happy for you two. Always remember God, and He will take care of you."

"Navi has already started shopping and planning to live in the US. We will have three children, she says!" Jaggi said, his face beaming.

The three of them sat down on a grassy ridge to drink tea. Bindo asked about his health, Navi's recovery, his interview at the embassy, and about Delhi and the Chawlas.

Jaggi fell into a relaxed routine once back home. He would wake up lazily and watch his mother make breakfast, clean the cutlery, wash it in a bucket of water, do the laundry, etc. If he ever tried to help, she wouldn't let him. "The doctor told you to take it easy," she would scold as if he were still a child.

Later in the day, Jaggi would go to the fields and try to help his father, but his father, too, would reject his help, insisting he sit and relax. Jaggi admired his father—a hard-working man, a faithful husband, and a devoted father. Though he rarely interfered with Jaggi's life, Jaggi could always count on his unwavering support.

Bindo had made a list of things to send with them. She knitted a sweater for Jaggi and a two-color cardigan for Navi. In her metal trunk, she had a never-used, heavily embroidered ceremonial shawl her mother had given her. *I will give this phulkari to Navi. It will look so nice on her,* she thought. She bought a few pieces of beautiful silverware for their kitchen and made a pitcher full of her trademark mango chutney.

I'll leave them behind, Jaggi would think with sadness. It's only temporary, he would rationalize, once we finish our studies and settle down, we will send for them to live with us.

Jaggi's excitement about going to the US paled to Navi's enthusiasm. Navi was ecstatic. "Jaggi, I can't explain how I feel. It's like being born again. I want to enjoy every bit of my life." She would call in the evenings, telling Jaggi about her shopping, her research on living in California, how far from the university campus they could get an apartment, and how much it would cost to rent. She would talk about their careers, places they would like to visit, and even where they would eventually settle down in the US. Navi had researched the vast weather and cultural differences among the states and was particularly interested in deciding the best place to settle.

"I want to settle in North Carolina, in the research triangle park area," she would say. Jaggi didn't care where he lived as long as it was not New York City. He had heard a lot about how crowded that city was and its unruly traffic—it sounded like a big Indian city.

Sometimes, Navi's feverish enthusiasm worried Jaggi. He thought she might be exerting too much. After all, she had a foreign organ in her body to let nurse, grow, and slowly adapt. He tried to persuade her to relax, but she was on a roll. Jaggi wanted her to be with him in Kundyan. However, she had still to be under the doctor's supervision, and he hesitated to go to Delhi into the unwelcome milieu created by Karmjit.

Then suddenly, Navi's calls stopped. On the first day, Jaggi assumed something had come up, and she got busy. But the next day, he began to worry. On the third day, he called the Chawla house. A servant answered the phone. With anxiety, she told Jaggi that the family was in the hospital, where Navi had been admitted with a fever three days prior. Jaggi hung up the phone in shock, his only thought being: why hasn't she called for me?

The following day, Jaggi was on the first bus to Delhi, telling himself the fever was from some minor issue, perhaps a small infection that would go away soon. That must be why no one called him. Karmjit, Jaggi could understand, but Parveen had always treated him as a true son-in-law. Still, he planned to stay in Delhi for at least a couple of weeks, even if it meant dealing with Karmjit. He missed her and regretted not having been with her.

Navi came to the hospital because of a lingering fever over the weekend. When the doctors found her bilirubin high at 3, compared with the average total of 1.2 mg per dl, they admitted her as a precaution. "It takes the body a little time to accept a donor organ," her doctor had tried to reassure her. Navi didn't call Jaggi that day or the following two days. She missed him terribly but didn't have the heart to tell him she was sick again. A part of Navi wanted Jaggi to be by her side, but another couldn't bear to make him suffer any more than he already had.

Navi turned in bed and raised her head to look at the clock. She had been awake, tossing and turning, for more than an hour. Sara would be here in ten minutes. Sara was the morning nurse who came at six-fifteen every morning, woke Navi up, took her vitals, and gave her medications. Soon the familiar soothing voice entered the room, "I'm here, sweetheart, wake up!" And the now-familiar routine began.

With her symptoms not getting any better, Navi grew nervous that something worse was happening inside her than a delay in accepting Jaggi's liver.

That afternoon, Navi looked at her frequent visitor, a small lizard sitting on the plumeria outside her window. Instead of looking for insects, it was staring at Navi. The door opened as Navi wondered if she was growing crazy, thinking of a lizard as her friend, and with delight, she saw Jaggi walk in.

"My love!" she said, extending her arms out. Jaggi came and took her in his embrace.

"Looks like all that shopping tired you out," he said playfully. Sitting next to Navi on the bed, holding her chin, all his annoyance at not being informed dissipated. He patiently listened as Navi caught him up on the past few days. Karmjit and Parveen visited her every morning and Raman every evening. Bitu was busy with his school and came to see her once. She did not tell Jaggi how much she had wished he was by his side, knowing it had been her fault.

"Tonight, I'll massage your feet, your temples, and anywhere else you like; you'll have a wonderful sleep," promised Jaggi, noticing her dark circles and the words she left unsaid.

Navi's eyes softened, and she squeezed his hand.

"The hospital has a little pond in the back, and they have a small walkway around it," Jaggi told her. "If you feel like it, we can go for a little walk; it should be warm and sunny."

Navi liked the idea, and they went about their walk around four in the evening. It was a two hundred meters long concrete walkway about the pond, and they slowly paced around it. Navi wore a thick sweater and a shawl. The sunshine provided additional warmth.

"Jaggi, do you think I will ever be healthy enough to live a normal life? I mean, go to the US, work on my PhD, be a wife to you, have children—all the things I always dreamed of doing?"

Jaggi squeezed her hand and stopped to look at her.

"What normal? No matter what life we have, as long as we are together, it will be normal; our normal, and it will be perfect," he said.

Jaggi's arrival reinvigorated Navi. Her appetite improved, she became energetic, and her fever disappeared; although she still had jaundice, her bilirubin levels decreased. Their walks became a daily routine; one day, they made two rounds of the pond. Navi asked Jaggi to bring her a new diary. She would mostly write sitting in her bed or scribble on leaves from her packet of loose pages. Once a day, she would make an entry in the diary. Jaggi found a tall wooden stool for himself to use as a table. He would work on his book when Navi was busy reading, writing, or sleeping—their comfortable routine.

Unfortunately, this peace did not last, and her condition deteriorated. Her strength began to decline again, and so did her appetite. Bilirubin was still at three. Her liver was tender to the touch and enlarged. Their walks became shorter until Navi was too tired to walk one day. Outwardly, she assured Jaggi she was fine, however. She became anxious that life was again slipping away from her. At times she would see Jaggi absorbed in his book and wonder if it had been fair of her to make him go through the transplant. She began to wonder if Jaggi would develop problems of his own from the surgery, whether his liver would grow back to its previous size, or if he would have any issues later in life. *God, please make him fully healthy; he deserves a good life,* she would pray.

Then one day, she asked Jaggi to take her for a walk. At this point, she could not walk, so Jaggi had to take her out in a wheelchair. It was a lovely day, slightly chilly, but the sun was bright and glistening playfully on the water's surface. She was attentive and wanted Jaggi to go slowly, trying to absorb the tableau around her. She couldn't shake the sense that she would not get another chance to see the trees or bushes she was passing. She wanted to listen to every cricket sound and bird chirp, knowing she may never hear it again. When she saw a squirrel stand on her hind legs to eat something, she made Jaggi stop to watch until the squirrel noticed and ran away in suspicion. Eventually, they had to return to the room and did so solemnly.

The following day when Sara was making early morning rounds, Navi took the rare opportunity of privacy to make a request without Jaggi's knowledge.

"Sara, can I ask you a favor?" Upon seeing her distracted nod of consent, Navi continued, "If I don't make it out of here alive, can you mail something for me?"

Looking up in alarm, Sara tried to protest. "Everything should be fine," she said, attempting not to indulge in the discussion.

"Please listen to me, Sara," Navi said louder. "I hope you are right, but I may not get another chance to ask if you are not. And I do need this favor, please." She pulled an envelope from under her pillow and gave it to Sara.

Despite her rapidly degrading health, Navi continued to write in her diary. She began to see her hospital room as a cage. The plumeria-covered window and her faithful companion, the lizard, provided her the only view into the thriving world outside. Writing in the diary had become a ritual for Navi. It was the only time she felt like herself; she cherished the retreat from her present.

The doctors found a fungal infection as the source of her sickness. The medicines were taking a toll on her; she developed a cough, and a chest x-ray showed she had pneumonia. She dissociated from the world around her. For the first time, Jaggi couldn't bring a smile to her face. He would just sit next to her and hold her hand. Soon she started to get skin bleeds. Despite all the pain, she would still gather the energy to sit up and write in her diary.

It was a Wednesday afternoon, five weeks since her admission to the hospital, when Navi was put on the ventilator. She was conscious and responded to verbal commands. That night, the hospital staff allowed Jaggi to stay in her room and even provided a cot for him. Navi was awake until two in the morning, and Jaggi sat with her on the bed, holding her hand. She gathered all her energy, pulled the diary from under her pillow, and signaled him to take it.

"Do you want me to write in it for you?"

She slightly shook her head and drifted off to sleep. Jaggi put the diary in his pile of papers and moved to a chair, pulling it close to her bed. He sat there numb, with a blank mind, refusing to let his mind wander. Having controlled his thoughts in a tight grip for the last five weeks, he slipped into sleep.

A slight commotion woke him up—Navi had begun to stir. He got up and sat on the bed next to her, holding her hand. The day had broken, and there was sufficient light outside the window. He looked at his watch; it was six thirty-two. Navi opened her eyes and looked at him. Her lips trembled as she mouthed, "I love you."

Jaggi responded, "I love you, too," and squeezed her hand. She closed her eyes again. His mind took him to Chacha Chimna's canteen, where they sat together alone for the first time, wandering back to when Navi was in Kundyan.

Navi went back to sleep, but when the nurses came to administer her medication a few hours later, she wouldn't wake up; she had slid into a coma.

Navi was Jaggi's strong arm, the love of his life, and his future. Though the doctors and nurses gave up on her in a couple of days, he was sure she would wake up soon. He would lash out and shut down whenever a doctor attempted to discuss an alternate outcome.

On the unresponsive fifth day, Jaggi was shepherded into an office. There were two doctors and a hospital administrator in the room.

"Mr. Jagjit Singh, we need you to listen to us. She is alive only because of the ventilator. At this point, we know she will never recover. You need to decide when we can take her off the machine." Numb, Jaggi could only nod in acknowledgment before returning to Navi's room. She looked so frail lying there, attached to all the machines, surrounded by the dullness of the room.

Eventually, he let himself feel for the first time, and his emotions burst forward in a crushing wave of despair. For hours he just sobbed, thinking of all their dreams shattered. *How can I let that go? How can I let you go?* When Raman came that evening, Jaggi said nothing. He wasn't ready to let go of her yet. Jaggi thought all night. *Maybe she would recover*, he pondered. He had heard many stories of people coming out of a coma long after doctors pronounced their cases hopeless. But what if she didn't? Should he let her continue to suffer?

The following day when Karmjit and Parveen came for a visit, he quietly shared what the doctors had told him. Karmjit did not react while Parveen began to stammer in horror, "No, no, she will get better. She can't leave us like that." Jaggi held her, unsure if it was to comfort her or himself. The Chawlas stayed there all afternoon, and unlike their previous visits, Jaggi did not leave the room. When they left, Jaggi had no idea what they wanted. He ashamedly realized he had been hoping for them to take the decision out of his hands. *I guess they finally see me as a true son-in-law*, he thought bitterly.

Jaggi went to see the doctor. "What are the chances that Navi might recover?" he asked. "Not much more than zero, in my opinion, unless you believe in miracles," the doctor explained. "Her blood has begun to hemolyze due to sepsis, and with her suppressed immune response, she cannot fight any more infections. All we are doing is prolonging her pain."

The thought of her suffering helped Jaggi steer himself to a decision. Around ten-thirty in the evening, he called Navi's parents, and they arrived a little before mid-night and Navi was taken off life support. With all the tubes gone, she looked like his Navi again. Jaggi prayed for a miracle once more, but in a few hours, in a quiet room punctuated by her parents' low sobs, Navi's heart stopped beating.

Two nurses came into the room. One went right to Navi and felt for a pulse on her neck; Navi was no more. She nodded to the other nurse, who quietly called for a doctor. Suddenly feeling suffocated in a room that felt too crowded but also too empty, Jaggi walked out, hearing a loud keening behind him. He managed to get to a phone and called Himmat in a flat voice, asking him to tell Bindo and Teja. "Please ask them not to come here. I will be home in a day or so." Jaggi knew they would try to make it there for the funeral, which, per Sikh customs, would have to happen that day, and he didn't think he could remain strong if his mother appeared.

Jaggi returned to the room as a doctor, and a nurse exited. The doctor stopped and put his hand on Jaggi's shoulder. "I am sorry," he said. Jaggi nodded and walked inside. Navi's parents were not there. The room was quiet without the gentle beeping of the heart monitor, the soundtrack to his life for what felt like an eternity.

Navi was covered with a sheet. Jaggi took a deep breath and pulled the sheet down from her face. She had relaxed into a peaceful, beautiful expression, her lovely head framed by her dark hair on the white pillowcase. Her face looked calm, as if she would wake up any minute. Jaggi held her head in his hands and bent down to kiss her forehead. Two tears flowed from his eyes and dropped onto her skin. One rolled down to the top of her lip, leaving behind a wet streak along her cheek as if she had been crying. He wiped them with his shaking hand.

Chasing Dignity

The morning sun shone through the window; his watch said seven thirty-five, but it didn't mean anything to him. He looked at the road through the plumeria branches. It was business as usual. The people, the cars, the scooters, the whole world was going on just as it always had. Didn't they know someone had died? How could their universe continue like nothing was wrong when his had been shattered? When Navi's heart stopped beating, he, too, ceased to exist. Without Navi, there was no future.

Dimly, he remembered Navi's diary that he had put among his notes. Jaggi began to read: The last five entries were poems.

November 30, 1999

Why give me hope
only to take it away?
Why give me love
but make my body decay?

December 1, 1999

Selfishly, I am glad you were mine
I had you first; our hearts intertwine
But you, my dear, must not Mourn
For the world to lose us both, this cannot be borne

December 2, 1999

Your sacrifice wasn't unwanted,
It made me fuller before I lamented,
My days as yours, were your skill,
Little camaraderie was His will.

December 3, 1999

All great tales must come to a close
All beginnings must have an end
My journey had barely begun
Can my story still be great?

<u>December 4, 1999</u>

Ready I am, not scared to die,
Hold my hand, bidding me goodbye,
Lighting my pyre
That you must, don't cry,
Pass me to Him,
with pride in your eye.

The poems ended with no entries on December 5, 6, or 7. There was only a single line on the 8th—the day she gave him the diary—*Goodbye, Jaggi, my love.* Overwhelmed, he looked at her still face, *You knew, didn't you?*—still hoping she would open her eyes and respond.

Jaggi sat with the diary open in his hands for a while—he was still in that position when Navi's parents returned with Raman and Bitu. Parveen collapsed over her daughter to embrace her and again began to cry. Bitu was touching her face in disbelief and shock. Karmjit was caressing her head, tears streaming from his eyes. Jaggi just stood in the corner, looking at them but not seeing them, lost in his world. He did not cry; he could no longer feel anything.

After a few minutes, Sara came in. "I am sorry for your loss," she said, hugging Parveen, going to Karmjit, and putting an arm around him. "Can I get anyone a cup of water or something?" she asked. But they gently shook their heads. "Navi was a wonderful person. She won everyone's hearts. I'm going to miss her. We will miss her," Sara said before putting a hand on Jaggi's shoulders and leaving.

Chasing Dignity

After a few minutes, the nurse returned to tell them the arrangements had been made to prepare the body for transport.

Anger flashed in Jaggi for an instant. How dare she call his Navi a body. Then, in realization again, he returned to numbness.

Navi was taken home in the hospital van; Jaggi, Parveen, and Karmjit rode by her side. It was a little before ten in the morning when they reached home. Word of Navi's death had already spread, and friends and relatives started to gather at the house. They arranged the wood and sent it to the cremation grounds, and a few people went to set up the pyre. A priest arrived to say the last prayers, and the ladies assumed the responsibility of giving Navi her final bath.

More than a hundred people had gathered on the premises. Every time new ladies came, they would seek out Parveen, embrace her and start sobbing or crying, empathizing with her grief. Parveen, however, did not weep any, not even a sniffle. Emotionless, she was helping her princess get ready for the final journey. Men would come to hug Karmjit or Navi's brothers without saying anything. Few would break into tears.

Jaggi stood apart from the scene, watching but unable to feel anything. It was as if he was standing in the middle of a movie. A man passing a clear plastic bag containing a white cotton garment to a lady got Jaggi's attention.

"Can you please take it inside? It's for Navi," the man said. Jaggi realized what was in the bag—a plain white garment they would shroud Navi in for the pyre—a dull, boring outfit Navi would have hated.

Jaggi recalled: I can't describe the exhilaration I experienced when I put on that dress. I felt no sickness during that moment. He decided she had to go forward with the same feeling; with full pride and dignity.

Raman as standing next to Jaggi. "Could you please ask them to dress her in her wedding dress instead?" he asked Raman.

Raman went in, returning a very short while later.

"It wouldn't look right, they say," he relayed.

It made Jaggi agitated. "I don't care! She has to be in that dress. Please go and tell them!" he said with his voice raised.

Karmjit signaled Raman to do what Jaggi wanted. He likely did not wish Jaggi to draw unnecessary attention, but Jaggi was grateful for the unlikely ally no matter the reason. With Karmjit in agreement, they conceded. With his outburst, people realized that Jaggi was the mystery husband they had never met, and suddenly he was swarmed with condolences.

Navi was brought out on a wooden stretcher, dressed beautifully in her wedding dress, and the priest started the prayer. Jaggi moved to stand by her side, looking at her, thinking back to all the time they spent together, about their wedding, and how hopeful they had felt.

When the prayer was over, four people lifted the stretcher and carried it on their shoulders, Jaggi and Raman supporting the front, and Bitu and a cousin, the back rungs. The procession was accompanied by the prayer chants "Waheguru, Waheguru, Satnam, Satnam." The cremation grounds were more than half a mile away, and more people joined the procession as they walked.

The stretcher was put on the ground by the pyre. Three people lifted Navi's body, Jaggi supporting her head and shoulders, and put it on the pyre's flush top. They placed new wood to cover her fully.

The priest said the last prayer, and someone handed a wisp of straw to Karmjit. Jaggi went to him, pleading, "Please." Karmjit gave him the tinder. They lit one end, and as instructed, Jaggi went around the pyre five times, lighting the kindling set around it. Soon the wood flared up and crackled, setting large logs ablaze. A spurt of wails emerged from the women.

The odd resonance of wailing voices and the licking flames stirred Jaggi, and grief overpowered him. He recited to himself the lines from her diary what seemed like a lifetime ago:

> *Lighting my pyre that you must, don't cry,*
> *Pass me to Him with pride in your eye.*

Please, God, take care of my love until it is my time to join her, he added in silence. He forced himself not to react to the burning flesh's sound and smell. Seeing and smelling her body disintegrate was heart-wrenching, and he closed his eyes. He could not bear to see her perfect body eaten by flames, a body that had given them both so much joy and pain. He stood in place until long after the crowd had left

"Let's go home," Raman said, gently tugging at his arm. Jaggi looked at the burning pyre.

"Come, they will take care of the rest," Raman said, looking at Bitu and three others tending to the fire.

Friends and family members started gathering in the evening to pay their condolences. Many brought food, and the ladies set it on the tables like a buffet. Jaggi barely knew any guests and didn't want to talk to strangers. The idea of explaining his presence was unbearable—without Navi, was he still her husband? He went up and confined himself in Navi's room. Later in the evening, Jaggi was sitting on the bed, thumbing mindlessly through the pages of *To Kill a Mockingbird* when Bitu came with a plate of food for him, put it on the corner table, and sat in a chair next to it.

"Bhaji, come on, have something to eat."

"Please leave it. I will eat later," Jaggi answered.

Bitu sat for a couple of minutes. He got up only to return a moment later with his plate of food. When Jaggi saw Bitu bring his food, he got up and joined him and, despite having no appetite, forced himself to eat some.

"I will leave tomorrow with her cremains," Jaggi said. "I will return for the *bhog*."

"I'll talk to mommy and papa. They planned to take the cremains tomorrow to Kiratpur Sahib." Kiratpur, a traditional immersion site for the deceased, was a few hours from Delhi but less than an hour from Jaggi's village.

They decided Jaggi would take the urn of Navi's remains to Kundyan. Karmjit and Parveen would meet him and his family at Kiratpur Sahib the following day.

The pyre had cooled down by late morning the following day. A few family friends joined Jaggi and the men in Navi's family to pick up her remains from the ashes. Jaggi was careful to put every little bone he could find in the urn and would cringe if he saw someone step on even the tiniest bit. Cranial sutures, considered divine writing by many, can occasionally be seen on a part that survives the fire. Jaggi found one such large piece with beautifully inscribed letters of some strange language. He held it out to the others, and they all gasped. "Oh, this is her kismet. This is where the creator writes it all!" proclaimed an older relative.

The urn was almost full when they finished. They collected the remaining ashes in a large burlap sack, and Raman put it in the trunk of his car for dropping in the Yamuna. Jaggi took the urn with him.

A few hours later, Jaggi was sitting alone in the window seat of a bus to Chandigarh, looking outside. The blur of trees, houses, and fields running backward was mingled with distant memories of Patiala, and his mind kept returning to Chacha Chimna's canteen.

"I want to buy Chacha Chimna a nice shirt," Navi said.

"What is wrong with that undershirt he is wearing?"

"That view of his naked belly and the hanging drawstring is not nice to look at!" she said, laughing, stuffing the remaining half of laddu in her mouth.

Jaggi's eyes welled up, and he let himself get lost in grief for the remainder of the ride.

When Jaggi arrived in Kundyan, only Bindo was home. He walked to her, and she gathered him into her arms. His forehead resting on the top of her head, he began to sob—feeling like a young boy again, in desperate need of his mother to make everything better.

Eventually, Jaggi pulled back to show her the urn. The sight of the pot in Jaggi's hand weakened her knees, and she sat heavily on her chair. This was not how Navi was supposed to return. 'There was no mustard oil on the threshold, no celebration, no blessings. It was all wrong!'

Soon, Teja came home—someone had told him about Jaggi's arrival. Jaggi got up to hug his father. They sat down somberly, tears pouring down Teja's face.

"She is gone. She left me; she left us all," Jaggi repeated incoherently. Bindo stroked his back like when he was a baby. Teja sat in a chair, watching. She got up and brought him a glass of water.

"Why don't you lie down, bete?"

With no resistance from him, Bindo guided Jaggi to the bed. He lay down, and she undid his shoes and put them away. She took his turban and put it on the shelf, sitting next to him, and caressing his hair until he fell asleep.

When Jaggi woke up, Bindo warmed milk for both of them.

"Putter, have some milk. God only knows when you ate last," she said, setting the glasses on the table between them.

Teja sat there quietly, his bleary eyes bloodshot.

The next day they rented a taxi to Kiratpur *Sahib*. Himmat was with them, and Karmjit, Parveen, Raman, and Bitu were already there. They all walked together onto the bridge. Jaggi emptied the contents into the water below. Typically, people dropped the urn into the water after clearing its contents; it symbolized breaking all ties with the deceased.

"Drop the urn, too," Karmjit said when he saw Jaggi backing off from the railing with the urn in his hand.

Jaggi did not; he could not.

PART VI

I am not one of those women who can stand things.

William Faulkner

Chapter 31

The following day Jaggi woke up late in the morning. Bindo made him breakfast, but he ate little before returning to bed in silence. After lying for a few hours, he felt restless, hating being left alone with his thoughts. He got up and went out for a walk. He decided to walk along the bank of Budki Rao, the seasonal stream that passed by Kundyan. For years, he and Himmat often walked there, but today, Jaggi wasn't in the mood to call upon his friend.

Jaggi had read stories of people waking after being in comas for years. *Did I make the right decision in letting them take Navi off life support? Should I have gotten a second opinion from another hospital or Dr. Gill?* The thoughts made his head spin, and he sat down, hugging himself tightly around the middle to fight off the rising bile.

Over the next few days, friends and relatives made condolence visits, but Jaggi remembered very little. Every little memory of Navi would make him retreat into a fog. When he did listen to their words, he became angry. People were trying to comfort him by comparing their losses to his. "Last year, my wife couldn't eat for three days when she lost her mother," a man said, comparing vibrant Navi to an 83-year-old grandmother. Some talked about Navi's death repeatedly, showing surprise, as if reminding Jaggi how young and healthy his wife had been would somehow bring him comfort. The worst was when people told him she was in a better place now, as if her rightful place wasn't alive by his side. Jaggi was polite with visitors but wished they left and let him wither in his misery alone. Why couldn't they see Navi was the cornerstone of his existence and that without her, he was nothing?

On the tenth day after Navi's death, Jaggi and his parents set out for Delhi to participate in Navi's last rites, the *Antim bhog*.

They got off the bus at the Kashmir Gate station in Delhi and hired a taxi to Navi's home.

Jaggi was sitting in the front seat by the driver. Looking out the window, he kept searching for Navi; her memory and the city were inextricably intertwined. How can she disappear, but the city remains? Shiv Kumar's lines stroked Jaggi's inner self:

Chit kre kake-kake,
raityan nu chum lavaan,
labh kiton, Sajna di perh

[The heart yearns to search the expanses, for the beloved's footprints, to kiss the crisp sands thereof.]

Jaggi had grown accustomed to the ache in his soul, created by a lifetime of rejection by the world. He did nothing to hide his face, uncanny if the driver sitting on the right noticed his grief.

The taxi dropped them at Navi's house. In the last ten days, no one from her family had called on Jaggi to see how he was doing. Neither, however, did Jaggi call to do the same. The familiarity was gone, and other than an obligatory greeting from Parveen, no one acknowledged them. Well, Jaggi thought bitterly, Karmjit got what he wanted. No low-caste son-in-law, after all.

The moment the prayer was complete, they left, feeling like unwelcome strangers, understanding that they would never meet these people, once family, again.

After returning to Kundyan, Jaggi became listless. He would eat when food was placed before him and sleep when instructed. Bindo did not know this wraith that occupied the house in the shape of Jaggi. She could handle his grief, but she did not know how to heal this shell of a man. Jaggi's new demeanor discomfited the neighbors, and they studiously avoided the house.

As she sat worrying on a Friday evening, there was a knock on the door. Wondering who it could be—all condolences had ceased. It was Rani, her beloved honorary daughter. She had taken a week off to visit them. Bindo opened the door and was swept into a big hug—"Chachi, I'm so sorry. I tried to come as soon as I heard, but I had to finish my exams. I've been emailing Jaggi, but he won't respond. Is everything okay? I've been so worried."

Gratefully, Bindo unburdened her worries, "He is not okay. I am so worried, bete. He has lost all his spirit. He is here in body, but I am so afraid his body will follow where his mind has gone," she explained.

With alarm, Rani rushed to see Jaggi, who was sitting unnaturally still in a chair with a vacant expression. She tried to talk to him, but while he would turn to look at her, there was no response or recognition in his eyes. After about fifteen minutes of one-sided attempts at conversation, she returned to Bindo. "Chachi, I see what you mean. I promise to help; he is my family too. I will be here every day," she swore, ignoring Bindo's halfhearted protests.

Rani held to her promise. She returned every day, sometimes talking to Jaggi about Nursing school and her friends there. She would tell him about the daily bus ride, the movies she had seen after class, and anything she could think of while helping Bindo around the house. Often, she would sit quietly reading or doing schoolwork while still unacknowledged by the silent Jaggi.

After three days of this new normal, Jaggi finally spoke. "Do you know Rani? Something has been eating me up inside," he croaked, in a voice dry from disuse. Rani sat completely frozen, saying nothing and hoping he would go on as he continued to stare at the wall.

Jaggi then described the last six weeks of Navi's life in excruciating detail, culminating in her coma and his decision to take her off life support.

"What if she had a chance to revive? What if they could use a different antifungal drug to control her infection? Why did I have to choose how long she breathed?" Jaggi was miserable, and he started to cry.

Hating his pain but relieved he was talking, Rani put a hand on his shoulder to comfort him and sat there quietly as he cried.

"I can see why you are second-guessing your decision. But someone had to make that choice, and Navi wouldn't have wanted anyone other than you to do it. It was not a simple matter of her being in a coma. A lot was going on with her lowered immunity; once the blood sepsis sets in, things go bad quickly. The doctors must not have had any hope."

"But having her taken off the support quickened her death. Can you tell me how many breaths I snatched away from her?" he stammered through the tears.

Rani then held his hand, "Jaggi, look at me," He turned, looking at her for the first time that week. "I don't know much, but I know Navi loved and trusted you. One would be thankful to you for helping one end pain. I know I would," she said, earnestly.

Jaggi didn't respond.

The next day, for the first time, Jaggi said hello and talked to Rani as she moved around the house. Cautiously, Rani brought Navi into the discussion on her own. "Do you have all the stories Navi didi wrote?" she asked. Jaggi looked at her quizzically. "I would like to read them. I mean, if you don't mind," she said.

"No, I don't mind," he said. "She also had a few unfinished stories and many beautiful excerpts in her diary. Let me see what I can find."

As she left with Navi's writings that day, Rani promised to return them safely. After another couple of days of slowly coaxing conversation out of Jaggi, Rani returned with a thick pile of papers one morning.

"I think Navi Didi's works will make an excellent book," she said, handing Jaggi the stack. Jaggi, eyes glistening, nodded his head. Looking through the papers, he realized Rani had put together a proposal for a collection of short stories.

Jaggi smiled, and while it was small, it was as beautiful as the morning sun cresting a horizon after an eternity of cloudy skies.

The day Rani returned to her school, she came to see them.

"I'd like to help you put the book together," she said to Jaggi.

"Yes," he said, "We'll do it."

She squeezed his hand and got up to leave. Turning back in the doorways, Rani shared a final thought, "When baau ji passed away, I missed talking to him so much, I didn't know what to do. One day, I wrote him a letter with everything I wished I had told him while he was alive. It made me feel a connection with him I'll never forget." And then she was gone.

After Rani returned to school, Jaggi slowly began reconnecting with the world, catching up with old friends by day and sitting with Himmat at night.

Jaggi went to see Professor Tara Singh one day and spent an hour with him. After learning about Jaggi's articles in the *Sunup*, his op-ed, and the book he was working on, the professor told him he was sure Jaggi would be a successful writer. One day, Jaggi visited his primary school teacher, Surjit Singh. He was now retired and living comfortably in his village. He had read Jaggi's Op-Ed in the *Sindhu* and was incredibly proud of his star pupil.

Jaggi's most pleasant visit was with Kuljit, his friend from middle school. Kuljit was now married, and he was still the same quiet boy Jaggi remembered, just now grown up. Though Kuljit dropped out after middle school, he had taken special courses at the Punjab Agricultural University. Kuljit had become a liaison between the university and other farmers of his village. He would introduce new farming techniques and better-yielding, disease-resistant crop varieties developed at the university to his fellow farmers. In a way, he had become a model for them. "Punit got married two years ago," Kuljit teased, remembering Jaggi's childhood crush. Jaggi could only laugh in response.

Eventually, Jaggi sent a letter to UC Davis, letting them know what happened to Navi so they could assign her position to the next person in line. He wished he could tell Navi about it, just like so many things he wanted to share with her. "Then I wrote him a letter," Jaggi remembered Rani telling him. He smiled at the concept's absurdity but decided to try it anyway. He went to the fields with his diary and favorite pen, pulled a cot into the sun, and started to write. It was the morning of January 17.

Dear Navi

It's been two months since you left. Being of a rational and sound mind, I know you will never return to me, and yet, in some ways, I can't stop thinking you are just a shout away. People are consoling and counseling me to move on with my life; they tell me you are now in a better place. Though it hurts to hear that there is a place better for you than it is here with me, I hope they are right. I'm supposed to get used to your absence and not feel the pain of losing you. But I'm afraid of losing the pain because it is a gift from you. They think I am weak if I can't get over you. 'You seem happy today,' someone told me the other day, 'didn't I tell you time heals everything.' People seem to put my pain on some sort of 'schedule. I wonder if such timelines exist and where to find them if they do.

I am writing this letter sitting in the fields where you came to connect with me and my past, where you and Rani rode the tractor, plowing around merrily. How happy you seemed together. I thought you two looked alike, like two sisters. The idea of writing this letter came from Rani; she thought it would make me feel better.

I want to share something with you I haven't shared with anyone. I had a dream of Rani dying. I saw her lifeless body on the ground while the grim reaper stood above her, looking at me. 'You don't deserve love,' he said. I shudder when I think of that 'thing's' comment. Of all those who came to visit us after you died, Rani was the only one I felt close to. She always seems to know how I feel. Now, I am terrified to go near her.

I am lost without you and see no path in life. I always wanted to go to the US, but now going there without you is meaningless. I wish you were around to steer me in the right direction. My family and close friends have all been supportive of me, but I need you; I wish you could hold my hand and tell me everything will be okay. I was hoping you could read my writings and laugh at my mistakes. I miss the red lines you used to mark my handwritten, half articles.

Don't you ever think I'll forget you one day. You were, you are, and you will always be part of me—forever in this life and the next.

Love, Jaggi

Feeling calmer, he looked over the expanse of the young, growing wheat. *It was more mature when you were here.* He smiled, put the pen in his pocket, and closed the diary.

One morning while browsing the newspaper, Jaggi saw an ad for a copywriter's position with the *Dharamshala Times*, a popular newspaper in Himachal Pradesh and Uttar Pradesh. Jaggi applied. The work was in Dharamshala, a beautiful hill station in the Himalayas. Jaggi could see it as the reprieve he needed from this place, this life, where everything reminded him of Navi.

Bindo was so happy to see Jaggi motivated again. However, Jaggi did not share why she could see the spark for life beginning to glow once again. While waiting for a response to his application, Jaggi reviewed Rani's proposal to compile Navi's works into a book and emailed her his suggestions. He decided to honor Navi's legacy by pursuing a career in writing.

It was the last Friday of January. Himmat was visiting when the postman delivered a letter. Jaggi looked at the return address and put the large envelope aside without opening it. The envelope was more prominent than typically used in domestic mail, and Himmat noticed "Northern Illinois University" in the top corner.

"Jaggi, this could be big news! Aren't you going to open it?" he asked.

"What's the point?" said Jaggi.

"*What's the point?* You worked so hard to get admission, and now you won't even open the letter? Just open it. Do it for Navi," he prodded.

Jaggi picked up the letter and gave it to Himmat.

Himmat opened it, then shouted. "You got it!" He read aloud: "You will be an excellent addition to our geography research group."

Jaggi took the letter and began to read. It was true: He had been accepted to their PhD program in Geography for the fall semester. He was offered a good-paying Research Assistantship with all tuition waived, just like Navi had from UC Davis. He could now apply for his student visa; his J-2 had become invalid with Navi gone.

Jaggi put the letter aside once again.

"So, when are you going for the visa?" Himmat asked.

Chasing Dignity

"Ever since I met Navi," Jaggi said, looking off into the distance, "I never imagined a life without her in the US. Now it all feels meaningless!"

"But don't you think she would want you to go?"

The thought suddenly sapped Jaggi's energy, and he said he wanted to be alone. He tucked the letter into his shirt pocket underneath his sweater.

Himmat showed up at his house again three days later, but Jaggi wasn't home. Bindo said he had gone to a neighbor's house and should be back soon. Himmat waited, and Bindo started to make tea for them.

"Has he talked to you about going to Delhi?" Himmat asked.

"Why would he want to go to Delhi? I don't think he should go there. At least not until he stops thinking about her all the time. What if he sees her parents or brothers in the street, and they ignore him? It will make him miserable!" Bindo said.

"So, he didn't tell you? I was worried about that," Himmat said.

"Tell us about what?"

Himmat told her about Jaggi's admission to a university in the US He explained that Jaggi's student-spouse visa had become invalid because of Navi's death. He needed a new visa in his name. After some time, Jaggi returned. Bindo brought them tea and pulled a stool to sit next to them.

"Puttar, Himmat says you need a new visa to go to Amrika."

He shot a glare at his friend before replying calmly. "I am not going to the USA, maa."

"But this has been your life's dream, bete!" Bindo said.

"Yes, admission to a university, living in the US, that is what *we* wanted…" he responded. They were both looking at him intently.

"But that was before. I was going to talk to you and baau ji about it. I'm not sure if I want to go anymore. So much has changed."

"Why not, bete?" Bindo asked, concerned.

"With Navi gone, I'm not ready to go to a new country, to live a life we were meant to live together. Not just yet, anyway. I'll write to the university to see if they will consider deferring my admission. Right now, I need to try something different," Jaggi said.

"And what would that be?" Bindo asked.

Jaggi got up and brought back a letter from his room. "I got this early today," he said, giving the letter to Bindo. It was a job offer from the *Dharamshala Times*. Jaggi explained the position to them. He would need to move to Dharamshala, about a five-hour bus ride from Kundyan. The money offered was modest but livable; best of all, he could start afresh. No pitying looks would follow him, and memories of Navi wouldn't barrage him.

Nodding with understanding, Bindo stood up to hug him. "Whatever makes you happy, puttar, is okay with us."

Chapter 32

It was the second week of February when Jaggi left for Dharamshala. The long ride from Kundyan also took Jaggi to a town much colder than he was used to. It was still winter, and Jaggi had never seen snow. As the bus approached the city, Jaggi could feel the mountains' chill, and the surroundings began to appear white. Dharamshala was a hill station perched upon the Kangra Valley's slope, 5,000 feet above sea level, significantly higher than Kundyan's 1,000 feet, set against the splendid backdrop of the lower Himalayas' Dhauladhar ranges. The exiled Tibetan leader, the Dalai Lama, was settled in the city along with tens of thousands of his followers, and their presence had brought a heavy dose of Tibetan culture to the place.

Everything in the city was covered in snow, including the roads, the buildings, buses, and other vehicles parked at the bus station. As advised, Jaggi had brought adequate clothing. He put on his thick cardigan, heavy overcoat, woolen hat, and gloves and wrapped a muffler around his neck. A staff member from the paper was at the bus station to pick him up, and they drove to a hotel arranged for him while he found permanent lodging. Jaggi was taken out to dinner that evening, where three other people, including Paul, the paper's editor-in-chief, joined him. The following day, they took Jaggi around the city to find a place to live. Jaggi selected a reasonably priced, small one-bedroom apartment on the hillside. The kitchen opened to the balcony, where he could see over the deep, wide valley covered in snow-clad coniferous forest. As he settled into his room, Jaggi felt he could take his first deep breath in a long time. No one's eyes followed him with concern, and no one asked how he was doing or gave him thin condolences. In people's eyes, he was just a young man for once.

Jaggi was assigned to a senior sub-editor, and he quickly picked up his responsibilities, settling into a busy, daily routine. On a typical day, he would wake up around 7 a.m.. He would be back in bed within half an hour with a cup of tea and a toast. Four national newspapers and a copy of the *Dharamshala Times* would sit on his side, and Jaggi would go through them all in a couple of hours. He would be at the office before noon. He would attend the daily planning meetings of the sub-editors to decide what news would be published on what page. The *Dharamshala Times* was a morning daily; their press cut-off time was midnight allowing for late-breaking stories and coverage of late events. The newsroom was busiest during the afternoons and evenings. During that period, Jaggi interacted with reporters, photographers, layout artists, and other copy editors. Jaggi's day would often go past 10 p.m., and sometimes he would be there until the press cut-off time. Everyone in the office admired Jaggi's discipline, hard work, and calm persona, and he enjoyed his job.

As time flew by, the Navi-shaped scar on his soul had become less painful, a constant dull ache rather than a scarring stab. He had found new hobbies, often hiking the Dharamshala trails and discovering a love for cooking in his environment alone. Soon, he was offered a promotion and became one of the paper's youngest sub-editors

Jaggi's new responsibilities meant working more closely with the chief editor and other sub-editors to decide which stories were important and which were not.

A couple of weeks after Jaggi's promotion, Mahesh, another sub-editor and frequent hiking buddy, canceled plans with Jaggi one day. He explained he had work to catch up on and wouldn't go. Dismayed but understanding, Jaggi decided to still go on the hike, needing to get outside. As he approached a branch in his favorite trail, he noticed Mahesh and Priya, a coworker who had been passed for promotion in favor of Jaggi, walking ahead of him. A bit surprised, Jaggi slowed down. They took the turn, and feeling hurt, Jaggi turned around to go back.

Chasing Dignity

The next day when Jaggi went to work, a piece of paper folded like a nameplate was sitting on his table with *KEERA* written in big, bold letters on both sides. Jaggi crushed the paper in his hand, threw it in the dustbin, sat in his chair, and cursed silently. Jaggi had never shared his caste with anyone, and no one was around from Jaggi's past. After contemplating for a few minutes, he decided to go about his work as if nothing had happened.

He turned to look in his news bin. Usually, it would have a thick stack of papers neatly organized and marked with notes. Today, there were only three items in it. He heard a voice from outside his door as he gaped, open-mouthed, at the bin.

"I wouldn't have taken this job if I knew I'd have to work for a Keera," someone said. A different voice, loud and deliberate, responded, "Where I come from, they aren't allowed to sit in a chair."

Though Jaggi had grown up with such behavior, the last year of his anonymity had lowered his defenses, and he was shocked by the ugliness of the words, especially coming from coworkers, all of whom knew him well and once liked him. After composing himself, Jaggi went to the sub-editors' meeting. When he entered, the room went silent. Six uncomfortable people were in the room, the other three sub-editors and three copywriters, including Priya. None would make eye contact with him. That meeting was short, and as everyone left, he stopped Mahesh.

"What's going on?" Jaggi asked. "Yesterday, you said you were too busy to go hiking, but then you went with Priya, anyway?"

"Why are you acting so surprised? You know well what you did," Mahesh said with a sneer.

"No, I don't know what I did. Can you enlighten me, please?" Jaggi said, already knowing where this must be going.

"Some of us are religious. We have been eating with you without knowing you were a Dalit. And now, we all feel polluted. The whole staff feels that way. Half of them will quit if you stay in this place," Mahesh spat, looking at him.

"I see. And thank you so very much for your kindness in the word *Dalit*, not *Keera*," Jaggi said, dripping with sarcasm. He was thirsty and went to the lunchroom to get water. There was a communal glass sitting by the water tap; for people to drink water. They would then rinse it and put it back.

"Don't touch it; bring your own glass," a sharp voice called across the room as his hand was outstretched. It was Priya, sitting at a distance, eating her lunch with malice in her eyes.

Jaggi stared straight back as he picked up the glass and poured water, "I suggest you bring your own glass and don't leave it by the sink if it bothers you that this Keera might touch it accidentally," Jaggi responded in a clipped voice and walked out, hand shaking in anger.

Kaushik, another sub-editor, came to his office a few minutes later. He was a nice guy, but Jaggi had never considered him a friend. "I'm sorry," Kaushik said, surprising Jaggi, "for how a few of us are treating you. Priya is a vicious person; she could not accept your promotion over her, and she has been digging into your past and talking bad about you in the office."

"We are a liberal newspaper, and this is a Buddhist city. I never expected such behavior from colleagues working with me for so long," Jaggi said.

"But more than half of the staff aren't local, and many, like Priya, are Rajasthani," Kaushik pointed out, drawing attention to the news of the caste-related killing from Rajasthan they had recently published.

Jaggi shook his head in disbelief. "I can expect this from strangers, but I never imagined it could happen here."

"I suggest you talk to the boss before things get out of hand. Either he'll be on your side or won't, but at least you'll know," Kaushik suggested.

"Thank you for your support Kaushik. I guess I have to," Jaggi said.

Paul, the editor-in-chief, was supportive. "I'm sorry, it happened to you, Jaggi. Unfortunately, this prejudice is deeply rooted in our society; let me think about how to address it effectively."

That afternoon, Paul called a meeting of the staff:

"A case of caste discrimination has been reported to me. I have spoken with the main shareholders of the paper. We are all shocked to hear that the *Dharamshala Times* being a leading, liberal newspaper in the country, any of our staff can behave like this. I realize caste is a contentious social issue, and we can easily get into a long, never-ending debate. But I have no intention of getting into that discussion. However, one thing is clear to me: We are all required to uphold our constitution, which we will focus on today. To ensure that we are all on the same page, I will read article fifteen of the Indian Constitution, the part relevant to our discussion." He then took a piece of paper from his pocket and read the entire article, explaining how the law prohibits discriminating against any citizen based on religion, race, caste, sex, and place of birth.

He folded the paper and put it back in his pocket. "Following the same principle, caste-based behavior or discrimination is unacceptable at this workplace. Anyone engaging in such behavior will face disciplinary action. If you have any questions, please speak up."

Priya's hand went up, and she got up to speak. "What about our religion? Our constitution provides us with religious freedom. The Manu Smriti, one of our shastras, clearly defines our social structure and how people from different Verna interact with each other within it. Don't we have the freedom to protect our right not to be polluted by the outcastes?"

Paul was about to reply when Jaggi raised his hand. "May I?" he asked, standing up. "Yes, Priya, you have the freedom to practice your religion as you deem appropriate, and you have the right not to be polluted by a low caste like me. But as someone said once, 'your liberty to swing your arm ends where my nose begins.' I am a Sikh, and the Sikh religion does not accept caste hierarchies. In my faith, everyone is born equal. I am a human being and a citizen of a free country, and I intend to enjoy every legal right given to me by the constitution. Like everyone else, I have the right to use the water tap, take any available chair I like in the lunchroom, and do my work with dignity sitting in a chair. You can bring your own if you don't want to eat or drink from the utensils I touch. It's pretty easy. We've done it for centuries." And then Jaggi sat, turning away from Priya's reddening face.

Seeing her mouth open, Paul intervened. "As I said, we are not getting into a debate. This discussion ends here. See me personally if you have any other questions."

The office was very uncomfortable for the following few days, and Jaggi could always feel eyes on the back of his head. After taking an unscheduled leave of absence, Priya left the paper. To Jaggi's relief, no one else quit, and while things didn't return to the old normal, Jaggi settled into a new normal, where he had fewer friends, but because of his hard work and discipline, he once again commanded respect.

Luckily, it worked out in Jaggi's favor, but he would never forget how easily his life could have been uprooted and his career ruined.

Jaggi worked through email with Rani to publish Navi's stories, though it wasn't easy between their busy schedules. Still, they completed two of her incomplete short stories; Rani provided a surprising astute insight into Navi's writing, seeming to understand the love and longing in her compositions. The work was healing for Jaggi. It allowed him to remember happy times with Navi, not only the sadness of the end.

Jaggi imagined Navi's reaction to the incident at work and smiled as he thought. First, of course, would be fury. She would curse, and he would have to talk her out of storming right up to Priya's house for a discussion. Then she would hold Jaggi close, trying to hug away a lifetime of pain. Finally, she would look at him with fire in her eyes and declare some grandiose plan to fix the problem. Jaggi would have laughed and pulled her to him, telling her the system would never change, but it would be tolerable as long as they had each other. Then he would silence her inevitable protests with kisses, making her giggle, and they would move on with the day.

But Navi was no longer with him. Still, a part of her lived in his mind, and his commitment to honor her memory. A realization dawned on Jaggi as he thought back to the last year. He may have given Navi a part of his liver, but she returned the gift tenfold. Where he once would have felt fear, he boldly took on an adventure in a completely new town with a new career, surrounded by people who spoke different languages. Once, a young woman's derision and mockery would have caused him to turn aside in shame, but now it brought anger and indignation. Once his reaction to casteism would have been to shrug and go on, but now he could choose a different path. It occurred to him that the book he started when Navi was alive had mainly been forgotten, along with memories once too painful to visit. But now, these memories strengthened him, and he decided to honor Navi by finishing his book. It may have only a small impact, but it would be well worth it if it could change even one person's prejudiced views.

Invigorated, Jaggi devoted all his free time to his book, waking early to work before work and sleeping late to work on it in the evenings. Writing consumed his weekends, but he finished it in only two months. Thanking Navi, he put copies in the mail, hoping one of the many publishers he was sending these to would take an interest.

It had been long since seeing his family, so as a reward for accomplishing the feat, Jaggi decided to take a week off work and return to Kundyan. His family was ecstatic to see him and wouldn't let him lift a finger to help during the visit. He spent the week catching up with old friends, but to his dismay, Rani wasn't available; she was finishing up her last year of Nursing studies. Nevertheless, the visit revitalized him, and he resolved to visit more often when his mother knocked on his bedroom door.

"Bete, I know it might be too soon, but I want to talk to you about a proposal your Baldev mama ji called me about." Immediately opening his mouth to protest, Bindo held a hand to silence him. "Just hear me out. It has been close to a year and a half. We all loved Navi, but she would not want you to be alone forever. This girl is only a couple of years younger than you and is doing her MBA in the US. She's from a good family, and they are from our caste," she said. Jaggi was taken aback at how much time had already passed since Navi's death and barely registered the rest of his mom's sentence. Misunderstanding his silence, Bindo quickly told him, "Think it over. They are in no big rush, but it is a good match."

Jaggi nodded absent-mindedly, not wanting to dash his mother's hopes so quickly but knowing he would refuse the proposal. Two years and still, Navi was so deeply embedded in his soul! No wife could accept him, knowing his heart belonged to another woman.

Chapter 33

The following day, Jaggi returned to Dharamshala. Thinking of Rani and wishing he had gotten to see her during his visit, he stopped into the office to check in with Paul and get caught up for work. People kept patting him on the back and, to his confusion, saying congratulations. When he finally reached Paul's office, there was a huge smile on Paul's face.

"Jaggi, why didn't you tell us?" Jaggi's only response was a look of confusion. "You know, about your book?" Paul prompted.

Unsure what he meant, Jaggi responded, "I've been working on it for a while. I promise not during work hours, sir."

"Of course, you haven't, Jaggi. We know you well enough! I meant about the publishing deal. Your editor tried calling for you this week."

With shock, Jaggi realized what he meant. "I have a publisher?" he said, nearly yelling. Realizing he must not have gotten the news in Kundyan, Paul let Jaggi use his phone to call the publisher back. Jaggi felt overwhelmed, realizing this wasn't a joke or mistake. Through a barrage of congratulations from his coworkers and an impromptu celebration lunch party, one thought kept going through his mind—I have to tell Rani.

At last, he could get away in the afternoon and immediately called her dorm. They rarely spoke on the phone because, besides their schedules not being aligned, Rani's dorm had only one phone, and it took time for someone to go and get her. But that time, miraculously, she happened to be close to the phone.

"Hello," she said

"Hi, Rani! It's me, Jaggi," he said excitedly.

"Oh, wow, that was fast. I just sent the email," Rani replied in an odd tone.

"I was so excited I had to call immediately!" Jaggi exclaimed, nearly bouncing in his seat.

"Well, thanks, I guess. Yeah, maa is excited too about the proposal, but I haven't yet made up my mind."

Jaggi's blood froze as Rani kept going.

"I guess his family is wealthy in America. He's an engineer, so he will well take care of me. They are in India now and want a quick wedding so I can go with them after graduation."

All Jaggi could hear was a faint buzzing. He managed to give her congratulations before hanging up. Later he realized he never even told Rani his big news.

His thoughts were racing. What is wrong with me, he thought. That proposal is excellent news. Rani is amazing; she deserves this match. Especially after losing her father, this was a boon for the family. Still, he couldn't shake the knot in his stomach and could not focus on work. In the late afternoon, he asked Kaushik for help finishing it. Kaushik playfully teased him about being famous, as he agreed. Jaggi did not argue and gratefully left the office.

Instead of going home, Jaggi walked toward the bazaar. The shops were busy with evening customers, and Jaggi thought of buying a wedding gift for Rani. He noticed a Tibetan artifact shop and went inside. A beautiful piece got his attention. It had a cylindrical wheel in the middle, with some mantra inscribed.

"What is this?" Jaggi asked the shopkeeper.

"It is a prayer wheel. We call it *Mani Chos Khor*," the man answered. "The monks rotate the wheel clockwise during meditation," he explained, pointing at the cylinder.

It was interesting, and Rani liked exciting things. He decided to buy it.

Chasing Dignity

It wasn't yet dinner time, but he was in an odd mood, so he looked for a place to eat. A roadside Tibetan restaurant with outside seating got his attention, and he went in. He ordered a usually delicious mutton momos plate, but Jaggi tasted only cardboard. After finishing his meal, he sat there until realizing he had occupied the table unnecessarily while customers waited to be seated.

Jaggi had a half an hour routine of writing before going to bed. But tonight, he ignored it and just sat in the bed, staring blankly into space. Instead of Navi, Rani occupied his thoughts. Jaggi felt as if someone was stealing Rani from him. Why are my thoughts so weird and selfish? She likes the proposal; she will go to the US and live a happy life.

I should have said more than just congratulations, Jaggi thought. Jaggi remembered the email Rani mentioned. He did not have a personal computer at home, so he decided to go to an internet café down the road. He read her email over and over again:

Maa called me today. She has a proposal for me. It is some engineer settled in the USA. They are specifically looking for a nurse, and he is currently visiting India with his family. The family came to our house and saw my pictures. They agree with what they saw and are waiting for my approval. Maa will be sending his pictures to me. They say it will be a quick engagement and a small wedding. Maa would like to invite you to the wedding and asked me for your address so she can send you an invite.

He replied to her email, giving her his address.

As he was about to leave the café, closing for the night, he saw she had sent another email. The email did not have a body, only the subject line, "Is that it?" He quickly printed the emails and brought them with him, holding the paper clutching tightly on his walk home.

Rani had been close to Jaggi all his life. When he stuttered, she was his friend; when Cheta humiliated him, she was there to console him; when Simmie rejected him, she had the words to soothe him. Rani was never judgmental and always had words of wisdom that calmed him every time. She was the pillar of support he needed after Navi died. Rani understood him more than anyone else, sometimes more than Navi, he thought, and the usual guilt didn't follow it. But now she will be married and gone, and he will have to let her go. No more emails, phone calls, or long discussions. Just news through the mother of the girl he once knew. Likely, he will never even see her again in person.

Jaggi was restless. What did she mean by *Is that it?* What did she expect him to say? When he woke up in the morning, he had a pounding headache and a fever. But he couldn't bear to stay alone with his thoughts, so he took some aspirin and went to work.

When he opened his email, he saw Rani had sent yet another email that morning. I need to talk to you. I'm coming to Dharamshala and will be at your place this evening, between six and seven, she had written.

What does she want to talk about? he wondered. His mind was not at work at all. Citing sickness, he took two days off and went home. Unabated random thoughts kept him occupied. She had his address, he remembered. I sent it to her last night—he reflected without giving it much consideration.

It was a little before seven when Rani knocked at the door. Jaggi let her in without saying a word or displaying any emotion.

The living room was lightly furnished, with three chairs and a table. Jaggi used the table as his dining table as well.

"Would you like to drink something before eating dinner?" Jaggi asked.

"What are we eating?" Rani asked.

Chasing Dignity

"I cooked *rajma* and *aalu-mattar*. I can cook rice or make chapatis, depending on what you prefer," Jaggi said.

"Oh, so you can make chapatis too," smirked Rani.

"Two years experience. I can make as good chapatis as any woman."

They settled on eating rice. They made small talk as they ate, Rani telling him about her studies and Jaggi about his work. She had not called him 'Jaggi veer' since she came, Jaggi realized.

"So, what do you want to talk about?" he asked, coming to the subject when they finished eating.

Rani did not say anything. After a couple of minutes, she got up and went to the balcony. It was past nine, but it was a full moon with clear skies. She stood looking over the vast valley.

Jaggi came to join her.

"This is a beautiful place," she said.

"Yes, it is," Jaggi said.

Rani was quiet again for a while. "What are all these trees?"

"Deodar cedar trees," Jaggi said, pointing to a large one slightly to his right.

Another silence followed.

"Jaggi, do you love me," Rani asked abruptly.

"Of course, I love you. Why you ask?"

"Not like that," Rani said hesitatingly. "I mean do you love me as a woman."

Jaggi did not respond.

"Please answer honestly. Do you love me?" Rani repeated.

"You have no idea what you are asking," Jaggi responded.

"I have thought about asking this question for a long time, ever since Navi died. I just could not gather enough courage. Now, I am at a fork in my life and have no choice but to ask you the question to make my decision. I wish to spend my life with you. The alternative will be to marry someone else and bury my wishes forever," Rani said slowly and calmly, pausing at each sentence.

Jaggi did not respond immediately. "Can we talk about it tomorrow?" he spoke after a while, "I don't want to give you a wrong answer. I need to sort things out in my mind," Jaggi said.

"Sure," Rani said. Soon, they decided to go to sleep. Jaggi set a mattress for Rani in the living room and went to bed, calling her good night.

He could not go to sleep for hours. The proposal from Rani took him by surprise. He knew his feelings toward her had, at times, ventured into spaces one wouldn't consider quite brotherly, and he always felt guilty about it. Watching her grow into a beautiful woman had not been without effect on him. But Rani? He never realized she also harbored similar feelings toward him.

It made his guilt disappear, and suddenly, he was thinking about Rani in the same vein as Navi. He always enjoyed Rani's company. She understood him the way not many people did, matched his intellectual caliber, and now had shown a keen interest in writing. In an ideal world, she would make a perfect partner for him.

But unfortunately, this was not an ideal world, and it was a dangerous proposition in their situation. Jaggi and Rani were from the same village. Any relationship between a man and a woman born in the same village was considered incestuous and was a big no. And the caste gap? A Jat boy marrying a Keera girl could perhaps have been palatable, but a Jat girl going into a Keera household? It would be a civil crime, sure to incite peoples' ire and possibly violence against the perpetrators. People reminded Jaggi of his low caste at every corner, but he had gotten used to it by now. But if they got married, Rani, who had no such experience, would be subjected to the same treatment. How would she handle it? How would he take her being insulted?

How would their parents react to the news? How would Rani's mother perceive it? Wouldn't she feel betrayed? After Rani lost her father, Jaggi and his family provided the support Lakhwinder needed. Wouldn't that look like just a game to win her trust? How about Rani's bhua and her family? Could any of them take matters into their own hands and try to deliver some 'honor-justice?' How about his parents? Jaggi knew they would support him if it were any other girl. But Rani? They had always treated Rani as their daughter. Jaggi could not imagine how they would accept her in any other relationship. Rani and Jaggi themselves had treated each other as siblings. How awkward would it be for them to see each other differently?

Then Jaggi recalled his dream that Rani had died because he didn't deserve love. The remembrance made him uneasy. He counted the pros and cons of saying yes to Rani. There were too many cons, and whatever pros he saw, they seemed to be his selfish wishes. Tumbled in the whirlwind of thoughts, Jaggi fell asleep.

Rani woke up a little after Jaggi. He already had the breakfast ready—omelets, toast, and tea, and they sat down to eat.

Rani was eagerly waiting for an answer.

"So what did you decide?" she asked.

"Rani, it's not that simple. How do you think your maa will react?"

"Not well, probably," she said.

"How about your bhua ji, your mama ji, and all the other relatives? How will they take it?"

"Jaggi, do you think I haven't thought about it? I am determined to take that chance. Do you love me enough to do it as well?"

A long silence followed. Rani watched the changing expressions on Jaggi's face as if he struggled to find an answer.

"Rani, I love you in every sense of the word. You will be the epitome of a life partner for me. I am ashamed to admit that even though you always addressed me as Jaggi veer, my feelings toward you were not always platonic. However, things are never as simple as they should be. You ask me if I love you enough to do it. The problem is I love you too much to give you a simple *yes*. All night, I've been struggling to reach the right decision. I worry our union will hurt you more than you might have considered."

Rani got quiet. "So what is your answer?" she said after a little while.

"I suggest we think it through a little more. Our decision doesn't impact just us. It profoundly impacts those around us as well."

"How much time do you need? I have to respond to maa," she said.

"How long can you wait?" Jaggi asked.

"One week," she said, giving her response a thought.

Jaggi nodded in agreement.

Rani returned, and Jaggi went to the bus station with her.

"One week, don't forget," Rani said through the window as the bus started to roll.

Chapter 34

By early evening Rani was back in her dorm. Putting her purse on the table, she noticed the envelope she had forgotten to put back in the drawer. Picking it up, she sat in her chair.

"I did the best I could," she spoke to the envelope and pulled the folded letter from it. She had read the one-pager numerous times over the past two years. Still, she unfolded it and started reading yet one more time.

> *Dear Rani,*
>
> *I hope this letter finds you in good health. I apologize for not giving you a chance to respond; I will be no more by the time it reaches you.*
>
> *I lived a short, nonetheless happy life. My only regrets are that from here on, I will not be able to share the joys and sorrows or be able to repay the debts of love and care I incurred from you all.*
>
> *The most significant debt I owe is to Jaggi. I'll not be able to care for him how he cared for me with everything he had and how he deserves to be cared for. He must be devastated by my abandoning him so quickly, so soon. I feel helpless, knowing I can't do anything about it. He deserves better.*
>
> *Jaggi always spoke about you with respect and affection. I did not understand why he idolized you the way he did until I went to Kundyan and met you in person. I noticed you had the same respect and affection for Jaggi that he had for you. I felt a connection with you as if you were the sister I never had.*
>
> *I will now come to the purpose behind this letter. It is awkward for me to broach the subject because you address Jaggi as veer, and he always mentioned you as*

his little sister. However, I believe you are the best person who can be the perfect life partner Jaggi needs and deserves. I know that you know it, but just in case, let me reassure you—Jaggi will take care of you in ways no other man can. However, knowing Jaggi, he won't propose to you because enticing you to marry him would be, in his mind, selfish. Therefore, you will need to take the initiative to be with him. I realize social issues will be challenging to surmount, but you two can conquer them together—where there's a will, there is a way.

Please tell Jaggi I'll be fine; there's no point in wasting energy holding onto me. I fully approve of you two being together. Goodbye Rani. I love you.

Affectionately,

Navi.

Rani folded the letter and put it back in the envelope.

"You were right, didi," she said, looking at the envelope. "He would have never taken the initiative."

Rani then stood up straight and lifted her head smiling. She felt taller than herself, a Punjabi girl from a small village controlling her destiny. He didn't expect me to approach him like that, she thought and took a few firm, precise steps.

What if he decides against marrying her? In that case, I'll never marry. The thought made Rani uneasy as it amounted to manipulating Jaggi to accept her proposal.

"Didi," Rani said, again addressing the envelope, "I have loved him all along, but I never thought my love was possessive until you came into the picture, and suddenly, I was not the focus of his attention."

Something was wrong with what she just said, Rani realized. She remembered being happy that Jaggi had found love in

Navi and recalled how she liked Navi. However, she also recollected being a little envious of Navi because all Jaggi did was talk about Navi.

"I loved you, didi; don't take me wrong. I loved you. The news of your death hurt me deeply. I had never wished you to part with him. You were his life, and he was devastated when you left. When I saw him lost without you, I craved you to come back, bring his happiness back."

Rani realized she was talking to the letter and not to Navi. The fact was Navi was gone and was no longer a part of Jaggi's life. Her death had provided Rani with the unlikely opportunity to be with him, to be his partner for life. She could not lose this opportunity.

Then she addressed Jaggi. "You need me just as much, but I don't understand your altruistic reasons. You think marrying me will hurt me. But don't you know not marrying you will hurt me even more? If I get married to this dude from the US, or anyone else for that matter, will I be able to give him my unconditional love, my soul? How will that be fair to him?"

"Didi," Rani said, getting ready to put the envelope back in the drawer, "you are alluding to the social obstacles in our way, but trust me, I can manage those. But what do I do with him, the biggest obstacle of all? How do I make him realize that we are made for each other?"

Harinder, Rani's classmate, and her best friend came to get her for dinner. Harinder knew about Rani's love for Jaggi and related social issues. Rani had even shared the posthumous letter she received from Navi.

"How did it go?" Harinder asked.

"Not well. He hasn't agreed yet."

"Did you show him Navi's letter?"

"No, I did not. Showing him the letter would mean manipulating him. Marrying me should be his free will. With all the social norms against us, at least we two should be the free-willing parties to this."

"So, what will you do now?" Harinder asked.

"Wait for his answer. I have given him a week."

"Do you think he'll come around?" Harinder asked.

"I don't know," Rani said sadly, "All the social issues aside, I'm not sure if he is willing to let go of Navi yet."

"What if he says no?"

"I haven't thought that far yet. I don't know if I should say yes to the guy from the US," Rani answered.

Rani spent a restless night, having difficulty sleeping. She had a dream of her nuptials with an unknown person. After the wedding, she forgot who she had married. There was a party, and she knew her husband was in attendance, but which one was he? After talking to a few, she grabbed a familiar-looking arm. The man turned around; it was Jaggi. "No, I'm not your husband," he said, waving both hands as he walked backward. Then she got lost in a big building and could not find her way back to the party.

The following day, the first thing Rani did was check her email. Not seeing any correspondence from Jaggi, she thought of sending him an email just to say hello, but restrained herself and went to her class. Rani and Harinder were part of the team planning their class graduation party. As a nice distraction, Rani assumed more responsibility than initially planned. She volunteered to arrange a photographer for the party and scheduled a meeting with one for the following evening.

The next day, Rani received the pictures her mother sent her of the gentleman from the US. Still, no email from Jaggi, and Rani began to get jittery. She even thought of calling her mother to consent to the proposal. Though she had given Jaggi a week to change his mind, her hope was waning. What's the point in waiting? she thought.

In the evening, Rani got a message that someone was waiting to see her in the lobby. The photographer—she had forgotten about the appointment. She ran down.

Rani stopped in her tracks to see Jaggi waiting for her.

"I thought I might give you a surprise," he said. Rani motioned him to follow her to a secluded sofa in the dorm guest room.

"I didn't expect you to come," Rani chirped.

Jaggi delivered his lengthy apology, telling Rani how stupid he felt after she left, how he saw missing the opportunity to put his life back together, and how upset he got by imagining her with someone else.

"I'm saying," he summarized, "it will be my utmost pleasure to spend my life with you. I'll honor you, cherish you, and respect you as my wife for the rest of my life."

Rani extended her arms to hold his hands. "Thank you," she said. "I understand why you are so worried. I'm worried too," she continued. "Once we are married, our life in the village or anywhere near it will be over. We will be on our own and need to find a faraway place to live, away from all this. I have been working on our move to the USA. It will be the farthest and the safest country we can move to."

Jaggi looked at her curiously; she had never talked about going to the US.

Rani had been preparing for CGFNS for a while. She explained how nurses were in short supply in the USA and how the US government encouraged qualified foreign graduates to fill that gap. To qualify for immigration, Rani had to take the CGFNS exam, considered equally, if not more challenging than the NCLEX exam the US-educated nurses take to get licensed.

"As my spouse, I will be able to apply for a simultaneous immigrant visa for you," she said.

Rani's final exams were in less than two months, and the next CGFNS exam was a week after her last test.

"No one will ever care about your caste in the US," she said.

Jaggi was impressed by how well Rani understood their complex problem and agreed that moving to the US was their best option. He took Rani in his arm. "It will greatly mitigate the social pressure our parents will face because of our marriage," he said.

Jaggi could not imagine living in the US without Navi just a few days before. However, the prospect of moving there with Rani did not flash any doubt in his mind.

Chapter 35

For the successful execution of their strategy, Rani's passing of the CGFNS was critical, and for Jaggi's papers to be processed simultaneously, they had to be married. If everything went according to the plan, it would be close to four months before they had their visas in hand.

However, the news of their wedding could trigger unpredictable consequences.

Rani suggested a court marriage and not announcing it to anyone. However, Jaggi argued that excluding their parents would hurt them.

"The court marriage is to get the process rolling. Later, if the families insist on a social wedding, we can have that. They won't need to know we were already married," Rani said.

Jaggi consented, thinking it through. "But I insist we don't consummate our marriage until our parents know about it."

Rani's face reddened as she nodded, looking down.

Jaggi stayed in a hotel for the night; the following day, they went to find out how court marriages worked. The process was unsettling. They had to submit a special notice of intent, which would be displayed in a conspicuous place for one month in the office of the Marriage Officer. A copy would also be attached to the Marriage Notice Book, which anyone could inspect. They had to provide documents of proof of their ages and residencies and bring three witnesses who knew them at the time of solemnizing their marriage. An objection by anyone would result in a court hearing.

The clerk answering their questions watched them keenly, and their nervousness did not escape his notice. He knew many sought a court marriage because they wished to keep it anonymous.

"Is it interfaith?" he asked quietly. Jaggi shook his head in a no.

"Inter-caste?" the clerk asked. This time Rani shook her head.

The clerk smiled. "I don't care what your problem is," he said, "but there's a solution if you don't want to advertise your marriage."

Both looked at the clerk intently, who took a piece of paper and wrote '1,000' on it. After showing it to them, he crumpled the paper and put it in his pocket, whispering, "No one will ever get to look at the notice or the register."

He gave them the application form. "Please bring it back completed with all the needed documents and the fee," he said, smiling.

"These people are so corrupt!" lamented Rani when they were outside. "We can just go to a gurdwara and ask the Granthi to do it," suggested Rani.

"I wouldn't trust a Granthi any more than this person. It alarms a Granthi to marry us without our families and friends, and there are higher chances of the word getting out from the gurdwara. Our best bet is to bribe this man; let's just pay him the money he is asking," Jaggi said.

"Once he realizes we are desperate, will he demand more money?"

"I don't think so; the man already knows we are desperate."

"And where are we going to get the three witnesses without disclosing? The only person I can trust is Harinder," Rani said.

That was a serious issue. "Wait a minute," Jaggi said after giving it a thought, "let's go back."

Rani looked at him, confused.

"Trust me," he said, turning back.

"We don't have three witnesses," he told the clerk in a low voice.

"How many do you have?"

"One," Jaggi mouthed, gently lifting his index finger.

The clerk wrote *500* on a piece of paper. "No problem," he said.

"If we bring the papers tomorrow," Jaggi asked, "when should we return for the marriage?"

"We'll do everything tomorrow. Make sure to bring all the documents," the clerk whispered. "And don't put any dates on the application."

"Unbelievable!" Rani said on their way out.

Jaggi didn't have enough money and had to bring his proof of residence and age. He left for Dharamshala to return the next day.

The following day they went back to the courthouse, Harinder accompanying. The clerk took the application, put a past date on it, and made an entry on an earlier page of the register. He had them sign the documents, having two of his friends already signed as witnesses. He then took the papers inside to get them signed by the marriage officer. A few minutes later, they had a fully executed marriage certificate.

"Congratulations," the clerk said, handing them the certificate, "now you are officially married."

Rani had not yet responded to her mother about the proposal from the gentleman from the US. Having decided her course of life, she gave her a call.

"Maa, how will you feel if I say no?"

Lakhwinder went silent for a short while. "Why, what's wrong with him?" she asked.

"Maa, there's nothing wrong with him, but I don't know him. There's another proposal I'm considering. This person is also in Amrika and will visit India in a few months. He has already seen my pictures, and we even spoke on the phone," Rani said, convincing herself it was not a total lie.

"How do you know this person," Lakhwinder asked.

"His sister goes to college with me. She and I are good friends." Rani thought it was just a little white lie, hoping it would end the discussion.

And it did; Rani's reply calmed Lakhwinder. However, the proposal had come through Gurdev, Rani's bhua ji. "Your bhua ji will be very upset," Lakhwinder reminded Rani.

"Don't worry, maa; she'll be okay when she finds out I found a better match."

Three months passed quickly. Rani finished her BS degree and made the required scores in the CGFNS exam. They had applied for visas and were to interview at the US embassy in New Delhi in a week.

Now was the time to share the news with their parents; they decided to do it in person. Since his parents would likely be more amenable to the proposal, Jaggi chose to go first.

Bindo and Teja were alarmed when Jaggi dropped the bombshell.

"Bete, I could support you on anything, but this? I thought we raised you better. Please don't do it; the whole village will spit at us; they'll be up in arms against you. They can hurt you." Bindo pleaded. Jaggi explained how it all transpired and how Rani had approached him. But there wasn't enough he could say that would calm them.

Bindo felt as if God were testing them. First, Navi came into their lives and left, giving Jaggi nothing but pain. She had dreamed of having a big wedding for her only child. "You can always throw a reception when Navi comes out of the hospital, well and healthy," Bindo recalled Dr. Gill telling her. Well, that didn't happen! Not only looked his marriage no more than a prayer party for his and Navi's lives but they were also humiliated by Karmjit, the ungrateful man who couldn't even embrace the man whose son put his life in danger to save his daughter. She couldn't forget the humiliation she felt at being ignored at Navi's last rites.

Bindo was so delighted when Baldev approached them with a lovely proposal. The woman was beautiful and educated to match his son's caliber. She was from the US, where he had always dreamed of going. And above all, the girl's family was also Keeras. They didn't have to hide the marriage from anyone. Bindo could finally have the wedding she had always dreamed of for her son; alas! It didn't have to be. 'It's our kismet,' she thought.

Lakhwinder had told Bindo of the proposal she received for Rani. 'Why couldn't the girl accept that proposal? Both she and Jaggi would have gone to the US. Their families would have interacted with each other as close friends the way we always interacted with Lakhwinder and Sohan Singh.' For the first time, Rani's image did not invoke feelings of love in Bindo's mind.

Bindo then recalled how Jaggi had retreated into a dark place after Navi's death and how Rani pulled him out of it. She is a lovely girl, Bindo thought of Rani. 'But that doesn't mean they have to be married to each other!'

Bindo spent a troubled night, staying awake all night.

The following morning Jaggi sat Bindo and Teja again for a talk.

"Maa, we will leave for the USA within a couple of weeks," he told them about their upcoming interview with the US embassy. He informed them that they had to be married for him to get a visa as Rani's spouse.

It didn't change anything. Bindo was sitting uptight, as she had when she realized he had to donate a part of his liver to Navi.

"You should go before anyone here finds out about it," Teja interjected.

"Nobody else knows about it yet," Jaggi said. "But yes, I will go. Please do come to meet us before we leave for the US. I'll keep you informed."

Bindo did not say anything, and Jaggi did not know how to console her.

"Be careful, bete," Teja said when Jaggi finally left for Dharamshala.

Now it was Rani's turn to talk to her mother. As expected, Lakhwinder did not take it kindly.

Rani had not told her mother that they were already married. Instead, she had asked Lakhwinder how she would feel if she married Jaggi.

Lakhwinder could not believe her ears. "What did you say? Jaggi?"

Rani nodded.

"Are you out of your mind? Is that why you refused the proposal your bhua ji brought?"

Rani nodded again.

"Over my dead body," Lakhwinder screamed. "I won't let you drag your father's turban in the mud!"

Chasing Dignity

Her mother was so upset that Rani's telling her they were already married was out of the question. I'll talk to her tomorrow, Rani thought, after she is over the shock.

The next day around noon, Rani was surprised to see Gurdev arrive. Lakhwinder had called her. Gurdev had been a frequent visitor to Kundyan, and Lakhwinder had become increasingly dependent on her emotionally and shared with Gurdev every little problem she encountered.

Gurdev's arrival alerted Rani, and she tried to stay close and attentive to what the ladies talked about. Lakhwinder brought up the issue when she thought Rani was at a distance and not paying attention.

"Bhen ji, once you talked about the boy for Rani, who you said worked in a bank. Is he still available?"

"Your daughter refused that wonderful boy from Amrika. Why do you think she will agree to that one?" answered Gurdev. "And he may already be engaged by now."

"Bhen ji, we have to find someone quick. I'm worried she may run away with someone she should not," pleaded Lakhwinder.

That made Gurdev intense. "You are not talking about..." she said, looking intently at Lakhwinder.

Lakhwinder nodded, "Yes, Jaggi," she said.

"I was afraid this might happen," Gurdev said. But then she went quiet. She did not talk to Rani about it at all. She left the same afternoon, telling Lakhwinder to "Keep a lid on it. Don't say anything to anyone about it."

Late that evening, someone called Lakhwinder. It was a short call, and Rani could not hear it. Whatever it was, it made Lakhwinder nervous. She started to pace around the house purposelessly. After about half an hour, she went out of the house. Rani assumed she must have gone to see a neighbor.

The phone rang, and Rani picked it up. It was Ginder, her sister. Ginder was married to Gurdev's husband's nephew.

"Did maa talk to you about it?" Ginder asked.

"Talk to me about what?"

Ginder told her that their bhua thought Rani brought dishonor to the family. Ginder had overheard them plan something sinister. They planned to forcibly take Rani and get her married to Ginder's brother-in-law, and if Rani refused, they would kill her. Ginder also heard something about them killing Jaggi.

"Did you tell this to maa?' Rani asked.

"Yes, I did. Get out of here if you can. I think they will come tomorrow morning, if not tonight," Ginder suggested and hung up.

'Why didn't maa tell me what bhua was planning to do?' Rani wondered, 'Is she with them?'

Rani saw her baau ji's scooter. Lakhwinder always kept its fuel tank full, so whenever needed, she could let it to someone to get things for her from the town. Rani had to get out of there as quickly as possible. She took the scooter off the stand, and it started on the first kick, to her delight. She was out of the house in a heartbeat.

Rani headed for Chandigarh, where she planned to abandon the scooter and take a bus to Dharamshala.

After she had gone a few miles from home, she stopped at a payphone and made two phone calls. The first was to Bindo.

Very briefly, she updated her on the new development. Then without getting into an argument, she said, "Chachi, I don't have much time to talk, but just as a precaution, please get away for a few days."

The second call she made was to her bhua.

"Bhua ji, please listen to me carefully. I am married to Jaggi. He is my husband now. I'll come after you if you hurt him or anyone else. I'll not hesitate to go to the police and will do my utmost best to ensure you get punished."

"You slut—" came the response, but Rani hung up and was quickly back on her way.

The sun wasn't even up early the next morning when Gurdev knocked at Lakhwinder's door. Tarlok, her brother-in-law, and his two sons accompanied her. Both the boys carried guns, and their father had a spear in his hand.

"Where is she?" Gurdev asked.

"She's gone," Lakhwinder said. Gurdev, not believing her sister-in-law, asked them to search the house.

"She must be with that Keeri," Gurdev said when they could not find Rani in the house. "Go and get her. If that boy is there, make sure he doesn't see another day's light. Teach the Keeri and her husband a lesson they won't forget," Gurdev said, fuming.

The men quickly went out but were greeted by a padlock on the door.

"They ran away."

"Didn't I tell you not to send her to college? Couldn't she find some Jat to eat that turd with? And you let that trollop escape? Do you know she called me last night? She dared to threaten me!" Gurdev lashed at Lakhwinder.

The men looked at Gurdev with confusion. "Did she call you? What did she say?" the father asked.

"She threatened to come after us and put us all in jail," Gurdev said with a sneer.

"Why didn't you tell me about the call?" Tarlok asked sharply. We could have come last night and taken care of her. God knows what she's planning now. What if she goes to the police? I don't want my boys to get in trouble for trash like that."

Rani and Jaggi obtained their immigrant visas to the US. They stood hand in hand inside the airport lounge, their eyes scanning the people coming in.

"If it were not for the caste, what a pleasant experience it would have been," Jaggi said.

"It is still pleasant. We have each other and are going to a wonderful new country to start our lives afresh. I think that's more than enough," Rani said, squeezing his hand.

Then they saw Teja and Bindo enter. Jaggi approached Bindo and took her in his arms. Teja carried a nice-looking handbag.

"Thank you, maa; thank you, baau ji, for coming," Jaggi said as he separated from Bindo and hugged his father.

Teja smiled. Bindo was more relaxed, but she did not respond.

"Maa, I'm sorry for putting you through all this. Please get your passports ready. Once we get settled, we will send for you."

Bindo nodded. Now her nod bore a slight smile.

"Chachi," pleaded Rani, "if you get a chance, please let maa know I love her, and I don't want to stay apart from her. Please help her get a passport. We will send for her too."

"Maybe in a few years. For now, you may want to forget about your mother," Bindo responded.

Teja handed the bag he was carrying to Bindo.

"I had planned to give these to Navi. Now they are yours," "Bindo said, handing the bag to Rani,

Chasing Dignity

"Thank you," Rani said, giving Bindo a long, warm hug.

Soon Rani and Jaggi took their leave, bidding goodbyes. With moist eyes, Teja and Bindo watched them disappear into the passengers-only area.

Epilogue

In the Chicago Metropolitan area, the village of Addison lies on the Salt Creek tributary of the river des Plaines. In an expensive neighborhood stands a beautiful cottage house, substantial like all the others around it. It has excellent curb appeal, a steep roof, cross gables, a gorgeous driveway, and a stunning arched entry door. Stepping into the foyer, one sees a broad winding staircase to the second floor; to the right is the magnificent sunroom, and to the left is the study with a giant Bay window.

It is a Monday, and 2010 will end in another four days. It has been the coldest winter Illinois witnessed in a long time. Bindo sits on a sofa in the sunroom, knitting a sweater for Sangita, her six-year-old granddaughter. Teja has set up a small table in front of him across the corner from Bindo, cutting unripe mangoes into small pieces and putting them in a metal basin. Bindo and Teja have been visiting from India for the last three months.

"Is it enough?" he asks Bindo, showing her the basin.

"No, this is not even half of what I need. I also have to make a container for Baldev," she tells him. The following week, they plan to visit her cousin in Texas. Teja is preparing the mangos for Bindo to make an Indian-style mango pickle—*mango-achaar*. She plans to fill two containers, one for Jaggi and Rani and the other to take with them as a gift for Baldev.

Across the lobby from them, Jaggi is sitting in his study, writing. He is currently working on his fourth book, tentatively titled *Nationalism, National Pride, and Human Rights*.

The four-year-old Natasha sits on the floor in the corner of the study playing with her make-believe kitchen. She gets up and goes to her dad.

"It's for you, daddy," she says, giving him a tiny cup filled with invisible tea.

Jaggi takes the cup from her and pretends to drink from it. "Mmm, delicious," he offers his tiny daughter.

"Do you want more yet, daddy?" the girl asks.

"No, thank you, Natasha," Jaggi says, "Why don't you take some to Grandma?" he says, pointing toward the sunroom across the foyer.

When Bindo and Teja arrived in the US, they were immediately captivated by this vast country's cleanliness, wide roads, disciplined traffic, huge stores, polite people, miles and miles of open stretches of uninhabited land, greenery all around, its hugeness in everything. But slowly, they got used to it, and the novelty of it all began to wear off. Since everyone spoke English, they could not communicate much with anyone outside the house. They depended on Jaggi and Rani to go anywhere, including visiting a store or seeing a friend. Suddenly they begin to miss Punjab.

One Sunday, Jaggi takes them to the Gurdwara. It is more prominent, and the congregation is bigger than their expectations. They love meeting so many Punjabis and making acquaintances on their first day. One day Jaggi takes them to Devon Avenue, Chicago's Indian market. Seeing so many Indian clothing, grocery, jewelry, and other stores in one place gives them the feeling of being back in India thousands of miles away.

Still, Bindo and Teja prefer living in India for reasons other than living among those who look like them, speak like them, and act like them. They like living independently, so they don't have to rely on someone else for basic needs like groceries or visiting friends and relatives. They have worked hard all their lives, and there isn't much for them to do here in the US. They are attached to their house in Kundyan work and lifestyle.

"As long as your baau ji and I are both alive and healthy to live independently, we would like to live in India," says Bindo.

"However, when we grow old and need help, we will come here. Just give us one room in the corner of your house, and that should be enough for us."

"Come on, maa," says Rani—now she too calls Bindo *maa*—"this is as much yours and baau ji's house as ours. If we lived in India, you would not ask us to give you a room in our home because our would be all of ours. Jaggi and I bought this house in mind, so it has separate rooms for our parents, including my mother. More than an obligation, it is our privilege to take care of you, all three of you, whenever you decide to move in with us."

"I think your maa is ready to make amends with you. She has started talking to me," Bindo said, exacting tears from Rani.

Teja and Bindo look forward to Sundays—this is their day to socialize with other Punjabis. Bindo helps in the Gurdwara kitchen while Teja sits and chats with the men he has befriended. Something happened yesterday, though, at the Gurdwara that unsettled Jaggi, and he has not been able to focus on his work since. Every time he tries to settle down to write, he gets up, starts pacing around in the study, goes to the expansive wall of glass windows, and peers at the snowy landscape. At one point, he looks at his bookshelf, and his gaze stops at *The Eighth Of December*. Jaggi got this book, which he and Rani had put together, using Navi's stories and excerpts from her diary published a few months ago, and named it to commemorate the last day she was conscious. He looks at the book with fondness before walking back to the window.

The incident that upset Jaggi involved two older men at the Gurdwara. They were talking when one of them, who had recently moved to the area, pointed to Teja, sitting at a distance. He asked the other who that man was. Neither realized Jaggi was standing behind them.

"Do you know that Keera who they say writes books?"

The other man nodded. "This man is his father," explained the old-timer.

Jaggi was taken aback. No one had referred to his caste for a long time.

"They are just jealous of your success," Rani says when Jaggi tells her about the incident. Jaggi doesn't discuss it further, but he could not get it out of his mind and had difficulty falling asleep.

The sound of the opening garage door signals Rani's return from work. After coming to the US, Rani returned to school to get her master's and worked as a Nurse Practitioner in a hospital. Her job ends at three in the afternoon. She is usually home half an hour later.

Bindo starts the tea. All four adults have tea together after Rani returns from work. Bindo has taken over the evening ritual so Rani can relax after coming home from work.

Before Rani can set down her bag and take off her heavy winter coat, Sangita comes running. She had been playing in the dining room. "Look, Mommy, look, I did it!" she says, waving a completed Rubik's cube in her hand. "I showed it to Daddy. He loves it." Sangita had been learning to solve the puzzle for the past three days.

Rani looks at the cube. She had done it correctly—each side, a single color. "Oh, that's perfect. Now you have surpassed your mommy," she tells Sangita, hugging her. She loves that her daughters are intelligent and have access to puzzles, learning, and challenge; how difficult it was for her to get the education she wanted as a young woman in India. "Did you show it to Dadu and Dadi?"

"Yes," Sangita nods gleefully and runs back to whatever she is doing.

"Let me run up and change, then we'll have our tea," Rani says after walking to the kitchen and paying her respect to her mother-in-law. Rani is holding a shopping bag and today's mail from the mailbox. She leaves these behind on the kitchen counter.

When Rani returns, Bindo asks Sangita to tell her dad and grandpa that tea is ready.

Instead of getting up from what she is doing, Sangita yells—"Dadi, Dadu, tea is ready."

"I want you to get up, go to them and tell them tea is ready," Bindo scolds the little girl.

"Okay, Dadi," Sangita says and runs to announce the teatime.

The four adults assemble at the dining table. Rani picks up the bag to pull out a few beautiful-looking children's garments.

"These are for Himmat's children," Rani says, putting the garments in front of Bindo, "something for you to give them as gifts." Himmat got married after Rani and Jaggi left for the US. Nina, his wife, is a high school teacher like him, and the two work in separate but nearby villages. Himmat and Nina also have two children, the older, a boy, Sangita's age, and the younger, a girl, six months older than Natasha.

"Oh, those are beautiful," Bindo says, spreading the garments one at a time to take stock of the gifts before putting them back in the bag.

"Can you please put them by my luggage?" Bindo asks Rani. Her 'Gifts' suitcase is now full; she has already packed nice jackets for Dr. Gill and Surinder Kooner and elegant neckties for their husbands. She still hasn't figured out how to wrap the beautiful, small bust of Abraham Lincoln that Jaggi has bought for Professor Tara Singh.

Rani, who has been opening today's mail, screams with excitement. "For you, maa," she says, putting a check in front of Bindo. It was a check for one hundred and seventy dollars.

"What is it?" Bindo asks.

"The first royalty check for Navi didi's book that Jaggi got published." They have decided to spend all royalties from Navi's book to provide education to the Keera Basti children of Kundyan. Jaggi has created another separate fund from his income for the same purpose.

That makes Bindo emotional.

"Our Navi will always be with us," she says, looking at the check. Happiness spills out of her eyes.

Rani discusses stories from when Navi visited Kundyan, and Bindo adds hers to the discussion. Navi's mention always brings a sense of pride and happiness to the table.

Jaggi has been quiet during the tea.

"Are you okay, Jaggi?" Bindo says. "You seem to have been distracted all day today."

"You are right. Something has been bothering me since yesterday."

"Did something happen at the Gurdwara?" Bindo asks.

"I thought we left our caste behind when we moved to the US, but it seems we did not," Jaggi says.

"Maa," says Rani. "Jaggi is a little too sensitive. People always say things unnecessarily, and he takes those to heart." She then tells them what happened.

"Bete, look around you. You have a grand house, two lovely children, and a beautiful, intelligent wife. People recognize you for what you do. How does it matter if a foolish person says something stupid?" Bindo says.

"Am I bothered personally? Yes, but that is not the point. It is more than that. I never declared my caste to anyone, but the Indians are so closely networked that everyone knows everyone else's caste. They not only know my caste, but they even know our marriage is inter-caste. When these little girls grow up," he points to his daughters playing innocently nearby, "they won't know what caste means, but the others will, and they will judge them unfairly. How will the girls feel when they learn that they are not as good as their friends because of me, their father? I thought this country did not condone the caste system, so we moved here. Why do Indians bring the oppression here with them?"

"Jaggi, you know you are wrong," Rani says. "You told me that the caste system is not unique to Indians and that there is no difference between racism and casteism."

"What do you mean? Do people here have a caste system, too?" asks Bindo.

"Maa, race issues are like caste issues. In the US, Black people are treated differently from white people. Not too long ago, Black people could not drink from the same water fountains as white people. They took seats separate from the whites on buses. They worked as legally enslaved people in white people's houses and farms for hundreds of years. Even after slavery ended, the government made laws. Jaggi knows well about these Jim Crow laws, created to maintain employment discrimination, forcing people of color into undervalued careers and legalizing differences in wages and benefits."

Rani paused before continuing.

"If a non-Indian looks at our girls, they cannot tell them apart from any high-caste Indian. But think of a Black child—how can that child mingle with non-Black children without being noticed? The race is a noticeable trait that allows people to be categorized and ranked quicker than our caste system," says Rani passionately.

Jaggi has always appreciated Rani's intelligence and rational thinking. He is well aware of racism and has included it in his writings on caste and its variations in American history, the apartheid policies of South Africa, the horrible genocide of Jews in Germany, and other examples from around the world. However, Rani's sermon on inherent human prejudice throws Jaggi into deep contemplation. For the first time, he realizes that unconsciously he has been chasing an ideal bias-free, caste-free society—something he knew did not exist.

Rani breaks the silence.

"Do you remember 'The Smoldering Sticks,' the story that Navi didi wrote?" she says, drawing everyone's attention.

"I don't recall her exact words, but it means that injustice has a permanent place in every society because it benefits the strong, and the strong make an active effort to keep it in place."

They feel like Navi is sitting among them, participating in the conversation. Jaggi tenderly takes Rani's hand into his.

Teja has been listening to all this with keen interest. "Be happy with who you are and what you choose to do," he says, without looking at anyone in particular. His words hang between them as if engraved in the space.

Acknowledgments

Fiction writing is uncharted territory for me. Still, I feel comfortable presenting this debut novel to my readers, and the credit goes to several friends and acquaintances who became my beta readers and provided constructive feedback. Their encouragement gave me a feeling that I had a supportive team behind me. I admire my team: Chuck Shive, Balwinder Kaur, Rupinder Purewal, Bajir Singh, Cathy Linkous, Amarjit Batth, Karmjit Kaur, Jagdish Gill, Dr. Raj Bajwa, Sukhi Bains and Terri Khera; every single person has been phenomenal. My most extensive suggestions came from Amitoj, Sunitha Venkatesan, and Jasline Sahota. My editor Jennifer Kurdyla turned out to be a remarkable editor for my style.

Finally, I am grateful to my wife, Manjeet, who has always supported me, no matter what.

Made in the USA
Monee, IL
24 July 2023

39848275R00216